BY ANY OTHER NAME

GiGi Gossett

Foreword by
Nikki Giovanni

Gossett, GiGi.
    By any other name / GiGi Gossett ; with a
foreword by Nikki Giovanni
    p.cm.
    LCCN 2004092886
    ISBN 1-58597-258-4 (softcover edition)
    ISBN 1-58597-280-0 (hardcover edition)

    1. Race relations--Fiction. 2. Extortion--Fiction.
3. Adultery--Fiction. 4. Billionaires--Fiction.
5. Passing (Identity)--Fiction. 6. Cincinnati (Ohio)--
Fiction. I. Title.

PS3607.O834B93 2004   813 .6
                             QB133-2033

A division of Squire Publishers, Inc.
4500 College Blvd.
Leawood, KS 66211
1/888/888/7696
www.leatherspublishing.com

To truth,
the pathway to reconciliation.

FOREWORD

Cincinnati is no mystery to me. I have lived there or there-abouts most of my life. I have friends who live in Avondale, Walnut Hills, Over the Rhine. I'm a valley girl, myself. Lincoln Heights. Home of The Isley Brothers, Hari Rhodes, Phillipe Wynne. I know how to order Chili (four-way hold the cheese); I know where the best airport popcorn is (in the commuter terminal); and no matter how bad they are for me, I have to have my White Castles every six weeks or so. It's what I crave.

I know Cincinnati has one of the top five breeding zoos in the nation; our Eden Park rivals any beautiful spot on earth, and now that Marge Schott is no longer with us, I can go out and cheer for the Reds. I'll always be a Sam Wyche fan whether he is coaching the Bengals or not, and I'll always be a Bengal fan despite the stupidity wrapped up in a package called Mike Brown.

The Underground Railroad Freedom Center and Museum is the heart between the arms of two stadiums. Ed Rigaud is a great and visionary man. I split that because not all great men are visionary and not all visionaries are great. Ed is both.

Cincinnati is no mystery to me. Coming north on I-75 as you lean into that Dead Man's hill, the city skyline reveals the promise of its lights. A basket full of buildings spills over the landscape and I gun the car. We're almost home. They say home is where, when you go they have to take you in. I rather like to think home is where, when you could go anywhere you would choose to be where you are. *BY ANY OTHER NAME* by GiGi Gossett is as much about Cincinnati as about passing. Many have thought the city itself has been passing for a northern city when it is really of the South. Some black people pass for white, but don't some white people, especially after dark, pass for black? Or was it only Strom in the closet after all?

The questions of identity are as much of place as person. The questions of happiness are as spiritual as they are emotional. Humans quest for ourselves looking to find and identify the best of us … isn't this what life is? And with detective Lynn Davis, a tantalizing mystery, a great city and a wonderfully inventive writer, there can be no better way to spend a rainy day at home. Grab a quilt, a hot cup of tea, ask your dog to sit with you. You're in for a great experience.

Nikki Giovanni
Poet

ACKNOWLEDGMENTS

A few years ago, a New York literary agent whose clients include best selling authors reviewed my first work, a non-fiction diversity book for use in business. She commended my writing style and strongly encouraged me to consider writing fiction for a mainstream readership. Thus, I told a friend, Shirley Serey, I wanted to write a mystery novel. Even though it would be my first effort, she expressed the utmost confidence in my abilities and encouraged me to go for it. I took her advice and wrote *By Any Other Name*. From the first pages to the very last, Shirley read every line and gave me constructive feedback along the way, and always she gave me encouragement to continue. An avid reader, when she told me my writing was as readable and interesting as many of the other authors she had read, I felt unstoppable.

I am fortunate to have a sister who loves literature, is extremely well read, and who willingly gave me the benefit of her outstanding insights and perspective. Marti Stafford provided much critical advice on my writing style, the characters and the events. Her counsel enabled me to create characters whose lives and personalities people would want to read about, to tighten up the plot and basically make numerous substantive improvements. Furthermore, Marti applauded my novel storyline. This was certainly an important confidence booster that made me excited to get this book finished.

Laura Jetkins from Los Angeles, Regina Smith from Baltimore, and Evelyn Ferguson, Kim McClendon and Al DeJarnett from Cincinnati read the book and gave valuable critique. Their excitement was contagious, and their enthusiasm drove me to complete this work.

Finally, I sincerely thank and acknowledge the generous support of poet, Nikki Giovanni. She is a brilliant artist who keeps a busy schedule touring, writing and teaching. Yet, Nikki's willingness to take time to read the book and to write the Foreword reflect her true spirit of love, support and friendship of humankind.

Thanks to all of you for your support.

PROLOGUE

CURSING LOUDLY, J.T. slammed the front door and stormed furiously to his basement apartment. It was four-thirty in the afternoon. He should be counting his money right now — five million dollars! Instead, his moneybag was empty. He'd just returned from a failed attempt to collect cash from Earl Remington, one of the city's wealthiest businessmen.

For over four torturous hours on this rainy April day, J.T. had waited in a park shelter for his much-anticipated delivery — a delivery that never came. Even though he was warmly clad in a navy hooded sweat suit and work boots, his hands and feet were chilled to the bone. The day's frigid, dismal rain had only added insult to injury, turning every minute he waited into sheer, wet, cold agony, especially as it finally dawned on him his money was not coming.

At first he chose to deny the obvious, telling himself he had somehow, as if that were possible, miscommunicated the time for the drop. So he'd waited, expecting, hoping for a delivery that in the past had been made like clockwork. As the hours went by, he painfully had to concede the clock had stopped.

What happened? His plan had always worked so excellently

before. For two years, old man Remington had paid on time, and quite generously, too, to keep J.T. from springing those juicy, incriminating photographs on Remington's wife — photographs that wove a telling tale of deep deception. J.T.'s two-year ride netted him nearly a million dollars — money he'd used recklessly since he'd had every intention of continuing that ride — two drops a year, $250,000 each time — indefinitely. Hell, he thought, why not? This is mere chump change to a man with Remington's dough. This money had slipped through his fingers like water, sometimes lasting him mere weeks. But he never worried about that. There was always more where that came from. Then suddenly, as J.T. thought about those bad guys waiting for him to repay his ridiculously huge gambling debts, he shuddered and mumbled desperately, "Dammit, I need my money!" And they weren't the only people wanting their money. He had other expensive habits to support and big money to pay to some guys who were pretty scary. Minutes passed, but the shock of coming home empty-handed was not subsiding. For not once had J.T. expected failure, nor did he have any idea how he was supposed to cope with it.

J.T. had only recently learned through the media of old man Remington's failing health. He couldn't have missed it, for this development was all over the daily newspapers and the tabloids. Even major television networks treated the story of Earl Q. Remington's impending death as prime-time news. Remington had been his ticket to riches, his ticket to the fast lane, so this news brought a gripping panic to J.T.'s heart. Was his clever moneymaking scheme about to come to a screeching halt? He wondered this, even as he knew his treasured photographs weren't worth the paper they were printed on if the old man was dead. Somehow, he had to keep his profitable little ruse from coming to such an abrupt end. He just had to. He needed at least *one* final big score.

Frantically, J.T. paced the floor back and forth and then stopped cold. He had to think. Crossing his legs, he leaned against a cool steel beam and looked up to the ceiling. As he harshly rubbed his unshaven face, he damned the old man for daring to play him from his deathbed. "We'll see who gets the last laugh, Remington.

You'll regret trying to pull a fast one on me," he doggedly avowed, although he had no idea what he could possibly do to the powerful Earl Q. Remington.

His plan had been simple enough. He would make one last score before Remington kicked the bucket. This time he had gone for the jugular, figuring it ought to be worth at least five million dollars to this rich old guy to keep his missus from learning the shameful truth. J.T. had moved rather quickly on his plan since, according to the papers, the old man didn't have much longer to live. But for reasons he was unable to fathom, Remington didn't pay. J.T. was dumbfounded. He knew five million dollars was a huge price to pay, but on the other hand, weren't these photographs priceless? Besides, a couple of hundred grand was a huge price, too, but the man sure coughed that up whenever J.T. demanded it. Was Remington bluffing? Worse yet, could he be planning a deathbed confession? Remington never wanted his old lady to know his secret before because it was known that she'd have taken him to the cleaners, big time. But now things were different. He was dying. J.T. suddenly wondered whether the old cuss had already gone and told her the truth. It was all he could figure, because for sure, Remington had never failed to meet his demands before.

J.T.'s mind continued to wander uncontrollably. He grabbed a beer from the refrigerator, opened it, took long, deep swigs and swallowed hard. Still he was unable to contain his frenzy, and moments later with his bare hand he absently crushed his half-full can of beer and hurled it wildly at the faded walnut-paneled wall. Beer flew everywhere, but J.T. couldn't have cared less because at that precise moment that beer container might just as well have been silly putty in his hand; something had to give. His fury had so consumed him that if J.T. could've put his hands around the old man's neck right then, he felt like he could have wrung the very life out of him. While he probably wouldn't go quite that far, the idea still brought him momentary consolation.

In his other hand, J.T. still gripped the cheap canvas sport bag that should have been filled with unmarked bills of mixed denominations. He opened the bag and peeped inside to be sure he was not just imagining that the money was not there. It was still empty. With his eyes fixed on the empty bag, he flung it to the floor in disgust. Then, breathing hard, J.T. paced the floor of his dimly lit basement desperately trying to reckon with his failure. He stared in contempt at the useless bag, then furiously kicked it across the room as if it were the enemy.

Totally frustrated, J.T. plopped down on a cold gray metal fold-up chair and placed his elbows on his old gray metal desk, his knuckles kneading his temples. Over and over, he shook his head in disbelief, hoping also to shake off the ugly truth: his fool-proof plan had failed. What was he going to do? Sweat was now dripping profusely from his forehead, and little droplets rested on his eyelashes clouding his vision. But with his eyes glazed over with anger, he couldn't see anything anyway. Unconsciously, he wiped the sweat from his brow, rubbed his eyes and thought about how much he was banking on that money. This was dead serious business.

"NO!" he moaned in frustration as the reality of failure continued to wash over him. He raised his arms and pressed his hands against his ears as if to block out the tortuous thoughts, then whimpered, "Where's my money, crazy old man! You owe me. You can't do this to me. I'll show your sorry ass!" J.T. jumped up from his desk and walked the floor of his small room from one end to the other in search of answers and relief. What the hell do I do now, he asked the tired walls and waited agonizingly for an answer. Then he dammed the train that sped by his back yard and cursed the sun that was starting to peek through the clouds sending streaks of light through the faded print curtains of his small window.

All of a sudden, out of the blue, something strange and wonderful began to happen. Even as J.T. acted out his resignation to defeat, from somewhere in the deep recesses of his mind a hope was welling up. Strangely, miraculously, it hinted that all might not be lost after all — there just might be another way. Was that possible? He thought hard about this incredible notion. And the more he thought about it, the more he began to revel in an exciting new sense of promise that there still could be a chance.

Thoughts of cash money danced through his head, and he embarked on creating a whole new strategy. His anger was waning now, fast being replaced by an all-important sense of confidence that he would win in the end.

Moments later, J.T.'s expression changed; a cunning smile replaced his angry scowl. His eyes rolled upward, and he laughed outwardly at the new idea dawning. "Hot damn; this is it," he yelped excitedly, for he now had a bold new idea, one that was sure to get him his money after all. He nodded his head in smug satisfaction and began to work out the details. Then, just 45 minutes after a distraught J.T. had entered his apartment empty handed, angry, forlorn and bitter, a daring new plan had taken shape. Triumphantly, he thought, this will work. All I need is a few days — a week tops. Just hang on, old man.

Two days later, Earl Quincy Remington was dead.

CHAPTER

1

IT WAS AN unusually hot Sunday afternoon in June, and Lynn Davis headed to her office in downtown Cincinnati. Although she had just returned from four glorious days in the Bahamas with her main guy, Donald, and should have been feeling great, something was bugging her, but try as she might, she couldn't figure out what it was.

Lynn's little inner voice was telling her that something was up. But what? She'd learned from her years on the Cincinnati police force to pay close attention to her intuition. Besides, she had grown up hearing her mother harp on this. "Listen to your still small voice," Rachel Davis would say, "and you'll hear everything you need to know." Even her mentor and role model, Uncle Eddy, who had served over 30 years on the city's police force, had this thing, too — sort of a finely tuned sixth sense.

So when she should have been relishing happy memories of the previous few days, here she was instead with this nagging sensation that something was about to happen. Suddenly, the radio commentator got Lynn's attention, announcing that the immediate area was under a tornado watch. Intuitively, she started driving faster. Could this be what's bothering me, she wondered, while quickly dismissing that idea since her feeling wasn't particularly bad or foreboding. Rather, it felt like something exciting was about to happen, like she was on the verge of an important event. Maybe I'm just a little excited about getting back to my office, she said. But in her heart, she knew it was more than that.

The revolving clock atop the Western and Southern building registered three-fifteen. Lynn noticed curiously that except for the occasional homeless person or small cluster of noisy teens waiting at a bus stop, the normally busy downtown streets looked more like a ghost town. Within minutes, the skies above Cincinnati had turned a strange hue of greenish-gray, casting an eerie pall over the city which moments before had been bathed in sunlight. What had started out as a 60 percent chance of rain had grown from a tornado watch into a full-fledged warning, and suddenly, as the sirens sounded and heavy rains began to fall, Lynn had to take cover immediately.

"I sure picked a helluva time to come downtown," she uttered nervously. Being only minutes away from her office, she pressed down on the accelerator and ignored streetlights as she drove hurriedly through the empty streets. Then, just as the skies opened up to loud clashes of thunder and lightening and sheets of torrential rain, a relieved Lynn Davis drove safely into her building's parking garage.

"Howdy, Miss Davis. Get on in here outta that storm," beckoned old Mr. Fred Thompson, the elderly black attendant, as he waved her in and handed her a ticket. "You'll hafta take cover down here for right now. They ain't letting nobody go upstairs. In fact, they're clearing the building. Everybody'll be coming down here to the storm shelter directly."

"Thanks, Mr. T. You're not going to stay out here much longer yourself, are you? It's getting pretty ugly out there."

"Naw, ma'am. Matter 'fact, you're the last car that's gettin' in here right now. Lucky you came in when you did. I was just 'bout to close it down."

Over in the shelter, Lynn waited with the 15 or so others from the building for the tornado threat to be over. After a long 40 minutes or so of pounding rain and howling winds, the all-clear was sounded. Lynn breathed a welcome sigh of relief and headed out with the others. Thankfully, there had been no tornado. Some folks went directly to their cars. Lynn and a couple of others took the elevator up to their offices.

Lynn was dressed in a casual plum-colored silk outfit — quite the contrast from her usual weekday attire of stylish business suits and dresses which were always complemented with just the right effects. In fact, this was the outfit Lynn wore on the plane when she and Donald traveled back earlier from their much-deserved hiatus in Nassau. On the elevator, she smiled to herself as she let her mind momentarily take her back to the Bahamas where she could still hear the music of the steel drums ringing in her head.

Arriving at her floor, Lynn noticed the sun had already come back out. Strangely, it looked as if there had never been any real threat of danger. So like Cincinnati, she mused. From the window at the end of the hallway, sounds of cars and people could be heard. Lynn glanced out the window nearest the elevator and noticed that the streets below had virtually come alive with activity just that quickly. It was almost magical. Still, she was keenly aware of that persistent feeling of anticipation.

Outside her office door in the prestigious Carew Tower in downtown Cincinnati, the sign read "LYNN DAVIS, INVESTI- GATIVE SERVICES AGENCY." Lynn let herself into her office, turned on the lights and immediately went to check the thermo- stat. Apparently the storm had knocked out the power, and with it the cooling system, because her office was stuffy and hot. Even so, it felt good to be back, and for just a moment, Lynn recalled the good fortune that landed her this great location.

In her work as an investigator, she sometimes took cases on a contingency basis. One such case had resulted in a huge settle- ment for her client, and Lynn received a substantial windfall as her percentage — enough to invest some for later years, while plowing a significant amount into her business. It was this settle- ment that enabled her to locate her office in the distinguished Carew Tower in downtown Cincinnati.

She was even prouder of her latest acquisition — a 20,000- square-foot, four-story professional office building right in the heart of downtown. Her present tenants included a dentist, a lawyer and a bookkeeper, and Lynn planned to move her agency into her own building within the next two years when her modernization project was completed. She looked around with pride at her present suite of offices. The sunlight streamed through the blinds that adorned her panoramic picture windows, and the warm peach-colored walls of her waiting room invited her in.

She and her partner, Ella Braxton, occupied the private offices, and Janet Clayton, their administrative research assistant who sometimes worked from home, used the workstation in the outer area. Janet was a petite blond whose husband was a vice-president at one of the major banks downtown. At first he had balked at the idea of Janet's taking a job with an investigation service. After all, her degree was in education, and he feared that detective agency work might be dangerous. But Janet loved the work and the atmosphere at the Lynn Davis Agency, and the chance to work at home part-time was very appealing. In addition to her administrative duties, she was gradually building an expertise in research, driven by the prospect that as her contribution and acumen grew, she might one day be able to buy into the partnership.

The waiting area where Janet's workspace was located was a spacious room with chairs of hunter green and deep blue. The carpet throughout was a tasteful pattern of blue, green and peach. Everything still had the delightful smell of newness from when the offices were freshly decorated for Lynn's occupancy, and Lynn breathed in the warm but pleasant aroma. On the deep ledges of the windows of both offices sat several healthy and recently watered plants. Lynn turned on her radio to put some atmosphere in the place, and smooth jazz resonated throughout the suite of rooms.

In her own office, Lynn picked up the stack of files Janet had left in her in-box. Then she took a seat behind her desk — a beautiful antique walnut piece she had acquired at an estate sale and later refurbished. Lynn's office was elegantly decorated. Behind her desk was a rich, dark-blue, tufted-leather swivel armchair. Seating was provided by an attractive arrangement of blue and wine-colored office chairs and occasional tables that Lynn obtained at an auction of office furniture once belonging to a prominent downtown attorney.

Awards and plaques touting Lynn's many civic and professional affiliations proudly flanked her college diploma from Yale. Her academic achievements throughout high school had earned her a number of attractive college scholarships. Of these, she had selected Yale because she felt a responsibility to help pave the way for other inner city, low-to-middle-class kids to Ivy League schools. Her friends had jokingly teased her, saying there would only be two blacks at the school — Lynn and the maid. When she thought about the isolation she had sometimes felt at Yale, she realized her friends hadn't been that far off the mark.

Her wall hangings formed a neat arrangement on a wall behind her desk. One day there would be another diploma to hang on the wall, as she was more than halfway through law school. Lynn had never forsaken her dream to become a lawyer, a goal she was pursuing in night school. She expected the study of law to be a real boon to her investigative work. In addition to other wall decor, two beautiful framed Robert Duncanson posters complemented the horizon blue walls of her office.

Lynn had only been in her new office 18 months. Before this move, she had shared space for almost six years with five other investigators in a practice started by the husband-and-wife team of Brad and Tracey Billingsley. Then, as their business grew, they'd brought on additional investigators. After about two years, this group of six became independent investigators, each sharing equally in the expenses of the office, an arrangement that worked out well for all.

Being an African American woman private investigator in a white-male-dominated field had proven extremely challenging to Lynn over the years. Outside of her firm, she knew of only one other black investigator in practice in Cincinnati — her friend, Harvey Chapman, a seasoned professional who had helped her get started when she first entered the business. Harvey had retired from the police department after 25 years and began a second career in private investigating. Lynn and Harvey worked on cases together from time to time. He had been her mentor, coach and trusted friend. In the early years of her practice, Lynn would have been lost without him.

Lynn's partner, Ella, had started in the business as an administrative research assistant at Billingsley and Billingsley and elected to join Lynn when she opened her office. Within a year, Ella had clearly demonstrated a strategic business focus that led to her being offered a partnership in the firm. Lynn felt she was the clear winner in the decision to bring Ella in as a partner. Ella had a willing, can-do attitude and was committed to the success of the agency as if she were sole owner.

Besides Ella and Harvey, Lynn found much of her support outside her profession in her mother, Rachel Pennington Davis; her dad, Grady Porter Davis; her mother's brother, Uncle Eddy Pennington; and her guy of five years, Donald Anderson, a tall, dark and handsome lawyer in private practice downtown.

Sitting in her office today, Lynn found herself still wondering what was coming. Whenever she got these nagging sensations, they tended to foretell of something out of the ordinary. She leaned back in her chair and pressed her fingertips together while considering the possibilities. After a while, her thoughts drifted and she decided it was time to get to work. She picked up her folder and began to review its contents. This work was what she loved doing — right here in Cincinnati where, in addition to her parents and other family members, many life-long friends still lived.

Family and friends were very important to Lynn. She had grown up in Cincinnati, and in spite of receiving several attractive job offers after Yale, she chose to return to her hometown to aid her parents in caring for her ailing maternal grandparents who had since both passed on. Before becoming a private investigator, Lynn, whose degree was criminal justice, decided to follow in her Uncle Eddy's footsteps and go into law enforcement instead of pursuing the study of law. Thus, she spent her first eight working years wearing the proud uniform of Cincinnati's Finest. She was greatly challenged by her work, and her career ambition had been to become the first female chief of police in the city. But the predominantly male bastion of the police department had created a wall of resistance she found too tough to crack. That, and Jack Dupree.

Glancing up from her files momentarily, Lynn's eyes fell on her wall hangings, and she was drawn to the Certificate of Valor she had received from the Cincinnati Police Department. She was reminded again, as she often was, of that fateful afternoon in April eight years ago when she and her partner, Jack Dupree, responded to a robbery in progress at a convenience store and Jack was fatally wounded. She remembered so clearly how something had been nagging at her that very morning, too. It had felt ominous, but Lynn had mistakenly shrugged it off. Did it cost Jack his life, she'd often wondered. The death of her partner had been very traumatic, and her recovery was difficult.

Lynn was still deeply engrossed in her memories when the sudden ringing of her telephone jolted her sharply back to the present. "Who could this be?" she wondered. Deciding it must be Donald, she answered with a coquettish smile in her voice, "Lynn Davis."

"Miss Davis," a voice said, sounding hesitant.

"Yes, this is she," Lynn responded in a more business-like tone. She did not recognize this caller's voice.

"Miss Davis, I wasn't sure I would reach you in your office today. I'm so glad you answered. I know you're probably a very busy woman, but I have to see you right away." She paused. "This *is* most important. I am Elizabeth Remington."

Lynn wasn't sure she'd heard right. She recognized the name and was too surprised to speak. The woman continued, "I need to talk with you about a matter of utmost importance at the earliest possible time. Can we meet tomorrow? " Lynn could not believe she was receiving a call from Mrs. Elizabeth Remington, *the* Elizabeth Remington. What could she possibly want with me, she wondered as she hurriedly scheduled an appointment with her for the next day.

While at Yale, Lynn had attended school with some of the richest kids in the country, and because of that experience, she was able to move very easily between two worlds — the inner-city middle class world she grew up in, and the world of the wealthy elite. Even so, the thought of being on the telephone with Mrs. Earl Q. Remington was mind-boggling. Although her calendar was rather full, Lynn would have changed her whole week around to accommodate Elizabeth Remington, who asked to come the next day at two o'clock in the afternoon. Lynn wished she had wanted an earlier time, as she was extremely curious as to why possibly the city's wealthiest woman was calling her.

When she hung up the phone, she speculated over what this matter could be about. Then, knowing she would have to wait and see, Lynn sighed and looked at her watch. It was already six-thirty, and she had done virtually no work. Even so, she decided to call it quits, for now she was much too excited to do anything else.

As Lynn left her office, it dawned on her that her little sense of nagging was gone. In its place was a curious wonderment. What does Elizabeth Remington want?

CHAPTER

2

LYNN WAS UP at her usual time of five a.m. She exercised, dressed, and ate a bagel and fruit with her tea. It was just before seven o'clock when she turned into the parking garage of her office building. She intended to review some files and get ready for her meeting at nine. Mr. Thompson greeted her, "Morning, Miss Davis. Looks like it's gonna be a much better day today," he said, waving her in.

Lynn smiled. "Good morning, Mr. Thompson. Thank goodness for this weather. That was some storm yesterday. Glad that's over with." He nodded, smiled, then waved her on as he greeted the next driver.

Once inside her office, Lynn put on a pot of water for tea. Then she settled down at her desk to review her calendar for the day. Other than her much-anticipated meeting with Elizabeth Remington this afternoon, she expected this day to be quite like the others at the Lynn Davis Agency — brisk, fast paced, and routine. Little did she know her practice would take a turn today and she would move fortuitously into a whole new world, never to look back.

She felt good, and even though she hadn't accomplished much

at her desk the day before, she was raring to go. Lynn still found herself curious about her afternoon meeting with Mrs. Remington and wished she could have scheduled the meeting with her this morning. Forced to wait it out, she took a deep breath. "Let's see," she said, "there's Mr. Darby at nine o'clock," and she pulled his file from the top of the stack and quickly reviewed the current status of his case.

Earnest Darby's son, Randy, had been wrongly accused of attempted rape on a college campus. Randy vehemently denied the accusations made against him and was eventually proven innocent, but not before his character and reputation had been severely damaged. Probably as a result of this incident, several of Randy's scheduled job interviews had been abruptly canceled, and Mr. Darby feared his son's job placement was in serious jeopardy. He was considering a defamation of character lawsuit against the young woman who accused his son of rape. His business with Lynn had her researching the background and character of the woman who had falsely accused his son.

Feeling ready for Mr. Darby, Lynn reviewed the files of today's other scheduled meetings. Then she still had time to look over the summary report Ella had prepared to bring her up to date on last week's happenings.

Lynn reflected, as she often did, on how glad she was to have Ella as a partner. Ella was dependable, conscientious and thorough, and she always kept her eyes open and looked out for the business. Lynn now had a rather substantial caseload and a diverse client base. She specialized in domestic, family and white-collar matters, with cases ranging from marital discord and infidelity, to lost family members or heirs. Only a fraction of her cases pertained to criminal activity.

The Davis agency generally took several new cases every month, and Lynn found herself referring a small number out to other investigators. At any given time, her caseload was demanding. It had not always been that way, for when they first opened the office, she and Ella were scrambling hard to cultivate new clients.

Lynn quickly learned it was one thing to share office expenses as she had done at Billingsley and Billingsley. But it was altogether something else to shoulder total responsibility for all expenses of running an office. Of course, she had brought along former clients she'd procured previously. But obtaining new clients was important. And this was where Ella had been tremendously helpful.

Though much of their agency's new business was generated by word of mouth, a good deal of it was owed to Ella's aggressive recruitment efforts. Ella had established relationships with other investigators in the area and across the country, and she was responsible for their agency's being placed on several others' referral lists. She designed an attractive web site for the Lynn Davis Agency that continued to attract new clients, and she networked heavily at seminars and conferences. In fact, they both did. This practice resulted in a significant amount of new cases, and now a portion of Lynn's business was even based outside of Cincinnati. Lynn and Ella enjoyed an excellent relationship in that they both cared for and respected the other.

"Hi Lynn, welcome back!" exclaimed Ella cheerily as she opened the outer door of their office. It was five before eight.

Glad to hear Ella's voice, Lynn responded, "Ella, good to see you."

"How was the vacation?"

"Fabulous! I'll tell you about it over lunch. In fact, I've got much to tell." Ella told Lynn she had a few business matters to talk about, too. Lynn added, "Now get ready for this. I put a two o'clock meeting on my calendar today," then with a smile, slowly enunciated the words, "with Elizabeth Remington."

"Elizabeth Remington!" Ella blurted in disbelief, convinced her ears were playing tricks on her.

"Yes, ma'am, that's what I said. I don't know what it's about, but as you can imagine, I'm definitely curious. She called while I was in the office yesterday. You know me. I came in to look things over, but I got caught in that storm and ended up spending most of my time in the storm shelter area. So I really didn't get much done, but I *did* take *her* call, and she sounded real serious, too. Then, trying to sound like Mrs. Remington, Lynn added, "She said it was *a matter of utmost importance.* This should be interesting."

Ella chuckled and said, "Well, alrighty then. I'll tell you what, partner, if this is what happens when you go on vacation, you need to take them more often." They both laughed.

Lynn's meeting with Mr. Darby went about as expected. The case was closed, and Mr. Darby appreciated the thorough and comprehensive research done by the Lynn Davis Agency. Then Lynn prepared to see her next client. Her last morning appointment was to be with Madeline Hooks. Thirty-six-year-old Madeline thought her husband, Ted, was having another affair.

When Madeline arrived at their office, the first thing she wanted to know was if Lynn had learned if her suspicions were true. Lynn told Madeline their investigation confirmed her suspicions. Madeline looked very hurt. However, the bigger shock was yet to come as Lynn told her that the person spending time with her husband was not another woman, but a man. Madeline couldn't believe it and asked what proof Lynn had. "Pictures," Lynn said. "They speak for themselves." Then she handed the photographs to Madeline, who looked at them in disbelief and began to cry. Lynn waited patiently, and when their meeting was over, she escorted Madeline to the door.

"That was tough for her," she told Ella after Madeline had left the office. "Care to get out of here for lunch. We can walk across the street and catch up on last week."

Out on Fountain Square, a blues band was providing noontime entertainment. Lynn and Ella brought their sandwiches to an empty table and sat down in the afternoon sun. They liked being out on the Square. The sun beat down relentlessly on the brick pavement; yet there was a cool, gentle breeze in the air. It felt good. Scores of people moved about the area as they did at this time every day. Some fed pigeons that frequented the area at lunchtime. Others sat at lunch tables, or on concrete steps, or on the fountain wall, eating and people-watching. Some just listened to the music.

"Down home blues," crooned the lead singer to the accompaniment of a guitar-playing blues musician and a soulful drummer.

"Down-home blues. All she wanted to hear was some down-home blues all night long. Every other record or two …" The bass guitar player rendered mellow, funky notes to this old favorite by Z.Z. Hill. People tapped their feet, patted their thighs and popped their fingers to the beat. An old black man jumped up and started dancing the soft-shoe in front of the stage. Lynn and Ella listened and observed in rapt silence, both enjoying being part of the pulsating energy of downtown Cincinnati. When the song ended and the band began playing another number, the magical spell of the moment seemed broken. People gradually resumed their normal routines.

Ella said, "Now tell me, what did you and Donald do in the Bahamas?" For a few minutes, Lynn shared some of the fun moments of her vacation as Ella listened eagerly. Then Ella briefed Lynn on a couple of current cases. After a while, they noticed the noontime crowd was thinning and the band was beginning to break down its equipment. The face of the clock on the top of Carew Tower registered ten after one.

"Well, this was a nice break. It was fun catching up, but we'd better get back," Lynn said. "I've got that two o'clock with Mrs. Remington. Can't wait to find out what that's all about."

CHAPTER

3

ELIZABETH REMINGTON ARRIVED at the Lynn Davis Agency just before two in the afternoon. She was accompanied by her driver, Arnold Taylor — a short, fiftyish, stern-faced man with a ruddy complexion who also served as her bodyguard. He was dressed in a black suit, a black chauffeur's cap nestled under his arm.

Mrs. Remington was a strikingly attractive woman. Tall and stately, she was smartly dressed in an elegant midnight blue suit with dark blue Ferragamo shoes and matching handbag. Her blond shoulder-length hair complemented her lovely face. According to the news media, she was 63 years old, but looked years younger.

Elizabeth Remington entered the office in such a regal manner that Ella, who happened to be in the front office, was taken by this woman's commanding presence which seemed to fill the entire office. Ella escorted her into Lynn's office. Upon entering, Mrs. Remington seemed startled to see Lynn. Her reaction was one Lynn and Ella saw often, and it occurred to them this woman may not have been aware that Lynn Davis was African American. They both wondered if it mattered.

Lynn arose from her desk and moved forward briskly to greet

her guest. As they shook hands, the two women sized each other up. Elizabeth Remington was satisfied with what she saw, for in spite of the racial *surprise*, the attractive black woman standing before her gave the appearance of competence and confidence. She liked that.

Lynn knew Elizabeth Remington through the media. Indeed, she was a media favorite, being constantly featured in both the local and national press for her attendance at prominent affairs, hosting dignitaries, making charitable donations, or frequenting art auctions. She was known to have an extensive art collection in her home.

Lynn thought, so this is Elizabeth Remington. Yep, I'm impressed. Proudly, Lynn considered that this woman could have anything in the world she wanted, and here she was, seeking the services of the Lynn Davis Agency. Or was she, for Lynn also could not help but think of how startled Mrs. Remington had been moments earlier when she'd first entered her office. To be honest, for a moment Elizabeth Remington had wondered if she'd made a mistake when she first saw who Lynn Davis was, but that thought began to vanish almost the minute she laid eyes on this sharp-looking woman standing before her.

Lynn offered her a seat and tea or coffee. Mrs. Remington took a seat but declined the drink. She would actually have preferred a glass of brandy right now and elected to say so. Lynn did not keep a bar at her office, but decided right then and there that if she took this case, she would have brandy on hand the next time Elizabeth Remington came to her office.

Meanwhile out in the waiting area, Arnold Taylor helped himself to a cup of black coffee and riffled through the stack of magazines on the table until he came up with *Sports Illustrated's* swimsuit edition. Ella observed that Arnold Taylor was not a talkative man. Her attempt at small talk was met with a taciturn look. So she ignored the chauffeur and returned to her office and to the research she was doing for another client.

In spite of thinking she was finally ready for this, Elizabeth Remington had to make a decision. She had put this meeting off for two months. Was she ready to go through with it now? And with Lynn Davis. If only Ferrel had done his job, she thought. Ferrel Whitmore was her family attorney, and she had asked him to handle her matter, but his firm did not specialize in locating missing persons, and he'd suggested a private investigator. Miss Davis' name had been selected by her secretary from the Yellow Pages for two reasons — first, she was a woman; and second, her office location which was upscale suggested a class operation. But there was nothing in what her secretary told her that would have indicated that this was a … minority agency. I'll have to speak to that one, she said to herself of her 50-year-old secretary, Fiona.

As Elizabeth Remington struggled, it occurred to her that very possibly this dilemma might be turned to her advantage. Perhaps Miss Davis could understand and relate to her problem much more than some others could. Besides, she thought, if she backed out now, she wasn't certain she'd be able to go through with this again. It will just have to work, she told herself as she reached into her handbag and pulled out a handsome platinum cigarette holder and lighter. Then she swiftly removed a cigarette, sat back and crossed her legs, lit her cigarette, and took a long, slow draw.

"Miss Davis," she began, then exhaled. "I am here on a very delicate matter. I need an investigator, a tenacious one, you see. I cannot have a failure here." Then she inhaled again and studied Lynn closely and continued, "I don't even know if you can handle my case, so I suppose I'd best tell you about it and we'll know soon enough. Yes?"

Lynn was thinking, lady, who do you think you are? Of course, I can handle your case. Hearing Mrs. Remington speak told Lynn this powerful woman was definitely accustomed to getting what she wanted. A little haughty, but I guess that's to be expected from someone with her money, Lynn thought as she responded that her agency had handled all kinds of cases, large and small, and she would commit to following a case to the end if she took it. She added, "I'd be interested in hearing about your situation, Mrs. Remington."

Elizabeth Remington gave Lynn a satisfied look. She was thinking that it seemed this Lynn Davis might just work out. She had a reputation for being a capable investigator, and she certainly appeared to be successful. Not only that, the Remington family attorney had checked this agency out after her secretary came up with the name — although no one had mentioned it was run by a black woman. Mrs. Remington wondered how everyone could fail to mention such an important fact. Even so, any uncertainties she had experienced were quickly assuaged as she observed Lynn.

As Mrs. Remington contemplated Lynn's words, Lynn watched the ashes of her guest's cigarette grow longer and longer. She'd had to contain herself when Mrs. Remington first lit a cigarette in her office because "no-smoking" signs were clearly in evidence all over the building. The rich apparently live by their own rules, Lynn mused, while deciding that she would not be the one to challenge them today. Instead, she placed a saucer on her desk for the ashes and made a mental note to buy an ashtray for her office for *occasional use.*

Lynn interrupted Mrs. Remington's contemplative evaluation to explain her practice of tape recording her sessions to be sure she didn't miss anything important. "Goodness no," Elizabeth Remington replied without hesitation. "What I have to tell you is not to be recorded. Definitely not," she added, looking at Lynn as if she should have known not to suggest the preposterous. Thus, Lynn prepared herself to listen and write. Then Mrs. Remington sighed deeply, blew out her last puff of smoke and put out her half-smoked cigarette in the saucer. "Let's get on with it, shall we?

"You are no doubt aware that my husband, Earl Q. Remington, passed away two months ago," she began. Lynn acknowledged knowing of this. Earl Q. Remington's death from lung cancer had been front-page news in all the local papers. As the founder and owner of a chain of department stores, several major shopping centers, chunks of prime real estate all over the country, CEO of the Remington Corporation, and with a net worth estimated at over a billion dollars, Earl Remington was one of the city's wealthiest and most powerful men. He also headed the Remington Foundation, a national charitable fund that contributed millions of dollars annually to various causes across Cincinnati and the United

States. Ten years older than his wife, Earl Remington died at the age of 73.

"I'll get right to the point. This is an intricate and sensitive family matter, and I must say, it'll be difficult for me to talk about. Okay. Let me start with some personal background." Then she paused, pursed her lips and said, "Heaven, spare me …" as she shook her head as if there was no way she could talk about this. Lynn gently invited her guest to continue, sensing that if this conversation was to be, it was now or never.

"All right then. My husband and I were married 40 years. We had a good marriage, and he was obviously a significant part of my life. His passing has been difficult for me; I've missed him." She looked at Lynn and paused again. Lynn nodded her head in understanding. "We have four children — two sons and two daughters. He truly loved those kids. Earl was an excellent businessman, but he was also an idealist. Our family foundation has funded a number of special community programs. You see, it was always Earl's vision to leave the world better than he found it."

She cleared her throat and continued. "I was at his side when he died. We were all there." Then, with a faraway look in her eyes and a demeanor that changed from unapproachable to caring as she spoke, she told Lynn how, one by one, their children took their place by his side, each wanting to have their final time alone with him. She said she was somewhat surprised when her husband dismissed the children so he could speak with her alone. Elizabeth recalled how she thought it was because he wanted to have a final private moment with her and, of course, she wanted that, too.

As Elizabeth began to recap the final moments of her husband's life, she thought of how he sounded; his voice had been feeble and so faint she'd had to lean very close to his face to hear what he said. "And then," she said, "he began to tell me some things that have haunted my every waking hour since, and I expect shall plague me for the rest of my life." She paused for a moment to evaluate how to continue. Lynn was awed by the fact that within a matter of minutes Mrs. Earl Remington had relayed intimate and private family matters and was showing such vulnerability in her presence. She couldn't help but wonder what was coming; she would soon know. The narration continued. "Earl said to me, 'Elizabeth, I love you with all my heart.' " For Elizabeth Remington, this had been an extremely emotional issue, and even now this usually composed woman was unable to hold back tears. As she spoke, she dabbed her eyes with a silk handkerchief.

After a moment, Mrs. Remington said, "Miss Davis, I thought I was ready to talk about this. I may have come here too soon." Lynn waited. Then, pausing a moment to get her bearings, she said, "But I must proceed. As it is, I do not have the luxury of time, and it's important that I tell you these details so you will have the full context of my situation. But as you can see, it's very painful." Lynn could only imagine how uncomfortable it was for Mrs. Remington to discuss a personal family matter with a total stranger and was hoping she could continue. Her story was beginning to get interesting and greatly piqued Lynn's curiosity.

"I cannot begin to tell you how seeing my husband like this affected me. Earl had always been so strong and in control. He was such a powerful man." With a dazed look, she added, "He had a noble air about him, you see." Then, forcing a smile, she added, "You know, the media occasionally referred to him playfully as *'The Earl of Remington.'* I sometimes had to remind him not to believe everything he heard. My husband was accustomed to getting what he wanted and I loved that about him. But now he lay helpless and powerless. As you can imagine, it was very hard to see him like this."

Then Mrs. Remington shook her head resignedly and paused for another moment. She had stalled long enough. It was time to get on with it. Softly, she said, "By now Earl's voice was a mere whisper. I had to move very close to hear him, but I heard every word." She wrung her handkerchief in her hand as she continued, "He said, 'My dear, it saddens me to have to leave you. I wish I could stay by your side always.' "

As she told this agonizing account to Lynn Davis, Elizabeth Remington remembered how wonderful she'd felt when her husband told her what a magnificent wife she'd been to him over the years. He told her how fortunate he felt to have her as his mate. " 'I love you deeply, Elizabeth,' he'd said, 'and I would never want to see you hurt in any way.' " Elizabeth Remington looked at Lynn and said, "I have recounted those moments so often that his last words are permanently etched in my mind." Then she added almost as an afterthought, "This very possibly is more detail than you need to know. And so be it. For telling this helps me get to why I am here."

Lynn responded with reassurances, "Mrs. Remington, that is perfectly fine. I appreciate that you have enough confidence in me to tell me the facts of your case. I assure you I will treat your information with utmost confidentiality. Please tell me as much as you would like to."

"Yes, of course. This is the first time I have discussed this with anyone, and no one knows any of this, except perhaps Arnold." She gestured toward the outer office where her driver waited. "He has been with us forever and probably knows everything about our family, including all our dirty little secrets.

"All right then." She paused again for a moment, then continued. "Earl said, 'Elizabeth, I have something to tell you, and I want you to know it is taking every bit of courage I can muster to do this.' I wondered," she said, "what on earth was he talking about. So I waited for him to go on." Elizabeth remembered the dreadful feelings that came over her as her husband spoke next. " 'I have done something terrible to you,' he said. That statement came as a complete shock, for Earl had always been a responsible, devoted husband. I just listened. He said what he had to tell me was something that had happened many years before. He said he knew it was going to hurt me deeply. I asked him what on earth he was talking about. I said, 'Earl, you've been a fine husband. Do not trouble yourself with worrisome thoughts at this time. It can't be that important.' You see," she told Lynn, "in the back of my mind, I had a feeling that I really did not want to know about this thing, whatever it was.

"But he insisted. He said, 'Elizabeth, you never deserved to be hurt, and I only wish it did not have to be. I have wanted for so long to tell you this, but somehow, I was never able to face up to what I had done.' I did not know how to take all this he was telling me, so I just kept listening as he said, 'I want to ask you to try and find it in your heart to forgive me. For, my dear, I have betrayed your love and your trust.' Of course, I had no idea what he was referring to. Earl had always been a good husband and father. I didn't know why he needed to tell me this at this time. We'd had a good life together. Oh, he wasn't perfect; of course, he had his faults like everyone else. I actually believed I would have forgiven most anything he had done."

At that moment, the look on Mrs. Remington's face revealed the pain she was feeling from this unpleasant ordeal. However, with a silent resolve, she continued describing her husband's final moments. "Earl told me, 'Elizabeth, I wanted to go to my grave with this story to keep from hurting you. But unfortunately, I wish it weren't so, but you were bound to find out. As painful as it is, I wanted you to hear it from me and not someone else.' " Although she tried not to show it, Lynn was growing more curious by the minute. What on earth was his hidden secret, she wondered as her imagination speculated on secrets ranging from espionage to organized crime.

Lynn listened considerately though, for it was clear Mrs. Remington was extremely ill at ease right now. Indeed, as she was now coming to the most difficult part of her story, she laced her fingers together and looked abstractly at her perfectly manicured fingertips while preparing to speak. She continued, "Earl told me 30 years ago he'd had a foolish indiscretion. I must say, when those words reached my ears, my heart stopped and I was truly afraid of what was coming." She looked up at Lynn, who now wondered why, in all her guessing, she hadn't considered adultery.

"I had always been aware that Earl had a roving eye. But why would he bother to tell me about a single incident, especially if it happened 30 years ago? I was barely able to focus on his words, even as he told me this had been his only *serious* incidence of infidelity during our marriage. Well, if that was supposed to console me, it failed miserably, I assure you. In fact, those stinging words kept running through my head, over and over. Then when he told me exactly when this thing happened, I realized it was at the time I had gone to stay with my mother 30 years ago. She was terminal.

"Almost as if reading my mind, Earl said, 'It happened when you were spending the summer in Virginia with your mother before she passed away. I missed you so much, Elizabeth, but I didn't want to be selfish. After all, your mother was dying. She needed you. So I tried to cope with your absence, but my brief visits to see you in Virginia were much too short.' " Then Mrs. Remington told Lynn how Earl's eyes began to water, and hers did too at what came next.

" 'I met a woman. I didn't intend for it to happen, but I got involved with her.' He explained that he'd been unable to break it off with this other woman, so even after Elizabeth returned from Virginia, the affair continued. Mrs. Remington paused briefly, remembering that she had never expected her husband to tell her he'd had a serious extramarital affair during their marriage. Her husband's confession of two months ago had devastated her, badly bruising her ego. Today, she obviously still struggled, but at one point she noted with surprise the relative ease with which she was speaking about this with Lynn Davis. Was it Miss Davis, she wondered, or am I more ready to talk about this than I had thought?

"It only got worse," she continued. "Earl told me he continued this relationship with this woman for more than ten years. Ten years! I was completely shattered when he told me all this, but I could have fainted over what he said next — he'd fathered her two children, a boy and a girl!" Each new detail added another dimension to this convoluted story, and Lynn could now see why it was difficult for Mrs. Remington to recount it. Still, she wondered what the case was about. She listened with great interest.

Mrs. Remington continued, "I first thought this had to be some cruel joke, and I wondered why Earl would tease about something like this, especially now. But deep in my heart, I knew he was serious. I was hurt beyond words, but troubled, too, for if this was true, how could it have been so?" Even as she told this story, Elizabeth Remington still wondered how her husband could have done this to her. How could he possibly have led a double life for so many years, and how had he pulled it off without her suspecting something? When had he had time for an affair?

"I asked him many questions. Who was this woman? Where

was she now? What caused their relationship to end after ten years? What about his children?" Mrs. Remington recalled how she had so wanted to hate her husband at that moment; how she even wanted to hurt him as he was hurting her. But she could do none of that, for he lay dying. She could only support him in his final moments.

Her next words got Lynn's attention in a hurry. "Earl told me the woman's name was Hattie Rose Williams." Lynn's mind stopped short, for the name of his mistress immediately got her attention. Actually, she was thinking that the name Hattie Williams was not a typical Caucasian name. In fact, the name, Hattie, was pretty common among African Americans down south where, in fact, Lynn had a cousin from Louisiana whose name was Hattie Marie. Hmmm. Now wouldn't it be interesting if Miss Hattie Rose Williams was black, she thought.

Mrs. Remington said, "Earl told me this Hattie Williams died in 1984 in an automobile accident. So that is what brought an end to their affair? Of course, I wondered, what if she were still alive? Would this thing still be going on?" Turning her head from side to side, she said, "I shutter to think…

"Earl told me their daughter was eight and their son six years old at the time of her death, and Hattie was only 30. He said no one knew he was the father. Even the children themselves did not know who their father was. He said he thought that Hattie Williams' mother took care of the children after she died. Anonymously, he sent money to their grandmother for their care at first, but he soon lost contact with them. When he learned that the children's grandmother, too, had died, he assumed they were sent to foster care. He didn't know where they were, or even if they were alive today."

Mrs. Remington paused to light another cigarette, took a long slow draw and studied the wafting smoke as she exhaled and considered her next words. "Miss Davis, I do not consider myself a prejudiced woman. Quite the contrary for, you see, Earl and I have always dealt with many kinds of people. But you cannot possibly know how profoundly shocked I was when Earl told me his Miss Hattie Williams was a Negro, a black woman!"

Although this was a major revelation, Lynn was not too surprised at this point, for she had already guessed as much. It still was quite something though. Mrs. Remington was now speaking rapidly, her agitation apparent, and Lynn judged by the change in her demeanor that this was an aspect of her husband's affair that was most troubling. Lynn began to catch the flavor of Mrs. Remington's next comments.

"It was frankly difficult to picture Earl in a long-term affair with any woman. But, for God's sake, a *black* woman! The very idea! And the fact that he'd been intimate with her, had had two children, well, I assure you, this was absolutely impossible for me to comprehend or forgive. I'm telling you, Earl could have stabbed me through the heart and I would have been less shocked than I was by his disclosures that day. This distressed me more than I can say. When he told me this, I just stared at him. I felt I did not know this man anymore." Then she took a series of short puffs, looked at her cigarette and absently replied, "Until two months ago, I had not smoked one of these damned things in years."

Lynn was intrigued by Elizabeth Remington's story, especially as the older woman talked about Hattie Williams. In fact, with her feelings so pronounced about Miss Williams' race, Lynn wondered had Mrs. Remington momentarily forgotten whom she was talking to right now, for she seemed completely oblivious to Lynn, who listened quietly.

Elizabeth Remington raged on. "Of course, Earl understood my horror at his having an interracial affair. He told me he did not wish to bring embarrassment to me for his actions and, in particular, for consorting with a black woman. Nor did he want to cause our own children any undue humiliation. He assured me he had always been very discreet, and that only a few people ever had any knowledge of this affair. I was disgusted at the thought that anyone else should have known of it at all. Earl also told me that while he thought no less of Hattie because of her race, he recognized that this world had not yet come to look upon black people with acceptance or tolerance. It troubled him deeply that if people had knowledge of his relationship with a black woman, of his two children with her, well, it could be problematic for all of us."

Lynn was completely immersed in this story. In her practice, she prided herself on being objective with her clients. And a good thing, she thought to herself, or I'd probably be getting a little ticked right now, myself. When Mrs. Remington paused, saying she needed a minute, Lynn once again asked if she would care for tea or coffee. This time, Mrs. Remington requested tea, and Lynn stepped to the door and gave Ella a look that said, you are not going to believe this. She remembered Mrs. Remington expressing a desire for brandy earlier, and at that moment Lynn felt she could definitely have used a taste herself. She returned with two cups of tea and placed them on the desk before sitting down and taking a quick sip of her own.

Elizabeth Remington was beginning to feel unsettled, especially now, as she thought about her husband's deathbed request. She dreaded talking about it, but felt she'd already gone too far to turn back.

Lynn sensed her momentary uneasiness and said, "Mrs. Remington, by what you've already told me I can appreciate how difficult this is for you."

Mrs. Remington took a sip of tea, and slowly placed the cup and saucer on the desk. "You are so right." After another long pull on her cigarette, she placed it in the makeshift ashtray and looked straight at Lynn and said, "Earl told me he didn't know the whereabouts of his two other children at this time. Their names are Erica and Perry Williams." Lynn jotted down their names. "Erica would be 28 now, and Perry, 26. Earl told me how he'd agonized over what to do about this, and he felt the need to do the right thing by his two children. He told me that after a great deal of thought, he had decided to name them as beneficiaries in his will.

"Now that nearly shocked the hell out of me. But knowing Earl as I did, this decision of his really shouldn't have surprised me all that much; it's so like him to try to be noble," she said, looking right through Lynn as she spoke. "He said those two were his rightful heirs, and until now, he had not done right by them. He said, 'I want to fix that now, and perhaps this will somehow make it up to them. However, to protect you and our children from scandal, Ferrel,' that's our family's lawyer, 'is instructed during the reading of the will, to identify Erica and Perry as children of a loyal employee — if need be.' "

Elizabeth's mouth felt dry. She took another sip of tea to moisten her lips, stared upward reflectively and shook her head as if she were still in utter disbelief. "Earl said, 'I know I'm about to ask a great deal of you, Elizabeth, but I want you to find my children.' He told me he wanted his other daughter and son to know who they were. You see, while Earl said he would have loved to see them again before passing on, he chose to sacrifice doing so as a symbol of his sincere regret for what he had done to me and our children. As I said, he could be very noble. Then he said he knew this would be hard on me — an obvious understatement — as it would our own children, and he asked *me* to tell them about it. Well, no one could ever imagine how put upon I felt at such an insane request." As before, Lynn found herself deeply engrossed in this story.

Elizabeth Remington told Lynn this wasn't the worst of it. Earl wanted his two children to be *accepted* by their half-brothers and sisters. "He even asked me to try and accept them, too. Now that will be the day." She couldn't imagine the total ludicrousness of such. "Earl said, 'Elizabeth, I know this is asking a lot of you and our children, and I realize you may not be willing or able to do this. But this is my final request of you.' And then he added, 'Whatever your decision, I know it will be the right one for you.'

"My God, I truly did not know what to do. How could he have asked such a thing of me?" She looked at Lynn as if she were seriously seeking an answer. "How could I ever accept his two illegitimate children? How were our four children to ever accept them? This was like a bad dream. I tell you, I wanted to wake up, but God knows, I wasn't dreaming. No, as much as I wanted to deny it, this was real."

Mrs. Remington then shared how she knew the end was near. She told her husband this had been the most difficult thing she had ever had to deal with. "Earl looked so pained." And as if suddenly remembering something important, she added, "I completely forgot to ask Earl why he believed this matter was going to be made known to me. I still do not know why he said that. I told him

I did not wish his final moments with me to be filled with such anguish. Although I did not know what I was going to do, I promised to sort out my feelings later. I told him he was right, I would have mixed feelings. Of course, I was already terribly upset for what he had done to me, and especially that he had waited until this moment to tell me about it. But for now, he just needed to know I did love him and would carry him in my heart. I wanted him to know I would try very hard to forgive him. I truly wanted him to be at peace in death. Earl could barely speak, but I knew he was relieved. I also knew it was time to call our children back into the room."

Mrs. Remington patted her dampening eyes while her husband's last moments whisked through her mind. For the hundredth time, she recalled her children and herself standing at his bedside, she tenderly stroking his face. Their daughters, Parker and Jordan, standing together on one side of his bed, both with tears glistening their eyes, gently touching him and holding his hand. In her thoughts, she saw their sons, Earl, Jr. and Ross, also patting him softly.

Earl had told his children, "I've had a beautiful life, and each of you has added so much to my joy. I have loved you four more than words can say." Elizabeth reflected on how her husband closed his eyes for a moment and paused, summoning the energy to continue. "I have asked your mother to share something with you after I am gone." The children looked at each other momentarily perplexed; then they all looked back at their father. "She will decide when the time is right. It will be difficult for you, but your mother and I have tried to teach you to be good people, and I hope you will understand. You must know that I would never want to hurt any of you in any way." How can I tell them about this, she had asked herself. This will surely break their hearts as it did mine.

Silently she remembered her sons' and daughters' professions of love to their father. After taking a moment to relive the final moments of her husband's life, Elizabeth Remington began weeping softly. Her head was down, her forehead resting on one hand. When she finally spoke, she told Lynn that when it was over, she gently kissed her husband as he closed his eyes for infinity. Lynn was at a loss for words. She wanted to somehow comfort this powerful woman but did not know how. She said only, "I want you to know, Mrs. Remington, I'll be more than happy to take your case."

Elizabeth Remington looked up momentarily. She regained her composure, sighed and stated, "I must find Earl's children, Erica and Perry Williams. That is why I've come to you. I have not told my own children about this yet, although I know they are curious about what their father wanted me to tell them. But with so much to tend to since the burial, I have managed to put them off. Quite frankly, I have only recently sorted out my own reactions to this. I certainly struggled with it a great deal.

"I so wondered why Earl couldn't have just let sleeping dogs lie. Surely, this was not his first time, and frankly, I'd much rather not have known about any of this. Over and over, I wondered why did he have to tell me? Why would Earl leave the burden of his past with me? Why couldn't this secret have died with him? I don't know if I'll ever have the answers.

"Before Earl died, he told me our attorney, Ferrel Whitmore, was to schedule the reading of his will exactly three months from the date of his death." Lynn looked puzzled, and Mrs. Remington noted her look, telling Lynn that Earl wanted to give her time to work through this. That is why it had taken her this long to speak with an investigator to locate his children. Elizabeth thought of the past two months during which she'd had to wrestle with this problem alone. If only she could have talked to someone about this, but she had no one with whom she could confide such confidences. Perhaps, she thought, that is why today I am telling all to this investigator; maybe I've held on to it too long. Thankfully, she is certainly easy to talk to, and appears objective enough.

By far, Elizabeth's toughest decision had been whether or not she would honor her husband's deathbed wish. Some days she had thought she would be able to, but there were many days when she felt she could never go through with it. What a mess! But here she was today talking with a private investigator about finding her husband's two children. Yes, she would comply with his last wishes.

She was finished. At last, it was out; this horrible secret was out. Elizabeth felt a great sense of relief. With their session ending, Lynn quickly scanned her notes and told Mrs. Remington she would need all the information she could provide her. Lynn told her new client how she and her partner, Ella, worked together on many cases, and would do so on this one. She told her that she sometimes hired the services of an outside agent. Mrs. Remington looked concerned that this matter would be discussed with others, and Lynn assured her that her case would be treated with utmost confidentiality.

Elizabeth Remington hastily agreed to a generous fee and expense arrangement that essentially gave Lynn complete authority to run this case. Then she told Lynn the Remingtons customarily paid a handsome bonus for satisfactory services, but Lynn quickly said that would not be necessary. "As you wish," Elizabeth Remington replied and left her office. Lynn wondered whether her pride had caused her to speak too quickly about that bonus.

What a day! It was almost four o'clock, and Lynn was totally zapped. She realized why. This whole day had been chock full of emotion and intrigue — a bit more than the average day at the Lynn Davis Agency, and this last case had been the gem of them all! Lynn was glad she didn't have any other appointments. She had to clear her head for a minute. But not before Ella brought the two of them a freshly brewed cup of herbal tea, sat down, and said, "What in the world was that about?"

Lynn told Ella the whole exhaustive story. Ella interrupted often with her own surprised reactions. When Lynn finished, she told Ella, "I'll get started looking for the children this afternoon." Ella said she would get on it right away, too.

CHAPTER
4

SEVERAL WEEKS HAD passed since that rainy afternoon in April when J.T. returned home from the park empty-handed. Hardly a single day went by when he didn't think of how shocked and angry he'd been that Remington hadn't paid up. Still, with every passing day, his resolve to succeed grew stronger. He had thought the old man still had weeks, maybe months to live. But, BAM! Just like that, he was gone. His sudden death had hit J.T. completely by surprise.

He often thought of the brainstorm that got him through that fateful day. While true, the idea of kidnapping a Remington had given him something to hold on to, he quickly ruled it out, realizing it was just too dangerous. Oddly, however, entertaining this notion had helped J.T. immeasurably, for it pulled him out of the doldrums and kept him from giving up. It took a while, but he finally came up with another angle. He had to, for without a plan, J.T. knew his sweet money well would soon be dry, and big trouble awaited him if he was broke.

Since he had believed there was an unlimited pot of money at his disposal, he had spent recklessly, invested foolishly, gambled excessively, and taken some costly chances. Hey, you only live once, he had told himself with each lavish expenditure. Now, not only were legitimate creditors hot on his back, so much so he stood to lose everything — maybe even his job. But there were also those tough loan sharks he had become hugely indebted to because of some tough luck at gambling and other bad habits. J.T. couldn't let himself go down like that. He would strike quickly while the iron was still hot. He figured old man Remington must surely have confessed to his wife. Why else would he have dared not pay me my money, he fumed. No problem. If his wife knows about her old man's unfaithfulness, we'll see if she wants the rest of the world to know about it, too.

J.T. decided the tabloid press would be his angle. He had scandalous pictures; they wanted scandal — especially pictures. He'd just threaten to sell these puppies to the tabloids, for surely all the editors would be eager to get their hands on a juicy story about one of the nation's richest men. So he would let the wife pay to keep her dead husband's story out of the headlines. This sounded like an airtight plan, because any self-respecting widow and mother would pay, wouldn't she? Sure she would. So now he'd need a way to communicate with her while staying out of the picture.

He sat at his metal desk, removed a packet of his infamous photographs from a locked drawer and studied them one by one as he had done many times before. It never ceased to amaze J.T. how he'd come by those pictures in the first place. It's like they dropped right in his lap like a gift from heaven. Cunningly, he had been able to piece two and two together. He figured out what those pictures represented and came up with his lucrative scheme, marveling all the while at his ingenuity.

J.T. always wished he could have seen the old man's reaction when he first got his package and saw those tell-all photographs of him and his dark little mistress. He'd laugh as he pictured Remington practically falling out of his chair in shock. "Remington," he said, "you owe me, big guy." He truly believed his life had been ruined due to the actions of Mr. Earl Q. Remington. These photographs had conveniently been both his passport to riches, as well as his pathway to sweet revenge.

Okay, now, to get to the old lady. J.T. had managed to cultivate a special contact that fed him priceless information about
the Remingtons. He hoped his contact would somehow give him
an idea of how he could get to Mrs. Remington. J.T. put in a call
to his source. Bingo! He got an earful. Her name was Lynn Davis.
He wasn't too thrilled to learn that this Davis woman was a private investigator who'd been hired to locate Remington's bastard
kids. *I don't need any interfering private eye snooping around
the Remington matter,* he thought. *I'll just have to teach her to
mind her own damned business and leave mine alone?* The wheels
were turning in his head. *Maybe I'll just use a little unfriendly
persuasion to get her to keep her nose where it belongs,* he sneered.

* * * * *

Every day Ella and Lynn discussed the status of their unsuccessful search for Earl Remington's son and daughter. The two
had put in many hours on an exhaustive search of traditional
sources, including census records, police records, state birth and
death records, Social Security employment and death records,
records from area hospitals, telephone service, voter registration,
Human Services foster care and adoption agencies, military, foreign and Internal Revenue Service, penal records, public and pa-
rochial schools, State Department, funeral records, and Ella
had surfed and swept the Internet until she could look no more.
They both kept several search irons in the fire. So far, however,
their efforts had been futile. "I can't figure it out," Lynn said days
into the search. "We've had absolutely no luck. This is crazy. We've
practically gone the whole route. Nothing." Ella's bewilderment
matched Lynn's. She placed her hands on her hips and gave a
look of frustration.

Lynn found it hard to understand how they were coming up
completely empty-handed, for both she and Ella were well trained
in search techniques. In fact, Ella had just completed an extensive certification program on locating missing persons. She had
even taken advanced courses on computer investigations and
research. They had never had this much trouble locating people
in the past. A perplexed Ella furrowed her brow and thought
hard. It usually didn't take this much effort to find people, even

when they'd changed their identities.

It had now been over a week since Elizabeth Remington had come to the office. Earl Q. Remington's Last Will and Testament was to be read in just three more weeks. Time was short. The only thing they had uncovered was some limited information about Hattie Williams. According to school and employment data, Hattie Rose Williams was born in Ft. Davis, Alabama, in May of 1954, to Sophie and Leroy Williams, but she grew up in Cincinnati.

"Frankly, I'm mystified by this one," Lynn told Ella. She decided to get her friend Harvey Chapman's viewpoint on where to go from here. Lynn and Harvey had worked together on a missing person's case a couple of years before. Harvey's many years of experience had taught him the most effective tools, techniques and sources of data. Lynn gave Harvey what information she had about Hattie Williams, and he told her he'd look into it. She decided also to talk to her Uncle Ed to see what tips he could offer her from his many years on the police force.

The first thing Uncle Eddy said was, "Now you know, Lynn, people don't just drop off the face of the earth," adding, "unless maybe they're in the witness protection program or something like that." Uncle Eddy's years on the force had honed his sixth sense, and Lynn respected his hunches just as she had grown to respect her own. She knew that in the unlikely event these two were in a witness protection program, they would be all the more difficult to find. But there were ways.

"Now you say you couldn't find any childbirth records listing Hattie Williams as the mother in the state of Ohio?" Lynn answered in the affirmative. Then Uncle Eddy asked how extensive her search was. "I guess you've already looked at Kentucky? How about Indiana?" Lynn confirmed that not only the tri-state area, but the entire United States had been searched. "You've got to consider these kids might have been adopted, or they could have been given a different last name from their mother, either at birth, or even afterwards." Lynn told him she had also searched for them in vain under the Remington surname.

Uncle Eddy paused for a moment while he thought. "This is pretty unusual. I think you did the right thing to bring Harvey

Chapman in on this. I want you to keep me informed about this case," he said cautiously, and Lynn acknowledged her agreement. "If I can think of anything helpful, I'll give you a call," he told her.

After Lynn finished talking to her uncle, she was left with a wariness. *What am I missing?*

"Harvey's on the phone," Ella announced, and Lynn invited her to stay on the line as she greeted him.

"Hey, Buddy," Harvey said. "I called to tell you to pack your bags. We're going to Alabama."

"Alabama?" Lynn and Ella both replied in unison. "What's up, Harvey?" Lynn asked. "And where in Alabama?"

"Ft. Davis — it's near Tuskegee. You know that's where they're from." Lynn could see Harvey leaned back in his chair, twirling the ends of his salt and pepper mustache as he spoke, his deep, dark eyes accenting his handsome chocolate-colored face. *Your Miss Hattie Williams had an older half-brother, Wilbur.*

"Apparently, Hattie's mother, Sophie, brought the little girl up here to Ohio back in 1960 a few years after her husband died. Hattie's brother, Wilbur, was 15 when they left for Ohio, and he was sent off to stay with a grandmother in Alabama. He's still in Alabama. I talked to him briefly today. He has some more information, and he may be willing to talk about it. But he wouldn't say too much over the phone, especially to someone he doesn't know. I did get that much out of him." Lynn and Ella listened intently.

Lynn was confused. *Hadn't Mrs. Remington said her husband told her Hattie had no relatives? Maybe Mr. Remington didn't know his lady friend as well as he thought. And if Hattie had family, could the kids have gone to live with them when their mother died? This was very interesting.* Excited, Lynn said, "This is great, Harvey. I knew I could count on you to come up with something." Then she quickly added, "I'll go with you." Harvey gave her his flight schedule.

Ella said, "Sounds like you may be on to something we can dig our heels into. I'll keep up the search here."

The plane arrived in Montgomery at 9:15 the next morning. During the flight, Harvey told Lynn that when she told him Hattie

34

was from Ft. Davis, he was able to learn that she had a half-brother, Wilbur Williams, through state birth records. So he called Ft. Davis to try and reach this Wilbur Williams and had run up against a brick wall. Then after several phone calls and wrong numbers, he decided to check under the name of Leroy Williams, Wilbur's father. There were a half-dozen Leroy Williams in the Tuskegee area. Harvey called four of them before reaching a Mrs. Bessie Williams. He identified himself and asked for Mr. Wilbur Williams, brother of the late Hattie Williams. She called Wilbur to the telephone.

Harvey said that Wilbur Williams was a friendly sounding man, but he had seemed very cautious. Wilbur did confirm for Harvey that little Hattie and her mother had left Alabama for Cincinnati nearly 45 years before. Harvey explained that he was trying to locate Hattie Williams' children about an inheritance, and Wilbur told him he didn't feel right discussing his sister's business with a complete stranger. He told Harvey he was more than welcome to come down to Alabama to talk to him in person, and he seemed surprised when Harvey told him he and an associate could be there the next day. After arranging his flight, Harvey called Wilbur back to tell him when they'd be arriving in Montgomery. Wilbur gave him directions to his home in Ft. Davis, about 100 miles away.

When their plane landed in Montgomery, Harvey called Wilbur and told him they should be there in a couple of hours. Then they got a rental car and he and Lynn headed for Fort Davis. They drove about an hour and a half down two-lane Highway 29 until they arrived in Ft. Davis, population 450. The landscape abruptly changed from the well-traveled highway to lesser-traveled rural back roads. Now, winding dirt roads would lead them to their destination.

They drove slowly. Dense overgrown trees crowded the side of the road. Occasionally, Lynn and Harvey would see a small run-down house or mobile home by the roadside. They passed an old school bus that sat disabled off the side of the road. For a while, two dogs of unknown breeding ran alongside their car. They passed a little red church house and saw a general store with an old Coca Cola sign out front where they decided to stop and get something cold to drink. Harvey and Lynn got out of their car and went into the store, grinding dirt from the hot, barren ground outside onto the worn hardwood floors inside. A stand-up fan blew air around in the store.

An elderly black man greeted them. "Mawning, how y'all doin' t'day?" Lynn and Harvey returned the greeting, both noting at once the strong, pleasant Southern atmosphere of the place. They picked up two ice-cold bottles of soda pop and handed the man two dollars. He made change from an old cash register, and they returned to their car thankful for their cold drinks, and took off again. By now, the houses were about as close as a football field from each other. From his shirt pocket, Harvey pulled out the directions he'd written down when he spoke to Wilbur, and looked for a turn in the road that marked the place where he was to go to the left. "So far, so good," he said, seeing he was on the right track. "We're almost there."

A little before eleven, Harvey pulled onto a dirt and gravel road that, according to the wooden mail box by the roadside, led to Wilbur Leroy Williams' place, a small, tree-shaded, neat little freshly painted white house. A blue 1984 Buick LeSabre was parked in the drive. Pecan trees graced the neatly cut yard, and weeping willows flanked a small fishing pond about 200 yards from the house. A rickety white picket fence surrounded the property. Gravel sounded beneath the slow-moving tires, and a chicken sauntered across the road in front of them. Harvey jokingly asked Lynn why the chicken crossed the road. She laughed. An older couple sat on the porch. As Harvey and Lynn headed up the dirt drive, the man rose to his feet.

After they pulled to a stop, Wilbur walked briskly over to their car. "Mr. Chapman, is it? How ya' doin? I see you made it all right. Wilbur Williams here," he said, extending his hand to shake Harvey's and saying, "Hello, ma'am," to Lynn, and she introduced herself. Then he said, "Come on over here and meet my wife, Bessie." Lynn and Harvey liked his warm welcome. They got out of their car, taking in a quick overview of this homey place, and formal introductions were exchanged all around. Then they went over to the porch and greeted Wilbur's wife, who stood up and gave them both a friendly hug.

Wilbur and Bessie told their visitors to make themselves at home. Then Bessie asked them if they wanted something to eat or drink. Lynn and Harvey declined, saying they already ate on the plane, and they were still holding their bottles of pop. They showed Bessie and Wilbur some identification and were invited to sit down on some old padded rocking chairs on the porch to talk.

Wilbur was a tall, lean, proud-looking, dark-skinned man. He had striking chiseled features and thick black hair. From what she knew of the story, Lynn calculated him to be close to 60, but he had the carriage and appearance of a man 30 years younger. His gait was quick and supple, and his shiny skin was smooth as silk. Wilbur was wearing a short-sleeved shirt, showing well-developed biceps and forearms. His overall fit physique was the apparent by-product of a lifetime of hard work. He had on heavy work boots that looked like they had seen their day around the farm. Wilbur later told Lynn and Harvey that he still worked his 80-acre farm and Bessie tended a nice-sized garden around the side of the house.

Bessie looked like she might have been in her 40s, but she was about the same age as her husband. She, too, was lean, fit and agile with pretty roundish facial features and flawless milk-chocolate-colored skin. Bessie was wearing a pink floral blouse, loose-fitting gray pants and cut-out flip-flops on her feet.

They talked small talk sitting up there on the porch and occasionally swatted at flies or fanned the air around trying to cool themselves. There was no breeze today, and the temperature was in the low 90s. "But it's cooler out here than in there right now," Bessie laughed and said, pointing through the screen door into their house. Then Harvey repeated what he had told Wilbur on the phone about why he and Lynn had come down to Alabama to see them.

Wilbur needed to know more. Exactly why did Harvey want to find his niece and nephew? What was this inheritance business? Who was the benefactor? Lynn and Harvey told him that a woman had retained Lynn's agency to locate Hattie's children.

They told him this was a very wealthy woman who was married to Erica and Perry's deceased father. Wilbur asked what their names were, and Lynn explained that they were not at liberty to say at this time due to a need for absolute privacy. He didn't like that, but accepted it and said he would help them all he could anyway.

Wilbur began talking about his younger sister. "She's been gone 30 years, but I still get sad thinking about her dying so young like she did. But when she was a young'un, that li'l gal was sure 'nuff a pistol," he said with reminiscent eyes and a sad smile. "She was bright as could be, I tell ya, but spoiled as all get-out, what with being the baby and all. Wouldn't mind her momma for nuttin'. She was a real cute li'l gal, you know — had them big ole' twinkly eyes and curly black hair that hung all the way down her back. Ma Sophie, Hattie's mother," he told them, " 'course now, she was my stepmother, you see, well, she was a bright-complected woman, near-bout white, but she sure wasn't stuck up and she coulda been, too, 'cause was she ever pretty. And was nice as she could be, too. Least my daddy thought so. He married her as quick as she would say 'I do.' " When he said to Lynn and Harvey who appreciated his openness, "I can show you some pictures if you want," they readily accepted his offer.

Wilbur went inside his house and came back with an old photo album. He opened it carefully because some of the stick-on corner holders had come unstuck. He turned a few pages and came to a particular group of photographs. "Here we go," he said, holding the album so Lynn and Harvey could see Hattie's picture. "Here she is right here. Ain't but 'round 'bout four maybe five years old. Got on her li'l Easter Sunday outfit."

The old sepia-toned picture he was pointing to was of a strikingly pretty little girl sitting demurely in a white ruffled dress, wearing long white stockings and black patent leather shoes. A little white bonnet covered her head and tiny white gloves, her hands. She had light brown skin, deep dark eyes and curly hair that draped her face and hung down under her bonnet across her shoulders. Her little feet were crossed, and she was holding her hands in her lap with a small black patent leather purse dangling across her wrist. Her head was slightly tilted; she was smiling coquette-like. She looked sweet and precious. Lynn couldn't help but say so. Everyone agreed.

Then they looked at the other pictures. Wilbur and Bessie pointed out and described each one. There were more pictures of Hattie, some taken when she was about five or six, and all were very pretty. There were also pictures of her mother, Sophie. Whereas her daughter had big almond-shaped eyes and a heart-shaped face, Sophie had keen features, fair skin and straight brown hair. Even still, there was a definite resemblance between her and Hattie. Photographs of Hattie and Wilbur's father, Leroy Williams, showed him to be a near imposing figure. He was tall with rich dark skin and deeply piercing black eyes, regal cheekbones, a wide mouth and sliver-thin lips.

They also saw pictures of Wilbur, a tall, lanky teenager who strongly resembled his father. Wilbur showed them a picture of his mother, Reba Heard Williams, a plump, pleasant-faced woman wearing an Afro hairstyle and a big smile. His mother and father had split up years before his father met Sophie. Lynn, and Harvey pored over the pictures while completely immersed in Wilbur's descriptions.

Wilbur shifted in his seat, his eyes briefly pinned to the porch ceiling while thoughts of his mother crept into his mind. Pointing to her picture again, he told them he was only ten when she died and he went to live with his father and stepmother, Sophie, and little baby sister, Hattie. When Wilbur was 12, his father died from a tractor accident, so he helped out as much as he could, even dropping out of school to go to work to help make ends meet. But the family still wasn't able to get by. So eventually Sophie and Hattie moved to Ohio where Sophie had a distant cousin and thought she could earn a living wage in her profession as a laundress. She wanted Wilbur to come with them, but in the end, it was decided that he would go to live with his grandmother, Flossie Heard. And that was that — the Williams family history, filled with both pride and sadness.

As the pages of the photo album were turned, Lynn looked at pictures of Bessie's side of the family, and of her and Wilbur's five children. Then she asked Wilbur and Bessie about Hattie's kids. Lynn repeated that their search had so far left them empty-handed. Sitting back and studying his two visitors, Wilbur furrowed his brow and said, "Now I'm gonna tell y'all why you haven't found those kids of Hattie's." This is what Lynn and Harvey were waiting to hear. He spoke on. "Hattie never used the Williams name when she had those kids. She was so ashamed of not being married and all that, she took her mother's surname, Dodd. Probably figured with a different name, folks would think she up and got married. Then, having them babies out of wedlock wouldn't shame her reputation. Naw, suh, you ain't gonna find no one named Erica and Perry Williams. But you probably won't have no trouble if you look for Erica Rose and Perry Earl Dodd." Lynn caught the children's middle names as she thought to herself, puzzle solved.

Now she understood why they hadn't been able to find the two and was excited about resuming the search. Wilbur continued, "Erica's birthday is September something or other. Born in 1976. Our baby girl was born that same year. And Perry, we remember, was born on Christmas day, nineteen hundred and seventy-eight.

We ain't seen those young'uns since before Hattie died. But don't you go thinking they gonna be glad to see you coming, 'cause them two prob'ly don't want to be found." Lynn and Harvey wondered why. Lynn asked Wilbur for clarification, and he carefully turned the pages of the album. He came to a page that had pictures of two little pale-skinned, blond-haired kids, a girl and a boy. The girl was the older child. She was a pretty, pixie-faced little girl with long, thick, somewhat wavy hair and looked to be about seven or so. The little boy looked like he was around four or five. He had long, straight hair and bangs, a mischievous look in his eyes, and a big, happy smile. Lynn and Harvey stared at the pictures, bewildered. Are these kids Erica and Perry, they both wondered as the answer began to dawn on them.

"I know what y'all thinking," Wilbur said, seeing the puzzled looks on their faces. "This is Erica," he said, pointing to the little girl in the picture. "And this is Perry. I guess you didn't 'spect to see 'em looking like that." Lynn nodded agreement. Wilbur continued, "With their light-colored skin, they musta took more after their daddy."

"Those are the last pictures we ever got of these two," Bessie added. Sophie was still living when Hattie died. You remember what Sophie looked like. You see, she could pass for white. So now, what do you think they did after it was just the three of them?" Bessie asked her guests, then answered her own rhetorical question. "They started living as whites. You know, passin'. Wasn't no reason not to, I guess. They musta figured they'd have it better off that way. She shook her head as if that was a pitiful shame.

"Miss Sophie dropped Williams from her name and went back to her maiden name, too. So now, all of a sudden, they was all Dodds. 'Course now, after that, they cut themselves off from Wilbur and me. Tore Wilbur's heart out. We was all the family they had left," Bessie added. "But we was still black, and they was now a'passin' themselves off as white." Sophie died a coupla years later, never recovered from some kinda ailment or other. Them kids got sent off to foster homes, and that's all we ever heard about 'em. Lost touch completely."

Lynn and Harvey's mission was accomplished. Lynn now had the information she needed to complete the search for Erica and Perry. After talking a little while longer, they thanked the Williams for the valuable information that was going to help them locate Earl Remington's two children. Their plane didn't leave Alabama until seven o'clock that evening. It was already nearly two o'clock. They had viewed pictures and chatted for close to three hours. Bessie said, "Now y'all just gonna hafta stay for dinner."

Wilbur added, "Y'all can't come flying all the way down here from up north without eatin' some of Bessie's fried chicken and mashed p'tatoes."

"And we've also got collard greens, and for dessert I got strawberry shortcake," Bessie added.

Lynn and Harvey gladly accepted the invitation, looking forward to the chance to just relax and visit some more before making their drive back to Montgomery. From her cellular phone, Lynn called to give Ella the news, and Ella said she would start searching for the Dodds. Then Ella told Lynn that Mrs. Remington had called and wanted Lynn to call her when she could. "Have a safe trip back and enjoy that down-home cooking. And eat some for me," Ella laughingly told Lynn.

Lynn hung up and immediately returned the call to Mrs. Remington so she could tell her of their successful trip to Alabama. Elizabeth Remington was surprised that Lynn had located relatives because she didn't know Hattie had any other family members other than her mother. She said she was glad to hear their trip was successful as she was getting concerned, what with the date for the reading of the will fast approaching.

"I have spoken to my attorney. He assures me that if all parties are not located by July 15, he is authorized to reschedule the reading for the following month. Frankly, I don't know how much more of this I can take. Whatever it takes, I want this thing over as soon as possible. I'm trusting this will give you enough time." Lynn assured her she felt they were now much closer.

Then Mrs. Remington told Lynn that while looking through some of Earl's things, she had come across a locked file in his desk marked *Private*. She had not run across this particular file before, so she opened it and was dismayed to find materials that obviously pertained to her husband's affair with Miss Williams. In this file, she found some letters she thought were from Hattie to Earl. These letters bore no return address, just the initials H.W. in one corner of the envelope. They had been sent to his office. She said the envelopes were yellowed with age, the words written in pencil slightly faded. Also in the file were bank statements, a sealed enveloped marked *Photographs*, and some other miscellaneous papers.

Lynn asked if Mrs. Remington had found anything in the letters that might offer information on the whereabouts of Hattie's children. She told Lynn she had not felt up to reading the letters. However, she did want to know what they contained. Then she asked if Lynn would examine the file with her. They scheduled a meeting for the following morning.

While Bessie prepared dinner, Wilbur showed Lynn and Harvey around his farm. Then they sat on the porch and talked about life in general. "Everything's ready," shouted Bessie, as she called Wilbur and their guests into the kitchen. It was now about three o'clock. Lynn and Harvey decided to depart no later than four in order to have plenty of time to get back to the airport. The kitchen was filled with the wonderful aroma of good home cooking. A large area fan was blowing, and occasionally a little air would come through the back screen door. Lynn and Harvey sat down at the kitchen table. Lynn noticed a small window air conditioning unit as she peered into the living room. Bessie saw her glance at the unit and said, "It don't work, honey." Then she adjusted the fan to be sure Lynn got plenty of air. Lynn smiled gratefully.

Bessie's table was covered with a red and white checkerboard oilcloth and loaded with a delightful meal. Harvey and Lynn helped themselves while complimenting Bessie's delicious cooking. After their leisurely meal, they thanked their hosts and prepared to leave. With handshakes, hugs and promises to inform Wilbur and Bessie of their findings, Lynn and Harvey pulled away from the Williams' house. As they headed back to the airport, they agreed that this day's deep immersion into genuine Southern hospitality constituted one of the special aspects of their work.

CHAPTER

5

Since the death of her husband, Elizabeth Remington had endured extensive, often torturous, personal introspection. During her ride downtown to deliver her husband's personal file to Lynn Davis' office, she again retraced their relationship as she had done many times, beginning with their meeting in 1963 at the Kentucky Derby in Louisville. Her father, Wade Forbes, a prominent Virginia businessman, and his family had been invited to a celebration party for the winner, Northern Dancer's owners. Elizabeth was only 22 at the time.

Earl Remington, the most eligible bachelor in the Tri-State, was in attendance. At the time, Earl was 32, ruggedly good looking, and even then, extremely wealthy. He was also smitten by Elizabeth. She was young and beautiful, sophisticated, college-educated, and from a fine upper-class family. Elizabeth had heard of Earl Remington before; his name was often mentioned in upper society's "who's who" circles. He had allure, charisma, and many interested women. But Elizabeth was not so easily charmed, for she had many interested gentlemen seeking her hand, herself. However, when Earl Remington began to pursue her, she was swept away. Their courtship was like a fairytale for the beautiful Elizabeth Forbes. Her many other suitors waited in the wings to see if she would emerge unattached. They lost out, and Earl Remington had his prize.

On her way into town this morning, Elizabeth Remington mentally walked through their eight-month courtship, which began almost the moment they met and intensified when she left Virginia to move to Cincinnati to pursue a graduate degree in art history, and to be near Earl Remington. She analyzed every phase of their four decades of marriage and recalled how when she first learned of her husband's affair with Hattie Williams, she had been completely unwilling to accept that he had been unfaithful, especially for such an obscenely long time.

How could he have done it? She had been a good wife who adored her husband and enjoyed the life they lived very much. However, now that she knew about her husband's relationship with Hattie Williams, things were beginning to add up more. She'd recalled long periods of time when Earl would appear disengaged, or detached, or just faraway. She had told herself these moods were the product of business pressures. Of course, they were, she had convinced herself, because he was otherwise devoted to her and their four children. Elizabeth remembered an extended period, wasn't it about 20 years ago, when Earl had been completely unlike himself for weeks, maybe months. He seemed to have fallen into a pit of depression, and nothing she or the children did would cheer him up. Was he losing the business, she had wondered. She remembered that during this time, Earl had actually missed Parker's debut in her school play. That had been unthinkable. Heartbroken though she was, Parker forgave him. Everyone always forgave him. That was just how it was with Earl. Parker's debut was in the fall of 1984. The year Hattie died? Although she did not know the exact date of Hattie Williams' death, Elizabeth couldn't help but wonder now if her death may have had anything to do with that terribly moody period Earl had gone through.

This type of introspection was a constant these days. When Elizabeth finally accepted the painful reality of Earl's affair with Hattie Williams, she searched herself to understand why she had chosen to ignore the signs, for surely Earl had always had an eye for beauty. Of this, she was certain. She also was not stupid. She knew he'd had his share of tête-à-têtes over the years. Some things you just forgive, especially since she'd been no angel herself at times. However, those little affairs of his had always been just fleeting nuisances, none ever seriously threatening her status as Mrs. Earl Q. Remington. But this Hattie Williams affair had not passed fleetingly, she thought. And, dear Lord, of all things, the woman was black!

As she approached downtown Cincinnati, the hustle and bustle of the busy streets brought her out of her reflections, and Elizabeth saw she was very near Lynn Davis' office. Even as she was trying to face the truth, she knew it would have been next to impossible for her to have examined the contents of this file she'd located in her husband's desk. She'd have been more inclined to burn them. It had been difficult enough just going through Earl's private things. Here's where Miss Davis will be extremely helpful, she thought with a sigh of resignation.

At eight o'clock, Elizabeth Remington was sitting in Lynn Davis' office. She was extremely hopeful this secret file might shed light on this matter, and she was curious. As they prepared to look at the contents of the private file, Lynn offered her client something to drink, and she readily accepted. This time Lynn was able to serve brandy in an elegant Waterford crystal glass on a silver tray from her newly appointed bar now stocked with Courvoisier and a few other premium alcoholic beverages, including Kahlúa, Absolut Vodka, Beefeater Gin and Chivas Regal Whiskey. Lynn was prepared.

Elizabeth Remington took a sip of her welcomed drink, then sighed and placed the file on the table beside her. Lynn studied the rich-looking aged leather portfolio. It looked mysterious. Then Mrs. Remington took a small key from her purse and unlocked it. Slowly she dumped its contents onto the desk; then together she and Lynn sorted the contents by type — letters, bank records, photographs, other miscellaneous papers. Curiosity as much as anything made Lynn want to dig right in, but she held back, for she hadn't forgotten how shook up Mrs. Remington had sounded when she talked about finding this file, and how she'd been hesitant to probe it. Lynn carefully sorted the letters by date, and selected the earliest postmarked one as the first to be read. It was dated June 2, 1974. Elizabeth knew that was the year Earl and Hattie met.

"Shall I?" Lynn asked, and Mrs. Remington gave a single nod. Lynn read:

My Dearest Earl,

Sometimes I think it was wrong to have fallen so in love with you. But then, I ask myself how could I have possibly not fallen for you? You are my everything.

Although it feels like we belong together, in my heart I know you belong to another. I have no choice but to accept your deep commitment to your family, and you have made it clear that you will remain so committed. God, she is a blessed woman to have your devotion. I know that I can only experience a portion of your precious love. I'll take what I can get. Nonetheless, this does not lessen my passion and desire to be with you always.

Earl, you are such a marvelous man. I have never known one of such strength, and yet such warmth and affection. When you touch me, hold me in your arms, I am all yours. What is this power you have over me, my dearest? Could it simply be the power of your touch, or is it your kiss? Perhaps it is your warm body next to mine, inside mine. Oh, Darling, I yearn for you so when I think of you like this. How is it possible to feel so strongly after the short time we've known each other?

I cannot wait until you are here with me again. Sunday seems so far away, but I know I will see you when you return from Virginia. So until we are together again, my love, I will remain your love captive. I want no one but you.

Always, HRW

Lynn finished the first letter. How compelling, those words. She'd had to make an effort not to read them with the tenderness they evoked in her. Even still, Elizabeth Remington looked terribly saddened. The message had been so poignant, so tender, but so wrong. She just stared blankly in deep thought. She earnestly wished this was a mistake, but she knew it was not. Her heart ached hearing those words of love expressed by another woman to her husband.

Earl, why did you save these letters? Elizabeth asked herself silently. Did they mean so much to you that you would bring them into our home? Oddly, she began to feel less anger toward the woman, Hattie. For the moment, she felt only anger toward Earl. In her mind, she continued her probe, Why, Earl? Why did you need someone else in your life? Were you not happy? How could you have betrayed me so? And why would you tell me about it the way you did? I would love for you to need to know the pain and anger you've caused me. Then with watery eyes Mrs. Remington said aloud, "This is damned cruel." For solace, she lit a cigarette and took a long, lingering draw and a comforting sip of brandy. Then another.

Lynn waited quietly. After a while, Elizabeth Remington said, "Miss Davis, as you can probably tell, I've heard quite enough. At the present time, I cannot listen to any more of this. I would like you to keep this file and go through it. If you find anything of importance to this case, feel free to use it and let me know. I don't want to hear any more of these letters. I'd probably shred this entire file if I took it back home with me."

"I understand, Mrs. Remington. Of course, I will," Lynn assured her. "Is there anything in this file you want to hold on to, or see? The photographs, perhaps?"

"They probably won't be any easier than those letters, but yes, I am interested in seeing them. Let's have a look?" She placed her burning cigarette in the ashtray Lynn had placed on her desk for Mrs. Remington's visits.

Lynn carefully unsealed the envelope that was marked *Photos*. Inside was a small stack of black and white and color photographs of assorted sizes. Lynn removed them from the envelope and laid them on the table. As she took the largest photograph from the stack, she observed Mrs. Remington's eyes hungrily scanning the photos as they were spread across the desk. Holding up the larger photograph, Lynn and Elizabeth viewed it together. They both stared at the black woman in the picture. For a moment, they were both spellbound by her loveliness. Finally, Lynn turned the photo over. The words on the back said, "To my darling, Earl, With love, Hattie Rose.

Lynn turned the picture back over. This woman had a very special beauty. Her hair was long and black. The features of her heart-shaped face were soft and sweet, and Lynn thought of the picture of the precious little girl Wilbur Williams had just shown her yesterday. Looking at her alluring photograph, Lynn could almost understand how any man, Earl Remington included, would find this woman irresistible. Lynn could almost imagine Mrs. Remington having the same reaction. Perhaps seeing this photograph might help her understand her husband's attraction to Hattie Rose. Elizabeth had been away for months on end. Earl, left all alone, had obviously been captivated by Hattie. Elizabeth's voice softened, and she quietly sighed, "She's quite beautiful."

The remaining photographs were almost as dramatic as the first. There were photos taken of Hattie and Earl together, and always there was the look of adoration on Earl's face. One picture was very telling. Hattie Rose and Earl Remington were standing by a Rolls Royce — he, a tall, powerful, wealthy white gentleman standing behind his young, lovely black mistress, his arms wrapped affectionately around her waist. Hattie was leaning back against him with her head tilted slightly, her arms draped over his with one foot perched in front of the other. Lynn could tell this picture was extremely difficult for Mrs. Remington to view. She quickly put it aside to view the others.

There were some pictures of newborn babies. On the back of one was written, *Erica Rose, born September 2, 1976.* The writing on the back of the other baby picture said *Perry Earl, born December 25, 1978.* As she viewed the children's pictures, Elizabeth Remington seemed puzzled, although Lynn already knew why, for she'd had the same reaction when she saw these children's pictures the day before in Alabama. These babies did not look biracial. Elizabeth and Lynn discussed this. Other photographs showed Erica and Perry a few years later, perhaps at ages five and three. Reluctantly, Elizabeth had to admit these two bore a striking resemblance to her own children when they were small.

Lynn explained to Mrs. Remington what she learned from Hattie's brother in Alabama. When she became pregnant, Hattie had dropped the Williams name and taken her mother's maiden name, Dodd. Therefore, the children had been born as Dodds, not Williams, which was why she and Ella had previously had no luck finding them. She told her that after Hattie died, her two children were placed in the care of their fair-skinned, gray-eyed grandmother who looked fully Caucasian. Elizabeth was surprised to learn that Earl's children and their grandmother had lived as whites from that point on. When their grandmother first died, the children were placed in a foster home with a family named Bridges. "We're on the right track now," Lynn told Mrs. Remington.

After Elizabeth Remington left her office, Lynn carefully studied the remaining contents of the portfolio. The rest of the letters from Hattie to Earl were equally passionate and torrid, and as with the first letter, they were written in a poetic, romantic style. Lynn thought Hattie was probably very well educated. These letters were quite compelling. It was probably best that Mrs. Remington had not put herself through the misery of hearing the rest of them.

The bank statements provided an easy trail of financial transactions. Quarterly bank drafts had been drawn on Earl Remington's personal account over a ten-year period. In 1974, the drafts were for $10,000. The amount increased steadily, and at the time of Hattie's death, quarterly drafts were being issued in the amount of $25,000. "Hmmm," Lynn thought, "Miss Hattie Rose Williams wasn't doing too badly back then." The last draft for $100,000 was dated October 22, 1984. Was that when Hattie died in that accident? Perhaps Remington had sent this money to Hattie's estate for the care of his children.

In the stack of miscellaneous papers were some of Earl Remington's handwritten scribbles; most were written in his own brand of shorthand. Lynn did not find much, but she was able to get the gist of some of these cryptic notes. For example, one note may have been a reference to birthdays and gifts. It said, *A jewel for a jewel,* and was hand-dated, May 17. Was that Hattie's birthday? Lynn found a receipt in the stack dated May 10 for $3,778 for a diamond brooch. There were several other receipts for equally elaborate items. It looked as though Mr. Remington showered Hattie Rose with expensive gifts.

Oddly, one note seemed to have an angry tone to it. It was written on the back of an invoice for the purchase of an automobile. It said only, *Where are you? Why aren't you at home?* Lynn thought it had a jealous, almost possessive tone.

There were a few other papers and newspaper clippings that Lynn had not noticed during her meeting with Mrs. Remington. The first clipping dated October 15 was a short article titled, "Fatality on the Interstate." It described the death of a young black woman, Hattie Rose Dodd, 30. The circumstances of her death were under investigation. It was believed that her brakes failed as she entered a downhill ramp off the interstate, and the car, a 1983 Town Car, went over the overpass. She died instantly. Another clipping was Hattie's obituary. The date of the clipping was stapled to the top of the paper: October 20, 1984. "... Accidental death ... survived by her mother, Mrs. Sophie Williams and children, Erica Rose, eight, and Perry Earl, six, of the home." There was no mention of her brother, Wilbur.

CHAPTER
6

DURING THE RIDE back to her home, Elizabeth sipped her drink and pondered the difficult meeting she had just left. Of that horribly depressing private file of Earl's, she thought angrily, what right did that woman have to write such things to my husband? And Earl, dammit, why would you keep them? Why must I suffer this ordeal? Isn't it enough to have to deal with becoming a widow after a lifetime of marriage, then this, too?

Furthermore, now that her husband's two other children were likely to be located soon, she knew she had to get on with the next unpleasant part of his last request — to break the news to her children and somehow convince them to accept these two strangers into the family. This was an unduly difficult task because she had not fully embraced the idea of accepting these two, herself. How can I expect my children to do what I am unable to do, she wondered. How could Earl have ever conceived of such an absurd notion? The very thought made her shudder. She did not know what she would say to her offspring, but she knew she must do this soon. She could tell they were eager to know what their father wanted her to tell them — why he had begged their forgiveness. Elizabeth had sensed from both Parker and Earl their desire to broach the subject, though neither had. Of course, she could understand their need to know. Elizabeth had absolutely no knowledge that her husband had shared his story with one of their children for the express purpose of providing a helping hand to her, should she need the support.

What had Father wanted us to know, Parker Remington wondered as she sat alone sipping lemonade after a vigorous tennis match with a colleague, Abbie Nash, who departed the country club right after the game. *I have asked your mother to share something with you after I am gone. She will decide when the time is right. It will be difficult … I would never want to hurt any of you in any way.* Those words still sent chills through Parker, and she wondered disconcertingly, why hasn't Mummie told us? Parker's curiosity had finally gotten the better of her, and she had called her mother earlier this morning intending to ask about this. Her mother told Parker that she did not have time to talk as she had business downtown. Parker thought her mother's tone sounded evasive. Her questions could wait.

An attractive blond of 38, Parker Remington was the eldest of Earl and Elizabeth's four children. She had obtained a law degree from Harvard University and was a successful tax attorney in a prestigious law firm in downtown Cincinnati. A private person and fiercely independent, she had only a small core of close friends and was generally seen as a loner.

Parker had been extremely close to her father and took his death very hard. In fact, she mourned his passing practically every single day. As she drank her lemonade, she thought about how their father's death was probably as hard on her siblings, though they never really talked about it. The four Remington children were not especially close with one another. Next to Parker was Jordan, whom Parker considered unsettled and immature. Earl was totally absorbed with retracing their father's tracks up the Remington corporate ladder, and her youngest brother, Ross, was an idealist who thought he could save the world.

As she sat with her thoughts, Parker toyed with the six-carat diamond ring on her left hand. She was engaged to Dale Lane, a stockbroker. Dale was tall and handsome, financially successful, and a good catch. Even her father had approved of Dale, unlike his usual opinion that *no man was good enough for his princess.* At one time, Parker's parents, okay, her father, had hoped that as their first-born child, she would settle down and bless them with their first grandchild. As she had never married, Parker had left his wish unfulfilled. Instead, it was her brother, Earl, who became the first of her siblings to have children. Instead of family, she had focused on her work, making the rapid rise to senior partner in her firm in quick timing.

Parker had always been the apple of Earl's eye, a position she relished. When he was hospitalized during his final weeks, she never missed a single day visiting him. They both looked forward to this daily ritual. Whenever her father was home from the hospital, Parker would abandon her luxury downtown condominium for the family mansion in Butler County. If she was going to ultimately lose her dad, she wanted to spend as much time with him as she could until the end. Her mother saw this devotion to her father as somewhat excessive and often encouraged Parker to spend more time with friends her age. She rarely did, however, choosing rather to be with her father.

Later that evening, Parker sat on the deck of her penthouse condominium overlooking the Ohio River, enjoying a glass of wine with Dale. The night air was warm, and reflections of the city lights on the river below made the rippling waters sparkle. A ferryboat heading up river sent gentle calliope music ringing softly into the peaceful night breeze. In the park below, lovers strolled lazily about. Quiet romantic piano music by George Winston emitted softly from inside Parker's apartment. She and Dale stretched out on chaise lounges and gazed at the stars shining brightly through the clear sky. Parker looked at Dale and reached for his hand. The mood and the moment seemed made for reflection.

Parker thought about what it was like to have grown up the daughter of Earl Q. Remington. The lifestyle of grandeur, power and plenty was all she had ever known, and it was something she took for granted. In spite of giving them everything their hearts desired, their father had particularly stern expectations of his wife and children, and no one in the family questioned or challenged him. Except me, she thought, and sometimes Mummie, of course.

As she wondered again about her father's secret that *M*other was to tell them, a particular event that happened long ago when she was very young crossed her mind. She and her father shared a secret long forgotten. He had taken her into the city to a woman's apartment. In fact, she lived on the river, too, and you could look down at the water and see the barges going by. He told Parker this woman was one of his business contacts. She was pretty and seemed like a very nice person. She had lovely candles burning in her living room, and Parker recalled thinking it might have been the woman's birthday, partly because she also remembered having ice cream and cookies in the kitchen, while her dad and this woman discussed business in the living room.

Her father told Parker that business bored her mother, so she was not to mention this little business meeting. He called it their secret visit, and Parker was proud to share a business secret with her dad. She had often wondered what became of that nice woman and whether or not her dad had ever gone back to that apartment. It hadn't seemed strange to Parker that this was an African American woman, because she had been to her dad's office several times and had seen black people there all the time. She was just glad to be able to go around with her father when she did.

Then, for some reason, Parker thought of something else, something she had nearly forgotten that had happened years before in her last year of high school. For a long while, her dad seemed to have been deeply affected. She had always sensed he had some kind of problem, and it seemed worse during the holiday season. Her father just hadn't been himself. What had been wrong? She'd asked, but never got a good answer. Her mother would explain his mood by saying her father was just tired, or that he had a business problem.

Now as Parker lingered in deep thought, she wondered for the first time, could something have been wrong between Daddy and Mummie? She thought again about her father's deathbed remarks. Daddy wanted us to know something. Could it possibly have something to do with that thing that had him so depressed a long time ago? After all, that had been the only other time she had seen him that way. Yes, she would have to talk to her mother soon.

"What are you thinking, honey," Dale asked Parker as he leaned over to kiss her shoulder.

The sound of Dale's voice brought Parker out of her memories. She answered, "Oh, Dale, I was thinking about my father all over again. I was all the way back to my childhood. You know how close we were. Sometimes I wonder, do people ever get over the death of loved ones?

"I've pretty much kept this to myself, but when I think about my dad and some of the things that happened in his life, I believe there are some important things about him that none of us knew about. I've never told you this, but moments before he died, he said something to us about being sorry and asking forgiveness. But he did not say why. He said Mummie would tell us when she was ready. It's been over two months and she hasn't said anything yet. I've really wanted to ask her about it."

Dale looked concerned. "Darling, that must be weighing very heavily on you. You have no idea what this was about?"

"I've no clue."

* * * * *

Thirty-six-year-old Jordan Remington was an absolute knockout. A brunette like her father, she was tall and long-legged with a drop-dead figure, an outgoing personality, and a gorgeous face. With her looks, she could easily have been a top fashion model, a movie star, or even a knock-'em-dead corporate executive. Her interests, however, and a somewhat rebellious streak, took her elsewhere. Always popular, Jordan made friends easily and plentifully. She was warm and playful, adventuresome and gregarious. People were drawn to her like a magnet. Unlike her more conservative sister, Jordan tended to be capricious and, at times, a touch irreverent. Her mission was to experience life to the fullest.

Also, unlike her brilliant sister who received several scholastic honors and went on to get a law degree, Jordan's passion was art and photography. Eager to leave Cincinnati, she was happy to attend the San Francisco Art Institute after high school. She loved northern California and adapted very well to its culture. As a photographer, Jordan was quite talented. This interest was a life-long passion that started when she was only ten years old after her nanny gave her an inexpensive camera as a birthday gift. From the moment Jordan snapped her first picture, she knew she wanted to be a photographer.

After receiving her Bachelor's Degree from the Art Institute, she studied for two years at L'ecole des Beux Artes on Paris' legendary Left Bank. It was there that she met Sergé Benoit, the dashingly handsome, successful and wealthy owner of a popular fashion magazine. Sergé was to become the love of her life. Although Jordan had been the consummate jet setter, Sergé swept her off her feet. With him, she experienced an excitement and passion she had not dreamed possible.

In spite of fancying herself the world's greatest playgirl, Jordan was ready to settle down with Sergé and expected he would ask her to be his bride. And she would wholeheartedly accept. But Sergé was quite the playboy, himself. He was often photographed with beautiful models and celebrities. A proposal for marriage to Jordan Remington was never in his plans.

Jordan eventually returned to the states alone, hoping to forget about her unrequited love. Still, she often thought of Sergé. Back in the states, she worked for a while as a free lance artist for a greeting card company in New York, but after a few years, she decided to pursue her passion for photography, her first love. Her profession took her all over the world; however, she returned to Cincinnati when her father became ill. These days, Jordan was an independent photographer living at the family estate.

One contemplative evening in her darkroom, she remembered that before Sergé came into her life, there was Gerald, one of her many college flings. Gerald was tall and handsome, a doctoral candidate, and an Olympic decathlete. Jordan recalled the summer following her sophomore year of college when she'd invited him to her home in Cincinnati for a visit.

She used to tell herself that she forgot to mention to her family that Gerald Franklin was black. Whatever the case, she definitely caught everyone by surprise, and the visit was awkward. Arnold, the family chauffeur, had picked them up from the airport. Even he could hardly contain the protective scowl that came over his face when he saw Gerald. Her mother had been the first of her family to greet them. Jordan remembered how embarrassed she had been at the rude reception Gerald received from her mother. When Elizabeth Remington saw him, she looked aghast, but forced a curt hello, never even trying to camouflage her displeasure. Although her parents had never come right out and taught them prejudice, it seemed obvious by her mother's cold reception that the sentiments were there all right, just unspoken.

Parker and Earl, Jr. had also been rather cool toward Gerald, but fortunately, her brother Ross had behaved quite civilly. Actually, it was her father who gave her the biggest surprise. When he arrived home in time for dinner that evening, Jordan braced herself for more discomfort. Instead, she recalled her father greeting Gerald in a congenial and easy manner that made him feel welcomed. It seemed genuine — not fake or contrived. Happily, her father's easy and natural reaction relaxed her mother, and the general awkwardness subsided a bit.

Jordan felt guilty for subjecting Gerald to this situation. When she apologized to him about it later, she was surprised to learn this had not been his first encounter with prejudice. His willingness to tell her some of his experiences as a black man brought a shocking new awareness to Jordan, who'd apparently been too sheltered to ever care about these kinds of things.

Sometimes Jordan worked in her dark room until the wee hours of the morning. She took great satisfaction in developing her own prints and was quite good at it. On this occasion while developing prints from her latest shoot, Jordan ran across an old negative of a photograph she had taken of her father and mother aboard their yacht. This brought memories of her father streaming through her mind, and she thought of the many fun hours they had spent aboard *the Rose*.

Earl Remington's death had affected her in a way that nothing ever had before. She didn't fully understand why, but his passing had taught her an important lesson in living. Now, she found she no longer took life so much for granted, nor did she have as much of a need to live on the edge. She found this lesson welcoming, but confounding.

Jordan studied the picture of her mother and thought of how she and her mother never had the fairytale mother-daughter type of relationship. She loved her mother, but Elizabeth Remington was not a particularly warm or affectionate person. With anyone. Jordan was aware that people generally knew when to get out of her way, because under the right circumstances Elizabeth could be extremely deadly. In Jordan's view, her mother would single-handedly stop a moving train if it dared to get in her way. These days, she rarely saw her mother except at suppertime.

With her father, she recalled, it was equally difficult. She remembered how tough and demanding he had always been toward her. In recent years he had let up on her and had become more easy-going. On infrequent occasions during her trips home before she came back to Cincinnati, the two of them would dine together. At such times they would talk openly and freely, and Jordan discovered that she was learning to feel very comfortable around her father. Now she missed him greatly. By the time he died, it felt to her that not only a father, but also a friend had passed.

In Jordan's mind, her father was a man of many faces. She sometimes wondered how he and her mother ever got together. To her, they were as different from each other as night from day. But he seemed very devoted to her mother, and Jordan was happy about that, for she knew that her mother loved her father. Occasionally, however, Jordan couldn't help but notice his wandering eye. She used to wonder, is it possible my dad has eyes for other women? Well after all, he is only human, she would reason. Besides, he treats Mother like a queen.

As she thought about her parents, Jordan again remembered that strange thing her father had said to them on his deathbed. It was about forgiving him for something. What could it be? Mother was to tell them what that was about. But when? Although she wondered about this often, she decided to let her mother tell them in her own time.

On second thought, it had been several weeks; what the hell. She thought she'd try to give it another week. If she didn't hear anything by then, she would ask her mother about it. Jordan didn't relish this prospect, and could hear her mother's cool response now: "Now, Jordan, did your father not ask me to tell you four when I was ready?" As Jordan could see herself responding yes, she could also hear her mother's brisk retort, "Then why don't we just wait until I am?" No thanks; Jordan decided to spare herself that encounter. But why won't she tell us, she wondered, hanging up her last print to dry as she prepared to exit her dark room. Daddy apparently wanted us to know. Jordan remained beset with wonder — what did he want us to know?

CHAPTER
7

THE SIGN ON the door to the executive office was bronze colored with gold trim and lettering. It read, EARL Q. REMINGTON, JR., PRESIDENT.   Earl, Jr. carried his name with immense pride. He was his father's first son and proud to be his namesake. Earl had studied Business Administration at Princeton University, and joined his father's company right out of college. Hard working and ambitious, he had become president of one of Remington Corporation's major divisions when he was only 30. His division was RemCap Development, which handled mammoth site development projects all over the country.

Young Earl had always dreamed of being at the helm of his father's company one day. Until a few months ago, this had merely been a remote dream. For even though his father was in his 70s, he had continued to run the corporation until his illness finally prevented him from making his daily trips to the office. Even then, Earl, Sr. still spent a few hours each day, often from his bed, reviewing business operations and making strategic decisions.

Earl, Jr. sat at his desk, unable to focus on the files in his hand. He was working on a project that had been especially important to his father. As he stared into space, he thought of how difficult his father's dying had been to him personally. Indeed, he considered his death to be a great loss to the city of Cincinnati, if not to the country. In his son's mind, Earl Q. Remington, Sr. truly was one of the great men of this world.

So many times, Earl, Jr. wished he could have been closer to his father. He would loved to have been taken under the senior Earl's wing. Yet, no matter how hard he tried, Earl, Jr. had never been successful at building the kind of relationship with their father that his younger brother had. Ross didn't even work at pleasing their father, yet he always seemed enthralled with his youngest son. This nagged at Earl, Jr. to no end, and he sometimes found it hard to disguise his agitation toward his brother. He was glad Ross lived in Colorado.

* * * * *

That Tuesday morning in late June in another part of town, old Jake Huber gazed out the window of his small office. His meager view was a busy freeway and barren grassland through which ran a railroad track. Out of necessity, he had learned to drown out the grinding sounds and was completely oblivious to the clanging of the train that presently passed through a nearby intersection. Huber was anxious about the phone call he was about to make to Earl Remington, Jr. He desperately needed it to be convincing and compelling.

Jake Huber was a skinny little man who looked like anything but the successful businessman. However, at one time, he had considered himself a business associate to the senior Remington, and occasionally, even a golfing buddy. In fact, the two had worked together on a profitable venture some six years earlier. They had designed a state-of-the-art shopping mall and work center. This was a unique concept that called for the top levels of the mall to house the usual department stores and shops, while work centers such as furniture upholstering, picture framing, wallpapering and the like would take up the entire lower level of the mall. These work centers would draw an entirely different clientele than the upstairs shops, while increasing their business.

This concept turned out to be a huge idea. It was sold to a developer in another state, and the mall/work center was created.

Following the success of this venture, these centers sprang up all over the region, ultimately making Jake Huber a rich man, and his relationship with Remington was sealed. However, a string of bad luck eventually cost Huber his fortune, and he was eager for the opportunity to partner with Earl Remington and the Remington Corporation again.

His second joint venture, however, turned out to be a major disaster. Daily, Jake Huber cursed himself for not having been more savvy. He had owned a prime piece of real estate which was slated to be the site of one of the future Cincinnati area home shows. This annual event attracted hundreds of thousands of people to sneak previews of new homes costing well over a million dollars. Huber used his property, estimated at two million dollars in value, to buy into the new venture. However, this was an ill-fated transaction and the venture crashed. Old Jake Huber lost everything. At first, he felt he had been shafted. Thankfully, Earl, Sr. told him not to worry for he would make him whole.

In his final days, Earl, Sr. relayed to Huber that everything in their deal had been legitimate. He had not dealt improperly with him in any way. Even so, he said that given their history, he would still help him acquire more property. He would talk to his son, Earl, Jr., who would make good his commitment. Unfortunately, the senior Earl died before he had a chance to discuss this with his son. And so far, Huber's conversations with the young man had been hopelessly futile. For Earl, Jr. did not believe Huber for one second, especially since all he had to go on was his word. Huber was in a real fix and getting more desperate every day. Finally, feeling ready to try again, Huber placed the call.

Brynn Jamison, Earl, Jr.'s secretary, alerted Earl that a Mr. Jake Huber was on the line. Oh, no, not that guy again, Earl thought. This guy had been pestering him ever since his father died. Earl decided to take the call, hoping this time to finally convince Huber to stop calling. "All right, Brynn, put him through."

Earl did not look forward to talking to Mr. Huber. If he'd heard his story once, he'd heard it a dozen times. "Your father ripped me off, gypped me out of my land and took advantage of me. I was a successful businessman. I put up my land to buy into one of his projects, and he practically swindled me out of it. Because of him, I lost everything, my money, my land, my resources, hell, even my family …"

"Hello, Mr. Huber, this is Mr. Remington."

Huber lit in again. His rampage was nearly the same as always, but this time, he added a new twist. "I have found a piece of property on the west side of town," he told Earl. "It's not as good as what I lost to your father; I don't think I'll ever find anything that prime again. But it will have to do."

"Sir, why are you telling me this," Earl, Jr. asked again in the same detached, patronizing tone of voice he always used when he spoke to Jake Huber.

"Because your father owed me. He promised to help me replace my land. Don't you hear me? Now someone over there had better take responsibility to settle this thing with me."

"As I have asked you before, sir, do you have a contract that shows my father owes you anything?" Earl asked him, sighing. "Because if you do, I will be happy to have our legal office review it and make certain we handle the matter appropriately."

"Listen, sonny," Jake Huber said, clearly angry over this same old yarn he'd heard from Earl, Jr. before. "You know damned well I don't have a contract. I've told you this before. What I have is your father's word to me that I would get what was coming to me. That meant I would get my land back, or *some* land — with his help. I sure as hell can't afford to buy this property. It'll cost close to a million dollars. But the land your father same as swindled me out of was worth twice that. I want my property, or I want the money. Do you read me?"

Earl said coolly, "Mr. Huber, as I said, if you will produce an agreement, I'll be happy to have it reviewed by our lawyers. You understand, don't you, I cannot take the word of every Tom, Dick and Harry who claims my father owed them something. Think about what you're asking here. We can't do business like that. Why, in one day, we could lose everything my father worked years to build. He built this business on solid values and practices. Personally, I can't believe my father would ever swindle you or anyone else. So now, if you will excuse me, I'm ending this call. Remember, if you can produce a contract, we will expedite this matter."

"Listen here, sonny boy, you're not ending anything," Huber said in a shaky tone. "Maybe you don't know who you're dealing with. I'm no fool. You'd better quit messing around with me and pay me what your old man owes me. I don't have to produce a contract. I have something better than that. I know an awful lot about how your father did business. And I'll tell you this much. It sure wasn't all about solid business values and practices. Don't force my hand. I can't afford to let this property get away from me. I want you to get back to me within 24 hours. Twenty-four hours — that's all you got, or you'll be hearing from me. And that's a guarantee." The conversation ended on that somewhat threatening note, leaving Earl very curious about what Mr. Huber planned to do 24 hours from now, and leaving Jake Huber wondering the same thing.

"Strange man," Earl uttered as he hung up the phone. This call unnerved him, primarily because practically everything that happened these days could affect his chances for the CEO position. The Board knew of these frequent calls from Jake Huber. How will they feel about Earl, Jr.'s not being able to get rid of this pest? The next quarterly Board of Directors' meeting was scheduled for September. At that meeting, Earl hoped to be elected Chief Executive Officer of the Remington Corporation, but that hinged on his being the selection committee's choice.

The Board had called a special meeting immediately after his father's death to discuss his replacement. But rather than appoint Earl, Jr. at that time as he expected would happen, they commissioned a search team to choose the CEO. This had been very upsetting to Earl, for he'd hoped the selection would have been automatic. He was, after all, the owner's son, and already a high-level executive in his own right. But there were four other people at the same level as he — three men and a woman. All four were very sharp, and each was credited with substantial innovative, moneymaking initiatives over the years.

The corporate by-laws stipulated that in the future the Board was to fill the CEO seat from within the corporation by appointing the most qualified person for the position. Earl, Jr. felt he had been groomed his entire life for this position. He couldn't under-stand why his father had agreed to those ridiculous terms in the corporate by-laws.

Whenever he thought of his father, it usually brought back memories of his final moments. Earl, Jr. cherished his father's final professions of love to his family. But he was still mystified over his puzzling comment about some secret his mother was to tell them one day. His mind was racked with concern and curios-ity, and he found himself completely unable to shake it from his mind. What could it be? Was there trouble? Surely Mother would have told us by now if something was the matter, wouldn't she? Earl, Jr. wondered in vain.

He secretly hoped it would be a surprise announcement of his selection as successor to his father's position. But Father would not have needed to apologize for that. Besides, Mother would let me in on that. I'm sure of it, he mused. He suddenly had an urge to speak to his mother. Of all Elizabeth Remington's children, 35-year-old Earl was actually closest to her, and he valued their bond. But could he question her about this? On previous occasions he had tried to bring the subject up, but the words would not come. He tried to convince himself that she would mention it in her own good time. Still, he wished he knew how to carefully broach the subject without infringing on her confidences.

His secretary told him his wife was on the phone. Shannon reminded him of his son's soccer game that evening. Earl, Jr. hung up the phone and remembered how he had been proud enough to burst when he witnessed the delivery of his first child. He was prouder to be the first of Earl, Sr.'s four children to present him a grandchild and a grandson at that. Earl, III was now eleven. Earl, Jr. had two other children, another son, Dexter, who was nine, and a daughter, Farrah, who was six. Earl, Sr. could not have been more pleased. He treated his grandchildren as if they were the most precious beings on earth. His son had done him proud. With the receiver still in his hand, Earl dialed his mother's home.

"What's up, old man," Ross asked cheerily upon hearing his brother's voice. As he often was, Earl, Jr. was miffed at Ross' intrusiveness. Ross, he felt, had hoarded his father's affections, and now here he was apparently trying to endear himself to their mother by hanging around. Earl greatly resented his brother for this. He was feeling pretty lousy right now, and had no desire to chat idly with his brother.

"How are you, Ross," he replied in a cool voice. "I would like to speak with Mother. Is she available?" Ross detected his brother's coolness and chose to ignore it. As far as he was concerned, Earl needed to relax sometimes. He was far too uptight, and Ross refused to get drawn into his sour moods. He called their mother to the phone.

While waiting for his mother to pick up the telephone, Earl, Jr. thought about the upcoming Board meeting. He was extremely curious how it would turn out. Heretofore he'd never thought beyond the possibility that he would get the job. What would he do if he didn't get it? That thought was too unbearable to fathom. If only he could come up with something spectacular or heroic, something that would make him the selection committee's clear choice. By the time his mother picked up the telephone, Earl, Jr. had once again talked himself out of asking about Dad's final words.

* * * * *

For years, Ross Remington, who was 31, had bounced around the globe, moving with his job from one country to another. Altruistic by nature, the last thing he would have ever wanted to do was to put on a suit and go to work at the Remington Corporation. His college major had been geology. At the time of his father's death, he had been living back in the states for a year. Now Ross resided in Colorado and spent his time studying the geological composition of some of Colorado's great mountainsides to isolate the conditions that produced massive land and rock slides. There he had fallen in love with and gotten engaged to Pamela Whitten. They were to be married the following year after she completed medical school.

Ross had returned to Cincinnati on an extended leave two weeks prior to his father's death, and stayed to support his mother afterward. He planned to return to Colorado after the reading of his father's will. Pamela had come to Cincinnati for the funeral, but returned to her classes after a short stay.

He sat in the great study at his mother's home surrounded by reminders of his father and considered how he might help her with what she was going to have to do. She would soon return from an appointment downtown. Ross knew she was laboring under a great burden, completely unaware he was able to help. He knew the reading of the will was near. Time was running out, and he wondered how to approach her.

Ross thought about his father and the unfair liberties he had taken in his marriage. Earl Remington was a known workaholic and stayed away from home a great deal. But Ross had been fairly certain his father's extended absences weren't all about work. His suspicions stemmed from having once overheard snatches of a phone conversation his dad was having from his study in the house. From what he heard, it was apparent his dad had been talking romantically to someone other than his mother. This had infuriated young Ross to no end. How could he do this to Mom, he fumed.

Today, as Ross absently studied the hundreds of books encased in the bookshelves, he recalled how he had wanted to tell his mother about that phone call, but he didn't do it because that would only have hurt her too much. Certainly, his father treated his mother very caringly, and she seemed satisfied with their relationship. But Ross could not forget what he had heard.

When he saw his father after that phone call, Ross boldly gave him an angry look. He was ready for a showdown. Ross knew that neither his brother nor sisters would have dared challenge their father, for they jumped at his every beck and call. Well, maybe Jordan didn't; even still, she would not have challenged him. But Ross did not fear his father. In fact, in his opinion Earl, Sr. was far too controlling anyway, and Ross was not to be controlled. He figured the worst thing his father could do would be to kick him out of his will. So what? Money did not define Ross Remington, and he would never let it or anything else run him. The usually stern Earl took in his son's look and walked out of the room.

As Ross sat in the family study, he reflected on how in recent years, at the prompting of his father, the two of them had begun to build a stronger relationship. Ross was extremely troubled by his death. A private visit at his father's hospital bedside in his last days was deeply embedded in his mind. Ross still did not know quite how to deal with that conversation, but he knew the purpose of it was for him to help his mother through her personal turmoil. In a heartrending talk, his father told Ross many things he had never told him before, including secrets from his past life.

Before divulging the shocking details of his affair, Earl, Sr. told Ross he'd always respected and admired him for his individuality. He said it did him good to see that characteristic in his son. This had been a surprising admission to Ross, for he'd had no idea his father looked upon his individuality as an admirable characteristic. In fact, Ross always felt his dad considered him a letdown because he had not followed in his footsteps as a businessman. Earl, Sr. told his youngest son that after devoting his life to attaining wealth and power which he had accomplished very well, he'd discovered too late that he had traded too much for this success. Money and power alone, he told Ross, were not the only important things in life. He'd had the storybook Horatio Algier life, achieving a status few people would not want to have. And yet, with all his money, he could not buy complete happiness. What a surprise this was to young Ross who'd always thought his father had everything he wanted out of life. I guess I never knew my father completely, he reflected.

During this surprising bedside chat, Earl, Sr. now told his son that by being the way he was, dogmatic and overbearing at times, he'd inadvertently driven Elizabeth to drink. And he accepted her drinking because at least alcohol gave Elizabeth the solace he was unable to offer. Now he saw it for the crutch it was, and told his son he hoped Elizabeth would eventually be able to draw on her internal strength versus relying on the false sense of comfort provided by alcohol. For years, Ross had watched his mother grow quite fond of her brandy, even using it as an escape from difficult realities, and he wanted her not to depend on it so. But Ross was amazed his father would admit to having contributed to her habit, for Earl, Sr. rarely admitted to being wrong about anything.

However, the most amazing aspect of that conversation was yet to come. It began when his father brought up a subject that was to completely stun Ross. Even as he thought about it today, he cocked his head in bewilderment. His father told him something that could have knocked him over with a feather. Ross recalled how his father's speaking was labored, but he was determined to say his piece. "I believe you may know of my unfaithfulness to your mother," Earl, Sr. had said to Ross who did not verbally respond, but his face told his father he'd had his questions. Although Ross had believed his father strayed at one time, he'd still always seen a good deal of outward affection between his parents, so he had thought things were okay. Why is father bringing this up now, he quietly worried.

His father continued, "I love your mother very much, but for a period, our relationship was not my top priority." To Ross' startled look, his father quickly added, "I feel I'm to blame for much of that. You see, I realize there had to have been many times over the years when Elizabeth needed more from me." He coughed weakly, and Ross held up a glass of water, which his father sipped slowly through a straw. Soon, he was able to continue. "But she never let on. She must have known I'd have disapproved, so she appeased me by remaining silent." Ross listened, puzzled by his father's surprising comments, puzzled also at the notion that his mother would be silent about things that troubled her. That certainly was not the Elizabeth Remington Ross thought he knew.

Then Earl, Sr. said, "Son, I must tell you something even more difficult. At one time in my life, I had a serious relationship with another woman." Ross gasped quietly and breathed deeply at this bold admission, and his father continued. "I never stopped loving Elizabeth. Quite the contrary. She has always meant the world to me. However, I loved this other woman, too. In fact, very much, and it lasted quite a while." Ross listened as his father talked. He did not know what to do or say, nor did he even want to know about this.

"Does Mother know?" Ross agonizingly asked his father.

"No, but she may have had her suspicions. I will speak to her about it soon. This has been very hard to face, and I know it will break her heart. But I must tell her and ask her forgiveness before I pass on."

"Why? Why not just leave it be? Does Parker know about this? Jordan, Earl?" Ross asked.

"No, son. No one knows. I only intended to tell your mother," his father said, clearly too weak to protest Ross' many questions. "I planned to ask her to tell you four about it."

"But why is it important for her to tell everyone? Why do you even need to tell her? Why do you need to hurt Mother like this? And why are you bringing this up with me, Father?" Ross, who was becoming angry, asked in a baffled, troubled voice.

"Because I'm dying and she will need you," a weary Earl, Sr. continued impatiently. If I could take this secret to my grave, I would do it. Believe me, son. I've had my share of indiscretions over the years, but most were never serious. And I've been discreet for I never wanted to hurt or embarrass your mother. But I need to tell you this." Ross was quiet. "I met this woman 30 years ago." Earl, Sr. paused to let his son absorb what he had just said before continuing, "Her name was Hattie Rose Williams. With her, it became very serious. So serious that even though my family meant the world to me, I couldn't let her go." Earl, Sr. then looked deep into his son's eyes and added, "You've got to believe that, Ross." Earl, Sr. was deeply troubled. He hesitated a moment because what he was about to tell Ross was even harder. "What I want you to know is, this woman and I had two children together, a daughter and a son."

Ross raised his head and stared at his father in utter disbelief. "Good Lord, Father! I don't know what to say. I can't believe it. You're telling me you had two children by some other woman? How could you?" Then he sputtered out one question after another. "How long ago was this? How old are they now? Where are they, Father? Where is their mother? Are you still seeing her?" Did you end this relationship, or is she still in the picture? You're telling me I have another brother and sister somewhere?"

Earl, Sr. looked wearily at his son as he told him the woman died 20 years ago. Ross found himself almost relieved to hear that the woman was dead. "The children never knew I was their father. They never had the Remington name. I provided some for their care after their mother died. For a while, they lived with their grandmother, but when she died a few years later, I believe they were adopted. That's as much as I know. As far as I was concerned, it was over. I was through with that unfortunate chapter in my life. I know it wasn't right, but it happened. And believe me, Ross, I was prepared to keep quiet, but somehow, I don't know how, someone got wind of this and has been blackmailing me. For two years."

"A blackmailer, Father," Ross exclaimed. "Good grief!" Again, Ross bombarded his father with questions. "Did you report this? Do the authorities know? Did you tell anyone about this? Do you know who it is? And how on earth did anyone find out about this? How did the blackmailer get this to you? How much did you pay him?"

Earl told Ross that the first blackmail envelope delivered to his office was specially marked. It said something like *Confidential and Highly Personal: No one must open this envelope but Earl Q. Remington.* The envelope was eventually presented to him. He laughingly told his secretary it wouldn't kill him to open one envelope. Inside, the photographs of him with Hattie and their children quickly wiped the smile from his face. After the shock of receiving the photographs and the letter demanding $200,000, he summoned his secretary. He told her that if any such mail came to him addressed that way again, it was to be brought directly to him as it would contain highly sensitive information that only he should deal with.

"So why would you pay some blackmailer?" Ross asked while shaking his head in astonishment.

His father's breathing was strained as he continued to talk. It was important that Ross know the whole story, for he was going to require something very important from him. "Because," he said, "whoever was behind the blackmail threatened to tell your mother." When his father said these words, everything became clear to Ross. Earl continued, "And I never wanted your mother to know about this. I knew it would hurt her too deeply. Unfortunately, this character is persistent and, of course, since my illness has been well publicized, he seized the opportunity to really put the squeeze on me for the last time. I paid him close to a million dollars before, but the crazy fool has now demanded five million dollars."

"Five million dollars! Good grief, Father, what are we going to do? You don't want Mother to find out about this, but on the other hand, you can't pay some swindler five million dollars either."

Earl told his son, "As I said, I will tell your mother about my affair. Then she will know, and the threat will be over."

Troubled, Ross said, "I don't know. Besides, can't he still make trouble for you, or for Mother? I mean, what if he carries through on his threat to send his information to the media?"

"Of course, if he did, it certainly wouldn't be the first time the tabloids have tried to sell papers at my expense. I do consider that a possibility, but only a remote one, for somehow I see no gain for him to do this. Mostly, I don't want Elizabeth and you children to suffer. And I don't want my other son and daughter, wherever they are, to suffer either. I have included them in my will, but identified them only as the children of a faithful employee. I have carried the guilt of abandoning them all these years. Ross, now I want to bring them into this family. Surely, they are entitled to know the rest of their family and to enjoy a share of my wealth. I will ask Elizabeth to locate them using every means possible."

"Father, don't you know how much this is going to hurt Mother?"

"If I knew of anything else to do, I would do it. I can only pray your mother will forgive me and that she will understand."

"You've been carrying this secret around all these years? I don't know how," Ross said. Then shaking his head, he exclaimed, "Man!"

Although Ross thought he had heard enough, Earl, Sr. said, "There's more, son."

"What, Dad? What more could there possibly be?"

"You need to know this, too. The woman I had this affair with was black."

Ross exclaimed, "What!" He could not believe what his father just said. Surely he wasn't serious. "Your mistress was black as in African American?" Ross asked in disbelief. He truly did not know how to think about this. In a low but demanding tone, he just said, "This is unbelievable. Damn it, Father, what on earth were you thinking?"

Earl continued in a resigned tone, "I know, I know. She was a wonderful woman, and I got carried away. I guess I just couldn't resist the forbidden fruit. I really can't explain any better than that.

"I want you to know something else, Ross. When these children were young, their complexion was very fair, their hair, blond. You could not tell they were bi-racial. The last time I saw them when they were little kids, they still looked Caucasian. You see, I believe Hattie's mother was white, too. I do not know if they were raised as white or black after their mother died."

"Goodness, Father, they must have had a very confused life. I just don't know what to say. How can I possibly help Mother deal with this?"

Earl's eyes were growing heavy. Ross could tell he wanted to close them now and sleep, but he continued. "My will is scheduled for reading three months after my death. I am going to ask Elizabeth to talk to you children about this, and to find my other son and daughter before the will is read. I know this will be extremely hard on her. She will need help with this," his father told him. "Obviously, I want her to handle it in her own time and in her own way. But if she falters, I want you to be there for her, son. Elizabeth will need a shoulder to lean on, a hand to hold. For some reason, you are the one I felt I could make such a request of. Your mother is going to need you, Ross. If she doesn't talk to you four about it in a timely way, you will have to decide when to bring it up with her."

Ross knew this had to be the end of the saga. There couldn't possibly be more, could there? He sure didn't want to hear anything more. He asked his father a few of the details about the blackmailing ordeal, then left him to rest. This is positively going to tear Mother to pieces, he thought.

Ross heard his mother return. Suddenly he knew it was time. He sought her out, and they had a very long talk right then and there.

CHAPTER
8

J.T. WAS HAVING a rough day; his big plan was becoming a source of tremendous anxiety for him. Furthermore, he was finding it difficult to stay focused because tormenting memories of his lost love dominated his thoughts. But he would persevere. He told himself he was doing this as much because of her as anything.

Intermingled with his thoughts was anger that the Remington woman had hired a private detective. Knowing why she hired her upset him even more. Now he would have to come up with a way to get rid of this outside interference. He wanted this Davis woman off the case. So she's a former cop. Big damn deal, he thought. But deep down, J.T. knew it really was a big deal because he definitely didn't want to get mixed up in any police business, which was precisely why he'd steered clear of that crazy kidnapping idea he'd come up with weeks before. He could just see himself being carted off to jail for doing something stupid like that.

He turned his thoughts to Lynn Davis and said between clenched teeth, "Why don't you just go away! The Remington affair is mine, not yours. You need to stay the hell out of my business." Although his basement apartment was cool and damp, J.T. was hot. Holding a cold can of beer, he rolled it across his perspiring forehead while sitting at his desk indulging his discontent. What if this Lynn Davis woman tries to convince the old man's wife not to pay? This concern and similar ones were wreaking havoc on his state of mind. Davis, he thought, you are trespassing on private property. Stay out!

He finally decided what he had to do. He would simply telephone Lynn Davis and convince her to back off. He sat back in his chair and thought about how to deal with her. She can't be that tough, he thought. So here goes. Let's see, a woman's voice will throw her, he cleverly decided. Then he concocted a short message that he figured would give her something to think about for a while. This should convince her to get the hell out of Dodge. I hope it works. That's for damned sure.

* * * * *

Lynn ran water for a relaxing bath in the Jacuzzi following an exhilarating run. It was a hot Sunday morning in late June. At times like these, her bathroom was indisputably her favorite room in the house. She was still ringing wet but feeling great. While the bathtub was filling, Lynn stretched to cool herself down from her run. She had started jogging back during her Police Academy days and continued the exercise over the years. It kept her physically fit and energized, and she had a terrific body — a perfect size eight — and a sharp mind to show for it. Still breathing deeply, Lynn lit some lavender candles and was about to climb into the tub when her phone rang, and she rushed to answer it. Hearing her catch her breath, Donald asked if he'd called at a bad time.

"Hey, sweetheart. Nope, perfect timing. In another ten seconds, I probably wouldn't have heard the phone ringing. I was just about to step into the Jacuzzi. What's up?"

Donald said, "Look, since we're both going over to our offices this afternoon, you want to catch brunch at the Westin, at about, say, noon or so?"

"I'd love to. Besides," Lynn said laughingly, "I miss you. Haven't seen you since," she checked her watch and, referring to the special night they had just spent together, said, "about, oh, three hours ago. Yes, hon, noon is great."

"Excellent," Donald said. "I'll see you then. Enjoy that bath.

Wish I could join you." Donald was a romanticist, and Lynn loved that special quality in him. He also had a brilliant mind and was a great sounding board to her.

Lynn stepped into her shower and quickly washed her hair before turning on the jets to her Jacuzzi. The thrashing water looked deliciously inviting. She climbed in and slowly lowered herself into the tub. Smelling the fragrant lavender aroma, watching the candlelights flicker, feeling the powerful jets massaging her body in all the right places, she sank down and let out a long, pleasurable sigh. It just didn't get much better than this, she thought.

Lynn was looking forward to brunch. After running hard this morning, she found herself with an enormous appetite. She generously applied lotion to her skin that was withered from her 30-minute bask. Then she meticulously applied her makeup, blew her black shoulder-length hair dry and pulled it back off her face using a simple shiny black barrette to hold it in place. Then she put on a stylish pale blue silk pantsuit and straw-colored mules, checked her purse, grabbed her keys and headed out the door, quickly glancing approvingly in the mirror, front and back.

Lynn lived only minutes from downtown, and she arrived at the Westin with time to spare. As she gazed in the window of one of the shops near the restaurant, she thought about their successful search for Earl Remington's two children by Hattie Rose Williams. Late on Friday afternoon, Ella had happily exclaimed, "I've found them. I've got them both, Erica Rose and Perry Earl Dodd." Locating these two gave Lynn and Ella much cause to celebrate.

After the arduous search they'd previously conducted for the Williams children, Ella easily located them, first under the name, Dodd, then Harrington. Now 28, Erica lived in Minneapolis. Her brother, Perry, 26, lived in Chicago. Ella had even learned that Paul and Kitty Harrington, a childless couple from Columbus, Ohio, had adopted the two Dodd children at a young age, and they had grown up in Columbus. Even though their names were changed to Harrington, a strategic search produced the whereabouts of the two. Lynn had immediately phoned Elizabeth Remington to tell her the news, and they set up an appointment for Monday morning at nine o'clock to discuss next steps.

Completely absorbed in thought as she waited for Donald, Lynn glanced up just in time to catch his reflection in the store window as he loomed over her shoulder. From behind, Donald put an arm around her waist. Lynn turned and greeted him warmly; then holding hands, they strolled into the restaurant and enjoyed a delectable brunch. While they ate, Lynn was able to gain Donald's perspective on some of the puzzling aspects of the Remington case. Afterward, she spent a couple of hours in her office.

Monday morning, Lynn awakened feeling a bit nervous but couldn't figure why she felt this way. As she prepared for work, something felt troubling somehow. This feeling rarely failed her, but she was unable to identify what was bothering her. She decided to check on her folks and made a quick phone call to her mom and dad. Rachel told her everything was fine and that her father had gone fishing with her Uncle Ed. She reminded Lynn of dinner, and Lynn promised she'd see them this evening, blew a kiss through the phone and hung up with her usual, "Love you."

Lynn had planned to call her uncle, but since he was out fishing, she took off for her office, wanting to get there in plenty of time to prepare for Mrs. Remington. She stopped for bagels before she got to her office. Mr. Thompson signaled her into the parking lot. "How're you, Miss Lynn. You're lookin' mighty spiffy today. That bright red color brings out your complexion right nicely."

"Thanks, Mr. T. I'm doing well. I didn't see you in here yesterday. Is everything all right?"

"Sure is, ma'am," Mr. Thompson answered with a smile. "Yesterday was my Sunday off. And I'll tell you, my wife, Mamie, had me so busy around the house this weekend, I couldn't wait for that alarm clock go off at four-thirty this morning. I said, thank goodness, it's Monday!" he replied, chuckling.

They both laughed and Lynn drove into the garage, parked, then headed up to her office. Still wondering what was up, she munched on a bagel while preparing tea. When Ella came in, the two discussed the nine o'clock meeting with Elizabeth Remington. Ella was to sit in on this meeting to detail her findings.

All at once, Lynn noticed her phone's message light on. She'd had no message when she'd left her office yesterday and figured someone must have called pretty early this morning. However, closer examination showed the phone call came in at 11:22 last evening. She played the message and heard an unusual sounding female voice saying, *"You're getting into someone else's business. The Remington affair is off limits. Whatever you know, you'd better forget."* Then the caller abruptly hung up.

"What the ..." Lynn exclaimed, curiosity and perplexity filling her voice. "What on earth is this?" Ella had a similar reaction.

Lynn pushed the play button again, and once more she and Ella listened to the message. Disbelief registered with them both. They continued to replay the message to make sure they'd heard right, and to see if there was anything that could explain it or at least give them an idea who the caller was. They noticed that the voice had some kind of foreign accent. Upon hearing the message a third and fourth time, they detected the slightly discernible sounds of a distant train. Could the call have come from a train station, from a pay phone near some railroad tracks, did it even originate in Cincinnati? The caller ID function on her telephone only registered, "number unknown."

Lynn was confounded, as was Ella. She decided to phone Harvey. "Harvey, I don't know what the hell is going on here," she told him. "But I just listened to a weird telephone message from someone who called about the Remington case of all things. It sounds like someone is trying to scare me off!"

"What? Tell me what happened," Harvey said, sounding troubled.

"Well, I just played a phone message that came in after 11 last night. Some strange-sounding woman said — well, wait just a minute; let me play it for you." She pushed the play button.

Harvey said, "Play that again," and when Lynn did, he said, "I don't like the sound of that. Tell you what. I was just on my way out. Why don't I stop by your office right now?" Harvey added, concerned that Lynn might be getting mixed up in something dangerous.

It was now a quarter before nine. Lynn said, "Okay, Harvey. But look, I'm meeting with Elizabeth Remington at nine o'clock.

I'm set to give her the details about locating the Dodds. Perhaps you can sit in on this meeting with me. Do you have time?"

Harvey said, "Sure, I can do that. I'd be interested in seeing if she has any idea who your caller might be. See you in a few."

Janet arrived just before nine, and Elizabeth Remington and her chauffeur arrived a few minutes later. Arnold removed his cap and opened the door, holding it open for Mrs. Remington and a young man Lynn did not recognize. Arriving just behind them was Harvey. Arnold sat in the waiting area with Janet, who soon became the next person at the Lynn Davis agency to discover that attempts at small talk with Arnold Taylor were futile.

The first few minutes of the meeting were spent in introductions of the unfamiliar parties and explanations why each was present. It was easy for Lynn to explain Harvey's presence, since the two of them had made the discovery in Alabama that led to finding Erica and Perry. Ella had previously met Mrs. Remington, but neither she nor Lynn had met her son, Ross.

Ross was around six-feet, one. He had a trim, athletic build, and was casually dressed in tan slacks, a pale blue polo shirt, a navy blue sport jacket and dark tan penny loafers. Ross' sandy-colored hair was cut stylishly short. As he was introduced, he removed his sunglasses and took Lynn's hand and held it firmly as he did his gaze. Lynn found herself looking into the eyes of one of the most charming and boyishly good-looking faces she had seen in awhile.

"My son is joining us because he knows everything," Mrs. Remington explained, adding, "Earl shared his secret with Ross a few days before his death. He did this so Ross could help me with this. I am finally ready to sit down with my other children." She continued, "Ross has already been a big help to me. I had no idea how to approach my family with this. My son," she said, looking toward Ross, "made it easy for me, because he came to me with what he knew." Mrs. Remington looked fondly at Ross, whose face showed concern.

She continued. "I have now learned there is another horrible twist to this story. You see, I still couldn't understand why Earl felt it was so important that I know about this, this …" accentuating the next word with distaste, "*affair* of his. He certainly could have left money to those children by identifying them as offspring of a long-serving employee, and no one would have had to know the difference. I believe that if Earl had carried this secret for 30 years, he had no doubt made peace with himself and was prepared never to mention it. However, Earl told Ross something he had not mentioned to me, although I believe he had intended to. It's quite an upsetting development, but at least it explains why my husband felt compelled to tell me his secret in the end." Mrs. Remington looked to Ross to explain.

"What Mother is getting at is Dad was being blackmailed, and this had been going on for almost two years." To Lynn's surprised look, he added, "As you can imagine, my father nearly bowled me over with this news."

"I'm sure he did," Lynn said. "Blackmailed, hmmm. By whom? Did your father tell you who the blackmailer was?"

"No, he never knew. The reason Dad decided to tell me this was because apparently when the blackmailer learned of his terminal condition, he came up with the preposterous demand of five million dollars."

"Five million dollars! That damn fool's serious," Harvey scowled. Mrs. Remington gave Harvey a sideways unapproving glance at his language. He got the message in her look and uttered an apology.

Ross continued, "Father decided that he had gone far enough with this blackmailer, and now he had no choice but to tell Mother. He thought that if he did that, it would diffuse this character's threat and the thing might end. He also knew that if he paid the five million, it might never end. The blackmailer could have continued bilking my mother, our family, out of millions. Father was pushed too far. He didn't pay him a cent. Thank God, he didn't hear from the guy after that."

Lynn said, "This is all very peculiar, and I'm afraid I'll have to add to the mystery. What you are saying about Mr. Remington being blackmailed just could have something to do with a phone call I received." Elizabeth and Ross were curious.

"Just this morning, I listened to a message that was left for me shortly after 11 last night. I don't know who it's from, but now I can't help but wonder if it could possibly have anything to do with your blackmailer. Here, you can listen to it." She touched her play button, and the voice delivered its cryptic message: *"You're getting into someone else's business. The Remington affair is off limits. Whatever you know, you'd better forget."* Mrs. Remington's hand flew to her mouth as she gasped in shock. Ross frowned and gave a look of puzzlement. They asked to hear it again. Before the message played again, Lynn pointed out the faint clanging sound of a train in the background.

Mrs. Remington looked troubled, "Who knows if it's Earl's blackmailer or not, but it makes sense that it could be. I'm sorry you're being dragged into this, Ms. Davis," she said to Lynn.

"When I heard this message, I realized Lynn might be getting involved in more than she bargained for — possibly something dangerous," Harvey stated emphatically.

"Maybe this should be reported to the police," Ross offered.

"Oh, no," replied Mrs. Remington, sounding shaken. "If the police get involved, then this whole thing will have to become a matter of public record. I don't want this aired in public." She turned to Lynn and continued, "Hopefully, Miss Davis, since you've completed the job I hired you to do, whoever is behind this call will leave you out of this. I certainly don't want you to be in any peril."

"Mom, are you sure this is not a matter for the authorities?" Ross asked. "We can't start caving in to this character now, especially after everything Dad must have gone through." Elizabeth looked at her son, but she truly did not know what to say.

Lynn said, "Mrs. Remington, you are right. I have done what you hired me to do, and as you know, I am turning this information over to you this morning. However, with this phone call, I'm not so sure it's over." She continued, "If you want me to stay on this case to help figure out who is behind this, I'll be glad to do so. I wonder whether someone really doesn't want Erica and Perry to be found or if it's something else, like maybe they're on a campaign to get you to pay blackmail money again." Again, Ross and his mother gave each other quizzical looks.

Ella rubbed her chin and said, "We think someone apparently wants Lynn off the case for a reason. I'm wondering what this person is afraid she'll find. But what I really find strange is how someone even knew Lynn was working on this case. Is it possible someone may have followed you here before?" she asked Mrs. Remington. "Or possibly could your telephone be bugged? This phone call to Lynn could end up being only a small piece of the puzzle."

Harvey said, "That's a good point, Ella. How did this person get Lynn's name? It does sound like he, she, whatever, doesn't want her involved in this case." He looked at Elizabeth Remington and Ross, and said, "Right now there's no way of knowing if this is a hoax, if it's only one person or whether or not others are involved. After all, this sounded like a female. Did your father mention whether the person blackmailing him was a man or woman?"

Ross answered that his father assumed it was a man, but he had never spoken with him personally.

"What shall we do?" Mrs. Remington asked.

"Harvey and I are former police officers," Lynn said. "We still have a lot of contacts at the Department. If it's all right with you, I can get someone there to listen to this tape and analyze it." She added, "I bet she'll call again. I would like to talk to this woman to find out what she's really after."

Mrs. Remington looked at Lynn and said, "Yes, do that. And I'd like you to stay on the case." Lynn told her she would.

Lynn, Ella and Harvey spent the next 30 minutes reviewing information they had obtained from their search for Earl Remington's other two children. Lynn shared with Ross the photos of the two that Mrs. Remington found in Earl's private file. Ross recalled his father telling him that the children did not look to be of mixed heritage. His father was right.

Ross, like his mother, did notice the striking family resemblance. These are Father's children, all right, he thought. Beyond that, Ross found himself intrigued by the lives of his half-siblings — the fact that they didn't know who their father was, their being reared by a grandmother and living as whites. He thought of how they'd been adopted, and of how fortunate it was that they had not gotten separated from each other.

When the photo of Hattie Williams was shown, it was apparent that Ross, too, was immediately caught off guard by her loveliness. Her photo had him momentarily spellbound. However, not wanting to hurt his mother's feelings for staring so hard, he nonchalantly set the photo back down without commenting on it. Harvey was also seeing the picture of Hattie as an adult for the first time. Just yesterday, he had seen the photo of the pretty little girl in the white ruffled dress. He picked up Hattie's photo and gazed at it, and said, "Pretty woman! Man, oh man, what a shame." Mrs. Remington did not hide her annoyance at Harvey's apparent fascination with Hattie's appearance.

"I was pretty surprised that Dad would cross the racial line," Ross glanced toward Hattie's picture. "Not that our father was a racist or anything; I just would never have thought he'd do something like that. Dad was pretty conservative. This woman was probably just out for his money." Ross paused for a moment and looked thoughtful, then said, "But then, when Dad talked to me at the hospital, I did see a different side of him, a more sensitive side. He seemed like he was really hurting inside." He quickly added, "Especially for what this news would do to Mother." Ross' eyes locked with his mother's in a moment of shared angst. He had said enough.

Lynn had previously told Mrs. Remington about the remaining contents of Earl Remington's private file, and about the trail of cash withdrawals from his private bank account, including the $100,000 drawn in 1984, the year Hattie died. None of this had set well with Mrs. Remington, for no matter how much she learned of this situation or how many times she heard about it, the minute details still sent a searing pain to her heart every time she had to hear about them. She told herself that one day she would surely be able to get past this.

"Now that we know the whereabouts of the children," she finally said, "we'll have to contact them and get them here, of course." Shaking her head, she thought, why, Earl? Why did you ask such a thing as this of me? She added as if thinking aloud, "Although I still can't imagine why on God's green earth we are

84

to put ourselves through this ordeal."

Ross replied, "Because, Mother, Dad wanted them to be a known part of his family." Elizabeth Remington looked at her son as if to say, that's impossible. Ross went on, "Since she is staying on the case, maybe Miss Davis can invite Erica and Perry here to meet the family. But first, Mother, you've got to talk to Earl, Jordan and Parker. Ross knew this would be hard for them, just as he knew how he, himself, had wrestled with this quite a bit. Nonetheless, they had a right to know the truth.

"This is simply dreadful." Mrs. Remington said.

Lynn replied, "Mrs. Remington, I understand how you must feel. This is a lot, especially when you factor in last night's phone call to me and this whole blackmail matter, plus the reading of the will being just over two weeks away. If you would like me to contact Erica and Perry, I will do it. I know you don't want to postpone the reading of the will for another month, because then you'd just have to deal with this that much longer."

Ross looked at his mother and said, "Mother, you are only trying to carry out Dad's wishes. He obviously knew the burden he was placing on you. I'm sure he toiled with this long and hard before asking such a thing of you, but I don't think he would have wanted you to struggle with this forever. Besides, these two people — Erica and Perry — they're not to blame for any of this. In fact, they had to grow up without their real mother, and without even knowing who their real father was. This is undoubtedly going to be as tough on them as it is on our family, but they have a right to know who they are. And whether we like it or not, they have a right to be heirs of Earl Q. Remington since that's what he wanted." Lynn liked this young man.

"Of course, you're right, Ross. I don't mean to suggest that they're to blame. Surely they're not. And God knows, it's not about the money," Elizabeth Remington said. "Let them have their inheritance. I am sure your brother and sisters will agree." Then looking thoughtfully doubtful, she added, "On second thought, I'm not so sure about that after all." Mrs. Remington turned to Lynn and sighed, saying. "Yes, Miss Davis, please contact them. Get them here as soon as you can — this week if possible. I have to admit, I would like to get this over with."

Lynn told Mrs. Remington, "I will contact them right away." Elizabeth and Ross Remington left the office.

"When you set a time to meet with them, I'll have Janet make their travel arrangements," Ella added.

Lynn walked to the door with Harvey as they talked. "Lynn, we've got to get to the bottom of this telephone call of yours right away," Harvey said. "Whoever this character is must have had some reason for involving you in this mess. Keep me informed of anything that happens. Okay?"

When Lynn returned to her office, she picked up the phone to call Erica and Perry Harrington. Since they were going to be asked to meet with the Remingtons, she would give them the scoop in person. Information like they were going to receive did not need to be delivered over the telephone. Luckily, Lynn was successful in reaching them both. Furthermore, she was able to convince them to come to Cincinnati with little difficulty. In fact, Erica and Perry both sounded keenly interested in the subject of family. Afterward, realizing she had taken them quite by surprise, Lynn reflected on her conversations with the two of them.

"Hello, this is Erica Harrington," Erica had answered in a pleasant voice. Hearing her use her family name, Lynn wondered if she had ever married. She'd then introduced herself and explained the purpose of her phone call.

"I know this will probably come as a surprise to you, Miss Harrington, but I've been hired by a family here in Cincinnati to locate you and your brother, Perry. They wish to invite you to Cincinnati as soon as possible to discuss a very important family matter."

"A family matter," Erica had said in wonderment, obviously having no clue what this could possibly pertain to. "Miss Davis, I don't understand. My parents are in Columbus, Ohio, and besides my brother and son, I'm divorced and have no other relatives to speak of. Please, what is this family matter?"

Lynn carefully explained what she could. She told Erica that, as it turned out, she and Perry did have relatives in Cincinnati, although until recently, no one had known of this relationship.

She told her that the woman who hired her wanted Erica and her brother to come to Cincinnati to meet with them. Then she told a still stunned young woman that this matter was extremely pressing, and the sooner they could arrange to be here, the better for all concerned.

Erica Harrington was mystified by this peculiar phone call. It caught her completely off guard. First of all, she knew of no other family. Their grandmother died when they were small children. Who could it possibly be, and why would they want to meet with her and Perry now? Erica could not fathom what type of family matter would require an in-person meeting.

While speaking with Miss Davis, her curiosity had abruptly turned to suspicion. Who was this Lynn Davis, and what did she really want with her? There were elements of her family life that she wasn't certain she had become comfortable with yet. What if relatives of her mother suddenly showed up? Erica did not want to put herself or her adoptive parents in a precarious position. In a way, she almost preferred that things just stay as they were right now. Maybe later, she could deal with this. But for now, she wasn't sure.

Yet as her curiosity intensified, she suddenly realized the magnitude of this development. Miss Davis was telling her that she actually *had* family in Cincinnati! Over the next few minutes, her attitude changed from suspicious to extremely curious. She had asked several more questions, but got little additional information. Even so, in her heart, Erica knew she would move mountains if necessary to get to Cincinnati.

She had told Lynn she would need to arrange for care for her young son and for coverage on her job. Then she could be on a plane. She asked if Lynn had already talked to Perry, and when Lynn said she had not, Erica told her she would call Perry first. "He's a civil engineer and usually he's out in the field, but I will page him. I'll tell him to call you right away."

"Do you think he'll be interested in coming to Cincinnati, too."

"Oh, you bet!" Erica stated emphatically. "Don't worry, I'll convince him if he isn't. But I'm sure he'll be just as interested as

I am. Perry travels a lot, but I don't believe he was traveling this week. We may be able to come there as early as this Wednesday. Would that be soon enough? I have to say, I will admit to being more than a little nervous about this."

"I'm sure you are," Lynn said, adding, "Let me know your availability as soon as you can. If you can swing it, this Wednesday would work for the people here."

Within minutes, Erica had her brother on the telephone, telling him everything. Perry was excited and inquisitive when he called Lynn just minutes after speaking with his sister. To his probing, Lynn explained, just as she had to Erica, that all their questions would be answered very soon. Perry confirmed that he and Erica could come to Cincinnati Wednesday evening. Lynn called them both minutes later to tell them what travel arrangements had been made for them. She arranged to meet with them at ten o'clock Thursday morning, then notified Mrs. Remington of this schedule.

Next, Lynn also called Wilbur and Bessie Williams to tell them of her success in locating Erica and Perry. The Williams were pleased to hear the news.

Suddenly, Lynn thought again of last night's weird phone call. It made her wonder for a minute if someone could have been listening in on her phone conversations. She felt a slight chill run up her spine as she remembered her Uncle Eddy's concerns when she first took the case to search for Hattie Williams' children. Lynn wondered what he could possibly have sensed, for other than that strange telephone call, she had been feeling pretty good about her successful search for and contact with the children of Earl Quincy Remington and Hattie Rose Williams. She couldn't wait to tell Uncle Eddy the latest developments when they met the next day.

* * * * *

Lynn was to accompany her Uncle Eddy to the annual Police Memorial program. This event was held expressly to honor Cincinnati's slain officers. Tuesday morning her uncle came by her office, and the two walked over to Fountain Square where the program was being held. Arriving early, Lynn and her uncle watched the crowd gather to pay homage. They noted that seated on the front rows were immediate family members of officers who had lost their lives in the line of duty.

As the Chief of Police offered an emotional tribute to the city's fallen heroes, Lynn searched the audience for Freda, the widow of her former partner, Jack Dupree. When Lynn spotted her, the memories came flooding back, and her mind was drawn to that fateful day eight years before when Jack was killed. Her memories seemed as vivid and painful today as the real thing. She recalled how she and Jack had been the first team to arrive at the scene of a robbery in progress. They were just stepping out of their squad car as two men came running out of a store. Jack called out to the suspects to stop, and shots rang out.

Lynn's remorse returned, remembering how she had had a wary feeling that day. She had wondered what it meant, and thought there may have been other burglars. She'd glanced away for only a split second. It was in that precise instant, her partner of five years was felled by a bullet to the head. Lynn, herself, had been grazed on the arm in the melee, but she'd been completely oblivious to her own injury. All she really remembered was seeing Jack fall to the ground. She tried to picture the sequence of events that followed, but could remember only feeling helpless and hopeless as Jack lay lifeless on the ground. Her memory of shooting one of the robbers in the leg and flattening a tire on the getaway car with a bullet, which led to the capture of the suspects, and even receiving a citation for bravery afterwards was a fog.

Lynn relived the saga of delivering the tragic news to Jack's wife. And she recalled every detail of the funeral — the ceremonial 21-gun salute; the long, slow procession; Freda in black, nobly putting forth a brave front; Jack's six-year-old daughter, Autumn, too young to really understand. Lynn's sorrow was relentless. This sad incident seemed permanently etched in her heart.

One by one, other speakers took the podium to give their somber salute. Then the audience sat grimly as a choral group began singing their tribute. The mood was solemn. Finally, the names of those men and women who had died in service to the city were called. Lynn waited for one name in particular. When she heard them call out Jonathan Henry DuPree, her eyes filled with tears. As she dabbed her eyes with a tissue, her uncle patted her arm to console her. Although this was a sad occasion, Lynn never missed a chance to honor her former fellow officers.

Over lunch after the ceremony, Lynn told her uncle about the latest developments in the Remington case. Uncle Ed told her that he was feeling uneasy about this case. The strange phone call she received that Sunday night gave him all the more reason to be bothered. He said he believed that the blackmailer was not finished and that Lynn would likely hear from that person again.

Uncle Eddy told Lynn not to rule out anyone associated with the Remingtons as a possible suspect. This included the chauffeur, other employees of the home, other employees of the corporation, the Remington children, the Dodd children, friends or associates of Mr. Remington, his lawyer, Mrs. Remington herself, Wilbur Williams, Erica and Perry's adoptive parents, and other possible Remington mistresses.

"Lynn, honey, you can't rule anyone out. You never know what someone is liable to do when money's at stake. Especially big money. I don't want to see you in harm's way over this. You keep your eyes and ears open, and call me whenever you need to. That's what I'm here for."

CHAPTER
9

AFTER THEIR MOTHER died, Erica and Perry went to live with their grandmother, Sophie Dodd. Soon afterward, Sophie moved from her small inner city home to a bigger, nicer home in the suburbs and quit her job in order to become the children's full-time guardian. Having only the best interest of her grandchildren at heart, one of the first things she was to change was their race. Sophie decided that there was no point to their being subjected to the racial prejudice that was sure to be their fate as biracials. Since they all looked the part, herself included, she figured that no one would ever know the difference. Therefore, they would simply pass as Caucasians like thousands of blacks and other races before them had done. So Sophie gathered her collection of photographs of her precious daughter, Hattie Rose, and stored them in a small keepsake box that had once belonged to Hattie. She did not want her grandchildren to see these pictures and become confused about their race.

Although Erica and Perry did not understand at first, it did not take long for them to accept that they were white. After all, why would their grandmother tell them something false? Since they had no photographs of their mother, her face faded from their memory over the years, as did her complexion. Years later when Erica and Perry learned their true racial identity, they would remember their grandmother's teachings about their race. Funny, race was never treated like a big deal; it was more subtle and suggestive. And they'd bought it. Even though learning of their racial heritage had been difficult for them to deal with, they believed their grandmother had done what she did so they would have an easier life. They knew she meant well. Sadly she had given up so much, including her cultural heritage, in their best interest, and they couldn't hold that against her.

Two years after they went to live with their grandmother, she passed away. Erica was ten and Perry only eight years old at the time. After her death, a social worker named Miss Arthur came and took them to a foster home where there were lots of other children. While they were afraid at first, they found their caretaker, Mrs. Bridges, to be a kind person, especially if they studied hard and did their schoolwork. Miss Arthur sometimes visited Erica and Perry to see how they were doing, and at times even helped them with their homework during her visit. Erica and Perry had only each other as family, and Miss Arthur assured them she would do everything she could to make sure they always stayed together.

One day, the two were introduced to a couple named Paul and Katherine, or Kitty, Harrington. Miss Arthur told them this couple might want to adopt them. Erica and Perry knew about adoption and had wondered if anyone would ever want to adopt them. The Harringtons thought the two were good kids. They were attractive and well behaved and worked hard in school. They told Erica and Perry they lived in a nice big house in another city not too far away from Cincinnati. If the children came to live with them, they could have their own rooms, a big yard to play in with swings and a tree house, and they could have their own dog. And the dog could have his own house, too!

Erica and Perry knew they would miss the Bridges' house because their friends were still there. And they would miss Miss Arthur. But the Harringtons seemed like nice people, and Erica and Perry thought their home might be all right, especially with that dog. They moved away to Columbus, Ohio, and began calling the Harringtons Mom and Dad. After that, they had a pleasant and ordinary childhood filled with dance recitals, music lessons, school plays and little league ball games.

From the day when Erica first learned of her racial identity, she was plagued with questions for which there were too few answers. She wanted to talk to her adoptive parents about this and had the chance a week later when she and Perry spent a weekend with them as her parents celebrated their 35th wedding anniversary. Erica and Perry were eager to learn what their parents knew about their background, their birth parents, and especially their race.

As the family gathered around the fireplace after dinner, Erica brought the subject up and noticed the furtive glances her mother and father gave each other. With worried eyes, her mother responded, "This is the conversation your father and I knew we would one day have to have with you two." At that moment, Erica and Perry realized their parents knew all.

"Do you remember Miss Arthur, your social worker?" her mother asked them. Erica did remember her. In fact, she'd always credited Miss Arthur with her own choice to enter the field of social work. Perry had sketchy memories of her, too. Kitty told them that when they talked with Miss Arthur about adopting them, Miss Arthur brought them the children's birth records. These records reported the race of the mother as black. Although his name was not provided, their father was listed as Caucasian. She and their father knew the children were bi-racial when they adopted them. Kitty and Paul thought that since Erica and Perry came to them when they were older, they surely remembered their mother, and therefore knew their racial makeup. And neither Kitty nor her husband could ever find any reason to bring the race subject up. For certain, they had not wanted to make a big issue of it.

"I wish you had told us," Erica said.

"Darlings, your dad and I have talked about this many times. You know, we were always very open with you two about your adoption. But we never knew quite what to do about the other. Funny, the longer we did nothing about it, the less appropriate it seemed. Over the years, we often wondered if it had been a mistake not to talk to you about your background, especially when we finally realized you probably didn't know. But please try and understand, we only wanted to do the right thing," their mother said sorrowfully. "To us, your race did not make a difference. As you know, Paul has a brother-in-law, your Uncle Alberto, who is Mexican, and I have other mixed race family members, too, and we've always thought of ourselves as a typical family. So we didn't want to treat your race as a special thing when it really wasn't a huge issue to us. We surely never wanted the two of you to be hurt by this."

This long awaited conversation had gone on into the night, leaving Erica and Perry much to think about.

* * * * *

The call from this Lynn Davis in Cincinnati had Erica's head spinning. She still couldn't get over the fact that she and Perry had been invited to Cincinnati for a family matter. What could this family matter be? Even though she asked Miss Davis, Erica was to learn no more details. She was brimming with curiosity. From the moment she received that phone call, Erica could think of little else. She had called her parents, and they, too, were very curious but had no idea what this could pertain to. Since that phone call, Erica and Perry had talked several times, and Perry was equally perplexed by this family matter. They planned to have dinner together tomorrow night in Cincinnati. Erica looked forward to seeing her brother.

As Erica prepared to travel, she found herself hardly able to focus. The notion that there was an important family matter awaiting her and Perry was almost too much to stand. After putting her son to sleep, she packed her bags. One big worry was eliminated when her ex-husband, Thomas, agreed to keep their son while she was gone. She poured herself a glass of juice and sat at her kitchen table to think. Her marriage to Thomas was on her mind.

At Ohio State University Erica studied sociology, and upon attaining her Bachelors Degree was offered a great job with the Federal Government in Washington, D.C. However, she and Thomas had recently become engaged, and just after graduation, they married.

Thomas was a ruggedly handsome man whom she began dating in her sophomore year of college. Having grown up poor in a small town near Cincinnati, Thomas went directly into the military service for two years after high school so he could attend college on the GI Bill. An athletic person, he was one of the popular stars of the football team. Thomas was also an achiever. He was very proud to be the first member of his family to go to college and worked hard to earn his Civil Engineering Degree, graduating the same year as Erica. Thomas had a number of job offers to choose from, and decided to take an attractive position with a real estate developer in Minneapolis, Minnesota. Since Thomas was a little older and had traveled around the world in the Air Force, Erica thought he was much more interesting than guys her age, and she declined the government job in D.C. to move with him to Minneapolis where she was able to land a position in her field.

In his new job, Thomas traveled extensively. Erica recalled that his job occasionally took him to Cincinnati, which gave him a chance to visit his folks. On returning from one particular trip there, he had boasted proudly about a huge business deal he had just signed on — a shopping plaza development project which his firm, Runyon Developers, had entered into with an outfit named RemCap.

As she thought of Thomas, she recalled their happier days. Other than his occasional mood swings which she'd attributed to his little-spoken-of military experiences, they were a happy couple. Thomas and Erica had been married two years when his father became ill. Erica remembered visiting her in-laws with Thomas one weekend in his father's last weeks of life. During that visit, her husband spent many hours alone with his father. They talked a great deal. He was greatly depressed by his father's illness and took his eventual passing extremely hard. Erica recalled how different Thomas seemed after his father's death.

Erica thought again as she had many times before about the difficult and painful breakup of her marriage. It had been precipitated by a terrible ordeal that took place after they had been married less than three years. This all started when she visited her parents one autumn weekend. For some reason, this particular weekend she decided to explore the contents of a cedar chest that had once belonged to her grandmother. This chest had always been there in the attic, and she knew in her heart it held memories from the past. Her adoptive mother had told her the chest and its contents were hers and Perry's if they wanted them. As a little boy, Perry was completely disinterested and had probably forgotten about the chest a long time ago. It had been in the attic gathering dust since Erica and her brother were adopted by the Harringtons. She had resisted looking in it before, primarily because it seemed eerie to dig up the past. Furthermore, when she was younger, she found the attic a spooky place. On this particular weekend, however, her latent curiosity finally compelled her to examine the possessions of a grandmother long gone.

Actually, sometime during her early teens, Erica remembered opening the chest once and taking a cursory look inside. But the touch of her grandmother's belongings had given her a strange feeling, so she quickly closed the chest and departed the attic, never to return until that fateful weekend years later. Now she was ready to see what was inside, so she looked more closely at the contents. This time, Erica discovered something that had previously gone unnoticed — a small intricately carved brown wooden box that was tucked away among the embroidered bedspread, handmade tablecloths, old costume jewelry, hats and clothing. The box was labeled *Property of Hattie Rose*. Recognizing the name, Erica had been ecstatic to find something that had belonged to her birth mother. Since it was nearly time for her to return home, she took the box with her. She couldn't wait to get home and dig in and didn't want to be rushed. Little did Erica know that once this little box was opened, her life would be forever changed.

Back in Minneapolis, Erica took the little carved box into their spare bedroom that she used as her sewing room. She wanted to relish her treasure in private. Upon finally opening the box, her most amazing discovery was some old photographs of her mother, both as a child and as a young adult. In some of the adult photographs there was a man with her mother. Erica was amazed at her find, for she'd never before seen pictures of her mother and had long ago forgotten what she looked like. However, the minute

Erica laid eyes on her mother's face, there was instant recognition; it was amazing. She felt suddenly warm and happy and tingly all over at the very sight of her mother. She was struck by how beautiful Hattie Rose was and by the sweetness and innocence that emanated from her youthful face. Erica felt safe and whole as her eyes gazed spellbound at these aged photographs.

All of a sudden, reality kicked in, nearly paralyzing Erica. As she stared at the lovely woman in the photograph, it suddenly hit her like a ton of bricks. Hattie Rose Dodd — her mother — was a black woman! The reality of this discovery left her stupefied. She stared at the photograph for what seemed like an eternity.

Her mind raced back to her childhood, and she frantically searched her memory for a vision of her mother. She asked herself in absolute bewilderment, how could this be? How could my mother be black if I'm white? Mortified as a shocking awareness struck her, she cried, "My God, if my mother is black, what does that make me?" Confused, Erica answered her question with another one: "I'm black?" The realization of her racial makeup was overwhelming to Erica. Even though she had vaguely remembered her mother, she'd had absolutely no recollection of her being black. For so long she had considered herself Caucasian. Everyone in her world — her grandmother, her adoptive parents, and her husband — were white. "This makes no sense. How can I be black? What about my father? Surely he was white."

As her racial heritage settled in on her, Erica pondered how society unfairly defined anyone with even one drop of black blood as black, completely discounting the other side of one's makeup. This seemed so unfair. She was at once abhorred at another notion society had taught her, one she admittedly had accepted without question — that black people weren't really quite as good … "Oh, God, perish the thought," she found herself speaking aloud, "as whites."

Erica didn't know quite how to handle the rediscovery of her racial identity. For a moment, she even blamed Hattie Rose. Mother, she anguished, how could you do this to us? Why couldn't you have just been white? Then Erica instantly hated herself for thinking such a horrible thing. She wondered why no one had ever talked to her and Perry about this, prepared them for this. And what should she and Perry call themselves now? Bi-racial? African American? Had their adoptive parents known about their racial identity? And if they had, why hadn't they told her and Perry? And why had she forgotten her light brown-skinned mother? How could she possibly have forgotten something so significant?

Erica remembered being thoroughly traumatized when she remembered missing her last monthly cycle, suspecting that she might be pregnant. So fresh was this new development that she had not yet even told her husband about it and had not planned to do so until she knew for certain. Upon this new discovery, all kinds of troubling questions raced through her head. What color will our child be? What if he is brown like my mother? Will Thomas be able to deal with that? Will I? The timing for a pregnancy could not have been worse. Moments earlier, Erica was looking forward to seeing her doctor in a few days to confirm her suspicions and announcing the news to Thomas. They both wanted a baby, and it should have been an exciting and joyous time. Instead, Erica was completely distraught.

She had to tell her brother what she had found. Erica remembered their conversation. "Are you sitting down," she had asked. He answered, "Sure, sis, what's up?" Excitedly, she told him she had found some things in her grandmother's old chest that had belonged to their birth mother, Hattie Dodd. "That's great. I'm glad you were interested in looking through that old stuff. I sure wasn't," Perry said laughingly. "So what'd you find, valuable stock certificates or some rare jewelry or something?" Ignoring his playfulness, Erica told him she found pictures of their mother. Perry immediately took note.

"Perry, do you remember what our real mother looked like?" Erica asked him in a serious tone.

"I don't think so," he answered.

"Do you remember anything at all about her complexion?"

"Her complexion? No, not really. Why?"

"Because, Perry, our mother was not white."

"Aw, come on, Erica. Of course, she was white. Or what are you saying? That she was Indian? I know, she was Hispanic."

"Neither, Perry, and I'm being serious. Our mother was African American."

"Yeah, right," he exclaimed impatiently.

"Perry, I'm trying to tell you, our mother was black. I'm looking at her picture."

"No way! Quit kidding around, Erica. This is nothing to joke about."

"Look, Perry," Erica said, "I'm not joking with you. As strange as this sounds, the fact is, our mother was black! Believe me, I'm finding this hard to believe, too. In fact, I'm really struggling here. You realize, don't you, that if our mother was black, that makes us part black, too."

Perry was silent on the other end of the phone. Erica continued to tell him of her findings. She told him that as hard as it was to believe, pictures did not lie.

"You are serious, aren't you, Erica," Perry slowly asked, no longer in a playful tone as awareness washed over him. "Gosh, sis, I really thought you were just kidding. Frankly, I don't know what to say. I don't see how a person can just change what they are in a single instant. I've got to see these pictures of yours. Maybe when I see for myself ... you know, I've always taken it for granted that I am what I am. I feel the same now as I've felt my whole life. And you know what, I'm still the same person I was before you dropped this on me. I still feel the same, and I still look the same. I don't know, Erica. Maybe race isn't anything but a word. Everybody's probably mixed anyway. Maybe we are all the same. After all, aren't we all members of the human race?" As Perry rambled on, Erica could tell that he was struggling with this revelation just as she was. They talked quite a bit more, and he had even called her back later that night.

"Listen, Erica," Perry told her. "I've been thinking a lot since you told me this earlier. And I've been trying to figure out what to do with this new information. I've made a decision." Erica thought her brother was handling this news much better than she. He seemed to have at least accepted it, while she felt she was still very much in denial. Then Perry told her he had decided this would change nothing in his life. "Look, Erica, we both have it made, relatively speaking. We have a good education, good jobs. We're pretty fortunate. Personally, I'm not willing to give up everything I've worked hard for. This racial business is my personal business, and I don't intend to discuss it with anyone else. I'm sure there are plenty of other people out there who are passing for white, too. We can't be the only people who look like this but are of mixed race."

Erica told her brother she understood and even mostly agreed with him. But she had been thinking about this, too, and she felt she did have to discuss it with someone else — Thomas. He had a right to know the truth. Perry told her she ought to just let sleeping dogs lie. When she told Perry about her possible pregnancy and her fears, he congratulated her, but said, "Me, I would still leave it alone if I were you, Erica. After all, what good will it serve? I don't think Thomas is that broad-minded. And it may cause problems between you two for no reason." They spent a long time on the phone that night. Even though Perry disagreed, Erica still knew what she had to do.

Now sipping juice as she prepared to depart for Cincinnati tomorrow, Erica again thought about this little wooden box which she later called her *Pandora's box*. She recalled how its contents had been the source of major joy, yet the worst crisis she and Thomas had encountered — one they would not survive.

She remembered fully that despite Perry's warnings, she hadn't foreseen how talking to Thomas was going to be that problematic. They had certainly faced other challenges in their short marriage. Granted, she thought he'd be shocked at first, maybe even upset, to learn his wife was bi-racial, and then he'd get over it. She hoped he'd be as accepting of this issue as Perry had been in the end. Unfortunately, her hopes were not to be realized.

Thankfully, Thomas was leaving town the morning following her discovery, and she was happy to let this wait until he returned. She'd have thought it through by then and would be better prepared to have this discussion with him. When Thomas arrived home a few days later, Erica had two important things to talk to him about, one being her now confirmed pregnancy. She decided to deal with the most difficult topic first. She often wondered if it would have made a difference had she told him first about the baby. Softly, she began to tell him about the box she had discovered days before in her grandmother's chest that contained some pictures of her mother. Thomas seemed interested. Erica told him that she had never seen pictures of her mother and had totally forgotten what she looked like. She told Thomas she did remember what her grandmother looked like and, of course, Thomas, too, had seen pictures of Sophie Dodd. Erica was relieved that Thomas seemed openly engaged and interested. She slowly handed him one of the black and white photographs of Hattie Dodd. What should have been a happy moment now filled her with dread, for suddenly Erica did not feel her husband was going to take this news very well. But it was too late to back out now. Thomas stared at the picture in puzzlement and asked, "Who the hell is this?"

Erica said, "Thomas, *this* is my mother." Thomas was baffled as he agitatedly asked, "What are you up to, Erica?" His mind was not letting him accept what she'd just told him. He decided she had obviously misspoken or that she'd been adopted twice — once by a black woman. Now why would an adoption agency allow black people to adopt little white kids, he wondered, growing angry. At least, they came up with the Harringtons? He'd heard enough. "This isn't anything to tease about," he admonished his wife impatiently.

Pointing to her mother's face, Erica said, "Listen to me, Thomas. This woman right here is my *birth* mother, Hattie Rose Dodd." Thomas turned and gave her a wild look, reflecting the extent of his total disbelief. His look was so fierce it actually frightened her. But she held back her fear and added, "As I said, I didn't remember what she looked like."

Erica now had Thomas' undivided attention. He mockingly said, "This black woman is my birth mother. Look, Erica, you're my wife. There's no way you're serious," he said adamantly, glaring at her questioningly. When she nodded, he stopped the denial. He knew she meant it, and a verbal denial would not reverse the horrible truth. For a moment he just looked at her in disbelief. Thomas was truly upset. He shook his head and stomped his foot loudly, causing the glasses on the kitchen table to shake. Now out of control, he began to talk to his wife in a way he'd never done before. He called her a liar and a phony. He even yelled at her and accused her of tricking him into marrying her. Erica had not expected this reaction from Thomas. It was appalling, and she was frightened by his ferocity. She knew Thomas had a pretty rough temper at times, but she'd never seen him this upset. She spent the next several minutes trying to quell his rage. Their discussion turned even more heated, and over the next several minutes more of Thomas' hidden bigotry surfaced. He stopped just short of hurling ethnic names at her. He told her he did not believe she didn't know what her race was. He accused her of knowingly deceiving him.

Erica was stunned. She reminded Thomas that they had never talked about race; she'd never told him she was white, just as he had never told her he was. It was just something they both just assumed. Erica told Thomas she couldn't see why it made such a difference anyway. She was still the same person she was before. Nothing had changed.

No matter what Erica said, Thomas would not calm down. He was on a tirade, ranting on and on, telling her his family had accepted her. Although his father was now deceased, his mother still treated her like a daughter. He wasn't sure how they'd feel now. Erica told Thomas that she did not wish to hurt anyone in his family. She reminded him that she had not married his family, she'd married him, and that should be all that counted. He was highly offended by that and told her he felt she had betrayed him and his family. She suggested they talk to their pastor or that they seek counseling. Thomas stormed out of the house in a rage. This entire ordeal had been almost too much to bear. Even today, it was still so painful, the very reminder of it brought tears to her eyes. After Thomas left the house, Erica tried to understand why he had reacted so negatively. Why had he been so hateful about this?

After several hours of drinking and who knew what else, Thomas came home and attempted to make amends. He was very calm as he told Erica that he'd thought a lot about their conversation and realized he had dealt rashly with the issue. He said he knew he should not blame her for something she may not have known anything about, but he did explain that he still needed to grapple with this. Thomas admitted to Erica having grown up in a very conservative household in a community of people who believed races were not supposed to mix, and that was that. But he loved his wife and didn't want to lose her.

Erica was grateful Thomas had at least calmed down, for his anger had troubled her greatly. She was even a bit hopeful that the worst was over and that they would get through this. Thomas apologized for his behavior, but she seriously wondered if he was sincere. With this incident, Thomas had shown Erica a side of himself she'd never seen before. His behavior had hurt and confused her, and although she had wanted things to work out, she wondered if their marriage could survive this. Even so, because she was now expecting a child, she decided to give it a try. The matter of her pregnancy was not brought up that day.

After a few weeks of relative calm, Erica knew that very soon her condition would become obvious. She was still not 100 percent certain that she and Thomas were on solid ground, and decided it was time to find out. So for the first time since that dreaded incident, she brought up the subject of her race. Surprisingly, Thomas was amenable to discussing the subject. In fact, he took over the conversation as if he had initiated it, telling Erica he had dealt with this issue and believed it was no longer a problem to him. He told her she meant more to him than his early racial indoctrination. He wanted them to stay together and maybe even start a family. Erica accepted this, partly because she wanted it to be true. She still loved her husband very much and really did not want to see her marriage come to an end, especially now that there was a child growing inside her body.

She hoped that in time this whole thing would be forgotten. Furthermore, she was now nearly three months pregnant. Erica decided it was time to tell Thomas about the baby. When he learned he was going to be a father, he seemed proud and happy, and at once the strain in their marriage vanished. Thomas even succeeded in being a doting husband during her pregnancy. Their son, Timothy Earl, was born a few months later. Thomas was very pleased that his firstborn was a boy. Initially, he accepted little Timmy and even claimed to look forward to giving him a brother or sister one day.

Erica was a proud new mom. However, because of their fiasco over her racial makeup, she couldn't help but wonder if Timmy would have her mother's complexion. She was admittedly relieved to see that when he was born, he shared his father's and her pale skin. Her relief was short-lived, however, when, within a matter of weeks, her son's pale complexion began to take on a light olive tone. Sadly, this sudden change also brought about an immediate change in Thomas and Erica's relationship, as Thomas could not handle the new development. He wondered how he would ever explain Timmy's coloration to his family. Furthermore, what would his friends say about his little black baby? What about his co-workers? He knew it was going to be very difficult to go out in public and face the stares. Thomas began to make racial references more often, and rather than confront his fears, he refused to go anywhere with Erica and Timmy. Not only that, his behavior had become erratic and he seemed to stay upset about one thing or another.

Once this corner had been turned, things only went from bad to worse for the couple. This was it. Although it was a hard pill to swallow, Erica had to finally admit their marriage was over. The ensuing divorce proceedings were acrimonious, and Thomas was basically hostile and angry, ironically even threatening to seek custody of his son. While this worried Erica, she didn't really believe Thomas would go that far, although by the way he was acting she couldn't be sure. He was such a different person now. She decided that when this was all behind them, she and Timmy might just move back to Columbus.

Even though the breakup of her marriage was an unfortunate development, Erica was pleased that through it all she had reconciled herself to her startling racial discovery of months ago. She was actually proud of the way she was embracing her dual heritage. While Thomas saw their son's appearance as problematic, Erica now saw only beauty in Timmy's golden complexion. She resolved that when the time was right she would help her child understand and appreciate both sides of his own racial makeup.

Erica had been deeply immersed in reliving these events. She finished her orange juice, and feeling a headache coming on, tried to clear her mind of these troublesome memories. Her bags were packed and she was all set to travel the next day. Although she wanted to enjoy speculating about her trip, she found it hard to shake the tormenting thoughts that filled her mind. Her breakup with Thomas had been so hurtful she couldn't help but be grateful they were now on good terms. Thomas now seemed to show more interest in their son and, in fact, he and Timmy got along well together. Knowing how important her relationship was with her adoptive father and how much she ached to know who her real father was, Erica felt it was important for Timmy to enjoy a good relationship with his father. Even so, these unpleasant memories gave her cause to wonder if she would be doing the right thing leaving Timmy with Thomas for a few days. She shook off her worries, assuring herself that nothing could possibly go wrong, and went into her bedroom.

CHAPTER
10

PERRY HARRINGTON WAS greatly looking forward to going to Cincinnati to see what this family matter was about. Like Erica, he was consumed with curiosity and had thought of little else since speaking with Lynn Davis two days before. With an hour to go before boarding his plane, he sat in a coffee shop near his gate, sipped a cafe latte, and pondered it all while trying to speed up the clock. Often, when he thought of family, his thoughts turned to his mother as they did now. He thought of her picture he carried with him at all times. Three years ago, when Erica had first discovered that picture among her mother's keepsakes, she'd quickly had copies made for Perry. He remembered how anxious he had been to finally see the woman who had given birth to him and Erica. He treasured her picture and removed it from his wallet, staring at it reminiscently.

Perry'd had no real recollection of his mother's face, for it had long been blotted from his memory. Thus when he first looked at the picture, he was in awe. Hattie Rose looked no older than he was now, and she was so very pretty. But Perry had also been stunned by her color, for even though Erica had told him what to expect, he still could not have pictured this look. Looking at her picture as he did now always gave him a warm sense of belonging and the stirrings of sweet memories. Yet his thoughts also brought with them a sense of forlornness that his mother was gone and a curiosity that Perry had always attempted to subdue. Who was my father?

Perry often wondered what it had been like when he lived with his mother. From time to time he was sure he could remember bits and pieces of his past, like the time he was swinging in the park. He felt positive the woman in his mind's eye was his mother smiling at him happily as he pumped himself higher and higher, trying to go all the way over the top. But his mother's face wasn't clear. And he was never sure if his memory was real or the product of an over-eager dream.

He thought he could remember being picked up from school one day in a big black car driven by a man wearing a black hat or a cap. Wasn't that his mother sitting beside him in the backseat with another person — yes, a man. Perry thought he could picture the man having shiny black hair. He seemed to remember that there was something unusual about his face, but he just couldn't remember what it was. Again, he didn't know for sure if this was a real memory or just his mind playing games with him. If it was real, who was that man? Could it have possibly been his father? Oh, he would love to know this; if only he could remember … There were times when a particular lullaby, a fairly well-known tune called "Mockingbird" would run through his head. Perry was positive he could remember someone, a woman, singing it to him as he lay in bed at night. She'd be sitting on the bed and stroking his hair. It always made things feel so safe and right. Perry was sure it was his mother whose singing he remembered.

The phone call he received from Erica some years ago ran through his mind. *Erica will probably never know how much that conversation taught me about myself and the world,* he thought as he reflected on the discovery of his bi-racial heritage. If one could feel a race, Perry Harrington felt white. This was how he had grown up. His circle of friends and associates were mostly white, as were his parents. This was the only world he really knew, and he was very comfortable in it.

He had told himself at first that race didn't matter, and to prove it, he tried an experiment. He decided to try to see the world through the eyes of a black man to find out if there was a difference. From the moment he tried that experiment, his entire perspective on race changed. Things as simple as watching television or going to a restaurant suddenly felt completely different through his eyes as an African American man. Perry found this experience disconcerting. It made him realize how much he had taken for granted all his life, even with his earlier hardships. In school, he'd worked hard and was rewarded with excellent grades and scholarships, the opportunity to work in the profession of his choice and be promoted on merit alone. He never had to wonder if things happened to him purely because of his race. He never felt any doors were closed to him because of it. This experiment in race gave him a totally new awareness. From a black man's perspective, Perry felt nothing could be taken for granted. Right or wrong, he drew an unexpected conclusion: that being a black person in America was hard.

This had been a sobering exercise, and in the end Perry decided to leave things just as they were. He saw no point in announcing to the world that he was not Caucasian. Just as he never talked about race before, he was not compelled to do so now. And life went on pretty much as before. In the three years since he learned the race of his mother, the one difference was that now Perry was much more attuned to worldly matters and issues than before. Without even realizing he had changed, he had become a vocal advocate for such things as civil rights and affirmative action.

Perry's deep thoughts were interrupted when a friend suddenly appeared and asked if he could join him. He looked up and greeted Lionel Simmons with a friendly handshake. Lionel was a black colleague with whom he regularly played racquetball. Lionel's flight to San Francisco was being delayed, and he had spotted Perry sitting alone. Perry welcomed the chance to talk to a friend. Lionel took a chair next to him and asked where he was headed. Perry told him. Then Lionel saw the picture in Perry's hand and said, "Hmmm, whatcha got there?"

For reasons Perry did not fathom, in spite of how he felt about discussing the race issue, he had no desire to continue the secret at that moment. Perhaps it was because of this mysterious trip he was about to take regarding a *family matter*. In any event, he passed the photograph to Lionel who said the woman in the picture was very pretty. Perry said, "Yes, she was very pretty." Then he took a deep breath, sighed somberly, and looking Lionel directly in the eye, said, "She was my mother. She died many years ago." His words sounded at once sad and resigned, yet pride-filled.

Although he was startled, Lionel managed to say, "Oh, I'm sorry." Then he waited for Perry to say more, because what he'd just heard made no sense to him at all. In fact, he was confused as hell. Wasn't the woman in that picture black?

"Yeah, I know what you're thinking," Perry nodded and said to Lionel, continuing, "have I ever told you we were adopted, my sister and I?"

"No, man, I never knew. Was this your adoptive mother?"

"Nope, this was actually my birth mother." Lionel furrowed his brow and looked dead at Perry. Perry understood Lionel's curious reaction. Without explaining the obvious question, Perry pursed his lips and slowly said, "Her name was Hattie Rose Dodd."

"Perry, am I hearing you right?" Lionel asked, still with a quizzical frown on his face. Then he pointed to the picture in Perry's hand and said, "This is your real mother? Excuse me, but isn't this woman African American?"

Perry added quietly, "That she is. My adoptive parents are Caucasian. Funny thing, I just learned about my mother's race a few years ago. See, she died when I was pretty young."

"Perry, man, wow. I didn't know. I sure didn't mean to pry or anything," Lionel quickly added.

"It's not a problem. I'll tell you though, it did take me by surprise when I learned I was bi-racial because, believe it or not, up until that point I had lived my life believing I was Caucasian." Perry gave a half laugh and a slight shake of his head. He seemed filled with bewilderment as he added, "Now here's the next twist. My sister and I thought we had no other family except our adoptive parents. Then suddenly, I get this phone call to come to Cincinnati about a family matter. I don't have a clue what this family matter is. Like I said, I am not aware of any family outside of Erica and our folks. But I will say one thing, Lionel, it's intriguing as everything. It's got me fascinated, so anyway, that's where I'm headed right now." Then Perry looked mystified and said, "And I truly don't know why I'm unloading all this on you at this time."

"Say, Perry, man, that's all right. It's really something. I sure hope you get some news you're happy with there in Cincinnati. I'm still thinking about living your whole life thinking you are one thing, only to find out that you're something else. Now that's deep. If you don't mind my asking, Perry, what happened to your biological father?"

"Couldn't say. I never knew him. Of course, as an adoptee, I never got any information about him. I don't even know his real name." The mere mention of the father he never knew shook Perry to his core. He was actually surprised at how much this was eating at him. He was also surprised at how all this stuff came pouring out of him. Had it been bottled up so long it was just time to let it out? He didn't know and really did not care to answer that question. All he knew was that it felt good to talk about it. Then Perry tried to shake off the sorrow he felt about not knowing his father by bringing up his mother again. "After our mother died, my sister, Erica, and I lived with our grandmother who was white. And that's how we grew up — as white. The subject of race never came up after that."

Lionel shook his head in surprise. "Man, I sure never would have known if you hadn't told me. Your adoptive parents had to be very special people, what with all the racial attitudes people have."

"Yes, they are special," Perry said. "The ironic thing is they thought we knew our race, so they never even brought it up." A soft laugh escaped his lips as he said, "I suppose they were just trying to protect us from all the prejudice in the world. They must have succeeded, too, because it's an odd thing: I'm half black and in my whole life, I have never really experienced race prejudice in America. I'm not asking for it, mind you. No, I feel very lucky I never had to deal with it because I know it's out there."

Lionel nodded his head in agreement and said, "Tell me about it. It's real, man. It most certainly is."

"Look, Lionel, you're the only person I've told all this to," Perry said, continuing, "I'm not sure I'll be talking about it to anyone after this. Just gotta sort things out right now, you know."

Lionel assured Perry he considered this conversation private. "Perry, man, I appreciate what you've had to deal with," Lionel said, "and as a matter of fact, I really admire you." After a bit, the two men chatted about work, the Chicago Cubs and other small matters until finally Perry heard the announcer call for his flight to board. "Good luck in Cincinnati," Lionel shook his hand again. "See you next week on the court. Meantime, I'll be around when you get back if you ever want to talk."

Perry took his seat on the plane, and as he sat back, he thought about how he had just talked openly about his bi-racial heritage for the first time. And it had been relatively easy. In fact, he was glad to finally discuss it with a friend. He and Lionel worked for the same engineering firm, played racquetball together regularly and from time to time, went to lunch together. They'd become pretty good pals. Still, he'd actually had no intention of going into all this, but this wasn't the first deep discussion they'd had. In fact, Lionel had come to Perry before to help him work through a highly confidential job matter that he had never discussed with anyone except Perry.

Perry patted his wallet to remind himself that he had put his mother's picture away. His family past had always been a mystery to him. And now it was off to Cincinnati for a family matter. Will Erica and I finally get some answers? God knows, he thought, I hope so.

* * * * *

During Erica's plane ride to Cincinnati, she actually closed her eyes and slept. The night before she had slept little. She'd been too excited and steeped in her memories. After reliving the saga of the breakup of her marriage, she had gone into her bedroom to go to bed, but was drawn to her closet where, on the top shelf, sat her mother's little wooden box. For a while she'd just stared at it and thought about how this little box had changed her life. She recalled Perry's admonishments to keep quiet about their mother's race, and she wondered if things would have been different had she not told Thomas the truth. Would she and Thomas still be together? What if she hadn't been pregnant? Would she have taken a chance on having children? In the end, she realized her breakup with Thomas was inevitable given their differences. Although she had accepted her bi-racial heritage, still, the topic of race did not come up in her everyday conversation, and basically, little else changed.

Erica hadn't been able to resist opening her little box again last night. It had probably been a year since she'd last looked in it. To this day, she still believed it contained more secrets. What were they? Once again, she was drawn to examine its contents. This small box held some fascinating objects. While the photographs of her mother were very special to her, they were not the only items of great interest. The box contained other things that had given her a special insight into her mother. There were additional photographs, including a few of her brother and herself when they were very young. Seeing these pictures of her and Perry always reminded her that she and her brother had had a life that predated the life she remembered as a member of the Harrington family.

A few black and white photographs showed her mother and a tall, distinguished Caucasian gentleman. These pictures all revealed a strong bond and an apparent intimacy between the two. In one picture, this man stood behind Hattie Rose with his arms around her waist while he looked adoringly down at her. They were standing next to a Rolls Royce. A chauffeur in a dark suit and cap sat inside the automobile with a serious look on his face. Erica always fantasized that the man with her mother was their father? She assumed this man was wealthy because of the luxury automobile in the picture and wondered what his name was and where he was today? Where were these photographs taken? It dawned on Erica as she looked at these pictures of her mother and this distinguished gentleman that she had never shared this set of pictures with anyone, including Perry.

Also in her box were several letters, apparently from some of her mother's suitors. Erica enjoyed reading these letters and loved how romantic they sounded. She always wondered about some cards and letters from a man named Jelly who seemed to have adored her mother, although he sounded more like a friend than a lover. Nonetheless, she wondered who he was and where he was now.

Then there were several letters from a mysterious gentleman who simply signed his name, "E." This man would end each of his letters with an affectionate phrase — *My beautiful Rose, with a love that knows no bounds.* One handwritten letter was placed inside a lovely *"wish you were here"* card. It was very romantic. Erica had read it many times before, and on this occasion she read it again.

My Darling Hattie,

Why did you come into my life? Why me? Why now? I ask myself this question daily, although I thank the kind hands of fate that brought you to me. I am reminded often of the first time I looked into your eyes. I don't remember if I was more attracted to your beauty, your splendid carriage, your gentle and loving character, or your fun-loving, exciting and spontaneous spirit. I feel so blessed to be in your life, my love, for you are indeed one of those wonderful beings whose life graces this world.

How can I show you that my love for you is boundless? I would gladly give you anything your heart desires. Oh, how I wish I could.

Every day I am with you is a day of magic, my darling. You make my heart happy and cause my soul to sing and dance with joyous abandon. You are, indeed, too glorious for words, and unquestionably, too marvelous for me. For every day, every hour, every minute you give me your love, I live a lifetime of joy. I will count the seconds until you are in my arms once more.

My beautiful Hattie, my special Rose. With a love that knows no bounds,

"E."

As always, Erica was mesmerized by the words of this letter. Being a romanticist, more and more she found herself yearning to one day enjoy the special kind of love and devotion this *"E"* professed to her mother. She believed her mother must have been a truly special woman to make a man feel this way about her, and she thought the man who could write such a loving letter as this was a master of words and charm. She could almost hear the voice — deep, rich, compelling. Who was this *E*?

Erica remained curious while she indulged her fantasies by reading her mother's personal memoirs again. She had always pored over Hattie's writings, totally submerging herself in them because when she read them, even when she simply touched them, she felt a strange connection to her mother. It felt tingly and quite special.

Hattie's writings were mixed. The earlier dated ones were joy-filled, but toward the end, they were very sad. From what Erica could tell, her mother's heart was broken. She was in love with someone, but it sounded like the man who stole her heart belonged to another. Although her mother made constant references to the hope of marriage someday, their relationship consisted only of stolen moments. For the hundredth time, Erica read the final entry in Hattie's journal. As it always did, it made her heart stop:

Today is a sad day for I am filled with longing.

I am falling deeper and deeper into a bottomless pit, and yet, while I find myself sinking fast, I cannot find the will or the strength to lift myself out of this hopeless situation. How I love this man with all my heart, yet I realize we will never spend our total lives together. That is fairly certain and I've known this from the start. Still, I want and miss him desperately.

I don't know how much longer I can continue this way. Would it be better to make a clean break. I wonder. Meanwhile, in spite of my sorrow, I will go on, I must — if not for myself, then for the sake of the two darling children produced by our love.

It hurt Erica to read her mother's prophetic words. She found herself reading them over and over and staring into space as the words rang through her head. She could picture her mother making that final entry, and the thought of her writing those words of desolation filled Erica with sadness. She sensed that she could actually feel her mother's pain. Always when Erica read this final entry, she almost hated the person responsible for her mother's broken heart. This time, however, tears came to her eyes, and she wept freely. "Oh, Mother," she lamented, "I wish you had not been so unhappy. I wish you were here today so I could tell you this, and so I could touch you and comfort you."

Hattie had not put the complete date on her memoirs — only the month and year. This last entry was dated October 1984, which was the exact month and year she died. As always, Erica was filled with questions. What had her mother's words meant? Whom had she been talking about? Why could they never marry?

The one question Erica never wanted to think always came to her mind. Had her mother known she was going to die? As unthinkable as it seemed, Erica even wondered if her mother had taken her own life. This was such a horrible thought that she could not bear the idea of talking about it with anyone, not even her mother, nor her brother. The one thing Erica could not let go were her mother's words about holding on for the sake of her children. It could not possibly have been suicide, Erica tried to convince herself. Our mother could not have chosen to leave us.

After reminiscing through her little box the evening before her flight to Cincinnati, Erica had carefully closed it and returned it its special place in her closet. It was well after midnight before she got to bed. By then, she slept soundly.

Now on the plane, more than three years after the discovery of her bi-racial heritage, more family matters awaited disclosure. Could it be she and Perry would learn more about their mother, their grandmother? Would they finally learn the identity of their biological father? Such would be more than she could hope for. She closed her eyes and, filled with an expectant anticipation, she rested peacefully on the hour-long flight to Cincinnati.

CHAPTER
11

THINGS HAVE ACCELERATED, Elizabeth thought as she prepared to have her long awaited talk with her children about their father's deathbed secrets. The search for Earl's other two children was over, and they were coming to town Wednesday evening. She had already asked Lynn Davis to coordinate a joint meeting this coming Friday for the express purpose of their all becoming acquainted. Lynn would run the meeting.

That decided, Elizabeth called her children to meet with her. Because of their varied schedules, she elected to talk to them one at a time. The fact was, she thought it would be more palatable to face only one set of eyes instead of three at once. She was grateful there would be only three talks instead of four since Ross already knew everything. Elizabeth was still uncertain of all she would tell her children. She would just play it by ear. However, she was not confident of her children's tolerance for others and decided against bringing the race matter up for now. How would they react to that? It's already going to be hard enough for them to learn that their father led a double life for many years and had two children by a secret mistress. She would cover only the basics for now.

Elizabeth Remington began these talks with a sense of resignation. One by one, she told her children, "I know you have wondered what your father wanted me to share with you. I'm now going to tell you, but remember first, that what he most wanted was your understanding and forgiveness. Your father never wanted to hurt any of you." And on she went until the story was told.

Even though they were anxious to learn the truth, the other three Remington children did not accept the news well. Each talk was met with surprise and indignation, although none of them let on to their mother that they suspected their father had sometimes been unfaithful. However, the details of his affair, including his having two children, shocked them all. Her children were clearly upset by their father's secret life. And as she suspected, none were the least bit interested in meeting the other two people their father claimed to have sired.

Parker was angry and hurt. All her life she had felt special, believing she was her father's favorite. When she learned of his illegitimate children, she felt betrayed. She did not want to think of sharing him with others. Parker did not want to have anything to do with these people, let alone have a relationship with them. The very idea of acknowledging them as Remingtons was itself ludicrous, and she told her mother she'd have nothing to do with that. To her mother's consternation, she conceded, "But I will meet them, Mummie, if I must." Elizabeth took this as a small win, for she knew to expect little more from Parker.

Jordan secretly thought the situation was ironic. As she heard the story, she thought to herself, I can't believe my father. He worked so hard on creating a powerful family image when it was all just a big front. She remembered how her dad had once practically given her an ultimatum to return to Cincinnati when she was jet-setting around the world — that or be cut out of his will. She always wondered what would have happened had she not complied with his demands. Now here were two people, in his will, no less, who never had to do a thing. Life was so unfair. Jordan told her mother she did not mind meeting them. But she knew in her heart that she had no interest in having anything to do with them. What could we possibly have in common? What was Dad thinking? She couldn't figure it out.

Earl, Jr. took this news even harder than the others. Although he felt badly for his mother, he wasn't really too shocked to hear about his father's affair because he was aware his father appreciated beauty, as did all men. Besides, he had seen the signals over the years. He never liked it, but he couldn't do anything about it. But it was these so-called children of his father that bothered him the most. This whole thing was preposterous. Earl, Jr. could barely stand the competition with his recognized siblings. What he did not need were two more people claiming they were his father's children and maybe even trying to climb the corporate ladder at the Remington Corporation, heaven forbid.

Frankly, Earl, Jr. was suspicious. Had these two people produced DNA results to prove they were Father's true children? Did anyone require them to take blood tests? How do we know this is not a hoax? Maybe they are just trying to cut in on the Remington wealth. "Remember all the claimants to Howard Hughes' fortune," he told his mother.

Clearly, Earl did not like this development. Meet them? "Now, why on earth would I want to do something like that?" he asked, simply appalled at the notion. He finally came around though, to appease her, not because he really wanted to.

Sipping a glass of brandy afterward, Elizabeth was grateful these talks were over.

* * * * *

"Downtown Cincinnati is pretty live," Perry commented as he and Erica watched the scurry of activity on the sidewalks and streets. They were both so young when they left here, they had no real memory of it. Surprisingly, it had the feel of a pretty big city, even to Perry coming from Chicago. Although they could have taken the internal route to Miss Davis' office through the skywalks from their hotel, they preferred to walk outside and see the people, smell the smells and hear the sounds of the city. They were both wonderfully excited.

The two walked the block toward the Vine Street entrance to Carew Tower. Their meeting with Lynn Davis was at ten o'clock, and it was only 15 after nine. They decided to kill some time by walking around. Erica ogled the window displays at Saks Fifth Avenue and Tiffany's. But she was merely pretending to care what was in those store windows. What she and her brother both really wanted to know more than anything was what this family matter was about.

They crossed the street to Fountain Square where they sat on a bench and speculated again about why they were here. Erica and Perry had had dinner together the night before which gave them a chance to catch up. It had been close to a year since they had last seen each other. Over dinner and again at breakfast, they'd guessed at why they were here. This morning as they waited, they picked up the topic of family once more.

"One thing I was wondering, sis," Perry said as he stared at the water dancing in the fountain. "Have you ever thought much more about why Grandma Sophie wanted us to think we were white?"

"A million times," Erica responded. "I've asked myself that very question over and over. And I feel the same way I always did about this. You know there is just so much prejudice in the world, I think she was just simply trying to keep us from being hurt by it." Perry agreed, saying that was the only thing that made sense. "And here's another thing," Erica said. "I think our grandmother knew who our father was, too. But just like she kept our race from us, I now think she kept that from us to keep us from being hurt. By what, I don't know." Perry told her sometimes he ached to know who their father was. "Me too," Erica said. "Just think, what if that's something we're going to find out today?" They both thought about that for a few minutes.

Then Erica reluctantly asked her brother a question that had plagued her for years. "Perry, tell me something. I know this is a dumb question, but," she paused and took a deep breath before continuing. "What do you really think about black people? I mean, do you believe they really are as good as whites? I want to know how you feel because I'm afraid growing up, I hate to say this, but I was caught up in all the negative messages, although I don't think I was really conscious of it. Even today, I think I feel more white than black because sometimes I catch myself thinking the way I used to about black people. That's pretty awful, I know. And I have to admit, I had a real struggle when I first had to come to grips with my bi-racial heritage. I'm ashamed to say so, but at first I felt like I wasn't as good as I used to be. Isn't that strange?"

"I hope you got past that, sis," Perry said. "As a matter of fact, I know a couple of other people who look just like us. I mean, they could easily pass as Caucasians. But they actually identify as African Americans and they're proud of it. One guy said his whole family looked that way, but they wouldn't think of giving up their family heritage to pass for some other race."

He shrugged in bewilderment and continued, "Yes, I heard all the hype about black people, too, but I always thought people were just being unfair to them. I've never been ashamed since I learned what my race is because I don't think one race is better than any other. But you know something — I would hate to be discriminated against because of my race. If I ever experienced it, I don't know how I'd handle it."

All Erica could do was listen and think. She envied Perry his easy acceptance of this. Her road had been far less easy. At times, she'd been bitter because her racial identity had cost her her marriage. At other times, she'd been angry — at her birth parents and her adoptive parents. It had taken a while before she was able to truly accept the reality of her racial identity.

"You know, Perry, here's where I have the most trouble. I was already eight years old when Mother died, and in my heart, I know I had to remember her. But it seemed natural and easy to fall right into being white and let myself forget what color my mother was. I've tried to understand why that happened like that, but it's a mystery to me. Still this whole race thing is pretty crazy. I think it's a strange and unfair system that says if you're part white and part black, you're still black. I don't understand that. Who defines what race a person is? And what are we anyway? What should we even call ourselves? Bi-racial? Black? Will black people accept us any more than whites will? I wonder how other bi-racial people feel."

"I understand your questions, Erica. I had some of them myself, so I know how you feel," Perry said. "But you can't keep worrying about this. It'll all work out; I'm positive it will. When you accept yourself, other people tend to accept you, too. That's how I look at it." Erica nodded in understanding, and Perry added, "Actually, the thing that bothers me most about all this is that I wish I had gotten a chance to know our mother better. In her picture she looked so young and pretty. She looked like such a wonderful person. I think about her a lot, and sometimes I think I can even remember her singing me to sleep, but I really can't remember too much other stuff. I always thought I remembered being in a car with her and a man, but I'm not sure these were real memories or just make-believe."

Erica said, "I've also thought about it a lot, Perry, and I'm pretty sure I can remember a few things, too. I do think she used to sing a lot, and I also seem to remember that she was always writing. Maybe she was a writer. I know she kept a journal because I found one among my collection. You remember, I told you about the box where I found her picture." Perry was looking at Erica thoughtfully. He nodded, and she added, "I wish I'd had a chance to know her better, too, because all I really have are a few scattered memories. But you know how I feel about our parents. They have been wonderful. I did used to wonder if they knew more than they told us about our birth mother and father, though. It's all so confusing, but right now I'm just so curious about what we're going to find out." She looked at the time and smiled wistfully. It was now 20 till ten. "Well, little brother, I guess we'll know soon enough."

They were glad it was time to go across the street to Miss Davis' office, as they were eager and curious. In fact, they could hardly wait. Upon their arrival, Ella greeted them and the three of them went into Lynn's office.

Lynn, Erica and Perry exchanged introductions. Lynn contained her surprise at the sight of Perry, for when he first walked through the door, she thought she was looking at a slightly younger Ross Remington. In addition to having similar facial features, like his half-brother, Perry was exceedingly handsome. He was also about the same height — clearly over six feet tall, with the same trim, athletic build. His light brown hair was cut in a short, neat style, and his skin looked richly tanned. The two even dressed similarly, with Perry wearing a white polo shirt, beige slacks, dark brown loafers and a navy blue sport coat. His sunglasses were tucked in the top outside pocket of his jacket. Perry had a casually confident air about himself, and when he and Lynn shook hands, like his half-brother, Ross, he had an easy smile and a sweet, sobering gaze.

Although she was much fairer-skinned than her mother, Erica bore quite a resemblance to the photo Lynn had seen of Hattie Rose. Erica was about five feet, seven inches and carried herself with an understated elegance. She looked to be a perfect size six in her pink two-piece suit and off-white blouse. Her skin was slightly golden in hue, and she had dark, almond-shaped eyes, thick, lovely lashes, a perky, keen nose, and pretty, full lips. Erica's dark brown hair was cut in a stylish bob that lightly skimmed her shoulders. A bright, ready smile accompanied her handshake.

Lynn and Ella gave each other knowing glances. These were two good-looking people!

When everyone was seated with small talk out of the way, Lynn said, "First, let me thank you for arranging your schedules to come here so soon. I know you're curious to hear what this is about, so I'll get right to the point." She noted the eager looks on the faces of her visitors as they acknowledged agreement. "I asked you here because a family here in Cincinnati has some very important business with you. In fact, the lady of the family asked me to locate you." Erica and Perry glanced over at each other, then at Lynn. They waited to hear more. "Have you ever heard of the Remington family here in Cincinnati? Of Earl Quincy Remington?" Lynn asked.

"Sure," they answered. When they lived in Columbus, the Remington name had been very prominent because of a huge department store chain there by the same name. Erica and Perry wondered whether or not Lynn was just chatting to get them relaxed. They wanted to get on with this family business. Erica politely said, "Miss Davis, if you don't mind my asking, would you kindly tell us why we're here."

Lynn said pleasantly, "I understand your readiness to know.

And as a matter of fact, I'm getting to that. You may have heard that Earl Remington died a couple of months ago." Of course, Erica and Perry had heard of his death since it had been national news. Lynn continued, "His wife, Mrs. Elizabeth Remington, hired me to locate you."

Erica and Perry reacted with bewilderment. They furrowed their brows and stared at each other in disbelief, and then back at Lynn, and Erica asked, "Why on earth would Mrs. Earl Remington want to locate us? What could she possibly want us for?" Crazy, exciting ideas raced through both their minds. Were the Remingtons trying to locate them for one of their employees? Did they know their father?

Lynn asked, "How much do you know about your father and mother?"

"We never knew our father, nor do we know who he is. See, we're adopted," Perry answered. "Our mother was Hattie Dodd. She died 20 years ago. Why, may we ask?"

Lynn said, "Erica, Perry, we know who your mother is, *and* we also know who your father is. That's what we want to talk to you about. I believe this is going to come as a very big surprise to you, and I know of no way to prepare you for what I'm about to say." Erica and Perry waited anxiously for Lynn to get on with it. They were both completely dumbfounded when they heard her say, "Your father was Earl Q. Remington."

They thought she was joking. They just gave her blank looks, then laughed, and then waited. They actually doubted if they had heard her right. Perry said, "Excuse us. I think we misheard you. It sounded like you said Earl Remington was our father. That's crazy, huh."

"No, no. What you heard is correct. I know this is hard to believe, and like I said, there's no good way to prepare you for this. But yes, Earl Quincy Remington was your father." Lynn then paused for a moment to give them a chance to digest the words. The two were speechless. They could only stare at her in disbelief. Lynn continued. "Of course, he and your mother were never married. In fact, when the two of you were born, he was married to Elizabeth Remington, the woman who hired us. Earl Remington and his wife were married 40 years. Together they had four children of their own — all of whom are older than you. Parker is 38; Jordan is 36; Earl, Jr. is 35; and Ross, their youngest, is 31."

Lynn might as well have said nothing else, for Erica and Perry hadn't heard a single thing since Lynn said, *Earl Quincy Remington was your father.*

Erica suddenly thought about their mother, Hattie Rose Dodd. For a moment, she wondered how her mother could have had an affair with a married man. Her strict grandmother would have surely disapproved. Then she remembered the love letters in her mother's little wooden box written by the man who simply signed his name *E. E* for Earl! Erica knew at once Earl Remington was the man who had broken her mother's heart. However, by the sound of his letters she'd read, one thing seemed certain — he had definitely been in love with her mother, too. From his letters, Earl Remington seemed to have been a very charming man, and Erica decided her mother must have been blinded by love. She could suddenly almost understand how her mother could have fallen for this charming, powerful, wealthy man.

Perry asked slowly, "You're actually telling us Earl Q. Remington was our father? The billionaire tycoon, Earl Remington," he said, his head slightly cocked as if to hear her better. Peering at Lynn through upturned eyes, he was braced to join her in shaking her head no. He was quite ready for her answer, *Oh, no. You must have misunderstood.* But instead, Lynn nodded. Then Perry said, "All these years. All these years, we have never known who our father was. And now, to find out that it was Earl Remington. Wow! You know, the way our grandmother used to talk about our father, we thought he was someone special, but we always believed he was dead."

"No, he just died in June," Lynn said. "And I know this has been shocking information, but I also need to tell you something else. The two of you are included among the heirs to his estate."

Erica held up her hand and said, "Miss Davis, you'll have to forgive us. All of this is just too much to fathom."

Perry exclaimed, "Oh, man!" He and Erica just stared at each other. Over and over, they shook their heads in amazement.

Erica finally asked, "So why would Mrs. Remington hire you to find us?" Given what they had just learned, somehow it didn't make sense that Mrs. Remington would have any business with them. Erica thought, this woman has to hate our guts. She certainly couldn't feel anything positive toward us, could she? After all, our mother obviously had an affair with her husband.

Ella said, "Like Miss Davis said, for one thing, you've been named as beneficiaries in her husband's will. The reading of his will was set for three months from the date of Mr. Remington's death. That is now less than two weeks away." Erica and Perry again were speechless, pondering the enormity of everything they were hearing. "And your presence is requested at the reading of the will," Ella explained.

There's actually more," Lynn said after giving them a moment to get past their shock. "Mrs. Remington wants to meet you, and she wants her four children to be acquainted with you, too." To the pair's bafflement, Lynn added, "I know it's hard to digest all this right now, but as her children are your half-brothers and sisters, she desires that the entire family will know each other.

"Now, at ten o'clock tomorrow morning they're coming here to meet you. However, this afternoon at two o'clock, Mrs. Remington wants to meet the two of you first. You see, it was her husband's final wish that she locate you for the reading of the will, and that you meet their other children. But I'll be frank, just as you were surprised by the news of your father's identity, Mrs. Remington was hit by surprise, too. She only recently learned about all of this, about her husband's relationship with your mother, about the two of you. She found out all of this on her husband's dying day. Her children just learned about everything this week. I'm telling you this so you'll understand and appreciate what they are going through, too."

Erica and Perry nodded in awe. They were blown away by this amazing news. They both experienced a sense of pride at the thought of who their father was, and of his wanting his other children to have a connection with them. They were genuinely overwhelmed. And they were also scared to death. What will they say to the Remingtons? What will this family think of them? Will they hate them? Then, having nearly missed the point when it was made twice before, Erica abruptly asked, "I'm sorry, Miss Davis, Miss Braxton. You said something about Earl Remington's will?"

"Absolutely," Lynn responded. "You have been named as heirs in his will."

"Man, this is unbelievable," Perry said.

Lynn then said, "Again, you are asked to be present at the reading two weeks from now. I'm sure you can arrange to be here. Right?" They nodded. "Okay then. Now I think you'll want to see these, too — it's a picture of your mother and father." She handed them two photographs — one, the portrait of Hattie Rose, and the other, of Hattie Rose and Earl Remington. Erica and Perry had seen their mother's picture. In fact, they both had a copy of the same photograph. For a moment they both stared at it fondly. But when Erica looked at the other picture, she suddenly quivered in shock and amazement.

"What's wrong, sis?" Perry asked, curious about her reaction.

Erica pointed to the man in the photograph and said, "This is our father? Why, I've seen this man before. In fact, I have this very picture."

Perry studied the picture of Earl Remington. He did not know what his sister was talking about. "Okay, I give," he said. "How do you happen to have this picture?"

"You remember when I came across that box of our mother's mementos, I found some other photographs. You know, I sent you this picture of her from that box," she said, pointing to their mother's picture. "I've never talked to anyone about this, Perry, but there was a picture of our mother and a man standing next to a Rolls Royce — this picture here, she pointed. And there were several other pictures of Mother and him. I always wondered who he was. I figured it was pretty obvious that he was wealthy, but I would have never dreamed …

"I even caught myself fantasizing sometimes that he was our father. I always believed there were clues to our father's identity in that box, and I had made it my mission to find him. Of course, I never turned up anything." Erica told Perry she even wanted to trace the license tags on the vehicle in the photograph. As it was, she'd been unable to make out the numbers, and that search had netted nothing. But she'd never given up hope.

Ella said, "Well, if you had a picture of this man, you were indeed looking at your father." Then as Ella looked at Hattie's picture, she added, "Your mother was a beautiful woman, and your father's not bad either."

Erica was shocked to discover that she'd had several pictures of her father all these years. Perry was visibly upset that his sister had not bothered to share the other photographs with him. She apologized, telling him it had not occurred to her to send him those pictures since she'd had no idea who the man was. Perry just looked at Erica, then acknowledged her apology with a nod. They both had better things to think about right now.

Lynn let that matter settle down, then told them about her visit down South. "You two've already had a lot to think about," she said, but I'd like to tell you about your uncle and aunt in Alabama." Again, Erica and Perry looked surprised. Lynn kept talking. "Another investigator and I went to Ft. Davis because we learned your mother had a brother who was still living. His name is Wilbur Williams. In fact, he was able to help us locate you."

"Our mother has a brother in Alabama?" Erica said as she and Perry looked at each other. "No, we definitely didn't know this either. Please, tell us about him," Erica said with much interest.

"Well, Wilbur and Hattie had the same father, Leroy Williams. But your grandmother, Sophie, was Wilbur's stepmother. We visited him and his wife, Bessie, in Ft. Davis, which is near Tuskegee. That's where your mother was born, but your grandmother, Sophie, brought her to Cincinnati after her husband, who was Hattie and Wilbur's father, died. Hattie was just a little girl." Then Ella added, "Your mother's name was actually Hattie Williams. She took her mother's maiden name, Dodd, when she became pregnant by Earl Remington. Your Uncle Wilbur said it was probably because she was not proud to have gotten pregnant out of wedlock." Erica and Perry were almost as surprised by these new revelations as they had been earlier when they learned the identity of their father.

Lynn told them, "Your Uncle Wilbur and his wife have five

children. They all live in Alabama." She continued, "Your uncle said that when your mother died and Sophie took responsibility for you, she severed all contact with them." A curious looked crossed Erica and Perry's faces.

"According to your uncle, your grandmother was fair-complexioned like the two of you, and she began passing for white. She passed the two of you as white, too. Therefore, it didn't fit to have a dark-skinned relative in the picture." Erica and Perry looked at each other in astonishment, for they were hearing for the first time that even their grandmother was of mixed race. They had thought she was white.

"Your Aunt Bessie said it broke Wilbur's heart when Sophie died and you two were sent away to a foster home, because they would have loved for you to come back down to Alabama to live with them. They were ready for you, too, but it was not to be." Lynn could see that Erica and Perry were totally absorbed in her story.

"Let me give you your aunt and uncle's phone number. You may want to call them. I bet they'd be thrilled to hear from you. They were very nice people who helped us a lot because we'd had no success finding you under the Williams name. Once your uncle told us you were Dodds, we located you very easily." Erica and Perry took their Uncle Wilbur's phone number and address. They would contact him and Aunt Bessie.

Lynn gathered the photographs and returned them to her files, telling the two to have lunch and return to her office that afternoon at two o'clock to meet with Mrs. Remington.

* * * * *

The morning had passed so swiftly. Over lunch Erica and Perry could not eat. They could barely speak, and they still could not contain their amazement. And now at a quarter to two in the afternoon, they were again sitting in Lynn Davis' office preparing to meet the wife of the man they'd just learned was their father. The prospect of coming face to face with her was extremely frightening. They expected she would probably be equally uncomfortable with them. Neither was looking forward to this encounter. "Mrs. Remington is here," Janet announced.

Hearts racing, Erica and Perry rose to their feet, as did Lynn as she walked around her desk to greet Elizabeth Remington and introduce her to her husband's two children. "How do you do?" Mrs. Remington said tersely, while giving the two a quick once-over. If she had secretly hoped this was all a big mistake, that hope vanished the minute she laid eyes on the two of them.

The sight of Erica actually jolted her. As she looked at this stunning young woman, it was as though she was seeing the image of Hattie Rose Williams, her husband's mistress. Lord! She thought. Perry, with his height and athletic build, his loose-limbed casualness and handsome facial features, bore an uncanny resemblance to Ross.

Lynn did her best to get everyone relaxed, then excused herself so the three could speak in private. Please don't go, Erica thought as Lynn walked out, for she was still uncertain of how this meeting would go, and could have happily used Lynn Davis as a buffer.

"And how was your trip to Cincinnati?" Mrs. Remington asked. As they tried to give a poised response, Erica and Perry couldn't help but be impressed by this attractive and extremely intimidating woman. Mrs. Remington seemed to be in complete command and not the least bit uncomfortable in this situation.

"I understand Miss Davis has explained everything to you?"

"Oh, yes, ma'am," Erica said.

"Sure thing," replied Perry, shaking his head in agreement.

"Then you know why you are here. Why I wanted to meet you, and why I will have my children meet you, too." She paused a moment, then said, "I personally wanted to see you, and to know the people I'm about to introduce to my family." Erica and Perry heard subtle insinuations in her comment. As Mrs. Remington spoke, she had a coolness in her voice. She was trying to treat this matter with indifference and was coming across that way, but she was not feeling indifferent at all. She was actually bitter now — at Earl — for asking her to do this unspeakable thing — meet his children by another woman. How could she bring these two to her family? What could this possibly gain, she wondered. Why did I ever agree to this? Erica and Perry detected the chill in her voice, and it made them more uncomfortable. Their conversation continued, but the atmosphere in the room was strained.

Mrs. Remington asked Erica and Perry about their lives, and they gave answers. Not being able to resist, she said, "Tell me about your mother," and they explained they had no real memory of her. When she asked them what their particular expectations were, they told her they had none in particular since they had not known what to expect when they were asked to come to Cincinnati.

It felt to them like Mrs. Remington had already pegged them as money-grubbers, eager to get their hands on the Remington fortune. This certainly wasn't true, and they felt bad but did not know what to do or say about that.

To Elizabeth Remington, this meeting was not pleasant either. Sitting here facing Earl's other two children was an instant reminder of his unfaithfulness and his apparently strong affection for their mother. She continued to speak to them as if this were strictly a business discussion. Erica and Perry continued to be uncomfortable. They sincerely hoped the meeting would end soon. At different points, they both felt a desire to retreat to their former worlds, leaving this newfound identity behind. Toward the end, Mrs. Remington asked if either of them had anything else to say.

"Mrs. Remington," Erica felt she had to speak. "We really don't know what to say." She paused then and very sincerely said, "We want to tell you that this news has been totally unbelievable to us. We are still trying to come to grips with what we learned just a few hours ago. You see, we never knew any of this either, and it has really taken us by surprise.

"Speaking for both me and my brother, I want to say that we're very sorry for everything that has happened. We're especially sorry for how you and your children must have been so hurt by this. But Perry and I want you to know that we're grateful that you chose to bring us here. What we've learned today closes a very important chapter in our lives, for we never had any idea who our father was. Now we do, and for this we thank you. I'm sorry. We don't know what else to say to you about this."

Elizabeth Remington had expected neither gratitude nor an apology. In fact, she wasn't sure what she had expected. She certainly had not counted on having any kind thoughts toward these people. Erica and Perry were actually an unexpected surprise. They seemed quite innocent of any ill intent, and to be sure, they were not responsible for what happened between their mother and Earl over 30 years ago. They even seemed genuinely sorry. Elizabeth did not know quite how to take them.

Oh, dear God, she thought, glad to end their meeting. This visit had lasted about 45 minutes. To Erica and Perry, however, it seemed like a lifetime. For Elizabeth Remington, it had been no picnic either, and she looked very much forward to getting back to the comfort of her limousine, lighting a cigarette, and allowing the smooth taste of Cognac to ease the throbbing tension in her head. She left Lynn's office in deep thought.

CHAPTER

12

IT WAS JUST before ten Friday morning when the long black limousine pulled up in front of the entrance to Carew Tower. This created a mild stir on the downtown streets as passers-by recognized Elizabeth Remington, and some stood around gawking, while one by one the Remington children, then she, exited the limousine and entered the building. Slowly the crowd disbanded.

Because of the large number of people attending this meeting, Lynn had arranged to use the huge office of a senior partner in a law firm next door to her office. The setting was comfortable and plush. Seating was arranged for nine. Inside the spacious executive office, Erica, Perry and Lynn waited.

Lynn thought Erica and Perry looked quite appropriate for the occasion of meeting the wealthy Remington family. Perry looked handsome and charming in a casual navy blue summer suit and brown tasseled loafers. The sun-bleached highlights in his hair cast a golden glow to his face, especially against a white Ralph Lauren polo shirt. Lynn could only sigh at his good looks.

Erica wore an attractive white sleeveless dress that highlighted her lovely figure and accentuated her skin's golden tone. The dress ended just above her knees, showcasing long, shapely legs. Her sunglasses were pulled to the top of her head, and her hair hung freely at her shoulders. Erica wore cream-colored pumps and carried a matching handbag that appeared to be a Coach. She gave the appearance of being well bred and well educated. One would not have known that Erica's charming mannerisms were the product of the countless instructions she received as a little girl from a strict grandmother who was determined that she and Perry would fit into any circle. Their Grandma Sophie had reared them with a stern hand, and the lessons of proper decorum she instilled in them were never forgotten.

Erica and Perry attempted to feel at ease, but in reality they were as nervous as they'd ever been. Lynn was eager to get the meeting underway. She would merely ask each person to take a turn at a brief personal introduction. She hoped this process would help to prevent moments of awkward silence. This is going to be interesting, she thought.

Ella greeted the group in the outer area and directed them into the office as Erica, Perry and Lynn rose from their chairs to greet them. Of the four Remington children, Lynn had previously met only Ross. She thought that, like their mother and brother, the other Remington children all made a striking appearance. Wearing expensive watches, diamond earrings, Gucci and Ferragamo bags and shoes and elegant custom-made designer suits, the entire Remington clan were the picture of affluence.

Parker looked the serious executive in her gray plaid hand-tailored suit that lent her a certain stateliness. She was attractive, tall, slim, blond and very composed, while Jordan was a real head-turner in a dark blue custom-made suit with a long side split and Manolo Blahnik shoes. Earl, Jr. made frequent shopping trips to Barney's, New York, and looked the part. Not quite as tall as Ross but just as good looking, he was dressed in a dark gray Armani suit, a striped blue shirt, a red diagonal-striped silk tie and a Cartier watch. He seemed very serious and business-like in demeanor.

Ross looked as handsome as a runway model in a casual summer-weight, custom-fitted navy blue suit, and as she always did, Elizabeth Remington was striking. She was wearing a black suit by Versace with a white silk blouse. A single strand of pearls graced her neck. Her hair was styled to perfection, and her face impeccably made up. Despite the apparent difference in income levels, Lynn saw little contrast in appearance between the two sides of Remingtons. Everyone looked elegant and attractive in his or her own way. They definitely appeared to be related to each other.

When all were inside, Ella closed the door. The tension in the room was high as introductions commenced. One by one, the Remington children shook hands with Erica and Perry who appeared to hold their own, although in reality they were truly overwhelmed. They had not yet recovered from all the major revelations of yesterday, coupled with the meeting with Mrs. Remington, and now they were facing five people with whom the only thing they had in common was Earl Q. Remington, Sr. Neither had known what to expect, nor had either anticipated that this family would be so attractive. All of them.

Erica looked at her handsome half-brothers and immediately recognized the resemblance between Ross and Perry. As she looked from one to the other, she decided their father must have been even better looking than his photographs showed. In addition to finding Parker and Jordan very beautiful, she admired their taste. Both were superbly dressed in exquisitely tailored clothing. However, she did notice the dramatic difference in style between the two sisters — one appearing to be conservative, and the other, just the opposite. Perry looked with great interest at his father's other children. He noticed that Earl, Jr., in particular, seemed somewhat ill at ease; Parker, too, looked uneasy; but Jordan and Ross seemed relaxed.

Lynn welcomed the Remingtons and invited everyone to take a seat. Then she introduced herself and Ella to the Remington children. She could tell some of the Remington clan seemed surprised when they saw her, and she decided their mother must have forgotten to tell them she was African American.

Ella offered refreshments and the meeting began.

Lynn gave some background information and explained the purpose for this meeting and her role. Then she proposed the format for the meeting. Everyone appeared willing to do self introductions, except Earl, that is. He breathed a sigh of exasperation and hid a fake cough with his hand.

Wanting to set the stage for her children for a cooperative meeting, Mrs. Remington was the first to speak. Again, she welcomed Erica and Perry to Cincinnati, and again, Earl, Jr. feigned a cough in agitation. She gave him a look, then repeated that her husband wanted them to meet the rest of his family, which was why they were asked to come to Cincinnati. Erica and Perry were thankful for her welcoming words.

Mrs. Remington then looked at Lynn and Ella and said that the Lynn Davis Agency had done a fine job of locating the two of them and acting as their intermediary. Of course, Lynn and Ella appreciated the acknowledgment. Then Mrs. Remington said that during her and her husband's 40-year marriage she had watched him grow the Remington Corporation from a one-division operation to its current five. She said she basically stayed out of the business while Earl was very much committed to it, and that she preferred working in the fine arts instead.

Erica and Perry were surprised by the graciousness of Mrs. Remington. Her tone was definitely different from yesterday's. Today she sounded much more accommodating, although admittedly, she was no less intimidating. They decided to get their introductions over next. They said they were happy to come to Cincinnati and, of course, they were very surprised at what they had learned about their relationship to this family. They told of being born in Cincinnati, living with their grandmother until she died, and eventually being adopted by the Harringtons of Columbus, Ohio.

Erica told them she currently lived in Minneapolis, but thought she might one day relocate back to Ohio. She showed pictures of her young son, Timothy, and said she and her child's father, Thomas, had divorced two years ago. Perry explained that he was an engineer at a construction firm in Chicago. He was not married, but had a girlfriend named Jennifer. He liked most sports, played many, and his favorite these days was mountain biking, of which he was becoming quite skilled. Erica and Perry's introductions were met with looks of indifference from the Remington children.

They were happy to be finished.

Parker was next. She told them that she practiced law, and glanced at Lynn when she said her office was right here in the Carew Tower. She didn't mention attending Harvard, but talked about her love of skiing, tennis and golf. She was engaged to Dale Lane, an investment manager. Parker sounded as if she was just going through the motion, while not the least interested in divulging personal information to perfect strangers. In spite of herself, she did think Erica was very attractive, and Perry looked a bit like her brother, but she was most eager to get this ordeal over with.

Jordan told of obtaining her degree from the San Francisco Art Institute, and of the years she spent in Paris. She mentioned her love of art and photography and her free-lance work with a New York company. As Jordan talked, she studied her two half-siblings, and wondered if Erica's tan was real or the product of hours under a tanning machine. Her little boy had the same rich tan. How'd they get so much sun up there in Minneapolis, she wondered. Through his suit, she could imagine Perry's muscular build, and wondered how his well-built frame would look on the beaches of Acapulco. She smiled as she scolded herself for forgetting this was, after all, her half-brother. Erica and Perry listened in fascination as Jordan talked, just as they had when they heard Parker's story. Jordan added how surprised she was to learn she had two half-siblings. Mrs. Remington gave her a quick glance to be sure she did not say anything inappropriate. Jordan said no more.

Since they seemed to be going in descending chronological order, Earl was a bit irked at the thought of having to be next. But he had promised his mother he would oblige. He had gotten a good look at his two half-siblings, and noticed Erica's beauty and demeanor and Perry's good looks, enhanced as they were by a touch of humility. He still did not like them, however, so without looking at either of them as he talked, he nonchalantly told of his marriage to Shannon, an interior designer, and of their three children. But he spoke with pride when he said he was president of RemCap, one of the five divisions of Remington Corporation. Then that was pretty much that. He made a half attempt to sound relaxed as he passed the baton to his younger brother. Erica thought the name RemCap sounded familiar, but she could not remember when she might have heard it before.

Ross was very comfortable since he felt like he already knew his half-brother and sister. He noticed that he and Perry were similarly dressed, and he liked the casual air Perry exhibited. Under different circumstances we could probably be buddies, he mused. He thought of Hattie Rose's picture when he looked at Erica. Like mother, like daughter, he said to himself, thinking that Erica was as pretty as her mother. He was actually surprised that their biracialness wasn't evident at all.

Ross told them he had traveled around the world and currently resided in Colorado where he was doing the work he loved — geology. He mentioned some of the countries he had traveled to, and identified some of the more interesting geological explorations he had taken part in. He explained that he was engaged to Pamela who was in medical school. Ross appeared friendly and natural to Erica and Perry. He actually talked *to* them, versus at them as Parker and Earl before him had done. Erica and Perry appreciated his friendliness, and asked a few questions of Ross about his travels.

Following the introductions, Mrs. Remington felt satisfied that her goal had been accomplished. Now they all knew each other, however, she knew of nothing she could do to make them actually like one another. She looked around the room at these six young people all fathered by Earl, and wondered were there others. Did I know the man as well as I thought, she asked herself. She told Erica and Perry that she had notified their family lawyer to schedule the reading of her husband's Last Will and Testament on July 15, and asked that they return to Cincinnati for the reading. Erica and Perry said they would return.

As Mrs. Remington mentioned the will, Parker and Earl exchanged looks of veiled displeasure. This was the first outward glimmer of the hostility they felt over having to share their father's fortune with strangers. They were unnerved at the very idea that their father would do something like this to them. Why on earth would he include these two people in his will? Apparently he didn't even know them, had not even seen them in 20 years. What had they done to deserve a share of their family's wealth?

Their looks to each other were not lost on Erica, Perry, Ross or Jordan. A few more words were exchanged, and the meeting ended as it began — with the appearance of cordiality. Lynn could feel something hanging in the air and could only guess at the probable resentment the Remington children felt toward their half-sister and brother. She thought of the racial differences, and to herself said, they don't even know the whole story yet.

When the meeting ended, Erica and Perry were mentally exhausted. They departed Cincinnati and headed to Columbus to visit their parents for the weekend.

Meanwhile, Lynn marveled at what had just transpired, because if she had thought about it, she would never have guessed such a peaceable meeting could have taken place.

CHAPTER
13

PAUL AND KITTY Harrington were astounded by the news of their children's meeting in Cincinnati. Of course, they were happy that Erica and Perry now knew the identity of their birth father, and they were amazed to learn who he was. But they were also afraid.

Kitty took Paul aside and confided to him her worst fears — that their children would turn away from them now that they had their own identity. Especially as they were now beneficiaries to the estate of one of the wealthiest men in the country. Paul tried to reassure her that they had nothing to fear. They had done a good job rearing the children, and surely Erica and Perry would never turn their backs on them.

Paul didn't want to worry his wife more, but he'd had his own concerns as well. Now that Erica and Perry knew who their real father was, even though he was deceased, he wondered if they would still look at him as dad? He reminded his wife that many other adoptive parents had gone through similar experiences and survived. They agreed to put their fears aside and hope for the best. In their hearts, they really were happy for their children. Later, they encouraged Erica and Perry to contact their Uncle

Wilbur and Aunt Bessie, which they did while in Columbus. Erica and Perry had a memorable, heartwarming conversation with their relatives and made a commitment to meet them in person one day soon.

After their visit, Perry returned to Chicago. He wanted to tell his girlfriend, Jennifer, all about his trip, but he knew that a matter of this magnitude had best remain confidential. Although it was hard to do, he kept the developments to himself, giving her only a sketchy account of his trip.

Erica returned to Minneapolis and went immediately to pick up Timmy. Although Thomas maintained his own apartment, she'd never seen his place, for he usually stayed with his girlfriend. His current girlfriend was his third or fourth since their divorce. She felt uncomfortable leaving Timmy with them, but Thomas insisted on keeping their son, even telling her he would take a few days off work to be with him.

Thomas still worked for the same real estate developer. To Erica, he seemed to complain about his job all the time. Thomas had always traveled extensively around the country, meeting people and making deals. He still traveled quite a bit, but almost appeared to be getting disenchanted with his job. Erica didn't know for sure, since the only thing she talked to him about was Timmy. At least, Thomas had been in town and was able to keep Timmy while Erica took this trip. He was waiting for her return.

"Well, what did you find out?" he asked, almost too quickly. Erica and Thomas had kept in touch because of their son. But they no longer had a close relationship — not after everything they had been through. So she had no intention of telling him everything. Erica had told Thomas she had to go to Cincinnati on a family matter, but she had no intention of telling him the details of her trip. "So did you find out who your father is?" Thomas asked. Erica told him she did, but she did not want to discuss it. He appeared to be offended.

To keep him calm, she decided to tell him about her uncle — her mother's brother that she hadn't known existed. Thomas seemed fascinated by this, and told her, almost patronizingly, it was nice that she was finally getting some real sense of family identity. He continued to probe, but Erica shared no more of her family details with him.

From time to time Thomas would go through periods when he would pester Erica to get back together. But to her, that was completely out of the question. Since their divorce, she had not gotten involved in a serious relationship. One person was becoming a trusted friend. Larry Porter had initially shown interest in her, but she explained that with her recent divorce she did not want to get involved with anyone for awhile, especially since she had a young son. Larry understood and did not pressure her for more. She appreciated their friendship and was proud to have expanded her circle of close friends to include African Americans. Erica knew Larry would be excited for her if he knew the nature of her trip to Cincinnati, but even though she, like her brother, was about to burst inside from holding it all in, she was afraid to discuss this matter with anyone for now.

* * * * *

The Sunday following the family's meeting with Erica and Perry, the Remington clan gathered for dinner out at their Butler County residence — a palatial mansion situated on a hundred acres. After dinner, Elizabeth told her children the rest of the story. She explained that there were some things she'd found too difficult to bring up before, but now she wanted them to know the rest. Ross sat calmly for he already knew, but Parker, Jordan and Earl were stunned to learn that Hattie Williams was African American.

When Elizabeth told them this, Earl, Jr. slammed his wine glass down on the table, spilling wine but fortunately not breaking the glass. "That's impossible. My father would *never* do anything like that!"

Parker and Jordan just looked bewildered; many questions went through their minds. Hadn't they just met their father and Hattie's two children the other day? Jordan said, "That would mean Erica and Perry are bi-racial. We just met them Friday. They looked as white as I do."

Parker looked disgusted. "I wonder, Mummie," she said angrily, "why you didn't just tell us this before we met them?"

Elizabeth Remington asked her daughter, "Now tell me,

Parker, would you have treated them any more indifferently had you known?" Parker's objection was stifled by her mother's chilly response. She was distressed, as much from the shock of learning Hattie Williams' race, as from her fear that this information might ever get out. That would be simply horrible. She worried about her family's image. Having heard quite enough of this business, she abruptly stood up from the table and turned to walk away. However, in a voice Parker knew not to defy, Elizabeth said, "Parker Elizabeth, sit down." Parker sat back down, but crossed her arms in defiance, hoping her mother would realize just how upset this news had made her and be sorry for saying what she did.

Jordan suddenly found all this amusing. Watching her sister, she couldn't help but remember the time she had brought her black friend home from college. And my, how the family had acted. But even as she remembered this, she thought of how her dad had seemed pretty comfortable. She always thought he had been just faking it, but now she wasn't so sure. Maybe Dad was for real. All she said aloud was, "Interesting."

Mrs. Remington added, "I know this comes as a shock to all of you as it did to me. But this thing happened. We have to face it and deal with it. However, you all need to brace yourselves, for this is not the worst of it."

All except Ross wondered what could possibly be worse than what they'd already heard. They settled back down and listened in dismay as Mrs. Remington told them that somehow, someone had learned about their father's affair and had been extorting money from him for two years prior to his death. Someone, possibly the blackmailer, had now even contacted Lynn Davis.

Parker, Jordan and Earl were horrified to learn there was a blackmailer out there. How dreadful it would be if the public ever got wind of this scandalous secret. They were glad their father had paid the guy to keep quiet. Who could it be, they wondered, as each of them began to point suspicious eyes toward the others. Their untrusting attitudes became obvious as they started throwing mean quips around the table.

Elizabeth was concerned with how quickly her children had turned on each other in the face of this crisis. If they were to survive this, they would have to stick together, she thought. She appealed to her children not to let this thing destroy their family. After all, she told them convincingly, if there is a blackmailer out there, the family needs to stand together now more than ever. There are still too many unanswered questions. For example, she added, how could anyone know about Lynn Davis? For no one except Ross should have known about the work she was doing for the Remingtons. Parker, Jordan and Earl wondered how any of this could involve Lynn Davis. Then, as if their mother's mention of Ross' name had just registered, they turned abruptly and eyed him curiously.

Ross quickly explained to his siblings that their father had talked to him about the blackmail. None of them could understand why their father had taken Ross alone into his confidences. Even so, they listened as Ross explained what their father had confided in him. First he told them how the extortion had taken place. Then he told them their father never knew who the blackmailer was, but felt the guy had him over a barrel. Therefore, he paid what was demanded of him. His father told him that his first payment had been $200,000 and he had made three other payments about six months apart of $250,000 each.

Parker, Jordan and Earl were as dismayed as Ross had been when Earl, Sr. first told him about this. He said their father considered this amount a "small price to pay" to keep from hurting his family. But when the blackmailer demanded five million dollars, their father had had enough! Besides, he believed that if he did not stop now, this extortion would never end.

Ross added that the blackmailer always demanded the money in small unmarked bills to be delivered to a public park. Their father was instructed to conceal a large brown envelope filled with the money in a newspaper that would be left on a park bench. The newspaper would be rolled up and held together with large rubber bands to prevent the envelope from dropping out.

That's all their father ever knew. He had hired an investigator to watch the transactions and find out who was picking up the money. However, the blackmailer apparently paid some kid to pick up the paper for him. Each time, the investigator saw and photographed or filmed a different kid zipping by, once on skates, the other times on bicycles. The kid would sweep up the newspaper and be gone in a flash, cutting through the park. Although the investigator always tried to follow, he invariably lost the person. Whomever the kid turned the newspaper over to remained a mystery.

When they were told about the mysterious phone call to Lynn Davis' office, they wondered why someone would try to stop her from searching for their father's other children. Could this be the same person who had been taking money from their father for two years? In the end, they all agreed they needed to work together as a family on this. They wondered what they would do if the blackmailer struck again. As it turned out, they would not have to wait too long to find out.

On the following Tuesday, Mrs. Remington had an appointment in the city. Arnold got the Mercedes ready and drove her downtown to meet with her attorney. A valet attendant parked the car, and Arnold accompanied Mrs. Remington to her lawyer's office where she was to discuss the final arrangements for the reading of her husband's will. Then he went back outside to wait for her. When the meeting ended a short time later and the attendant delivered the car, he handed Mrs. Remington a plain white 9x12 envelope that he found on the front windshield of her car. Curious, she opened the envelope and found a single piece of paper containing a message that had been written in large lettering using a standard type font on a word processor:

I HAVE SOMETHING YOU WANT. YOUR HUSBAND OWED ME AND I INTEND TO COLLECT! IF YOU THINK YOU ARE NOT GOING TO PAY, THINK AGAIN. I CAN GIVE A VERY CONVINCING INCENTIVE. BE CAREFUL DRIVING YOUR VEHICLE. YOU NEVER KNOW WHEN YOUR BRAKES MIGHT FAIL! THE NEXT TIME, YOU WON'T GET A WARNING. YOU WILL SOON GET DETAILS ABOUT HOW TO PAY.

"What in hell!" Elizabeth exclaimed as she read the note. Arnold looked curious. He asked if there was a problem, and she told him to find out from the attendant where the envelope had come from. The parking attendant said it had been placed under the automobile's windshield wiper in the parking garage.

Mrs. Remington told Arnold that she was concerned her brakes may have been tampered with and told him to have them inspected right away. Arnold asked her why she thought the brakes were faulty, and she told him the note she received from the attendant indicated there might be a problem. While he was getting them checked, she returned to her lawyer's office and phoned Lynn Davis, telling her there was an urgent development and she needed to see her right away. Then Mrs. Remington's attorney had his driver take her to Carew Tower where Arnold would pick her up as soon as he had the automobile checked out.

Ella showed Elizabeth Remington into Lynn Davis' office and closed the door behind her. Arnold arrived some time later and waited in the outer office. Ella noticed that he seemed to be extremely nervous. While he waited, he watched the door to Lynn's office intently and seemed jumpy.

Meanwhile, in Lynn's office, Elizabeth had said, "I just left my attorney's office, and this letter was placed under the windshield wiper of the car while it was parked. The parking valet gave it to me. Unfortunately, no one saw anything. I didn't know what to do," she told Lynn. Both women suspected this was the work of the blackmailer.

Lynn handled the envelope with great care, although she thought if there were any prints on it, they were probably blurred by now. She removed the single sheet of paper and read aloud the note. As she read, Lynn noticed that Mrs. Remington looked very upset. She told Lynn, "I'll have a drink if you don't mind." Lynn poured her a glass of brandy.

Elizabeth explained that Arnold was having the Mercedes checked to see if anything had been tampered with. Lynn said, "It's too bad no one saw anything. How long were you in the building?" She answered that it had been less than 30 minutes.

Lynn said, "Mrs. Remington, this is very serious. At this point, you may want to think about reporting this to the police." To Elizabeth's look of startlement, Lynn added, "You won't have to divulge what you know about the blackmailer. Furthermore, it's not conclusive that this note came from the same person. Even so, I wouldn't take a chance with this character."

Mrs. Remington said she was not ready to talk to the police about this. Lynn said, "If you prefer, I can get someone at the department to check out this note, look for prints, that sort of thing, without disclosing all the details." Mrs. Remington accepted Lynn's offer.

"Obviously, someone is starting to play for keeps," Lynn said. "This is going beyond blackmail. And your hands are tied because you have no way of knowing if this person means business, or if he or she is just making an idle threat to frighten you into giving up some money. We've got to find out what's behind this? What's his angle? Why would someone think you would pay?" While asking these questions, Lynn suddenly thought of another line of questions and asked, "Mrs. Remington, how long has your driver, Arnold, worked for you? And how much can you trust him?"

"Oh dear, Arnold has worked for us for over 35 years," Mrs. Remington answered protectively. Then she added, "If we can't trust Arnold, we can't trust anybody."

"Are you aware if Arnold knew of your husband's affair with Hattie Williams?"

"I would expect that Arnold knew everything about Earl," Mrs. Remington said as she furrowed her brow. "He drove him everywhere. And he always kept his ears open. I'm afraid if anyone knows our family secrets, it's Arnold."

Then Lynn asked, "As far as you know, were there ever any disagreements or arguments between Arnold and your husband?"

"No, I'm not aware of any such thing. Earl took very good care of Arnold."

"In what way?"

"For one thing, Arnold supports an invalid mother and has taken care of her for years. Earl paid him generously and even provided additional medical benefits so he could take care of his mother. In return, Arnold has been very loyal to Earl and to all of us." Then Elizabeth paused for a moment, looked directly at

Lynn and asked, "Why are you asking these questions about Arnold? Surely you aren't thinking he had anything to do with this, are you?"

"At this point, Mrs. Remington, I'm not sure what to think," Lynn commented. "But think about the phone call I got the other day. How many people could have known of your connection to me? And Arnold would certainly have every opportunity to tamper with your car. He didn't sit in on your meeting with your lawyer, did he?"

"Oh, no, of course not," Mrs. Remington replied. "But Arnold doing anything to harm any of us is extremely unlikely. He is very protective."

"I certainly hope you're right," Lynn replied. "But if you can think of anyone else who might have known I was working for you, let me know. To me, that's a big mystery." Then, holding the envelope, she said, "Listen, I will run this over to the Department this afternoon. I can probably know something by tomorrow."

"Yes, take it, please," Elizabeth said. "I would like a copy to share with my children, and I'll be waiting to see if you learn anything. I must admit, I'm concerned about harm coming to my family over this. If it's money they want, I'll gladly pay whatever it takes to keep my family safe and be done with it. Frankly, I don't know else what to do. If only Earl were here."

"I understand how you must feel. Do you want me to arrange protection for you?" Lynn asked.

"No, my dear, we have a full security force in residence. Extra security is not what we need."

"All right," Lynn said. "Just tell the rest of your family to be watchful. Also, you should alert your security chief about this. You'll want them to check your vehicles daily. While they're at it, I would have them check your house and all your cars and phone systems for bugs. You wouldn't want anyone listening in on your conversations." Unnerved at the very idea, Lynn silently thought, I'd better do the same thing. On the drive back, Arnold told Mrs. Remington that everything had checked out. The car had not been tampered with. Everything was fine. Yep, sure was.

* * * * *

147

Miss Birchway was the executive secretary to the CEO. Since Earl Remington's death, Miss Birchway had maintained his office as before, although a replacement CEO was as yet unnamed. Daily she opened the mail addressed to Earl Q. Remington, CEO, and forwarded it at her discretion to the various officers for handling.

She wasn't certain what to do with the shoe-box-sized package that had been delivered to her office that Tuesday afternoon. It appeared to be some sort of gift delivered through the interoffice mail system. This particular package was marked *Personal, Confidential and Highly Sensitive. To be opened by addressee only.* There was no return address. Surely everyone knew Mr. Remington had died, she thought, while wondering who would send a gift.

For reasons unknown, she put the box up to her ear to shake it gently to see if she could tell its contents. As she did this, Miss Birchway detected a fairly audible ticking sound coming from inside the box. She froze, horrified at the thought of a possible bomb, she managed to contain her urge to drop the package and cautiously set it down on the edge of her desk. She was shaking as she stepped into the next office and called Security. "I believe I may have possibly just received a bomb that was delivered to Mr. Remington's office," she excitedly told the guard. He told her he would call the bomb squad and advised her to vacate the office right away. The entire 15-story Remington headquarters building was evacuated within minutes, and the bomb squad examined the contents of the box.

A few minutes later, the all-clear signal was sounded and people returned to the building. Wayne Johnson, chief of security, came over to Miss Birchway's office. "Here's your ticker right here," he said holding a small battery-operated toy animal, obviously relieved at the find. "With the on-off switch where it is, it could not have switched on by itself. The person who sent this must have turned it on and then sealed the box. The toy was still clacking when we looked in the box. We've taken it apart, and all we found were batteries inside. I guess this is someone's idea of a joke — a right sick one," he said, turning the switch on and off. "Do you know who brought this delivery in here, ma'am?" he asked Miss Birchway.

"Why, yes, it was delivered with the afternoon mail run. Kenneth from Mail Services brought it over."

"Well, it doesn't look like anything more than someone's prank, miss," he said in agitation. "It's harmless, but who would send something like this to the CEO? We'll have a talk with this mail carrier and see what he can tell us."

Earl, Jr. told Miss Birchway he had a pretty good idea where the box may have come from. I'm going to get that damned Jake Huber, he said to himself. He called Johnson from Security over to his office, then they called in Kenneth, the mail handler. "Can you tell me where this box came from?" Earl asked him.

"No, sir. When I was sorting the mail, looked up, there it was. Someone had to put it on the cart because it was too big to go through the mail slot," Kenneth said.

"Who put it there then?" Johnson asked him.

"I couldn't tell you. All's I know is when I was sorting the mail, there was this box. It was marked *personal* and stuff, so I put it with Mr. Remington's other mail and took it up to his secretary."

"Didn't you notice or hear anything suspicious?" Earl asked him.

"No, can't say as I did. But now, with all the noise in the mailroom, I won't say that that thing wasn't clacking. I just never heard it."

While Johnson questioned Kenneth, Earl, Jr. rummaged through the crumpled wrapping paper inside the box and came upon a folded sheet of paper that had almost gone unnoticed at the bottom of the box. He stared at the paper. It read, *THE NEXT TIME YOU MIGHT NOT BE SO LUCKY. CONSIDER THIS A FAIR WARNING.*

"What the ..." he exclaimed, holding the note in one hand as his other hand went to his forehead in disbelief. He then read it aloud, passed the alarming note around for others to see. Then he reached for it to make a copy. Handing it back to Johnson, he asked the chief of security to check it out thoroughly, although, he said, he was sure whoever sent that box would be smart enough not to leave fingerprints. Johnson was wondering how he and his men missed the note and couldn't figure it out.

"Listen, Kenneth," Earl said in an authoritative tone, "if anything suspicious ever shows up around here again, be sure to notify Security right away. Anything that doesn't have a return mailing address is not to be distributed to anyone. Security will check out all suspicious mail before it is delivered to anyone in this firm. Again, I don't want you to distribute any unidentifiable mail that has not been checked by Security." Then Earl told Johnson to notify the mailroom right away of this new procedure.

When Kenneth left, Earl told Johnson, "I didn't want to say anything until I was certain, but I have an idea who could be behind this." Johnson was all ears as Earl told him about the call he'd received from Jake Huber earlier that very day. "That guy said he was desperate. He was talking real crazy," Earl said to Johnson, then told him the gist of Huber's conversation with him. Johnson wrote down Huber's name and said he would look into it.

Shortly after the evacuation ended, Harry Rogers, an office clerk, stopped by Miss Birchway's office. "There sure was an awful lot of commotion over that box that was delivered in here," he told her. "When I was coming in the building around noon, a woman stopped me and said the package was for the CEO's office."

Surprised, Miss Birchway said. "Oh? Go on, Harry."

"I told her Mr. Remington had died. She asked if I would drop the package in the office mail anyway, and it would probably get routed to the right place. So I took it, figuring there was no harm in helping her out and dropped it in the mail cart for sorting."

"Harry, this is very serious. Who was this woman? What did she look like? Did you know her?"

"No, ma'am. Never saw her before. In fact, she was just a plain-looking sort. Kind of tall, long brown hair. Nothing special about her. Looked like she was about 30 or so."

"Security is looking into this. Will you stop over there and tell Chief Johnson what you just told me?" a worried Miss Birchway asked Harry.

"Sure, no problem."

"And Harry, don't take anything else from strangers," Miss Birchway said, adding a weak smile.

* * * * *

Mrs. Remington gathered her family to talk about the note left on the Mercedes. As she explained to her children what had happened earlier that day, everyone was duly alarmed. Mrs. Remington said she feared someone might get hurt if this character tried to make good on his threat. The family discussed the seriousness of this development, and Ross said, "I wonder if this is the same person who was blackmailing Dad."

"If it is, what is he after?" Parker asked.

"If it's the same guy, he wants money and plenty of it. Remember, he hit Dad up for five million dollars in the end," Ross answered.

Then Earl, Jr. spoke up, "Mother, this was obviously the day for craziness. This morning that pesty character, Jake Huber, called again. He's the one who claims our father swindled him out of his land. This time he said he had something on Father. He also said he was desperate. Now you remember that phone call the blackmailer made to Lynn Davis and she heard a train in the background? Well, I could hear the sounds of a train when Huber called today, too. Then later this afternoon, a box shows up addressed to our father, and it was ticking. So thinking it might have been a bomb, of course, we evacuated the entire building." Earl's family looked shocked at the thought of a bomb at Remington headquarters. "Turns out," Earl continued, "it was just a battery-operated toy turned on. But we found a pretty serious note in the box. It said he was giving us fair warning and the next time we may not be so lucky."

Everyone was horror-struck. "What on earth's going on?" Jordan asked. "Do you suppose these notes were written by the same guy?"

"The note on the car was not handwritten. It was typed or produced on a word processor," Mrs. Remington explained as she pulled the note from her briefcase.

Earl said, "So was the note that came to the office. Here, I made a copy before I turned it over to Security."

Everyone looked on anxiously as copies of the two notes were compared to each other, and all were excited to find the lettering appearing to be identical in size and style. "I just bet that guy, Huber, is behind this," Earl said. "That guy's a real nut case if you ask me. We've got to put a stop to him before he really does try to hurt someone."

"You think it was Jake Huber who was blackmailing Dad the past two years?" Ross asked, sounding hopeful that maybe this case could be solved this easily.

"Who knows? I've already given his name to Johnson in Security. Tomorrow we're bringing him in to question him so we can get to the bottom of this," Earl said, adding, "maybe we can find out if he's connected to the note Mother received also."

In his heart, Earl believed that Jake Huber truly was a bad guy. By stopping him now, he hoped to stop both the blackmailer and the con man who was apparently out to swindle money from the Remington Corporation. Earl was proud of how he was handling this case. He wanted his mother to be proud of him, too.

14

FROM HIS RELIABLE source, J.T. learned that the woman detective had been successful in her search for Earl Remington's kids. Damn it! Why couldn't she have just stayed the hell out of this? Finding those two could possibly complicate matters, and he did not need that. Apparently his phone call hadn't made Davis pull out as he'd hoped. He should have called her again and again until he was sure she'd gotten the message. J.T. was starting to feel that calling Lynn Davis at all might not have been such a hot idea. She was, after all, a private investigator. He didn't need someone like that on his tail. The only good thing he knew for sure, however, was Lynn Davis didn't have a snowball's chance in hell of finding out who he was. His plan was just too solid. But now that he had established contact with her, he would just figure out a way to use her to his advantage.

J.T. had another problem. He didn't yet know how he would get information to Mrs. Remington. It suddenly occurred to him that this Lynn Davis might just be the answer to his dilemma, for who better than she would be in a position to deliver his message to the old lady. After all, this Davis woman must have some clout with those people by now. I'll get her to persuade them to cooperate and we'll all be happy, he thought, realizing now that he would have to play it smarter to ensure that Lynn Davis, herself, cooperated with his plan. J.T. had already set up his foreign bank account. He would get Remington to deposit the money there and be home free.

He spent a few minutes crafting his next message and practicing his voice. This call would be very important. He had to plant the seed, and it had to land perfectly. When he was all set, he dialed the telephone.

* * * * *

Lynn didn't learn too much from the police department about either the strange phone call she'd received or the note left on Mrs. Remington's car. As expected, they found no good fingerprints on either the note or the envelope. The detective she consulted suggested the note on the windshield and her phone call were likely related, and he profiled the person responsible as dangerous and very possibly, desperate.

Lynn relayed this information to Mrs. Remington the same evening. She was curious if there had been any new developments on her end, and was surprised when Mrs. Remington told her about the evacuation at Remington headquarters earlier that day. Lynn listened as she described the episode and told her Earl, Jr. thought he knew who was behind it. Security at Remington had notified the local law enforcement authorities about this incident. To Lynn, this bomb threat business was going pretty far, even if it was a hoax. If this character truly was desperate, the sooner they tracked him down the better, before he decided to turn up the heat. Lynn felt the perpetrator was a man, not a woman, although it sounded like a woman's voice she heard on the telephone message.

The next morning, with all kinds of questions going through her head but no firm answers, Lynn decided to talk to her friend, Harvey Chapman. She phoned him and after telling him about the bomb scare at Remington headquarters, said, "Harv, I'm still wondering why on earth someone chose to involve me in this with that phone call. What do they think I could possibly have to do with anything?"

"That's a good question, Lynn," Harvey said through fingers

that stroked his mustache. "On the surface, it looks like someone just didn't want you to locate the Dodds. But why? Most likely that's not it at all. They could just be trying to scare you off the case. That way, they'd have Mrs. Remington all to themselves without any outside interference."

"Could be," Lynn said, pensively. "However, it's been almost two weeks and whoever it was hasn't called back. Maybe they've given up on me. If they didn't want Erica and Perry here and are getting inside information, they may know now I've already found them. I'll admit though, I am still curious about that driver, Arnold Taylor." As she talked, Lynn ignored another call that was coming in on her line so she could finish her conversation with Harvey. She knew Ella would pick it up.

Suddenly Ella poked her head into Lynn's office and said excitedly, "Lynn, you'd better take this call. I don't know, but it sounds like that same voice."

Lynn looked at Ella, disbelief registering on her face. "The blackmailer?"

"I do believe so," Ella answered.

Lynn said, "Harvey, I think we must have talked this person up. Ella thinks that's who is on the line now. I'll get back to you." She told Ella to listen in, then pushed a button on her phone to record the call, and said, "Hello, this is Lynn Davis." She noticed her caller identification registered *number unknown.*

"I'm only going to say this one time," a whispery voice with the English accent said. As Lynn listened, she studied the voice and decided this definitely was the same person who called her before. This time she noticed that the voice sounded more like a man using a high-pitched falsetto voice to sound like a woman. The person continued, "You'd better tell your Remingtons to cooperate. Those out-of-towners have no business coming here. But since you went and found them anyway, you're going to have to do what I tell you or someone will be sorry. It may even be *you* if you don't cooperate."

Lynn heard the threat and quietly said, "May I ask who this is and why you are calling me? What do you want with me?" She hoped this person would slip up and reveal something important.

The caller answered, "It doesn't matter who this is. All you need to know is that I mean business."

"Tell me, how did you get my phone number? And what makes you think I'm working with the Remingtons," Lynn asked.

"Let's don't play games, sweetheart. I know all about your case," the caller said.

Lynn felt she was getting nowhere. She definitely didn't want the caller to hang up until she got something to go on. Again she asked, "What do you want from me? What do you think I have to do with this? Who are you, anyway? How can I get in touch with you?" She threw out these questions and hoped he would answer at least one of them.

"I've told you all you need to know. You can influence the Remingtons. When I tell you to, you'd better do it," the caller said and hung up the phone.

"Dammit," Lynn said in frustration. Ella came into Lynn's office. She too thought the caller sounded more like a man, but didn't get much more from the call. Lynn told Ella she had just been talking about this person with Harvey. She got Harv back on the line. "Ella was right. It was that mystery caller again."

Harvey said, "I'll be damned. Obviously, this chump still has his plan, and it apparently involves you. Gotta figure out why he wants you in this, Lynn, and why he *or she* may not want Erica and Perry to show up here."

Lynn replied, "He says he wants me to influence the Remingtons to cooperate. In paying a ton of money, no doubt. That'll be the day. You know, Harvey, I wonder if Erica and Perry have to be present to collect their inheritance. Could that be? Then, remembering the tension in the air when the Remington children met Erica and Perry, she said, "As a matter of fact, a part of me wonders could one of the Remington kids be involved. A couple of them certainly didn't seem any too pleased about these two new heirs to their father's fortune. I'm going to check with Mrs. Remington to see if she spoke with her lawyer yet. If you get any new ideas, let me know.

"Here's another question, Harv. What do you think about that package that was delivered to Remington headquarters yesterday?

The notes and the bomb scare prank send a different message. Yet, I feel these notes must somehow be related to the phone calls. What do you think?"

"It would sure seem that way, Lynn," Harvey answered. "Especially with everything happening at once like this."

"Well, it may be time to let Erica and Perry know someone wants to keep them away. But first I'll call Mrs. Remington." When Lynn and Harvey hung up, she phoned Elizabeth Remington and told her about her second telephone call and its message about her influencing her when he gave the word. "About what, he didn't say, but I presume it's about money, although the caller also mentioned that Erica and Perry had no business coming to Cincinnati." Then Lynn asked Mrs. Remington if she knew of any particular stipulations about their attending the reading. Could that possibly be an issue?

"Ferrel did tell me it was imperative that everyone be present for the will. If they are not, his instructions were to delay the reading for 30 days. Frankly, I don't want to have to delay this. I'm quite ready to get this matter behind me." Elizabeth agreed Erica and Perry needed to know about this new development.

Lynn left a message at Perry's home number and reached Erica at her office. Erica told her she had been so excited since returning to Minneapolis that she'd thought of little else besides her trip to Cincinnati. She admitted the revelation of her father's identity was still hard to believe, and she was literally in a fog over the fact that she and Perry would receive an inheritance. Whatever it was, it would be a welcomed gift. Erica told Lynn she might end up with enough money to relocate to Ohio. That would make her life a whole lot simpler. However, Erica was baffled by Lynn's story of the two threatening phone calls. Who could want them out of the picture? And why? The very thought of this made Erica shudder. Blackmail and threats? "I can't believe it," she exclaimed, then stated with conviction, "Well, whoever it is, they certainly won't stop me from coming. I'm sure Perry will feel the same way. I'll talk to him."

"I wanted to alert you to what's going on here, Erica. I definitely think you should come, and so does Mrs. Remington," Lynn told her. "I'll keep you apprised if there are any new developments. Just be careful on your end."

"Thank you, Miss Davis. I'm sure Timmy and I will be just fine," Erica replied. "You know, Thomas is still here in Minneapolis. I suppose I can depend on him if I need anything." Erica then left word for Perry to call her. Next, she called Thomas and asked if Timmy could stay with him for a few days since she had to return to Cincinnati the following week.

"What's up, Erica? Why are you going to Cincinnati so much?" Thomas asked. Erica had never told Thomas the whole story behind her travels. She said she had some unfinished business to take care of there.

"Well, I won't be able to take care of the boy because I have to be out of town that week, myself. You may just have to drop him off with your folks in Columbus. Tell me, what's all this sudden business in Cincinnati? I never remembered you having any business there." Erica was thinking about how to answer when Thomas asked, "You're not taking that Porter fellow with you, are you?" referring to her friend.

Erica was shocked by this question. It came from out of the blue. First of all, it was none of Thomas' business what she did, or with whom. But secondly, she and Larry were just friends. She had never even talked to Thomas about him. What could it matter to him who her friends were? She asked, "What are you talking about, Thomas, and why is what I do of any concern to you?"

"Because frankly, I don't want that guy around my son. I don't want him teaching Timmy any of *his ways*."

"Thomas, you're being ridiculous. What, may I ask, do you mean by *his ways* anyway*?*"

"I think you know exactly what I'm talking about. I don't want Timmy acting black," Thomas retorted.

Erica exclaimed in exasperation, "Timmy *is* mixed. I'm his mother, remember. I'm bi-racial. There is no such thing as *acting black*, or *white*, for that matter. What's with you, Thomas? And what's with all these insults? You know, I don't need you teaching Timmy any of your *ways*, either. I don't want my son growing up to be some kind of bigot. I thought we had gotten past this craziness a long time ago."

"Just you listen to me, Erica, This isn't crazy. Timmy is my son, too. And I have something to say about who he goes around." Thomas was almost shouting now.

Thomas' tone of voice was unsettling. Erica was already disturbed over what Lynn Davis had just told her. And now this. Once again, Thomas was sounding like a tyrant on the race issue. Their marriage had ended because he had obviously never forgiven her for being bi-racial. That really was when she thought his obsession with race began, and it had gotten steadily worse.

Still holding the phone, the memory of their terrible break-up crossed her mind. She remembered that shortly after learning she was pregnant Thomas had begun to act more normal. But in spite of his attempts at being a loving father-to-be, things were never quite the same again. Over time, Thomas was unable to contain his disdain for Erica, sometimes even for their child, and for people of color in general. Erica had known she wouldn't be able to put up with this situation much longer. But she made a noble effort, mostly for the sake of their son. The final straw came when she and Thomas had sat watching the local news on television one evening and Thomas started hurling racial epithets around. Hurt and shocked, Erica knew this was the end. Thomas had changed so. His negative attitude seemed to consume him. He appeared to be bothered all the time. His last comments had sealed the fate of their marriage. It was over. With these painful memories running through her head, Erica was reminded of how far Thomas was capable of going on the race issue. She hoped he would settle down before she ended their conversation.

In a calm voice, Erica finally said, "Thomas, I've got to go. It's obvious you're still carrying around all this anger toward me for being bi-racial. I truly never understood why that made such a difference to you. Whether I'm black or white, I'm still the same person I was before," she said.

Thomas was incensed. "That's where you're wrong, Erica," he said. "There's no way you're the same person I married. I married a white girl, but you turned out to be black. It's good you never took my name. You don't deserve to be *my* son's mother. I should sue you for custody and take him away from you!"

Thomas had threatened this before, but Erica never thought he meant it. Mostly, she thought he was just trying to be hurtful. Now she didn't know what to think. In spite of her hope to calm him down, their phone call ended on that acidic note. Erica was confused. She couldn't understand why asking Thomas to keep Timmy again could make him this angry. This thing he had about African Americans seemed to be flaring up again, and this outburst was the worst she'd experienced in a long time.

They may end up in court one day, she thought, but it will be to take away Thomas' visitation rights, for she was beginning to wonder if with his views, he could be any kind of father to Timmy anymore. His behavior was becoming so volatile and erratic, she actually wondered if he was using some kind of illegal drugs. In her job as a social worker, she had come in contact with drug and alcohol addicts. Thomas was almost beginning to act like one himself. In her heart, she wondered how she could ever have been married to such a mean-spirited person.

CHAPTER
15

THERE WERE STILL too many unanswered aspects to this case, so Lynn asked Ella to see if she could find out anything more about Erica and Perry Harrington. Lynn hoped she'd find something that would help explain this mystery and identify the culprit behind these puzzling phone calls and notes. Ella scoured the old neighborhood where Sophie and Hattie had lived years before, and finally, going door-to-door, she struck gold, locating an old woman who used to know the family. Her name was Bertha Waters, and she still lived in the old neighborhood. Ella explained to Miss Waters that she was trying to get information on the Dodd family because of an inheritance. Miss Waters told Ella to call her Miss Bertha and invited her into her home to talk.

Miss Bertha sat down in a large, cushy rocking chair and offered Ella a seat on the couch. The first thing she asked was, "Why do you keep calling them folks Dodd? I knew Sophie and Hattie, but their last name was Williams." Then before Ella could say anything, Miss Bertha said, "Now wait just a minute." She began rocking back and forth and thought about it a while. Finally she said she did remember something about Hattie changing her name from Williams after she had her first child. At first, everybody thought she went and got married or something. But she never married that man. No siree, Bob.

Eighty-five-year-old Bertha Waters was a small, dark-skinned woman with a big heart and sharp mind. She wore a little blue cotton dress with large red and pink flowers and puffy sleeves. It was starched and pressed and neat looking. Miss Bertha was the kind of person who prided herself on knowing a little about everybody in the neighborhood. She said she had been a friend of Sophie's ever since Sophie came to Cincinnati, way back in the 1950s. A spry, cute little woman who had never married, Miss Bertha wore her long, thick white hair parted down the middle and two braids that she twisted to form a bun at the back. She lived with a widowed younger sister, Lela, and a big dog named Walter in a small house in a section of town called Over the Rhine.

They drank fresh-squeezed lemonade while Miss Bertha told Ella how she sometimes used to babysit little Hattie Rose when Sophie made evening plans with that nice gentleman she occasionally saw. "His name was Mr. Washington. He was older than Sophie by about 10 or 15 years or so, and he wanted to make her his wife." Ella learned how this man had a good job with the County, and how he had been a widow for several years when he met Sophie.

"But Sophie, who was just a young woman herself at the time, wasn't about to marry Mr. Washington or anybody else for that matter," Miss Bertha said, shaking her finger toward Ella, who smiled at the fact that she was getting way more details than she had bargained for. " 'Cause, oh, was she devoted to that little girl. All Sophie was interested in was making a good life for herself and her little Hattie," she told Ella.

"So, here was Sophie Williams, a pretty woman. Had menfolk tripping all over her, but all she did was work and take care of that little girl of hers. Sophie died when she was in her early 50s. Shame she had to die so young, leaving those two kids of Hattie's."

Miss Bertha said she remembered Hattie Rose growing up to be the prettiest little thing on the block. "Big bright eyes, dimples in her cheeks so deep you could sink a ship in, a happy smile, and long black wavy hair. Boys hung around her like flies, but young

Hattie would just smile at them and walk on by. Stuck to herself, you know. Always had her schoolbooks with her. Even in the summertime, she was always reading. That child was so educated, she could hold a conversation with the President of these United States."

Miss Bertha told Ella when Hattie finished school, she worked as a secretary at a big law office downtown. Now what'd they call it? Whipple, Whitmore, or something or other. They say she couldn't keep the lawyers away from her. "Everybody loved Hattie Rose. But she wasn't studying none of them." The name of the law office struck a chord with Ella. She'd remembered Lynn mentioning that Ferrel Whitmore was Mrs. Remington's lawyer and wondered if that was where Hattie Williams had worked, and if so, was that how Mr. Remington came to know her?

"Then, one day," Miss Bertha continued, "Hattie must've let her guard down. She started seeing this man. At first nobody knew who he was, but, of course, I knew all about it," she said. "You see, Sophie told me it was this powerful rich man named Earl Remington. Matter of fact, when she learned he was married, she didn't want her daughter seeing this man. But you know how young people are. Don't listen to their momma sometimes. Hattie wasn't but around 20 years old, you know, and Sophie thought this man was just taking advantage of her youth and innocence. Because she knew her daughter would never have taken up with someone else's husband. Sophie had taught her better.

"But you know what? The girl fell in love. You could see it in her face a mile away; she'd be just a'glowing all over the place." Miss Bertha smacked her jaws and kept rocking and talking. Ella smiled and nodded and listened with interest. "Was that man ever sweet on that girl, too. I'll tell you, he set Hattie up in a fancy apartment somewhere and took real good care of her. Then she up and had not one, but two kids by him. Now Sophie was proud of her grandchildren, but she was sure not happy they didn't have a father at home. So now as I recall, that's when Hattie changed her name to Dodd. On account of trying to pretend she was married, you know. She sure did. You see, Dodd was Sophie's family name before she was Williams. So Hattie wasn't married, see, but child,

I'll tell you, that man bought her and her kids everything they wanted.

"Now you wouldn't have known those two little kids were Hattie's if you hadn't seen them with her. 'Cause they looked just like their daddy. What I mean to say is, they looked white, just like him. He gave Hattie plenty of money to live on, and Hattie even used to give Sophie money every month to help her pay her bills so she wouldn't have to keep working so hard."

Miss Bertha said this affair of Hattie's went on for several years, but Sophie thought something strange was going on toward the end. "Hattie started acting different. She told her mother this man was jealous. He didn't want her to be around other folks. Probably afraid somebody would take her away from him, Hattie believed he would probably have hurt anyone who tried. Sophie was afraid he might even harm Hattie.

"On the other hand, Hattie was getting confused, you see. Because after a while, she decided she didn't want to be no mistress anymore. Now she wanted to be somebody's wife. And he already got a wife. So now there's a problem. To make matters worse, both of them were jealous of each other, and you know that's no good. Hattie stopped coming over to her mother's and began sticking to herself. Sophie knew this man had a real tight rein on her. She wanted Hattie to leave him and come back home with her kids. Sophie told her she'd help her get on her feet. But Lord have mercy, Hattie Rose wanted this man. It got to be a real mess, child."

Ella was intrigued by this account and asked if by chance Miss Bertha had any pictures of Hattie and her kids. "Sure, I got some pictures around here. Would you care to see them?" Ella said yes. Miss Bertha got up spryly from her rocking chair to get a photo album. Ella looked around her cozily decorated little living room where sepia-toned family photos were hung in antique wooden frames on brightly flowered wallpaper. Crisply starched and ironed doilies under the lamps on the end tables added to the homey comfort of the place. Miss Bertha returned with the album and opened it to show some pictures of Hattie Rose, Sophie and Hattie's two kids.

Ella had not seen pictures of Sophie Dodd before. On these snapshots, she looked to be in her late 30s. She was a fair-skinned, pretty woman with long straight, light brown hair. Although she was smiling on this picture, her face registered the telltale signs of stress and strain. Sophie looked like the serious no-nonsense type.

Next, Ella viewed a picture of Hattie Rose Williams, and one of Hattie with Erica and Perry, who looked to be about two and four years old.

"Hmmm, now that's strange," Miss Bertha uttered in a confused tone. "I'm looking for one picture in particular. Miss Bertha furrowed her brow as she tried to remember where she'd put it. "Oh, it was really something, honey. Hattie was standing in front of this big fancy car with that man, Remington. And he had his arms all around her like she was some kind of trophy or something. It's around here someplace." She kept looking. "Matter of fact," Miss Bertha said, "I had quite a few pictures of the two of them. Sophie showed them to me, then forgot and left them behind. I distinctly remember those pictures were in here with the rest, but they're most certainly not here now. Maybe they got put away in another album.

"Lela," she called her sister into the room and introduced her to Ella. Miss Lela was a few years younger than Miss Bertha and resembled her older sister, except her hair was jet black. "Have you seen those old pictures of Hattie Rose Dodd and her gentleman friend? I'm sure I had them in this album? You remember them, don't you? You remember how Hattie's mother, Sophie, used to come by here all the time."

Lela was carrying a pitcher of lemonade, "No, ma'am, sister, I'm afraid I ain't seen 'em. Y'all want some more lemonade, do ya?" Ella took a refreshing refill as she studied Miss Lela who was not nearly as talkative as her sister. Miss Lela went back into the kitchen, and Ella and Miss Bertha resumed their talk.

Ella was totally absorbed in the story she was hearing, especially the way Miss Bertha could spout off details of these events just like they'd happened yesterday. She seemed to have the memory of a hawk. Miss Bertha spoke up, "I'll tell you something else, too. Sophie never thought things added up right about the way her daughter died. You know she was in that crash, supposed to have lost control of her car? Sophie thought that just didn't sound quite right. 'Course, now, the hospital claimed she was under the influence, if you know what I mean. But Sophie knew Hattie Rose never touched no liquor. So if she had alcohol in her body, her mother wondered how it got there." Ella was taking notes on Miss Bertha's point-by-point account. She nodded her head as the elderly woman talked.

"Now, there was even some talk about the brakes going out in her car. So now what was it? Was she drinking, or did the brakes go out? You see what I'm getting at?" Then Miss Bertha frowned and said, "Sophie thought that sounded suspicious what with the car being almost new and all. So you'da thought everything would have been in fine working order." Miss Bertha looked Ella dead in the eye and said, "If you get my drift?"

Ella was very surprised at what she was hearing. "Miss Bertha, are you saying Mr. Remington had anything to do with Hattie's accident?"

"Well, I can't say he did, and I can't say he didn't," Miss Bertha answered noncommittally. Then she looked down and studiously brushed at the gathers of her dress. "All I know is what Sophie told me she suspected."

"Then, why didn't someone report their suspicions to the police?" Ella asked.

"Honey, now what do you think the Police Department was going to do with an important man like that Remington fellow? Look at Sophie like she was crazy, I 'spect."

Ella looked pensive. Unfortunately, this made sense.

Then Miss Bertha stared straight ahead and continued her chronicle of events. "That funeral of Hattie's was something, honey. It's like everybody that girl ever knew showed up. School friends, co-workers from the law office she worked at, some of her momma's friends. But I'll tell you what was pitiful. Those two little kids of hers sitting there huddled against their grandmother. To tell you the truth, I wonder if they realized their momma was gone for good. But you still couldn't help but feel sorry for them.

"And Jelly was there, of course."

Ella looked puzzled. "Jelly?"

Miss Bertha explained, "Oh, Jelly's Lela's boy. My nephew. I'm telling you, this whole thing tore him to pieces. He loved that Hattie so.

" 'Course, now there was this one distinguished white gentleman at her visitation. I believe it was her man friend. He just sat in the back by himself. And you know, honey, I was not all that impressed. I suppose he looked all right, but mostly I remember he had this big ole' scar or birthmark over one eye. Very unusual-looking mark, wasn't like anything I'd ever seen before." Ella hadn't remembered seeing a mark on Earl Remington's face, but when she thought about it, the facial features were not real distinct on those old photographs. Perhaps with a magnifying glass she could find this mark. She made a note to look for it.

Miss Bertha finished her story by telling Ella, "This man dumped a whole lot of money into the bank account Hattie shared with Sophie. That way, her momma and kids would have something to live on. As far as I know, that may have been the last Sophie heard from him. Said she wasn't never gonna tell those kids about their daddy cause she didn't want them feeling funny about being illegitimate and growing up with some kind of complex. I told Sophie those kids ought to be able to know they were kin to this big shot. But she wasn't hearing it. I really think it was because she suspected he was involved in Hattie' death. So then, Sophie took them grandkids of hers and moved to a big fancy house. I remember now, that's when Sophie changed her name back to Dodd so she'd have the same name as her grandkids. Then she quit that job of hers so she could take care of them.

"With Hattie dead, I heard they all started passing for white folks. You know Sophie looked white anyway. And you couldn't have told those two little kids from any white kids you saw. So that's all there was to it. I never saw Sophie after they moved, but I heard about her dying a couple of years later. That was a real pity cause she was so young and, of course, who was going to look after those grandbabies of hers. I always wondered what happened to those kids. I knew Hattie had some kinfolks down in

Alabama. I figured they probably went back down home to live with them."

Ella asked Miss Bertha if she knew of any other people who had any knowledge of the Dodds, or Williams and Mr. Remington. "You mean other than everyone in the neighborhood," Miss Bertha said with a chuckle, but added that most had all moved away or passed on. But back then, everyone knew everyone, and they knew everyone's business, too.

"How did other people feel about Hattie and this man?"

"To be frank, everyone around here was kind of proud that our little Hattie had this big rich white man wanting her. I'm sure you know what I mean."

"I think I do."

"But you know, no one ever talked much about Sophie's suspicions about Hattie's death. I think the only one I ever told about it was Jelly — Jeremiah's his given name, you know. He lives in High Point, North Carolina. Used to be a big executive at a company that made hair products, but he retired a couple of years ago. He was a supervisor or something like that. Now Jelly was older than Hattie. See, my nephew will turn 60 on the 12th day of October. But he sure was sweet on that gal. 'Course Hattie didn't give Jelly the time of day, but that didn't stop him from being crazy about her.

"Jelly was always curious; he especially wanted to know exactly how Hattie died. I remember talking to him about it when he was in town some time back. Turns out I probably shouldn't have told him about all that because he got real upset. I mean he fretted and fumed and pored over those 20-year-old pictures of Hattie like they was taken yesterday."

Ella asked, "Do you remember when you told Jelly about this, Miss Bertha?"

Miss Bertha looked up to the ceiling to think. "Yeah, I think it was when Jelly was back here for Pop Dawson's funeral. Pop Dawson was his barber, you know. That was about, hmmm, two, three years ago."

As their conversation began to wind down, Ella felt that she'd scored a big hit in this visit. She thanked Miss Bertha for the information and told her she'd like to check back to see if she found those other pictures. If she found them, Ella said she'd like to come back over and take a look at them. Miss Bertha promised to look through her other albums.

Miss Bertha and her sister, Lela, really enjoyed having company come by. After Ella left, they discussed what a sweet and business-like young lady she was. Miss Lela wanted to know why Ella Braxton would come all the way back over to their house just to see some pictures. Miss Bertha told her sister, "I see your point." Then she said curiously, "Lela, you don't suppose I said too much about Sophie's business, do you? You know how I get to talking." Lela told her sister she always did run off at the mouth, and they both laughed. However, they decided Miss Bertha might have said more than she needed to say, but no harm done. This was, after all, ancient history. Anyhow, maybe she'd just have to be a little more tight-lipped next time.

Late that afternoon, Ella told Lynn about her visit with Miss Bertha Waters.

Lynn was pleased with Ella's find and quite interested in the whole story, particularly their suspicions about what caused Hattie's accident. "You mean they think Remington had something to do with Hattie's death?" Lynn asked.

"Kind of sounded like it," Ella answered. "His jealousy, possessiveness, alcohol supposedly in her system, the possibility of the automobile malfunctioning. I mean, Miss Bertha as much as said Sophie suspected he had something to do with it."

"If they thought he was behind it, why didn't they go to the police?" Lynn asked.

Ella explained how Miss Bertha had answered that same question. "I guess I can see why they didn't try to do anything about it. They didn't think anybody would listen to someone blaming one of the most powerful men in town for the death of a young black woman."

Lynn said, "This is really good, partner. Great job finding out about all that. It gives us something to look into. I'll see what I can dig up from the Police Department about Hattie Williams' death."

Next, Ella and Lynn examined the photos in Mrs. Remington's private file, looking for that mark on Mr. Remington's face that Miss Bertha talked about. Using a magnifying glass, they saw it. A crescent-shaped mark over his right eye. "There it is! That's exactly as Miss Bertha said," Ella exclaimed. Lynn did not know exactly what the relevancy of this new piece of data was; none-theless, it was an interesting discovery. She was particularly in-terested in Miss Bertha Waters' missing pictures and wondered whether Ella had not serendipitously happened upon the key to unlocking the blackmail mystery. Ella said she would check back with Miss Bertha to see if she had located the pictures. She tele-phoned her the next day.

"No, child, I haven't found nary a one of those pictures. I looked through all my picture albums, and they are just plain gone," Miss Bertha said.

"Miss Bertha," Ella said, "didn't you say the last person who looked at those pictures was your nephew, Jelly, from North Carolina."

"Yes, that's the last I remember of them."

"Do you suppose he might have removed them from your al-bum for any reason," Ella asked.

"Honey child, crazy as he was about Hattie, no telling what he might have done. Of course, now, did I tell you Jelly was mar-ried over 25 years himself? But about four years ago, his wife had a stroke one day, and don't you know, she died the next. He's been widowed ever since. Never did have any children of his own. But you know, Jelly may have got to thinking about the old days when he was running around here with that big ole' crush on Hattie Rose."

"What's your nephew's full name, Miss Bertha," Ella asked.

"Jelly?" Miss Bertha chuckled at the nickname. "Why, his real name is Jeremiah. Jeremiah Brownlee, but we always called him Jelly." Still laughing, she added, "Jelly says we called him that because he was just as smooth and sweet as could be." He grew up right across the street. Went to Taft High School."

"You know," Lynn told Ella, "this question about how Hattie died makes me wonder about Jelly. In other words, could he have wanted to avenge Hattie's death. I mean, think about this. Could he have taken those photographs from his aunt's album, copied them, and used them to blackmail Mr. Remington."

"Sounds plausible," Ella said. "I mean, it's all right there. Possible motive and everything."

"There's just one thing," Lynn said. "If it was him, why would he or someone call me about keeping Erica and Perry away from here?"

"You've got me there. I was hoping we were getting somewhere," Ella said. "But somehow, this doesn't sound like something a lovesick old man would do."

"What if," Lynn said to Ella, "God forbid, there are two blackmailers?"

"Damn! Now that's a frightening thought," Ella replied. Lynn and Ella decided they'd better do a little checking up on Jeremiah Brownlee of High Point.

Lynn decided to ask Mrs. Remington if she could locate any correspondence, records or anything from the blackmailer to her husband. "There are a few of Earl's things I haven't gone through yet. I'll look through them. Perhaps I'll get Ross to help me," Mrs. Remington said, while thinking to herself, *Earl, how many more secrets am I going to uncover?* Then she asked Lynn, "Why do you ask? Have you found anything out?"

"No, we really don't have anything definite right now, but we have learned about one of Hattie Williams' former would-be suitors, and we're checking to be sure he's not involved in any way. We're exploring every possibility." Lynn spoke cautiously, not wanting to mislead Mrs. Remington's into thinking they were on to something concrete. She added, "Mrs. Remington, I'm hoping you'll find something to help us here."

"Of course, Miss Davis," she said. "I'll look through Earl's things."

Police records of Hattie's death indicated that a maintenance check had been done on the wrecked automobile, but nothing unusual or suspicious was found.

CHAPTER
16

"UNCLE EDDY, YOU went to Taft High. Did you ever know anyone named Jeremiah Brownlee?" Lynn asked that evening. "He's probably your age."

With a pensive brow, her uncle said, "Well, now, that's a name from the past. Jeremiah Brownlee." He rubbed his chin, then laughingly told Lynn, "Why sure, I remember Jeremiah. He was in my graduating class. In fact, he was in my homeroom class. We used to call Jeremiah *Old Sly Fox*, 'cause that boy was as crafty as the day is long. You could never figure him out; nobody knew what he was going to do next. People thought he'd be dozing off in class, but when the exam grades came back, Jeremiah'd be the one who aced the test. Fact is, he was a brain; went on to study chemistry in college."

Uncle Ed nodded his head and smiled. "Yep, old Jeremiah was really something. I remember that guy'd do some crazy things." He explained, laughingly, "Well, at least we thought it was crazy back then. Today, people would only say old Jeremiah was just a little different. But back in the 50s, people thought he was nuttier than a fruitcake.

"Give you an example. Jeremiah was real competitive, see.

Now it didn't matter what he had to do to win. He'd do it. So I remember this chitt'lin-eating fund-raiser at the church. I think they called it something like *Platters for Platters,* or something like that. And Jeremiah out-ate everyone around. That boy ate six or seven heaping platters full of chitt'lins just so he could win a pair of tickets to a concert. Of course, the headliners were the Platters and some other groups like maybe the Coasters or Moonglows. Won the tickets, but then, come time for the concert, he was too sick from eating all those chitt'lins to go." Uncle Eddy laughed at his trip down memory lane.

"I haven't thought of old Jeremiah Brownlee in 30 or 40 years. "How'd you ever come up with his name anyway?" he asked an amused Lynn, who was still trying to figure out what in the world were the Platters, Moonglows and Coasters.

Lynn told her uncle about Ella's visit to a woman named Miss Bertha Waters, and about their comments about Hattie's accident. She said that Jeremiah Brownlee was Miss Bertha's nephew and they called him Jelly. Lynn told her uncle how Jelly had this major crush on Hattie, and she told him about the missing photographs. "So it may be stretching, but I'm just wondering," she said, "if Jeremiah Brownlee could have had anything to do with the blackmailing. Maybe he used those missing pictures of Hattie and Earl Remington to do the job."

Uncle Ed's laughter turned into a thoughtful frown. He told Lynn he remembered Jeremiah Brownlee being pretty different from other kids. But a blackmailer? No, he couldn't see him doing anything like that. Even so, he said, anything was possible, and she ought to check it all out anyway.

Lynn said that she had asked Mrs. Remington to look for correspondence or photographs from the blackmailer. "Good idea," he told her. "Maybe she'll run across the pictures the blackmailer sent. Now if you can get copies of those pictures, you can see if Miss Bertha Waters will tell you if they're the same ones missing from her album. If they match, that would certainly point the finger at Jeremiah. But what can you do? You can't expect those women to identify pictures that could implicate their own kin in a blackmailing." Then he said, "Besides, like I said, Lynn, this doesn't sound like the Jeremiah Brownlee I remember. Of course now, I know people can change all right."

The next morning Lynn called her mother to catch her up on things. Her mother was troubled at the idea that Lynn had received a second phone call, possibly from the Remington blackmailer, but relieved to know her brother, Ed, and Lynn's friend, Harvey, were continuing to advise her on this case regularly. Before they hung up, Rachel called Lynn's dad, Grady, to the phone. After spending a few minutes bragging about the catfish he and her Uncle Ed caught and fried up the other day, and about how much he was enjoying his new retirement status, they hung up with a promise to have lunch together soon, just the two of them.

Early Wednesday afternoon, Mrs. Remington phoned Lynn and excitedly told her she had found some photographs that might have been used by the blackmailer. She'd located them in a locked drawer in her deceased husband's closet off the master bedroom. "Excellent," Lynn exclaimed. "I'd like to see them as soon as possible."

"I'll have them delivered to you this afternoon."

"Terrific, Mrs. Remington." Then Lynn remembered her doubts about Arnold, and asked, "Perhaps I can just pick them up instead?"

"Oh no, I'll just have Arnold bring them," Elizabeth Remington said, and then, thinking further, said, "No, better yet, I'll have Ross bring them to your office. I'm sure he can get there within the hour." Lynn preferred having the delivery made by Mrs. Remington's son versus by her chauffeur, whom she was still not convinced was completely trustworthy.

Elizabeth said, "Miss Davis, out of curiosity, I looked at the pictures and they were quite something." Her voice trailed off before adding, "Interestingly, one was the same picture I saw in Earl's package I brought over the other day — the one with Earl and the woman standing by the Rolls. It made me wonder, could someone connected to her have something to do with the scam? Perhaps we'll never know. But I must tell you, seeing these pictures was just as hard as before. I don't suppose I'll ever get used to this."

Lynn thanked Mrs. Remington and told her she hoped the photographs would prove helpful. She thought about this one photograph that kept popping up. Seems everyone has a copy of Hattie Williams and Earl Remington standing by the Rolls Royce: Erica, the blackmailer, even Miss Bertha Waters. How did the blackmailer come by it, she wondered.

"Ella, good news," she said, stepping to the doorway of her office after she hung up the phone. "Mrs. Remington found some photographs. She thinks they may be the ones used to blackmail her husband, and she's sending them over now."

"Super. Maybe I can take them over to Miss Bertha's house this afternoon," Ella said. "I'll give her a call."

"Good," Lynn said, because at least one of these pictures fits the description of one of Miss Bertha's — how'd she describe it? Hattie and her man standing by some big fancy car?"

"Oh, oh," Ella said, thinking they might be on to something. She and Lynn discussed the possible explanations for everyone having this same picture.

Within the hour Ross arrived, dressed casually in off-white slacks and shirt and tan-colored dockers. He had the package. Ross told Lynn his mother had found the pictures to be pretty upsetting. Lynn told him she was eager to take a look at them. Before tearing into the envelope, she chatted with Ross a minute, asking about his plans for returning to Colorado. He said he had taken an extended leave from his job and didn't intend to leave Cincinnati until this matter was completely settled. His mother needed his support, and he thought the whole family should be together. Lynn thanked him and said she would phone his mother if there were any new developments.

Ella and Lynn sat at Lynn's desk and opened the envelope. Inside were four black and white pictures 8x10 inches in size. The grainy quality of the photographs suggested they were enlargements of smaller snapshots. There was the photo Lynn had seen before in Earl Remington's private collection showing him and Hattie Rose standing by the Rolls Royce. As she looked at the picture again, she saw a driver seated in the car. "Why, that must be Arnold Taylor, their chauffeur," Lynn replied as she studied the picture. "Mrs. Remington said Arnold had worked for them for over 35 years. So he obviously knew about Mr. Remington and his girlfriend." Lynn told Ella that Erica had mentioned having this very picture in her collection of photographs, too, and she and Ella thought it might be the one Miss Bertha referred to as well. If so, that would certainly raise more questions about her nephew, Jelly.

The other pictures were also suggestive of a deep affection between the couple. One depicted them embracing on a balcony. Behind them was the Ohio River. Another pictured the two of them seated on a large plush sofa in what appeared to be a beautiful room. In this scene, Earl Remington had his arm around Hattie, whose head was tilted back resting lightly on his shoulder, and they both looked very happy. Lynn and Ella wondered if this one had been taken in Hattie's apartment. If so, nice digs, they both thought.

The last picture was taken aboard Remington's yacht — a spectacular vessel named *The Rose*. A beautiful red rose was painted on its stern. Knowing that Hattie's middle name was Rose gave Lynn and Ella cause to wonder. Hattie and Earl were both wearing swimsuits. Earl in white trunks, deep tan and trim physique looked at home on his boat. Hattie's attractive light-colored swimsuit accentuated her smooth, creamy skin and svelte figure. "I can see why Mr. Remington would not have wanted his wife to see these pictures," Lynn said. Lynn and Ella both noticed that with the photos blown up as big as they were, the prominent mark over Mr. Remington's right eye was quite visible.

Miss Bertha agreed that Ella could come back over that very afternoon. When Ella arrived at the sisters' home, she immediately detected a different atmosphere from the first time she was there. Miss Bertha didn't seem quite as neighborly or talkative as she had been during that first visit. And Miss Lela didn't offer their guest any lemonade this time.

They exchanged hellos, and Miss Lela, Jelly's mother, greeted her with a disinterested look on her face. And this time, she sat in the room with Ella and Miss Bertha while they talked. Why does it feel so different today, Ella wondered as she removed the pictures from their envelope. She said, "Miss Bertha, as I told you, we have located some pictures, and I wanted to know if you would look at them and tell me if you've ever seen any of them before. Could they possibly be some of the same ones you had in your album?"

Miss Bertha said, "Surely, I'll look at your pictures," and Ella handed them to her. Ella thought Miss Bertha had an obvious reaction as she studied one picture, then the next. By her reaction, Ella thought that she recognized the pictures. Before she finished viewing them, probably out of habit, Miss Bertha turned each photo over to see if anything was written on the backside. Then, Miss Bertha said, "No, these aren't the same."

Ella was taken by surprise by her denial. She had expected a different answer from Miss Bertha, especially judging by the expression on her face when she first looked at the pictures. Furthermore, Miss Bertha herself had told Ella about the picture of Hattie and Remington and the big fancy car.

"Are you sure, Miss Bertha?" Ella asked. "I mean, didn't you mention the picture with the car? Are you positive that isn't it?"

Miss Bertha looked at the pictures again and furrowed her brow, and looking very sincere, said, "You know, now that you mention it, it could be. I don't know for sure. Child, it was so long ago that I saw them, I just can't remember." Then, real sweetly she said, "But these are certainly nice pictures, though."

Then Miss Bertha handed the pictures to her sister, and Ella noticed that she looked Miss Lela in the eye as she handed them over. Miss Lela looked at them slowly, one at a time. She had apparently seen her big sister's startlement and braced herself not to react similarly. Miss Lela said that she, too, could not remember seeing those pictures before. Ella was confounded.

What's going on, she wondered, as she realized the two sisters were apparently not telling her anything more.

Making an effort to sound casual, Miss Bertha asked, "Now why, may I ask, are you so interested in my pictures, and how did you come by these particular pictures anyway?"

Her questions put Ella on the spot. She wasn't certain how to answer and was actually feeling somewhat guilty for asking Miss

Bertha and Miss Lela about something that could possibly implicate Jeremiah Brownlee in a blackmail scheme. She felt compelled to level with them. So looking from one sister to the next, she said, "Miss Bertha, Miss Lela, the reason I wanted to know if you had seen these pictures before is a very serious one. You see, I told you I work for a private investigation company, the Lynn Davis Agency. Miss Davis was hired by the Remingtons to locate Hattie's children."

"And why are they trying to find those children?" Miss Bertha asked.

"Well," Ella answered, "Mr. Remington died a few months ago. And they are beneficiaries in his will."

"Well, now, that's something. You mean they're finally going to do the right thing by those children."

"Yes, but the reason I wanted to know about those pictures is that ... well, actually, someone had been threatening Mr. Remington with those pictures," Ella said.

"Threatening? You mean like blackmail, child?" Miss Bertha quizzed.

"Yes, I'm afraid so. And now, someone is even making threatening phone calls to our office. So as you can imagine, we're quite interested in getting to the bottom of this." Miss Bertha now knew she and her sister had done the right thing to keep their lips sealed. What has Jelly gone and done, she silently wondered.

Miss Bertha and Miss Lela slyly gave each other the eye. Then Miss Bertha said, "I wonder who could be doing such a thing." And she honestly didn't know. For some reason, she and her sister had smelled trouble when Ella produced those pictures, and the honest truth was that they did think the photographs looked an awful lot like the some of those missing from their album. While they really weren't absolutely certain, they hoped Jelly hadn't done anything rash. He had always done things his way.

As she looked again at the picture of Hattie Rose and Earl Remington on his boat, Miss Bertha remembered that even the name of Remington's boat, *The Rose*, hadn't set well with Jelly. Sophie had told her years before that Remington sometimes called Hattie pet names like *Angel* and *Princess* and *his rose*. Jelly would say, "None of that matters; cause a rose by any other name will still smell as sweet." She remembered how he used that expression a lot when he talked about Hattie Rose and her white man.

Ella had really hated telling the two little old ladies about the blackmailing, and she could see this information bothered them. She thanked them for their time, and asked that they call her if they had anything more to tell her. Miss Bertha said they would most certainly do just that.

Miss Bertha and Miss Lela were confused, and when Ella left, they talked this thing through. Jeremiah had been so infatuated with Hattie, he was jealous of any man who got next to her. He used to talk about Hattie all the time. In a way, neither Miss Bertha nor her sister would have put it past him to do something crazy to get back at Earl Remington. Blackmail could have been his way of punishing old Mr. Remington for winning Hattie Rose.

Then the two old sisters remembered that Jelly did come into a large sum of money a few years ago. Went and took a big cruise and everything. Jelly had told his mother he got the money because he'd invested right. Miss Lela started thinking some scarier thoughts then. Could that have been blackmail money?

Although they were worried, they breathed a little easier when this Miss Braxton told them someone was calling her private investigation firm. This did not sound like anything Jeremiah would do. The sisters tried to figure this thing out, but in the end they weren't sure what to think. Lela decided to telephone her boy and just ask him. She placed a call to North Carolina, but Jelly was not home, so she left a message. "Jelly, this is your momma. I want you to call me just as soon as you get home, you hear me."

"I don't think Miss Bertha and her sister were telling the truth, Lynn," Ella said, "I hate to say this, because they're such sweet little old ladies. But the way they were looking at those pictures, I could have sworn they recognized them. Somehow they must have gotten scared. And I don't know if I handled it that well either. I told them afterwards what this was about, so now, more than before, they definitely won't tell me anything. I think I should have leveled with them up front. I guess I was afraid to scare them off. But I don't think I'm wrong. I do believe they recognized those photos. If they are covering up, I can only assume it's because they think Jeremiah could be involved."

* * * * *

Since their conversation, Ed Pennington had been thinking about what Lynn told him about Jeremiah and his unfulfilled attraction to Hattie Dodd. He told his wife Maggie about it. "Now Jeremiah was a pretty strange guy. But was he crazy enough to pull a stunt like blackmail?" Ed questioned, but in his own mind, he still thought the answer was *no*. "But I guess it depends on how desperate the man was over Hattie, or money," he told Maggie. "We can't forget it has been over 40 years since I last saw the guy, and chances are I wouldn't recognize him if I saw him today. I've got to remember that people can change their ways."

Maggie had been a sophomore the year Ed was a senior. She told her husband, "I cannot remember Jeremiah Brownlee, Eddy. Wouldn't his picture be in your yearbook?"

"Should be. Let's look in my senior yearbook."

Maggie located the stack of yearbooks at the bottom of the bookcase in the den and pulled out the one from 1962. Dusting it off, she began leafing through it and enjoyed the reminiscent journey through its pages. She stopped on one page to admire and smile at Ed's senior class picture. He was handsome then and still handsome now, she thought. His motto listed beneath his photo was *To whom much is given, much is required*. She remembered how appropriate that saying was for Ed, or Mr. Big Heart as she sometimes called him.

Next Maggie found Jeremiah's picture. Full name, Jeremiah Tecumseh Brownlee. "Oh, so that's him," she said when she saw the senior class picture of a fairly nice-looking young man who looked younger than his years. Big mischievous smile, freckles. "You know, I think I do remember that boy. Didn't he play basketball?"

"Yes, Jeremiah Brownlee was a big man on the varsity team."

Then Maggie said, "Now listen to his motto, *A rose by any other name will still smell as sweet*. That's a nice one," she mused. "Wonder what's the significance of that."

CHAPTER
17

EARL, JR. WAS to sit in with Remington's Security head and a detective from the Police Department as they talked to Jake Huber. They had located him easily based on information he had given Earl in his many phone calls to Remington Corporation. Huber had been agreeable to this meeting and came in for it willingly. In fact, he was excited, for he thought the Remington Corporation was finally prepared to deal with him fairly and squarely and he'd now get what was coming to him.

Earl wanted to be sure he got credit for his thoroughness and follow-through in leading the detectives to Huber. He made it a point to mention that he'd been suspicious of Huber all along, and the cryptic note in the box simply confirmed it for him. He was pretty certain security would find Jake Huber to be the culprit.

This will really look good for me, Earl thought as he prepared for his upcoming interview with the CEO search committee. They'll have to be impressed with how quickly I jumped on this and solved the problem. And we'll be rid of that nuisance, Huber, once and for all. After all, there's no way my father would have ever made such a ridiculous offer. That guy must think we're complete idiots to believe we'd actually fall for a story like that. Earl was still a little curious, though, about what Huber meant when he said he had something on his father. He thought it was entirely possible that Huber was the one blackmailing his father the past two years.

Life had not dealt kindly with Mr. Jake Huber, and his appearance bore the signs of hard times. He was a rather smallish man who appeared to be in his late 50s. He had thinning dark hair that was sprinkled with gray, which he wore parted on one side to cover a hairless spot on the top of his head. He had a long beak nose, and the skin on his face had deep pockets which were only partly covered with a thin dark mustache and a short, scraggly, salt-and-pepper-colored goatee.

Huber wore an inexpensive brown plaid sport coat and stove-pipe-fitting dark brown slacks, a brown-and-white-striped-shirt, a cheap tie and a runner's watch. This was Earl's first time seeing Huber face to face. He thought this little sleazy character easily looked like someone who might try to pull such a stunt. Huber certainly looked desperate enough.

Jake Huber started talking. He wanted to take this opportunity to explain to the group what he had been trying to tell Earl, Jr. for the past several weeks. Mr. Johnson, Chief of Security, immediately stopped him and said, "Mr. Huber, you are here because we called you in to talk to you about an incident that took place here at Remington headquarters this week. We have reason to believe you might know something about it. Huber looked from Johnson to Earl, Jr. with a curious frown on his face. What in hell was this about, he wondered. What was this incident, and why would they want to talk to *him* about it? Unless, of course, it had something to do with the land deal.

Huber listened closely as Johnson explained who he and the other gentlemen were. Then Johnson proceeded to tell Huber that on Monday, the day he last phoned Earl, Jr., a package had been delivered to the Remington building by an unknown party, and the contents were suspicious. In fact, Johnson told him, on the fear that it might have been a bomb, they evacuated the building, but ended up finding nothing more than a small toy.

For a moment, Huber looked amused. He thought to himself smugly, so things aren't so peachy keen at the great Remington headquarters after all. Serves the tightwads right. But what in heaven does this have to do with me?

Chief Johnson continued, "If it weren't for the note we found in the bottom of the box, we might have taken this for a harmless prank, although it was definitely a tasteless and costly one for sure. But with that threatening note, well, now we're considering this a serious offense.

Jake Huber suddenly became very nervous. Was young Remington trying to pin something on him to make him forget about the old man's commitment to him? He wondered this as he sat in apprehensive silence. In desperation, he had claimed to have something on Earl Remington, Sr. Now he wished he really did. It could come in handy, especially if they were out to get him.

"We understand you've been making some pretty outrageous claims about the deceased Mr. Remington's owing you some land or something," said the detective, Mack Martin. "Can you tell us what that's about?" Old Jake Huber was fast becoming distracted by what was beginning to sound like an accusation of some kind of criminal act against the corporation. There's no way they can pin anything on me, he silently affirmed, while wondering, or can they? For he remembered who he was dealing with; these were, after all, the mighty Remingtons. They could do damned near anything they wanted. Are they trying to set me up?

"Do I have to repeat the question for you? We understand you've been calling Mr. Remington here with some unfounded claims and, I might add, some idle threats. Is that right," Martin asked sharply. "And if not, can you tell us exactly what these calls have been about?"

This time, Martin's words were loud and clear to Huber. In response, he nervously explained why he'd been calling young Earl there. Huber gave them intricate details on the land deal, and on the senior Remington's commitment to make him whole. Huber told them apparently Earl, Sr. hadn't had a chance to discuss this with his son, because every time he tried to talk to the junior Remington, the guy just dismissed him as if he was making it all up. He told them, "Now, that's just not right. What the hell's a businessman supposed to do?"

"Depends on what you have to back you up about this so-called promise. So whatcha got?" Martin queried, and Huber told him he had only the old man's word. Martin replied coldly, "I'm afraid the word of a dead man may not carry much weight around here. Unless you can produce some tangible evidence of your allegations, I agree with Mr. Remington here, you don't have anything."

The word of a dead man! Earl, Jr. felt singed by the crass way the detective had just referred to his father. He didn't have to be so brutally disrespectful. This wasn't just any dead man he was referring to; it was Earl Q. Remington, Sr. But Earl resisted his urge to haul Martin over the coals. Instead, Earl said to Johnson, "Why don't you ask Huber about the package and the note?"

Mr. Johnson gave Earl a look as if to say, I think I know how to do my job, but he chose to comply. He turned to Huber and said, "We aren't here to talk about the validity of your allegations. Let's get back to the matter at hand. What we want to know is whether or not you had any involvement with the box that was delivered here the other day."

"No, absolutely not!" Fear sounded in Huber's voice. "I don't even know what you're talking about. I don't know anything about any toy or any note." Huber was trying hard to sound convincing. Never mind, he was also upset about how that brief discussion regarding his lost land went, but he sure didn't need anyone trying to pin anything like this on him. He was the victim here, and it sounded like they were trying to turn things around on him. And Huber was certain they could do him in if they wanted to. He'd already experienced how the Remington power worked and certainly didn't want to experience their wrath again.

"Where were you this past Tuesday afternoon?" Martin asked Huber.

"I was in my office," Huber responded. He felt somewhat comforted by the fact that at least he was with other people all that afternoon trying to put together a business proposal. Thank goodness, he had a tight alibi.

"Was anyone else there?"

"As a matter of fact, sir, yes, there was. My part-time secretary was in. Becky Hamilton is her name," Huber said, sounding slightly self-satisfied.

"Was it just you and this Becky Hamilton?" Martin asked.

"Well, no. I had back-to-back appointments all afternoon. I have been working with some important people on a new deal, and I was busy from before lunch until after six o'clock. I can give you their names if you want me to."

Earl, Jr. said, "That doesn't mean anything. Harry said he took the package from some woman. This guy could have had anyone deliver it over here." Huber gave Earl a disgusted look, and shook his head.

Johnson said, "Mr. Huber, why don't you just give us a list of the people you met with Tuesday afternoon, and the times you met with them. We'll need to check this out, of course." Huber said he would have this information for them just as soon as he called his secretary. Johnson continued, "Of course, Mr. Remington is right. You could have had someone else deliver the box. What we're saying is that we know you had a bone to pick with the Remingtons, and for all we know, this could have been your way of getting their attention. Well, let me tell you, my friend, if we find that you had anything to do with this, it will be very bad for you."

Nervously, Huber dialed his office and was relieved that Becky was at her desk. He asked her to give him his appointments for Tuesday afternoon and prayed she had kept a record of all of them. Fortunately, she had, and she gave him the names, phone numbers and times. There were no gaps. Johnson took the information, and he, Martin and Earl, Jr. saw no reason to keep Mr. Huber any longer. They bid him leave with a fair warning: leave the Remingtons alone. And if the phone calls continued, he was told, Remington would seek an injunction against him and possibly even sue him for harassment. If the law enforcement officials learned he had anything to do with the package that was delivered there, or any future coercive tactics, they promised Huber would be charged with a felony.

Huber left their office shaken. He hoped he had convinced them he had nothing to do with the bomb scare. After this smoke cleared, he would definitely continue his pursuit of what was rightfully his. He would just have to get a lawyer to speak for him in the future, just as soon as he got his hands on enough money to hire one, that is.

A check of the names on the list of Tuesday afternoon appointments verified Huber's story. He had been in his office all that afternoon. Johnson and Martin talked about possibly putting Huber under surveillance, although deep down, they felt that pursuing Jake Huber would be a big waste of time.

CHAPTER
18

ARNOLD TAYLOR PACED the floor of his small two-bedroom cottage on the Remington property. He was completely distraught over what he had done, and even more, over what he had to do about it. Arnold had worked for the Remingtons most of his life. He was well treated here, well paid for his services, and his compensation package included fringe benefits and a generous retirement pension. Arnold had enjoyed a privileged relationship with Mr. Remington, and he even believed it was possible he might be included in his will. At least, the old man had hinted at it a time or two. In a way, he considered the Remingtons sort of like the family he always wanted.

He reflected on his many years as the Remington chauffeur and on his particularly favored status of occasional confidante to Earl, Sr. Over the years, Arnold was privy to a lot of the family's personal business, and he and Mr. Remington sometimes talked about things as he drove him around. In fact, Earl, Sr. kept few personal secrets from him. Arnold had also known about the blackmailing because he was the one who had delivered the money to the park benches. He was relieved the blackmailer had finally dropped out of the picture, and he knew that if he'd ever had a chance to get up close and personal with this character, he'd have made mincemeat of him.

His boss was a rich and powerful man, and somewhat attractive to boot. Arnold had always been aware of the stares and come-hither glances cast Mr. Remington's way by scores of women. He saw it all the time. However, in spite of all he'd seen, he knew Earl, Sr. to be basically a devoted family man. Oh, he still had an occasional rendezvous, like his little fling with that hot, leggy airline stewardess, Mikki. Yep, the old man did like the pretty ones.

But there was that one long-lasting deal. In fact, he'd heard the old man mention more than once how absolutely wild he was about that woman, Hattie-something. Called her *his rose*. And here's the damnedest thing about that one — this woman was black! Most unbelievable thing Arnold'd ever seen. Even so, that was his boss' business, and Arnold tried not to judge him or form any opinion one way or another. He knew Mr. Remington cherished his wife and would not deliberately hurt her for all the world. Yet, there was scuttlebutt floating about that Earl, Sr. had confessed all to his wife, even told her about his two kids by this woman! What a crazy stunt! That would have just about damned near killed Mrs. Remington, he figured.

Arnold had also known all about those two little kids, had even driven them places sometimes. Earl, Sr. told him after their mother died, he had taken care of those kids financially, but he wanted no part of their lives. He couldn't stand anything that reminded him of her. Said it was just too painful. Arnold always wondered what ever became of those two, but, of course, he had the good sense to never ask. Some things are just better left unsaid. That was his philosophy. Mind your own business.

One thing Arnold knew for certain was that Mr. Remington had been completely tormented over that woman's death. Of course, he tried to drown his sorrow in his work, but he never completely recovered fully. Through his rear-view mirror, Arnold could swear he even saw the old man shed a tear now and again. It took months, but Earl, Sr. eventually seemed to snap out of his slump and get on with his life. But now Arnold, himself, was near tears. These new developments were getting to be just too much.

He agonized over the situation and even discussed it with his mother. In fact, he usually discussed everything with his invalid mother. Even though Carrie Taylor couldn't get around anymore, she still pulled Arnold's strings. All his life, she had manipulated him by accusing him of being responsible for the condition she was in. She had suffered a stroke when he was just a teenager, and she, a single mother whose husband had walked out of their lives when Arnold was only six months old. Mrs. Taylor blamed Arnold for her husband's leaving, and she also blamed him for her stroke. She basically made him believe he was just a dumb nobody who would never amount to anything.

Accepting the blame for his mother's problems, Arnold had dropped out of school when he was 16 to take care of her, hoping somehow to make it up to her for her terrible losses. This happened at a time when he had just won the Golden Gloves championship in his welterweight category and had hopes of making it onto the 1968 American boxing team for the Olympics in Tokyo.

But Arnold's dream of making it in the boxing arena had to be deferred. He still wore the fading tattoo of boxing gloves, underscored by the word *Champ* on his upper right arm. Mr. Remington always required him to cover it up when he was on the job. But every chance he got, like when he washed the family vehicles, Arnold would roll up his sleeves and proudly show off his tattoo, and since he also lifted weights, his thick, well-developed muscles, too.

Other than his brief marriage to Minnie Barber, Arnold virtually devoted his entire life to his job with the Remingtons and to the care of his mother, who still practically directed his every move. After two years of marriage, Minnie had become fed up with her critical, bossy mother-in-law who never liked her anyway, and she left Arnold for a bus driver. Broken-hearted, Arnold carried on. His mother had drilled it into his head that he was nothing. He worked hard, largely to prove her wrong. Although he was weary of his domineering mother, he still tended to do exactly as she told him to do. Until now.

"Don't tell her anything!" Carrie had ordered in her shrill, high-pitched voice when Arnold talked of telling Mrs. Remington what he had done. Arnold was feeling so guilty he could hardly think straight. Mrs. Remington's own son, Earl, had made him do something that now scared the living daylights out of him. His mother didn't think any good could come from his telling what he had done, and Arnold might have agreed with her had it not been for that call he received from Johnson, Remington's security chief.

Johnson called Arnold over to his office at the Remington headquarters to ask him a few questions about the note found on Mrs. Remington's car. How the hell does he know about this, Arnold wondered, then guessed Mrs. Remington must have talked to him about it. Although his palms were sweating and his heart was racing, Arnold had vehemently denied knowing anything. He might have continued doing so had Johnson not finally thrown out what Arnold clearly heard as a direct threat: "Believe me," Johnson told Arnold, "we're going to find the person responsible for this. And when we do, I guarantee you, this character will rot in hell before he ever sees the light of day again."

Frankly, Arnold was scared to death. He wondered if he may have been caught on a surveillance camera in that parking garage while he was placing the envelope under Mrs. Remington's windshield wiper. Worse, he wondered, would Earl, Jr. turn him in if anyone started getting too close to the truth? And if they tried to pin this thing on him, would anyone believe him, Arnold Taylor — a chauffeur, against the word of a Remington president? No, he couldn't take that chance. He had to 'fess up, even though he knew he was probably damned if he did and damned if he didn't.

I've got to tell Mrs. Remington, Arnold painfully acknowledged as he commiserated with himself. He came to this conclusion in spite of his mother's admonishment not to do so. He had been lucky enough to have worked for the Remingtons since he was just 17 years old. And now, everything he'd worked a lifetime for was in serious jeopardy. He hoped Mrs. Remington would understand and forgive him and let him carry on like before. While he knew this was a long shot, he felt he had no other choice. He just had to tell her.

Nervously, Arnold sat before Mrs. Remington now. She had a stoic expression on her face which unnerved him. He'd never been more frightened about anything in his life; even so, he had to give her the whole story. In a shaky voice, Arnold began by telling Mrs. Remington he didn't want to cause any trouble to anyone, least of all, Earl, Jr. At the mention of her son's name, Elizabeth looked surprised. Arnold noticed her look, though he wished he hadn't; then he swallowed hard and continued. He said he had something very important to say. Elizabeth Remington was getting impatient for Arnold to get on with it, and although she could plainly see how uncomfortable he was, she had no sympathy for his anxiousness. "Arnold," she said, "please get to the point. You mentioned my son's name. Now I'm very curious." Arnold took a deep breath and told her that when Earl approached him to get him involved in his scheme, he hadn't known what to do. Then Arnold realized he'd better start with some background, so he told Mrs. Remington that shortly after Mr. Remington died, knowing that the senior Earl sometimes confided in him, Earl, Jr. had pumped him for information. Particularly, Earl seemed desperate to know what his father had said about his becoming CEO of Remington.

Mrs. Remington had rarely ever had a real conversation with Arnold over the years, so she had no idea what to expect from him. She sat motionless and stared at him coolly while waiting to learn what had compelled him to come and talk to her. However, as she began to get the gist of Arnold's message, she knew she wasn't going to like this. Arnold said that he reluctantly told Earl, Jr. that his father had expressed some concerns about his maturity level and doubts about his ability to lead as a CEO. Mrs. Remington winced as Arnold told her this. She had not known what her husband felt about Earl, Jr.'s capabilities, as they did not discuss these things. And she was genuinely surprised to learn this now. But as unexpected as Arnold's words were, he sounded believable. She continued to listen.

Arnold said that Earl, Jr. had gotten very upset upon hearing this. He had cussed Helen Newman and the other Remington presidents, saying that no one but himself, the owner's son, had a right to the position of CEO. Then Earl, Jr. even cussed his father. Arnold said that as he watched Earl, Jr.'s reaction to this, he immediately realized he'd made a huge mistake to have told him all this. Maybe he should just have lied or told him he didn't know anything. What Arnold told Mrs. Remington next shocked her. He said that Earl, Jr. vowed to turn things around so he could gain approval and favor in the eyes of the CEO selection committee. He said it was then that Earl decided to cash in on the blackmailing. Then Arnold looked sheepishly at Mrs. Remington as if he'd just let a cat out of the bag and said questioningly, "I'm guessing you know Mr. Remington was being blackmailed."

Mrs. Remington did not react. She was surprised that Arnold knew about the blackmailing. But she was even more puzzled at how Earl, Jr. would have known about it. She remembered how her son had reacted in shock when she and Ross first told the others about it. "How could my son know about this?" she asked Arnold.

Arnold held his head down and meekly confessed, "I'm afraid I told him, ma'am." He quickly added an apology.

Mrs. Remington, herself, looked dismayed. She said, "Arnold, how did *you* know about it?"

"Well, you see, Mr. Remington, himself, told me," he said. "He told me about it because he needed me to deliver the money."

Mrs. Remington asked, "Arnold, if you knew about this, did you ever know who was blackmailing my husband? Did Mr. Remington ever tell you? What exactly do you know about this? What you know could be very important."

"That is everything I knew, Mrs. Remington. The bare essentials. I always took the money like I was told and dropped it off. Never saw anybody, and Mr. Remington never talked to me about it. I wish I had known who was behind it. I'd have rung that guy's neck."

Mrs. Remington looked appalled, then turned and gazed off in the distance as she thought about this. She said nothing. "Are you all right, Mrs. Remington?" Arnold asked.

After a moment, Elizabeth Remington said, "This isn't everything you came to tell me. What else is it, Arnold?" She looked him directly in the eye. This made him even more nervous and afraid, but he knew he had to finish what he'd started.

Here goes, he thought to himself, then said, "Now I know you're gonna kill me for this, Mrs. Remington, but Earl, Jr. had me put that envelope under the windshield wiper of your car that day you went downtown to your lawyer's office." At hearing of her son's involvement in that ordeal, Elizabeth felt that she'd been struck. Although stunned at hearing this, she listened with deathly stillness.

Arnold continued, "I thought it was a joke; I sure didn't suspect anything foul. Earl, Jr. told me this was just an innocent little thing. He said no harm would come to anyone. I didn't see as how I had a choice when he same as ordered me to do it. Of course, I didn't even know what was on the note, and I thought if I didn't do what he said, he'd probably see that I was fired."

"Arnold, do you realize what you are saying? You're telling me my son ordered you to put that threatening note on my car."

"Yes, ma'am. But like I said, I didn't know what was in that envelope. Honest, I didn't."

"Now exactly why would Earl, Jr. do such a thing?"

"Ma'am, that's just it. I don't know why for sure," Arnold answered. "But I think it had to do with him wanting to solve the blackmail thing."

This made no sense. Mrs. Remington was suddenly very suspicious of Arnold. She remembered Lynn Davis asking her if he could be trusted. She had answered yes with certainty. Now she wasn't so sure. This situation was planting disquieting seeds of doubt in her mind. Could Arnold have been the blackmailer, she wondered. Then she thought of his mother, and wondered if by chance he may have needed extra money for her care. Mrs. Remington was lost in thought for a moment, and at first, she didn't even remember what her question had been. She asked him, "Is anything going on with you? Is everything all right with your mother?"

By this line of questioning, Arnold was afraid Mrs. Remington probably didn't believe him. He said, "My mother is the same. Our nurse, Miss Ritter, takes real good care of her." Then he said, "I hope you believe me, Mrs. Remington, I didn't have nothing to do with this. I would never turn against you or your family. Mr.

Remington was real good to me. You have been, too, and I would never betray your trust. You gotta believe me. I didn't want to tell you about this at all, but it just seemed like I had to. That's why I've come to you with this now."

Arnold had his head down. He began to rub his moistening eyes. He was praying that Mrs. Remington wouldn't hold this against him. "I swear to you, that's the honest to God truth, ma'am," Arnold pleaded.

Mrs. Remington thought a while. In spite of Arnold's involvement in this hoax, he had several qualities she valued. Among them, loyalty, dependability, longevity, persistence. No matter what, even though he was quite an insecure little man, she knew she could always count on him. And she was certain he would never betray the Remington family. He wouldn't dare. He sat in front of her in trepidation, waiting for the other shoe to fall. Mrs. Remington spoke. "Arnold, I feel you are telling me the truth, and although I did not appreciate what you had to tell me, I like that you came to me with this. But I must tell you, I am truly troubled by it all, and I'm upset and disappointed in you for taking part in this thing. Of course, you had no way of knowing it was such a horrid note. However, where I am coming out right now is that you needn't worry about your job. You've been with us a long time, and you'll probably be around a lot longer. You need to know that the only person who can fire you is me, Arnold, and I don't choose to do that at this time. However, I won't hesitate to fire you if you give me reason. Is that clear?" Arnold nodded sheepishly. "I believe this conversation is over."

Whew! Arnold hoped he'd heard right. He was so relieved and grateful for Mrs. Remington's kindness and generosity, he almost could have dropped to his knees and kissed her feet. While it was true he'd had a few rough moments over the years since he'd worked for the Remingtons, this incident still posed the greatest threat he'd ever felt to his precious job. He had always been loyal to this family and the corporation. His loyalty had never been seriously questioned before, although it was true, he'd had a little explaining to do from time to time.

Once, Arnold was overheard bragging on the telephone to his

friend about some celebrities he had picked up from the airport. It was pretty cool. He even started naming some of the places he had taken his boss that day. Shortly afterwards, Arnold was reprimanded by the head of security. He was reminded that it was a serious breach of security to tell anyone where Mr. Remington went. Arnold understood the rules, but he had seen no harm in friendly conversation, especially since his friend lived all the way out of town. When Arnold was told that this could not be tolerated and any further breaches would be reported to Mr. Remington, he quickly jumped to attention, saying he would never do such a thing again. That reprimand and the threat to tell his boss had been a close call, but it was nothing compared to today when he had put everything on the line. After his conversation with Mrs. Remington, Arnold was so relieved to still have a job, he could have cried. Knowing he would eventually have to face Earl, Jr., he still felt a bit like crying. But for now, he'd survived the big one. Did he ever have a reason to rejoice.

Arnold could hardly contain himself as he walked out of the Remington house. He was so relieved he didn't know what to do. He wanted to stand at the highest mountaintop and shout "hallelujah" at the top of his lungs. That's just how happy he was that Mrs. Remington had understood. Oh, how he wanted to tell someone, anyone, about his good luck. Telling his mother was out of the question. She still never thought anything he did was worthwhile, so he'd receive no kudos from her. Besides, he'd gone against her advice, so that was that. Subject closed.

Actually Arnold knew of only one person who really understood him, who seemed genuinely interested in what he did and who would likely offer him any praise. His friend. He desperately wanted to talk to his friend right now, but unfortunately, the guy lived in another state and was always traveling. He'd told Arnold he'd just check in with him from time to time. Arnold never even got his phone number. Arnold's friend was actually a business acquaintance of the Remingtons who had once initiated a conversation with Arnold that developed into a friendship. Most people didn't pay much attention to Arnold, so having this person as a friend made him feel very important. He'd first met this guy several years ago, and in the last couple of years he'd seen him at Remington headquarters two or three times a year. He sometimes called Arnold just to keep in touch. Arnold would just have to wait until his bud phoned him again.

As luck would have it, Arnold got a call from his out-of-town friend that very afternoon. He figured he must have miraculously willed this guy to call, because he usually didn't call that frequently, and he'd just phoned a couple of weeks ago. They chatted a few minutes about what Arnold had been up to lately. Arnold was pleased this big shot guy thought enough of him to stay in touch the way he did. And, although Arnold remembered his stern scolding from Security some time back about talking too much, well, Remington was dead now. And what harm could it do to talk to someone about his job. After all, other people talked about their jobs, didn't they?

So Arnold laughingly told his friend about the hot water he had gotten himself into, laughingly adding that it was all he could do to stay out of trouble these days. Arnold was trying hard to sound like the mischievous little boy who lived in every man. The friend laughed and congratulated Arnold for his ingenuity in handling a sticky situation. Arnold felt smug. Kudos at last! He had his friend interested now and tried to think of more interesting things talk about. So he told him about the recent excitement at the headquarters building with the evacuation and everything, adding that luckily this turned out to be a prank. Then, wanting to sound in-the-know, he added that although Mr. Remington died several months ago, it was business as usual from where he sat. When his friend didn't respond, Arnold kept trying to think of more things to talk about. He mentioned that immediate family members were coming together soon for the reading of Mr. Remington's will, and that he still missed the old guy. Stuff like that.

Arnold thought it was so great talking to his friend because he was always so interested in what Arnold had to say. It made him feel pretty important. They chatted back and forth for a few more minutes. It wasn't all one-sided with Arnold doing the only talking. Arnold's friend told him some things, like about a fight that had broken out at the baseball game he had gone to the night before. In fact, he said he was lucky 'cause he'd almost been drawn into the fight himself. Arnold was so pleased to share such camaraderie with this guy. When their conversation was over, the friend promised to call him again soon. Arnold thought it would be nice if this guy lived in town where they might go around together once in a while. Since he had no real friends, he missed out on the male bonding that occurred among guys. He thought he'd ask his friend for his telephone number the next time they talked so he'd be able to call him sometimes, too.

* * * * *

Before phoning her son, Earl, Jr., Elizabeth called Lynn Davis to tell her about this new development. When Lynn picked up the phone, she told her, "I've got some very distressing information."

"What is it, Mrs. Remington?" Lynn asked, hoping there were new developments that would shed light on the mystery.

"Well, I just finished speaking to my driver. Of course, you know Arnold Taylor. I have to tell you, you were right to question his possible involvement in this."

Lynn was surprised. "Are you saying that Arnold had something to do with this? Did he put that note on your windshield?"

"I'm afraid he did," Mrs. Remington told Lynn. "But it's not what you think. Actually, it's much worse than that. You see, Arnold was only doing what he had been told to do." She paused momentarily, "By Earl."

Lynn thought for a moment that Mrs. Remington had misspoken, but something in her voice told Lynn she had heard right. She said, "Your son, Earl, Jr.? Why would he do that, Mrs. Remington? And how did you learn about this?"

"Arnold told me. We just finished talking. My son's action was intended to look like it was connected to the blackmailing. He apparently had some notions about solving it."

Questions were running through Lynn's mind. "This is quite a development," she said. "Did your son have prior knowledge about the blackmailing?"

"Yes, I'm afraid Arnold told him about it," Mrs. Remington answered. "You see, Arnold knew about it from my husband. In

197

fact, I've just learned that he's the one who delivered the blackmail money for Earl."

Hearing this, Lynn became hopeful that Arnold might know something about the blackmailer. She said, "Perhaps I can talk to him about this. He may be able to give us some information that could help us nail this character."

"I'm afraid Arnold was the delivery man, nothing more. I asked him what else he knew about the blackmailing, and he knew nothing else. He says he never saw anyone, nor did he have any idea who was behind it," Elizabeth said.

Disappointed that Arnold might not be helpful, Lynn then asked Elizabeth whether she thought her son, Earl, might have had anything to do with the blackmailing.

"Earl? Oh, no. I hardly think that," Elizabeth said, then continued, "This note thing was supposed to look like the work of the blackmailer. Heaven only knows why. Arnold suggests it may have something to do with his eagerness to become CEO. I'm about to get him over here right now and get to the bottom of this. For now I just wanted to let you know how that envelope got on my windshield."

"I understand," Lynn replied, feeling compelled to pose the next question before she hung up. "Mrs. Remington, I hate to ask this, but is it possible Earl may have had something to do with that package that was delivered to the Remington building earlier this week?"

Mrs. Remington said, "Dear God, that possibility had not occurred to me. I certainly hope he didn't, but now that you mention it, when we compared the two notes, the copy looked exactly the same. But Earl said he thought he knew who was behind that package."

Lynn said, "It will be interesting to see who he says is behind all this. You know we are still trying to determine if there's any connection between those notes and the two phone calls I've gotten from this person. It's hard to imagine Earl, Jr. having anything to do with those calls. But if it wasn't him, that means someone else is still out there up to something."

Mrs. Remington groaned and said, "Oh, my word. The very

idea that Earl could be involved in any of this is almost too much to think about. I must speak with him right away. I'll tell you what comes of this," she told Lynn before hanging up. Then Mrs. Remington asked her secretary to get Earl, Jr. on the phone.

These days, the Remington case consumed most of Lynn's time, while Ella picked up most client appointments. However, Lynn did see some clients and had one scheduled this very afternoon. Lynn looked at her clock. She and Mrs. Remington had talked longer than she'd anticipated. Thinking her next client was probably waiting in the outer office, she stepped to her doorway to apologize for running late and saw that Ella was already handling the case of a woman who wanted to locate a missing deadbeat ex-husband in order to collect child support payments. After Ella had finished, Lynn filled her in on Mrs. Remington's surprising phone call.

* * * * *

Earl, Jr.'s secretary announced that his mother was on the telephone. Mrs. Remington told Earl she needed to see him immediately. "I'll be there right away," he told her, while wondering, what is wrong with Mother? She sounded upset.

Earl had been daydreaming about giving his acceptance speech. Daily, he thought about being appointed CEO of Remington Corporation; he'd have done almost anything for the chance. From the time he was a small child, he had fantasized about following in his father's giant footsteps. He had truly felt that one day he would step in behind Earl Q. Remington, Sr., proud founder of this great corporation. Now that day was close at hand. And Earl was worried.

Since that awful day when he learned from Arnold how his father felt about his ability to be CEO, he had been stuck in a blue funk. His colleagues and family felt he was still going through the grieving process over his father's death. That, too, but in reality, he was grieving the possibility that he might not get the CEO job. During this period, the usually sedate young man experienced a gamut of emotions ranging from intense rage to extreme sadness.

At times, he would be especially angry toward his father. "I've worked my butt off for this company! Why would you think I'm not ready, Father?" he would exclaim as he faced the gilded-framed portrait of his father hanging behind the desk in his office. "How could you possibly say these things about me? I've done everything I could to prove I'm ready to take your office as CEO. I'm your son, for Christ's sake. Doesn't that mean anything at all? Would you want to see someone who's not a Remington sit at the helm of our company? I've always tried hard to live up to your expectations. I've tried to emulate you in almost every way I could. What more could I have possibly done to show you? The CEO position is mine! That position is mine, Father!"

And on and on, a tormented Earl would rant until one day he came up with a brilliant idea. He would simply manufacture a huge problem, one that no one else would be smart enough to solve — a scare tactic from the blackmailer and a bomb threat at headquarters. Then he, Earl Remington, Jr., would solve it. Mother will be impressed with my part in identifying the blackmailer. She's on the board and can influence the committee. Besides, the Search Committee will be so impressed with my quick thinking and leadership in fingering the culprit responsible, they'll realize I'm definitely the right person for the position, he had thought.

"Thank goodness for Jake Huber," he had said to himself. "The old guy fell right into my plan, and it should have worked, too." Earl had kept a record of his calls, and when he came up with his idea, he was suddenly glad Huber had called so often. If nothing else, it showed the Board this guy was off his rocker. Earl believed Jake Huber was a real nut case to think he could take Remington for a million dollars, and he was very possibly a thieving blackmailer. He thought that if he could get rid of Huber, it would look very good for him. No one else seemed to know what to do about that pest. I'll handle him, Earl had schemed. He had intended to point the finger at Jake Huber for both the evacuation situation at headquarters and for placing that threatening message on his mother's automobile.

But after the meeting with Detective Martin from the Police Department, Security Chief Johnson and Huber earlier today, Earl feared his plan was foiled. "Damn it! This isn't happening like I planned!" he had fumed, frustrated that the Huber investigation hadn't proven more conclusive. Earl had been so sure the investigators would find Huber to be behind this recent action. But Johnson and Martin hadn't been convinced, especially after the old guy denied the allegations so strongly, then provided those cozy little alibis for his whereabouts on Tuesday afternoon.

I'll have to come up with something else, he told himself. Earl, Jr. asked Brynn to put away the files on his desk, and he headed out to his mother's house.

CHAPTER

19

E<small>ARL</small> ARRIVED AT his mother's house 30 minutes after he received her urgent phone call. "Mother, is everything all right? Has something happened?" The two sat down in the study and Elizabeth Remington gave her son a firm gaze and began telling him what she knew. With her first words, Earl, Jr.'s world shattered instantly. He was visibly shaken by the realization that his mother knew everything. He felt exposed and angry. That damned Arnold blabbed on me, he thought.

"Why, Earl? Tell me. Aren't we going through enough already?" Elizabeth so needed to understand this. Earl tried not to let it show, but while she spoke, he was getting more and more furious at Arnold for telling her. Man, was he going to get that little guy.

As if Mrs. Remington could tell what was going through his head, she added, "And Earl, you will do nothing to get back at Arnold. It was out of loyalty that he came to me. I value that. In fact, you could take lessons from him about loyalty."

That remark stung and insulted Earl, for he did truly not want his mother to think badly of him. But he quietly said, "Of course, Mother, I understand why Arnold would tell you," although he really did not understand. Why couldn't the guy have just kept his mouth shut? Earl continued, "This is all a big mix-up. I had my reasons, and I'm so sorry you had to find out about it. But it's nothing serious, really. Please don't bother yourself with it, Mother."

"Why, of course, it's serious, Earl," his mother's voice was steady, but she was alarmed that her son did not seem to understand this. He sounded so cavalier and callous about it. "That note of yours nearly gave me a heart attack. What on earth would make you do such a thing? What did you possibly expect to accomplish?"

Earl agitatedly responded to her barrage of questions. "Well, Mother, you know I wouldn't want to cause you a heart attack. I surely wouldn't want anything to happen to you. But I'm afraid I didn't consider what effect the note would have on you. So for that, I was being irresponsible and thoughtless and I'm sorry. I truly am. But, Mother, I did have a very good reason for what I did. I think you'll agree with me." Elizabeth could not imagine her son sounding so blasé. He seemed completely comfortable with what he had done. He even expected she'd agree with him! Who was this person sitting across from her?

"Earl, before we go any further, answer this. Did you also have anything to do with that package and note sent to the office on Tuesday — the one that turned into the bomb scare?" Elizabeth looked her son straight in the eye as she queried him.

As shocked as Elizabeth was to learn that Earl, Jr. had been responsible for the note on her windshield, she was absolutely mortified when he admitted that he had also cooked up the bomb scare, too. With this plan, he explained, he could kill two birds with one stone. First, it would get that guy, Jake Huber, out of their hair once and for all. But more importantly, his fast action at helping to point the finger at Huber would make him look good in the eyes of the search committee. "They'll have to be pleased with how I took care of that situation," he said naively.

Earl, Jr. sounded clearly proud of himself as he reminded his mother that Huber was the man who had been trying to extract a million dollars from their company. In a manner suggesting this was all too intuitively obvious, he told her that by solving the case, it would show the CEO selection committee that he knew how to handle even the toughest situations. This, plus no more harassing phone calls from Jake Huber. It was as simple as that. Earl, Jr. wondered why his mother couldn't see how he only did what he had to do. Surely she knew what his father had thought of his chances of becoming the next Remington CEO.

Elizabeth Remington had always been so proud of Earl, Jr. But now, she was completely dismayed at this foolish plan he had come up with and executed. Worse than that, it disturbed her greatly that he was willing to blame his actions on another. This was a major transgression in her eyesight, and her son would have to accept full responsibility for what he had done. She vaguely remembered this Jake Huber. Years before, her husband had talked excitedly about a shopping development project. She was sure it was Huber he had worked this project with. She even remembered her husband saying this guy, Huber, was a genius. She never knew exactly how Earl had come to acquire Huber's land, but she remembered he'd proudly mentioned more than once that he now owned it.

It was inexplicable how Earl, Jr. showed no sense of right or wrong as he explained his plan to her. "After all, Mother, how would you feel if some total stranger were sitting in Father's office?" he asked, as if she should naturally understand why he *had* to do what he did. At that precise moment, Elizabeth felt that Earl, himself, was the stranger. This was not the son she'd reared — the one who'd always shown such a strong sense of family pride and fair play. The young man sitting in front of her lacked character. It did not matter to her if Earl was CEO of Remington. What meant more to her was that Earl was a man of principle who knew right from wrong. Something had to be done about this, and it occurred to her that he must make amends. So much to Earl's dismay, his mother told him he would have to admit responsibility to the security chief at Remington.

"What!" Earl almost shouted. "Mother, you can't be serious. How am I going to march in there and tell Johnson I had anything to do with those things? It would blow every chance I had at being CEO. In fact, if my name wasn't Earl Remington, I'd probably be lucky to have a job at all if I admitted to doing something like that." Earl was completely flabbergasted that his own mother would suggest such a thing. He said, "There must be something else we can do."

"I don't know of a better way, Earl. You have to atone for your actions," his mother said. Being far more interested in her son's moral fiber than his title, she was not compromising her position on this.

"So you really expect me to do this," Earl asked as his mother gave him a resolute look. Before she could say more, Earl said, "Well, Mother, if I must go through with this, then I have an idea." He had come up with a possible approach — the truth. It might work, he thought. "I can just tell them, yes, I did it. But I did it because I felt that would be a way of getting that pest, Jake Huber, off our backs. Everyone knows he has been a real thorn in our sides and a first-class nuisance these past several weeks. Did I tell you, Mother, he also threatened that he had something on Father. I don't know what he was talking about, the jerk. But for all I know, he *could* have been the blackmailer. As I understand it, Father never knew who was blackmailing him. You notice, don't you, that we haven't heard anything from the blackmailer lately. I think we scared him off, but good."

Not convinced, Elizabeth gazed at her son and said, "Earl, you are simply going to have to own up to what you did." She continued, "However, if you explain why you did this, perhaps the committee will see your actions merely as poor judgment, which indeed it was. They may feel that you were obviously misguided, though maybe well intentioned." Then she added, "I'm concerned about you, son. I had no idea you were so anxious about moving into your father's position." Earl was relieved that his mother was about to acquiesce from her hard line. After all, he really did not want to own up to anything and was hoping she would change her position.

Before he could think of what to say next, Elizabeth added, much to his chagrin, "However, you're going to have to clear Jake Huber's name. You can cannot go around accusing an innocent person, essentially damaging his reputation just to serve yourself." As she talked, the entire picture was coming together in her mind, and she suddenly remembered the two phone calls that were made to Lynn Davis' office. Elizabeth asked her son if he had made those calls.

Of course, Earl, Jr. knew about the phone calls because his mother had discussed them previously. In fact, the reason he had hired a woman to deliver the package to their headquarters was so they would draw a logical connection between her and the female voice behind the phone calls. However, did he make the calls? "Mother, of course not!" he exclaimed indignantly, genuinely insulted that she would even ask such a thing. "I don't know who made those calls, but I can tell you I most certainly did not!" It was now dawning on him for the first time that this situation was much more serious than he had been treating it. Someone out there, heaven only knew whom, was still out to extort money from their family. Although he wanted to believe Huber was the one, deep down, he no longer felt he was.

Elizabeth was relieved and grateful her son hadn't gone so far as to have made those phone calls. But no sooner had she breathed a sigh of relief, agony set in. Then who, she wondered. There were no answers. Also, something else was occurring to her. She would have to try to learn more about how her husband acquired Jake Huber's land. Surely there was something in the records. If Huber was indeed telling the truth about all this, she would have to recommend to the Board that he be compensated as her husband may very well have intended.

* * * * *

After Earl left her home, Elizabeth was at a loss and felt like a good stiff drink right then. Over the years, she had come to rely on the therapeutic benefits of alcohol, particularly in times of distress. Searching for just the right tonic to supplement her coping skills, Elizabeth settled for brandy. Courvoisier had been her drink of choice for many years.

For months, during her husband's illness and subsequent death, she had put forth a brave face, concealing the torment his confession and deathbed wish had caused her. However, this meeting with Earl, Jr. was the last straw. Her facade was crumbling. Seeking solitude, she went into her bedroom where the private atmosphere provided the perfect setting to languish. From her bedroom bar, she fixed a drink. Then she lit a cigarette to help herself think. She was tired and upset. The drink helped. She took a long, slow draw of her cigarette and paced the floor.

What she had learned about Earl's involvement in the hoax was so troubling, it nearly impaired her. She felt a sense of betrayal and found little comfort in her son's admission of his actions. How had it come to this? After several minutes, her brandy was doing little to allay her despair, and for an uncharacteristic moment, Elizabeth indulged in the relief of self-pity. What had gone wrong?

Of all her children, Earl, Jr. was the last person in the world she'd have thought would do such a thing. She knew he had always tried so to be like his father. However, the more he tried, the less he seemed to meet with Earl, Sr.'s approval which he so earnestly sought. Although these thoughts of remorse did not assuage her anger over what he had done, she was torn, for she also pitied her son at this moment. "My child is in trouble. He needs help," she thought, while making a mental note to talk with her therapist about this. She decided to recommend that Earl talk with his therapist about this as well.

Elizabeth sipped her drink and took another warm, welcoming puff of her cigarette. As she slowly exhaled, she thought of her other children and started to question how good a mother she had really been. Certainly Parker had turned out fine. However, Parker was such a serious young woman. She rarely laughed. Elizabeth wanted to see her daughter enjoy life more — be a little more like Jordan — well, perhaps not too much. The good thing was that Jordan would always have a zest for life. At times, Elizabeth thought she had a little more than her share. Maybe Jordan could stand to settle down more. Be just a touch like Parker.

Ross, she mused, had never placed much value on position or wealth. Elizabeth did not understand his values and drive; however, Ross was a decent, hard-working young man who would get through this life just fine. Of that she could be sure. But Earl? Now Earl was her crown jewel. Of all her children, he was closest to her, maybe because he was the most vulnerable, and although he hid it, the most sensitive of all her children. And now he had done this terrible thing. Why Earl, she wondered. Would you sell your soul to become CEO?

Elizabeth finished her drink and walked over to her bar where she poured herself another. She still looked to her alcohol to give her the strength she needed. Finally, she collected her wits and phoned Lynn Davis to inform her of what she had learned about her son's involvement in the recent scare tactics. After talking with Lynn, Elizabeth felt better. It suddenly occurred to her how assured and hopeful she felt whenever she spoke with her. It felt comforting knowing Lynn Davis was on the case, and a feeling swept over her that, in spite of all the turmoil of the moment, things were going to work out. Elizabeth Remington was beginning to genuinely appreciate Lynn Davis.

* * * * *

The Search Committee scheduled a meeting with Earl, Jr. the following morning at nine o'clock. This was to be one of several interviews each of the presidents under consideration for the CEO position would undergo. As the meeting got underway, Earl found the questions in this interview to be essentially elementary, like talk about your major accomplishments here at Remington. What is your vision for this company? Where do you see Remington Corporation in five years? Ten years? How will you lead the Remington Corporation forward in this millennium? Why do you want to be CEO?

Earl answered these questions and others like them with ease and confidence. He'd prepared for them often enough, for heaven's sake. But the question he could not have been prepared for came next. *Now tell us, please, about your involvement with that package.* Oh, no! Earl could hear the question echoing in his ear. He wanted to play dumb and ask what package. He wanted to ask how they knew about his involvement. Instead, he was compelled to answer. Besides, he knew right away how they found out.

Earlier that morning, at his mother's behest, Earl had gone to see Johnson in Security. Johnson was in his mid-50s. He'd worked for the Remington Corporation for over 30 years. As much as Earl dreaded doing so, he explained to Johnson that he had falsely accused Jake Huber. But he explained his actions in a manner designed to exonerate himself of any wrong doing. He did say he had placed the note in the box, but he just couldn't admit to everything, like his staging this whole thing. After all, those details aren't really necessary and the note he admitted to was incriminating enough. Earl, Jr. asked Johnson to consider the matter closed and told him he would deal with Huber's land issue separately. He said the two issues — Huber's land claim and the fake bomb — were not connected, unlike what he had led them to believe. Although these admissions were painful, he feigned nonchalance, pretending that this was no big thing, really. Just a simple misunderstanding was all.

Johnson, who had never particularly liked Earl, Sr.'s arrogant, know-it-all son, was almost gloating. Over the years, the son had flaunted his authority and treated lower-level people, Johnson included, like dirt, addressing them with an offensive air and a superior attitude. Of course, Johnson read between the lines of Earl, Jr.'s story, so he didn't buy that pure and innocent theory for a minute. And Johnson had no intention of letting him off the hook that easily. Where'd he get off trying to blame some poor innocent man for his doings? Although Johnson had also found Jake Huber a bit off-center himself, Huber still didn't deserve to be framed, and he did not appreciate that this young executive sitting before him had willfully accused someone of something he did himself.

Johnson told Earl, Jr. he would have to write up a report of this issue for review by the board president. Drats! Earl thought. Why can't it just be closed here? In actuality, it could have been, but Johnson had the authority to decide what was to be sent forward, and he had already decided this matter would definitely be sent forth. In fact, he would make it the first thing he did this morning. Now, Johnson knew young Earl was going after the CEO position and he wasn't trying to knock him out of his chance for the gold. He just wanted to bring him down a notch or two. Build character. Make him stronger. What the hell, Johnson said to himself, laughing at the fact that he was not about to consider the matter closed, I guess I'm not willing to give the guy a break. So sue me.

After Earl Jr. left his office that morning, Johnson typed the summary in record time and had it hand-delivered. Chairman of the Board, E. Franklin Daniels, called Johnson and they discussed this little situation in more detail; then he notified the head of the Search Committee, James Reiner. The two Board members agreed this situation may not necessarily mean the end of Earl, Jr.'s chances for the CEO position, but it certainly gave them cause to be concerned about the young man's judgment, and they would definitely raise it with him. Hence, the question before Earl now: *Tell us about that package.* Reiner wanted to see how young Earl would handle the question. Earl could not believe how Security Chief Johnson had wasted no time getting his report over to the Board.

With all the sincerity, maturity and well-meaning innocence he could muster, Earl sounded relaxed as he offered the committee an answer that seemed convincing. He told them how he genuinely had the best interests of the company at heart. Based on his many recent conversations with Jake Huber in which Huber badgered him for recompense in land or money for what he claimed his father had promised him and his veiled threat about something clandestine, Earl said he was convinced that Huber was going to try something desperate. He just wanted to scare him off, to stop him before it happened.

He suggested that Huber could easily be the type of person who would storm into their office building one day waving a gun around and shooting up any and everyone he saw. Earl, Jr. was only trying to put him out of commission before anybody got hurt. And he was trying to save the company a great deal of money negotiating over some verbal agreement his father was alleged to have made. By now, Earl was sounding so convincing he almost believed his story himself. So he waxed on about why he was only doing what he thought was best for the company and all.

Mr. Reiner concluded the meeting by telling Earl, Jr. there would be more scheduled interviews. Earl breathed a sigh of relief as he walked out the door. Under his breath, he uttered a simple wish, "I sincerely hope you guys believed that."

"MISS BERTHA WATERS just called," Ella said to Lynn. "Got time to talk?" Ella and Lynn usually got together a few times a week to review cases and talk strategies. Other than to catch each other on the run, they'd not had the chance to do so this week. It was mid-morning, and it just happened to be a good time for Lynn who had come in early to prepare for a client. The first thing Lynn had noticed coming into the building was that old Mr. Thompson was not in the parking lot. When she inquired where he was, she was told he'd had a heart attack. This unexpected news was upsetting to Lynn, for he was such a dear person. When she got to her office, she ordered flowers and a card. Mr. Thompson was very well regarded throughout the building, and Lynn was certain her flowers would just be one bouquet among the many niceties he was sure to receive. Over tea Ella told Lynn, "After you told me about Arnold's admission to Mrs. Remington yesterday, I think I understand now why he was acting so strange that day."

"Oh, how so?" Lynn asked taking a sip of herbal tea.

"Well, when Mrs. Remington went into your office to talk about that note she'd found on her windshield, Arnold was not here yet. When he showed up after getting the brakes checked out, he sat out here as usual." Lynn nodded, remembering that episode all too well, and Ella continued. "You know, that guy usually sits back, reads, has a cup of coffee, and says nothing, you know, totally into himself. But that day, he was definitely different. He seemed real nervous, and he kept looking toward your door. It's like he was trying to hear what was going on in your office. I bet if Janet and I had stepped away for a minute, he'd have put his ear to your door. He seemed just that eager."

"Oh, really. Well, now we know why. He had just planted that note on his boss' windshield," Lynn said.

"He may have been wondering if somehow she knew it was him. You know, Arnold makes a good suspect," Ella said laughing. He'd better stay away from poker. If that guy ever did anything wrong, he'd probably give it away with his body language alone."

"We'll have to remember that about him," Lynn said.

Then Ella told Lynn that Miss Bertha said she and her sister had tried in vain to reach Jeremiah. The day after they left him a message, he called to say that he was spending a few days in Atlantic City with his lady friend whose name is Angel. But Miss Bertha and Miss Lela had been outside puttering around in their garden when the call came, so they hadn't heard the phone ringing. And Jelly didn't leave a phone number, nor did he say when he was returning to North Carolina. They said they'd keep trying to reach him.

Miss Bertha also told her she'd found a picture of Hattie Rose and Mr. Remington, her man friend. But neither she nor her sister thought it was one of the pictures Ella had shown them. Miss Bertha told Ella she could come by and see the picture for herself if she wanted to. "And, by the way," Ella added, "Miss Bertha said she and her sister were wondering if we'd found out anything about that blackmailer yet. She still seemed uneasy."

"I can certainly understand that," Lynn said, "especially if Jeremiah did take those photographs, and they matched the blackmailer's. Then I'm afraid our Mr. Brownlee would have some pretty serious explaining to do." Lynn poured herself and Ella a refill and sat back in her chair, thinking.

Ella said, "You know, it would make this case real easy if we learned that it was Jeremiah Brownlee. Then all we'd have to do would be to fill in some missing pieces and it would be case closed," she said, snapping her fingers. "But, you know, as much as I want this case resolved, I really hope it isn't him. Those two little ladies don't deserve anything like that. Boy, would it be hard on them."

"I know how you feel," Lynn said. "That would be too bad. But I'll tell you, it certainly doesn't look good so far. I know it's all circumstantial, but look — this man was in love with Hattie, and he apparently hated her being with this rich white guy. Plus, this extra money shows up in his retirement fund, and now he's up in Atlantic City. And it's possible, unless we learn otherwise, that he has Miss Bertha's pictures. Of course if he does, the chances of our ever seeing them are practically nil. We would have to watch him very closely to tie him to anything.

"However, Ella," Lynn continued, "my uncle still doesn't think the guy he knew from school would do such a thing. Uncle Ed gets these hunches, and he's pretty strong about this one. So I don't know. We have to keep checking it out because someone is still making these phone calls to me. And I do believe these calls are connected to the blackmailer."

"I agree, but why on earth would a blackmailer be calling you? You don't have any money, do you, partner?" Ella smiled, then said, "Well, at least not blackmail kind of money?"

They both laughed and Lynn said, "You got that right, Ella. But who knows, maybe some day ..."

After discussing a few more cases, the two returned to their work, and just as Lynn was preparing to phone Donald, Erica Harrington called her from Minneapolis. "Hello, Erica. What's going on? You'll still be here next week, won't you?" Lynn asked her.

"Yes, I'll be there. Wild horses couldn't keep me away. In fact, I was planning to get into town Tuesday morning, but now I'll have to stop by Columbus to drop Timmy off at Mom and Dad's, so I won't get to come to Cincinnati until Wednesday morning," Erica explained.

"Oh, I'd suggest you not cut it that close if you can help it. You never know what could tie you up, and it's imperative that you be here. Anyway, I thought you were going to leave your son with his father again," Lynn said in a concerned voice.

"Oh, no," Erica answered. "Absolutely not. Actually, Thomas told me he has to be out of town. I have no one else here to leave Timmy with, so I have to bring him with me to Ohio."

"I see. Still, it will be best if you can get in Tuesday. You know the reading is at eleven o'clock the next morning. I'd hate for you to have to rush around Wednesday morning to get here," Lynn told her.

"Thanks, Miss Davis, but I don't really have much choice. My parents have an important commitment Tuesday evening. My dad is being honored by the Rotary Club at their annual dinner. It's real special, and I don't want to ask them to change their plans for me. They don't have anyone who could sit with Timmy on such short notice, so that's why I'll have to leave Columbus Wednesday morning. I'll be driving down," she said, "because I couldn't get a convenient flight. But it's only a hundred miles or so, and I'll be sure to leave good and early. I'll be there in time all right. I wouldn't let anything keep me away from Cincinnati next Wednesday. Now Perry will be getting in early Tuesday, and we're both staying at the same hotel as before."

Lynn suddenly had an idea. "Look, Erica," she said, "how would you like to bring Timmy to Cincinnati? My mother's a schoolteacher, and she's out of school for the summer and is probably available. If you're interested, I'd be happy to ask her if she can keep Timmy. I know she wouldn't mind. She's wonderful with kids. How about it? He'd have a great time with Mom."

"What a kind thing to offer, Miss Davis," Erica said, having decided at once to accept. She had come to respect Lynn Davis very much, and even though she did not know Lynn's mother, she felt good about the offer. "It would sure solve my problems. I'd be able to arrive early Tuesday and have plenty of time to get ready. Oh, yes, that would be great. Would you mind asking her for me?" Lynn told her she would.

Then Erica said, "I'll tell you the truth, I don't know what's getting into Thomas. He has been so hateful lately. I really don't understand it. He's acting really mean. He's even threatening to take Timmy away from me."

"What?" Lynn said stunned.

"Well, I know he didn't mean it. He wouldn't want Timothy full-time anyway. But he's just being spiteful. He got pretty angry when I asked him to keep our son while I came back to Cincinnati."

Lynn was surprised to learn that Erica and Thomas did not have an amicable relationship, especially with their son in the picture. Lynn realized Erica probably needed someone to talk to. She had opened up to her rather quickly, and now she was confiding in her about Thomas. Lynn was happy to be a sounding board for Erica. They spoke a bit longer, and Lynn told Erica she would call her mother now and call her back to let her know what she said. She was glad to help her out in this arrangement, and she knew Rachel would be happy to have a small kid around the house.

Lynn called her mom, and as she expected, Rachel agreed to keep Timmy. Erica was delighted when Lynn phoned to give her the news. "I don't know your mother," she told Lynn, "but she must be pretty wonderful." Then she asked Lynn if she could call Rachel to introduce herself and thank her. Lynn gave Erica her mother's phone number and told her to let her know when she got into town next week so they could arrange to take Timmy over to her mother's house.

Then Erica asked, "By the way, have you received any more strange phone calls?"

Lynn said, "Thank goodness, no. But still, until we know who's doing this, we don't consider ourselves out of the woods."

After that phone call ended, she began dialing Donald's number just as Janet buzzed and told her he was on line two. She picked up the phone.

"Hi, baby," Donald said on the other end. "Are you all set for tonight?" Lynn and Donald had a Bar Association dinner that evening. Lynn wished she could get out of it, especially since she had an early appointment tomorrow morning and these dinners had a way of running on and on. But it was one of those non-optional events, so bowing out would have been out of the question.

Such is life, she thought, and told Donald she was all set. They agreed on a time, and Donald said he would see her later on.

* * * * *

That afternoon, Ella had a chance to go over to Miss Bertha's house. "Hello there, Miss Braxton. Hot enough for you today?" Miss Bertha asked as she sat on her front porch swing cooling herself with a fan in each hand.

"Hi, Miss Bertha, it's nice to see you again. Yes, ma'am, it is quite hot enough for me." Ella walked briskly up their sidewalk and stood at the foot of the steps to catch her breath. "Weatherman never said it was going to get up to 95 degrees today."

"He sure didn't. I believe they were talking about a little rain cooling things down this afternoon. Come on up here. We can go in the house and get outta this heat," Miss Bertha said as she rose from the swing and pulled open the screen door, beckoning Ella into her house. Inside, electric fans were blowing hot air all around. Fanning herself, Miss Bertha said, "Child, service man left here this morning to get a part for that air conditioner. Hasn't made it back yet. I'm telling you, no one ought to live like this." She offered Ella one of her fans.

Ella had settled down and was finding it fairly comfortable already, although she tried to imagine sleeping in a house this hot, and the thought was not pleasant. She said, "Well, I hope he gets back over here today. At least, it doesn't feel too bad right now."

"Would you ladies care for some lemonade?" Miss Lela asked as she walked in with a tray carrying three glasses of ice and a pitcher full of the most welcome-looking drink Ella had laid eyes on in a long time.

"Hello there, Miss Lela," Ella said with a warm smile, "Yes, thank you. I would love some." Then she took a glass and filled it to the top. Hmmm, she observed as she sipped the refreshing lemonade. Today the atmosphere is a lot different than it was during that second visit.

"I would like some, too, Lela," Miss Bertha said. The three women sat in the small, comfortable living room, and Miss Bertha told Ella, "I 'spect you're wanting to look at that picture we found, aren't you?"

Ella told her she did, and Miss Bertha reached for a tattered brown photo album that had an aged leather bookmark holding the right page. She opened the album and pointed to the picture. Ella sat her drink down on a coaster and reached over for the album, but Miss Bertha held on to it. So Ella got up and leaned over her shoulder to get a good look.

The small black and white picture was slightly out of focus, but Ella could tell it was Hattie Williams and Earl Remington. The picture was taken from a balcony. Ella compared it to her copy of the photograph showing the couple on a balcony. However, she saw that this picture was obviously taken from a different point. The Ohio River could not be seen. On the blackmailer's copy, it could. And the clothes they were wearing were different.

Ella concluded that this was not one of the blackmailer's pictures and told Miss Bertha so as she sat back down. Miss Bertha and Miss Lela looked relieved. All three women sipped on their cold drink. In Ella's mind, Jeremiah was becoming less of a candidate. She could not imagine Miss Bertha having two pictures of the same two people taken on a balcony. She asked the ladies if they had heard from Jeremiah yet.

They answered, no. "We don't know why that boy hasn't called back. I left him a second long-distance message," Miss Lela said, and added, half smiling, "I guess he's having such a good time with his lady friend, he can't stop what he's doing to call his momma."

Upon hearing the reference to long distance calling, it suddenly occurred to Ella that these two women were probably on a fixed income. Making those calls to Jeremiah may not have been in their budget. She took a ten-dollar bill from her purse and offered it to them saying, "May I pay you for those long distance calls?" Miss Bertha and Miss Lela both declined the money, saying they wouldn't hear of it. Ella decided to leave the money anyway, placing it on the end table next to where she sat her now empty glass. Then she asked the two elderly ladies to contact her if they learned anything else. She left their house, hoping it would be concluded that Jeremiah was innocent.

* * * * *

217

Jeremiah Brownlee was almost 60, and his girlfriend, Angel, only 36. And Angel was the closest thing to Hattie Rose he had ever come across. When he asked his deceased wife, Juanita, to marry him, he hadn't wanted anyone in his life who reminded him of his Hattie — the woman he could not have. Juanita had been an altogether different kind of woman. When they first married, she was tall and thin, but when she died at the age of 54, she had put on quite a few pounds and could be described as stout. She was a no-nonsense, serious kind of woman, and she and Jeremiah got along just fine. Because of a hysterectomy Juanita had when she was in her 30s, the two never had any children.

He was pretty torn up when she died, and it took him a while to recover, but even so, it was nothing like the years he spent mourning Hattie Rose. In fact, he was sure that memories of Hattie would plague him until he died. Now with Angel in his life, he thought he had finally gotten over her.

Jeremiah wanted to show Angel a good time, so he had taken her to New Jersey for a few days. They had spent the prior evening at a Cabaret show at a swanky hotel in Atlantic City. Now he sat in the casino and watched as his little Angel shrieked in excitement whenever she won at the Blackjack table. As he watched her gamble, he suddenly remembered that his mother had left a message for him on his home phone in North Carolina. He told himself he'd have to call her when he went back to his room. For now, he watched his woman having fun and thought of how lucky he was to have such a gorgeous lady in his life.

Jeremiah was now retired and living the life of leisure. He was tall and still slender, had light brown skin, hazel-colored eyes, and freckles dotted his face. His curly reddish hair had become sprinkled with white, so for a more youthful appearance he dyed it and came out with a fake-looking dark reddish-brown color. Angel gently hinted that he might let a professional salon color his hair, but Jeremiah thought he did a pretty good job himself. Colored that gray. Overall, Jeremiah wasn't bad to look at, and with his nice brick home in North Carolina and an El Dorado Cadillac to drive, there were any number of women who considered Mr. Brownlee a pretty attractive package.

When he first started seeing other women well after Juanita died, he just wanted companionship. It was never anything serious. But Angel was different from the others. He smiled to himself as he watched her and remembered how he had nearly fainted when he first spotted her walking through a shopping mall. She was the vision of Hattie Rose Williams. This young woman looked like Hattie Rose, walked like her, and just like Hattie Rose, she had this nice curvy figure that swayed when she walked. But she also had an air of sweetness and confidence about herself that reminded him so much of his lost love. She had passed Jeremiah in the mall and smiled. He was thrilled at her attention and took it to mean he was special until he turned back to watch her and saw that she gave that same greeting to others she approached. Even still, he was warmed. For the longest time, Angel was completely disinterested in him as anything more than a friend. It had taken a long time and a lot of work on his part to get her to think about him as more than just a friend. He had pulled out every old trick and used every line he knew, until finally she relented.

Angel Clark worked as a saleswoman at a department store and had two teenage daughters. She was divorced from her children's father and received no help from him for the care of their children. She was proud to be able to rear her children by herself. When she first met Jeremiah, she had just ended a long-term relationship and wasn't seeking another love interest. At the time, she was only 33.

At first, Jeremiah was just like a family friend. This was sort of how it had been with him and Hattie, too. He'd enjoyed being Angel's confidante as she discussed her life, her kids and her troubles with him. Sometimes he and Angel would talk on the telephone, but sometimes they would communicate by dropping each other a few lines in the mail every now and then. Actually, it was Jeremiah who did most of the writing, but Angel occasionally sent him a greeting card. In any event, he was finally successful at winning her over, and for the past two years he'd been on a fast roller coaster ride with her. She was one of the most exciting and beautiful women he had seen in a long time.

At first, Jeremiah thought Angel was everything Hattie would have been, but Angel turned out to be nothing like the real Hattie. She had a wild side, and at times was a bit impulsive. Indeed, his Angel was costing him a small fortune. Time and time again, she found herself in financial trouble, and time and time again, Jeremiah came to her rescue. But he held on to her, because as long as he had Angel, although it was cheating a little bit, he felt like he had Hattie Rose in his life. And as long as Angel had Jeremiah, she knew she had a sweet older man who would do most anything for her. So this relationship worked well for the both of them.

He wasn't sure what his mother wanted when she called. The message just said to call her, but when he remembered to call her the next day, no one answered the phone. He tucked it away in his mind and told himself he'd call her again when he got a chance. But it was hard to get that chance, because up there in Atlantic City, Angel was acting like a kid in a candy store. She loved Roulette and Blackjack, and quickly advanced from the one-dollar to the five-dollar slot machines. And she lost tons of money.

Jeremiah tried to show Angel other ways to have a good time besides just throwing money around. He obtained some great show tickets to see James Brown and Etta James. Angel went, but begged him to also take her to see Boys II Men and Destiny's Child. Who on earth were these people, he wondered, while watching these young singers perform songs he'd never heard of. Jeremiah took Angel to fine places to eat, but in spite of all his efforts, Angel still loved gambling more. She was costing him an arm and a leg, so not wanting to return home penniless, he finally decided they would head back down to North Carolina on Friday morning rather than stay through the weekend as he had planned. Jeremiah completely forgot to call his mother again.

When he and Angel arrived back in North Carolina, Jeremiah dropped her off at her place, stopped at his barbershop to get a haircut and chat with the guys, and then he went by the post office to pick up his mail. By the time he got home it was around four o'clock in the afternoon on Friday. He took his time unpacking and looking through his mail before he checked his answering machine to see if there were any messages. It dawned on him then that he still needed to call his mother. As he listened to his messages, there were two more from her. He would call her right away, just as soon as he made himself a cup of coffee.

He went into his bright, spacious kitchen and took a coffee mug from the cabinet, poured a spoonful of instant coffee in it and filled it with water. Then he placed the cup in the microwave oven. As his coffee boiled, Jeremiah swept up some grounds that had spilled on his black and white tile floor. Then he sat down at the chrome dinette set on one of his orange floral vinyl padded chairs, stretched the telephone cord over to the table, doctored up his coffee, and called his mother. This time she answered.

"Momma, this is Jelly. I got your messages. Is everything okay?"

"Jelly, boy. Where you been? How come you didn't call me back anyhow?" his mother scolded.

Now his curiosity was steeping. What in the world was wrong with his momma, he wondered, as he heard the agitation in her voice. "Now I called and told you I was in Atlantic City. Didn't you get my message? I called you back just the other day."

"Yes, you did, Jelly, but that was Tuesday when you called me. I can't figure why you didn't call me back again. I know you got my other long-distance messages, didn't you?"

"Not until I got home, Momma. Why don't you just tell me what's wrong. Ain't nothing the matter with Auntie Bertha, is it?"

"Naw, your Aunt Bertha's doing just fine. Listen, Jelly, now, I wanna ask you something. And I want you to answer me straight, you hear?" Miss Lela didn't wait for Jelly to answer. She continued, "Now you remember your Aunt Bertha had a bunch of old pictures of Hattie Rose Williams or Dodd, or whatever you want to call her, and her white man friend?"

"Yeah, sure, I remember," Jelly answered. "Now wait, Momma. Don't tell me that's what you been calling me about, 'cause those ain't nothing but some old pictures."

Miss Lela went right to the point. "Jelly," she asked, "did you take those pictures out of your Aunt Bertha's picture album?"

"Why you asking me 'bout them pictures, Momma? Yeah, I might have taken some pictures, but we're talking about a long time ago. What's wrong with that? Didn't nobody but me want those old pictures anyway."

Miss Lela asked Jeremiah how many pictures he had taken from their album, and he told her he didn't know for sure. It was probably four or five. But still Jeremiah couldn't figure what the big deal was. So his mother told him a woman from a private investigation office had come by to talk to them about Hattie Rose and those two children of hers. Miss Lela told him that when they went to show the woman some pictures, they couldn't find them. There was that one picture of Hattie and this man standing by some big fancy black car, as well as other shots of him and Hattie. And they were all missing.

"Why was some private investigator coming to your house to ask about Hattie Rose and her kids? What's going on? Did something happen?"

Miss Lela said, "Well, you know that man, those kids' father, he died, and he must've left them some money or something in his will. So the woman was just trying to find out what she could."

Jeremiah was pretty shocked at this news. "Well, I'll be da …"

"You watch your mouth, Jelly," Miss Lela quickly cut him off.

"I'm sorry, Momma. So what is the big deal about those pictures? Why you and Auntie looking for them?"

" 'Cause somebody been blackmailing Mr. Remington," Miss Lela answered. "Apparently they was threatening to show some pictures to his wife. So Remington was paying the blackmailer. 'Course now like I said, he's dead," she added.

"Well, that's just too bad, Momma. But what's that got to do with me?" Jelly asked. "Is that all you been calling about?"

"Listen, son," Miss Lela interjected. "You don't need to go getting on your high horse about me asking you these questions. 'Cause if those pictures that woman showed us are the same ones we used to have, then they would probably figure you as the blackmailer, 'specially the way you were so crazy 'bout Hattie Rose for so long."

"Momma, I wanna tell you, and I'm telling you straight. I haven't had anything to do with no blackmailing. Now you gotta believe that. It's true, everyone knew I was crazy about Hattie

Rose. Would have done anything she asked me to do. But I'm not a criminal. If he wasn't dead already, somebody needs to be talking to that Remington guy. They need to ask him how Hattie died."

"Well, you don't need to be worrying about how Hattie died. And that man is dead, may they both rest in peace. And I hope to God you're telling the truth," Miss Lela said. " 'Cause I didn't raise no criminals around here. Now do you still have them pictures? 'Cause I want 'em back if you do."

Jeremiah answered reticently, "I don't know, Momma. They're probably round here somewhere. I haven't looked at them in a while," he answered, all the while knowing he really did not want to own up to cutting Hattie's white man friend right out of every one of those pictures with the sharpest scissors he could find.

"Well this is important, son," his mother said. "Now I want you to look for those pictures and send 'em on back to me. I need to know for myself that they ain't the same ones. You hear me?"

"Yeah, I hear you, Momma. Don't you worry. I'll look for them." Jelly was trying to figure out how to mend those pictures. "But tell me this," he said. "If there ain't no pictures, how are the police gonna be able to say I did any blackmailing? Way I figure, if that's all they got, they got nothing on me, 'cause you ain't got no pictures."

Miss Lela said, "I hear what you're saying, Jeremiah. But it don't make no never mind what you got to say about them pictures. I have already seen the blackmailing pictures. And now I want to see them pictures with my own eyes. 'Cause some of them blackmailing pictures put me in the mind of the ones come from our house."

"Okay, Momma. I'm gonna look for them, and when I find them, I'll tell you about it. And I'll send them to you, too. I'll do that.

"Now, look, Momma, I gotta say this. I try to tell you and Aunt Bertha 'bout letting strangers come up in your house. Y'all can't be letting any and everybody come inside your house all the time. And you shouldn't be showing nobody anything either. It ain't their business. I worry about y'all," Jeremiah told his mother, who assured him she and her sister knew what they were doing.

They talked for a few minutes more about his vacation. Miss Lela asked him about his girlfriend, Angel, and he asked about Aunt Bertha. When they hung up the telephone, Jelly poured out his coffee. It was getting cold anyway, and he poured himself a shot of bourbon. He thought he'd just sit for a while and think about all this.

Miss Lela talked things over with her sister who called Ella. "Well, we just talked to my nephew, Jelly, and he told his momma he thinks he might have taken some pictures from here. But it was so long ago, he says he don't know if he still has them or not. She told Jelly what you said. That somebody'd been blackmailing Hattie's man friend. So Jelly promised he would look for them and if he sends them back to me, we'll be sure to let you know."

Ella thanked Miss Bertha and passed the news on to Lynn. Lynn and Ella figured they were back to square one because they were pretty sure Jelly would never *find* any pictures that could possibly tie him to a blackmailing. Somehow, this wasn't altogether too disturbing to Lynn, because for some reason, she just did not feel that Jeremiah Tecumseh Brownlee was the blackmailer. What Lynn did know, however, was that something was up. She could just feel it.

CHAPTER
21

TUESDAY MORNING, THE day before the reading of the will, Earl sat in his office lamenting. After those crazy notes and that fake bomb fiasco of last week, he had come to grips with his folly and desperately wanted to get back in his mother's good graces. He didn't like it when the two of them were at odds with each other, and he wanted to set things straight between them. Besides, his mother had taken a seat on the Remington Board of Directors to fill a void created by his father's death, and now she had a vote on the CEO position. Mother has to think I've lost my mind. How can I ever make this up to her, and prove to her that my head is on straight now?

He knew his mother was trying to pull all six of his father's children together because his dad had made some crazy dying request that everyone become one big happy family. Ordinarily such an idea would have been totally ludicrous to Earl. But now, as he searched for ways to make up with his mother, he decided he could help her comply with his father's wishes.

An idea was stirring. What if he were to offer Erica and Perry Dodd or Harrington, whatever, a tour of Remington Corporation. Now that would be a real friendly gesture. His mother had mentioned that they'd be arriving in town today. This idea sounded like a winner. Not only that, Earl could take care of the arrangements himself. He'd send Arnold downtown to pick them up from their hotel and bring them over to Remington Headquarters. He could give them the flowery orientation presentation, show the Remington public relations video, and take them on a grand tour around the facility. If the need for introductions came up between Erica and Perry and people in his firm, he would decide later how to handle that. Earl, Jr. thought for sure his mother would be pleased at his very magnanimity.

Everyone was getting antsy about tomorrow's big event — the reading of the will — and Mrs. Remington thought Earl's plan was, indeed, a surprisingly gracious idea. Earl left word for Erica and Perry at their hotel. They, too, were surprised at the offer, but happy to have a welcoming gesture from a Remington and grateful for an activity that would help eat up their afternoon. They promptly called his office and arranged a time.

At two o'clock that afternoon, Arnold arrived at the hotel in the limousine to pick up Erica, Perry and Timothy. Arnold and his passengers exchanged brief introductions, and as soon as they were seated, Timmy cuddled up beside his mother and laid his head across her lap to resume his nap.

Inside the limousine, Erica and Perry separately found themselves experiencing strangely warm sensations of familiarity. Perry experienced an exhilarating moment of déjà vu. Somewhere in his mind was a picture of a big black car being driven by a man wearing a black cap. He had a faint recollection of sitting in the back seat and going who knows where. Was this the same kind of vehicle, the same driver?

Just as he sat admiring the fine detail of this elegant carriage, he was struck by the fact that this was probably the way Earl Q. Remington, *his* father, had traveled to work every day. Perry was genuinely impressed; it felt good to be a Remington. His father had to have been quite a remarkable man. But more specially, Perry felt that his mother, Hattie, must have been a very special woman to have been sought after by a man like Earl Remington.

For Erica, seeing Arnold and the limousine was reminiscent

of the photograph of her mother and father standing by the Rolls Royce. She remembered seeing a driver seated in the car in the picture. I wonder if this is the same person, she thought to herself excitedly, as she suddenly began to feel an extraordinary connection to her birth parents. She mused, I could be sitting in the exact same spot where my real father has sat. I wonder if my mother ever got to ride in the limousine. It might have been Erica's imagination, but she believed that every now and then, she actually picked up a faint whiff of her father's perfume, and she gently stroked the soft black leather of the seat with her hand as if she were touching his. She imagined she could feel his hand patting hers back.

Erica then realized that all this time, she had really not given any thought to Earl Remington as a person or a father. She had only dealt intellectually with the astonishing biological relationship that existed between them. It was now beginning to register that this man was, indeed, *her* father, and she suddenly ached for the chance to have known him. Somehow, catching a hint of his scent, she could sense his essence, almost feel his presence. It felt at once other-worldly, and she let herself be carried away in this feeling. *My father*. She smiled at that novel thought. Erica basked in this special moment and did not want it to end.

While she loved her adoptive father, she had gone a lifetime not knowing her complete identity. Now she knew who she was, and as Earl Remington's daughter, she felt very special. She also felt sadly envious of his other four children for having grown up with him. However, a small part of her wanted to lash out at him: Why did you leave us like you did, Father? Don't you know how much it ate at me and Perry to never know who you were? We were extremely lucky that Paul and Kitty Harrington took us into their hearts and made us a part of their family. Even so, Perry and I have always had a strong need to know. Erica could not hold her anger long, and in the next instant she felt elated by the sense of her father's love.

As Erica thought about her wonderful adoptive parents, she experienced a sudden surge of guilt for entertaining these loving, though mixed, emotions about her birth father. She quickly reasoned that she was doing nothing wrong, for she loved the Harringtons no less than before. Certainly, she had a right to be curious, even awed by her famous father, so she decided to let herself freely experience the love and gratitude she felt toward him, especially for bringing her and Perry into the picture, even if on his death bed. That had to mean he was thinking of them; perhaps he had thought of them often. And again, she felt a warm feeling toward him, although she ached to know why he had removed himself completely from their lives after their mother died.

After a while, Erica let herself wonder what her father had left her and Perry in his will. He was immensely wealthy. What if he left them money? She found it hard to picture herself as a wealthy woman, although it was a delightful and pleasant thought. He may have left other things, like books. Or what if he gives me jewelry my mother had owned, a friendship ring, a pendant, or a broach perhaps? The thought of receiving things her mother had owned pleased her. The air conditioner had chilled the car, but Erica felt cozy and comforted by her thoughts.

Suddenly, Perry broke her train of thought. "This is great, isn't it, sis? I mean, I can feel it. Don't you? Feels kind of like he is sitting right here in this limousine with us." Erica nodded and smiled, knowing she and her brother were sharing a similar wave length. However, she really didn't want to speak just yet, for she was still relishing the moment privately and did not want Perry to interrupt her now. But he continued, "I'm just trying to take it all in. This is kind of crazy. You know, I think I remember that driver. When we stop, I want to ask him how long he's worked for Mr. Remington, I mean, our father. Man, it sounds strange saying that — *our father*."

For a while, Erica and Perry rode along in silence. Then Perry interrupted his sister's thoughts again, "I think that was real decent of Earl to invite us to tour the Remington Corporation. Frankly, I'm looking forward to it. Aren't you?" he asked his sister.

"Yes, I am." By speaking aloud, Erica realized her magical moment was broken. Stay with me, she thought to herself, but to Perry, she added, "I didn't think he was that friendly when we first met him, but this is definitely a thoughtful gesture. It will be fascinating to see the company that was built by Earl Remington." Erica realized she had no idea what to expect. Her picture of corporate life was a bland, stark office building with people in conservative dark suits carrying briefcases and scurrying around like busy bees.

* * * * *

As he drove along, Arnold took quick glances toward the back seat of the limousine through his rear view mirror. Although Earl, Jr. had directed him to pick these three people up, he had not disclosed to Arnold who they were. Arnold thought smugly, young Earl obviously doesn't realize I knew pretty much everything that went on. For sure, I knew exactly who these people were, except the little tyke, of course. Then he tried to picture Erica and Perry as the little children he had taken here and there over 20 years ago.

He was surprised at the striking resemblance the young man, Perry, had to his father. Even to Ross. This kid was tall and lanky, with similar facial features, and he stood very erect, just like his father did. And Arnold was most taken aback by Erica. Other than having a fairer complexion, when he looked at her, he could have been looking at her mother.

Arnold remembered Hattie Rose. Although she was black, she was one of the most beautiful women he'd ever seen. She could probably have taken her pick of any man. No wonder Mr. Remington fell for her. When he glanced back at Erica, he once again saw Hattie, the woman her boss had been mad about. Hattie was always so radiant and dazzling. She had a beautiful smile — laugh, really. And she laughed easily and often, revealing beautiful white teeth. Hattie had been very friendly to Arnold. He appreciated that. Because most of the other women Mr. Remington took around were real snobs. Other than that perky and friendly little Mikki woman who worked for the airline, most of the others were like cold fish.

Arnold had always been pretty amazed that Mr. Remington's kids didn't look like they were black when they were younger. He still was, and he wondered about that. It seemed that the offspring of a white-skinned person and a black-skinned person would be someone in-between, not someone who looked white as snow. Beats the hell outta me how that works, he thought to himself.

Along the way, Arnold pointed out a few landmarks, such as the world-famous Baldwin Piano headquarters and a few other notable structures as he drove north on Interstate 71 to Montgomery Road. Erica and Perry appreciated his attempt at being friendly and nice. Meanwhile, little Timothy remained asleep on his mother's lap during the ride to Remington headquarters which took less than 20 minutes overall.

Arnold pulled off the interstate, and after a couple of blocks into the parking lot of Remington headquarters. He said, "Well, here we are." Erica woke her son. Arnold parked in the executive parking area in a reserved space beside two other drivers who were chatting as they stood outside their vehicles. Then he stepped out of the limousine, greeted his driver friends and opened the back door of his limo for his passengers to exit. Erica and Perry looked around. This place looked beautiful — not at all what she had pictured. Several large, lush floral gardens added color, sweet aromas and beauty to the grounds around the building.

The focal point of the entry area outside the building was an elaborate, ornate fountain that turned its cooling sprays of water into something that resembled a clear, moving sheet of glass. "How beautiful," Erica thought as she took in the fountain and the scenery. She was conscious that she probably looked like a tourist viewing tall buildings in New York City. But she didn't mind that, for she was utterly thrilled by this place.

Erica, like her brother, had to keep reminding herself that Earl Remington really was their father. She felt great pride that this corporation and its headquarters were his creation. Similarly, Perry was impressed. However, he was eager to get on with the tour. Erica just wanted to take her time and admire the beauty here.

"It's this way," Arnold said. As the three walked alongside him chatting, they learned that Arnold had worked for the Remingtons for over 35 years. It *was* him, Perry thought to himself. He didn't want to come right out and ask Arnold if he could remember driving him around when he was a little boy because he wasn't sure how much Arnold knew about any of this.

They entered the lobby of Remington headquarters. Shiny white marble floors accented by brilliantly polished brass door frames and handrails welcomed them. A rich-looking dark blue carpet runner enabled them to walk across those glazed marble floors without feeling like they were on ice skates. In the center of the lobby, a small waterfall poured into a beautiful fountain filled with lilies and goldfish, and huge live green plants and flowers were placed around it. This beautifully appointed lobby made a grand statement about the Remington Corporation, and it created a welcoming atmosphere into the building.

Arnold asked the receptionist to notify Mr. Remington that his guests had arrived. Erica and Perry looked around while they waited. At times, they just caught each others' eyes and smiled. Words weren't necessary. They both felt it. This place was very impressive! Wait until we tell Mom and Dad, they thought.

Moments later, Earl, Jr. bounded out of the elevator and briskly approached them in the lobby. As he walked toward them, he extended his hand for a friendly shake and welcomed them both. He also acknowledged Arnold. Earl and Arnold had not talked since Arnold had pulled the rug out from under his little envelope on the windshield caper. But Arnold knew it was just a matter of time before he would have to come face to face with this guy, and he wasn't looking forward to that.

Earl didn't have his suit jacket on, but he still looked like he had just stepped out of the pages of the latest men's fashion magazine. He was wearing an expensive blue-striped custom-tailored shirt, navy blue slacks and a brilliant multi-colored silk tie. Earl also sported a rich tan, and his straight blond hair was stylishly combed, although it looked slightly tousled in an attractive sort of way as if he had just run his fingers through it.

Truly, this man, their half-brother, was the picture of success. Erica and Perry thought Earl acted very sociable this time, quite different from the way he came across in that first meeting when he had been aloof and unfriendly. He started the tour, pointing out some of the glass-encased art, famous paintings and corporate awards the company had received that were showcased in the expansive lobby. As they went toward the elevator, Arnold went back outside the building to chat with the other drivers while he waited. A security guard greeted the group as they arrived on the eighth floor — Earl's floor — RemCap Development Company.

They came into his executive offices, and Earl introduced everyone to Brynn Jamison, his secretary. "Have a seat," he offered as they entered his suite. The first thing Erica and Perry noticed was the life-sized oil painting of their father on the wall behind Earl's desk. Looking into Earl Remington, Sr.'s deep dark eyes that stared back at them intensely, they were spellbound. The portrait was in a gilded gold frame, and a light shone down on it, adding a touch of reverence to his countenance. Erica's eyes were riveted to the life-size face of the man she had seen pictures of before, and whom she now knew was her father. The figure in the painting was a perfect likeness of the face she had studied so many times. Perry, too, was mesmerized. He fixed his gaze on the image of a father he had not seen since he was a small child.

In this painting, Earl, Sr. looked to be about the same age as he was in Erica's photographs. Earl, Jr. noticed them staring at the painting and said, "Yes, that's Father — the founder of Remington Corporation." Earl, Sr. had a peculiar half-moon shaped mark just above his right eye. Erica asked about it, and Earl told her it was a birthmark. It gave him a distinctive look. Earl Remington was very handsome. He reminded Erica of the swashbuckler type or maybe Rudolph Valentino from the old black and white movies she sometimes watched. He wore his straight black hair slicked back, and he had very compelling eyes and a thin perfectly arched mustache. Earl told them their mother had commissioned a world famous artist to paint this portrait when their father turned 50 years old.

Up until his death, this painting had hung in the lobby of the building along with other art displayed there. However, after his father died, Earl, Jr. asked to have the painting relocated to his office, especially since it was going to be replaced by an updated one depicting his father in his later years. He was pleased to have his wish granted, for he felt that as the next CEO, the huge wall

behind his desk was a most appropriate place to display a render-
ing of the corporation's founder, his father, Earl Quincy
Remington, Sr.

Earl asked if his guests wanted something to drink, and they
asked for iced tea. When Earl told his secretary to bring refreshments, Erica and Perry nudged each other. They could hardly believe how posh and elegant Earl's office was, from its massive
size and expensive furnishings, to its spectacular view of the lush
green golf course below. Earl's office featured a beautiful hand-
carved mahogany desk and a dark brown leather sofa along with
several matching chairs. An executive conference room adjoined
his office.

Brynn brought Timmy some paper and colored pencils, and
Timmy sat on the sofa to draw and color. Then, Erica, Perry and
Earl made small talk about their trips to Cincinnati and weather
in Cincinnati, Minneapolis and Chicago. Erica and Perry commented on how attractive the building and grounds were, and Earl,
Jr. told them that in a little while he would show them around the
place.

This attempt at conversation wasn't extremely comfortable
for any of them yet. But as he talked, Earl, Jr. seemed to become
more at ease and natural. He gave them a brief background of
Remington Corporation. Although she was interested in the story
and listening eagerly, Erica's eyes were continually drawn to the
eyes in the painting on the wall of Earl Remington, Sr.

She and Perry learned how the senior Earl had made his first
million in real estate development before he was 22 years old.
And he only got bigger and more successful over time. He was a
brilliant and forward-thinking businessman who easily out-thought
his competitors and stayed abreast of emerging trends. The five
divisions of Remington were commercial real estate development,
shopping center development, information technology, investment
banking and housing. A president headed each division.

"Will you replace your father as CEO?" Perry asked Earl.

"Well, I would certainly like to think so," Earl answered. "The
selection process is underway now." Then he changed the subject,
giving them copies of the corporation's annual report. For a single

moment, Perry wondered what it might be like to work at Remington Corporation.

Next, Earl, Jr. told them about the public relations film that was developed for use in introducing Remington to potential clients, business partners and new employees. He explained that it would give them an all-around orientation into the company. This video had been made a couple of years before and was used regularly. Erica and Perry were ready to view it to learn more about the Remington Corporation. Timmy had lost interest in his paper and pencils and ambled over to sit on his mother's lap. He was a little fussy today, what with traveling this morning and all.

Earl inserted the disc into his DVD player and pushed the play button. Fast, upbeat music and the special graphic effects of the film's introduction designed to get the viewer's attention immediately captured Erica's and Perry's. The opening moments of the film showed panoramic views of Remington divisions and products — shopping malls, housing developments and construction projects. Sprinkled throughout these scenes were happy workers and apparently satisfied customers. While all of this appeared on the screen, a deep, resonate male voice told the Remington Corporation story — what the corporation stood for, and what it meant to the City of Cincinnati and to other cities across this great nation.

Next a cast of employees spoke of the privilege of being part of the Remington Corporation family. This was followed by the executive group — Earl and the other four presidents — each talking briefly about the role of key leaders at the Remington Corporation, and about the values and principles that guided their business. Then the presidents described their divisions as scenes of their particular projects filled the screen.

Now, the pace of the music became slower and softer, signifying a change in format as the illustrious leader, Earl Q. Remington, Sr., appeared on the screen to make brief inspiring comments about the corporation. This was Erica and Perry's first animated view of their father. They loved it. Hearing his strong, rich voice and just watching him move fascinated them both. He was no longer just a picture on canvas to them, but a flesh and blood real human being. They were hungry to see more of, but his piece was over quickly. His segment was followed by brief testimonials from satisfied customers.

Again the music changed, and as the video was nearing its end, the camera panned the facility. Timmy distractedly dropped his pencil on the floor, and Erica bent over to retrieve it. At that precise moment, Timmy said, "Daddy." Erica thought her son was just speaking abstractly. Scooping up the pencil, she said, "Honey, you know Daddy's not here." Timmy looked puzzled, and then pointing his finger toward the television, he said, "Wook, Mommy. There's Daddy." Erica looked to see what Timmy was pointing at, and sure enough, although she caught only a glimpse, there was Thomas standing in the lobby of Remington headquarters. He was viewing Earl Remington, Sr.'s portrait, the one that now hung behind Earl, Jr.'s desk. "That *is* Thomas!" she exclaimed in surprise, while wondering, how could that be?

Now Earl, too, was curious. "You recognized someone in the film? Would you like me to rewind the tape?"

Erica said, "Yes, please." Perry also waited for Earl to replay that scene. He was curious because apparently Timmy and Erica thought they spotted Thomas. That would be a bizarre coincidence. He hadn't noticed Thomas himself, since at that moment Perry had been studying the Earl Remington portrait on the lobby wall and not the man looking at it.

Earl rewound the film to the beginning of that last segment which showed people coming and going in and out of the lobby and moving around. Suddenly, there he was again. It was Thomas Harrison all right. He was standing and looking intently at their father's picture. Thomas was only on screen for a few seconds, but even with the camera catching him at a slight angle, it was unquestionably him. They might never have noticed him had Timmy not spotted his daddy. Timmy said, "See, Mommy, there's Daddy."

At first, Erica was thoroughly confused. Then she thought about Thomas' many business trips. Some had, in fact, been to Cincinnati, and now, in the back of her mind, she remembered he had told her a long time ago that his firm did some business with the Remington Corporation. Thomas was in the real estate development business, and his specialty area was shopping centers. So this was the business that had brought him to Cincinnati. Such a small world, she thought to herself.

Still in shock, Erica explained to a puzzled Earl that the man they were looking at was her ex-husband. She told Earl about Thomas' work with Remington and asked if he remembered Thomas Harrison of Runyon Developers. Earl paused the film to study Thomas.

"Thomas Harrison," Earl murmured. Then his face showed a glimmer of recognition, and he said, "As a matter of fact, I do remember doing some business with that guy a few years ago. Yes, of course, he was from Minneapolis. That's right. In fact, his firm partnered with us on the development of a shopping complex somewhere. I think it may have been Nebraska. RemCap did the design work and provided some other consulting services. In fact, we met right here in this office several times. Helen Newman, the president of our shopping centers division, was part of that deal, too.

"Well, sir, so that was your husband," Earl said to Erica. "This is definitely a small world. And a pretty amazing coincidence. Lucky your son just happened to catch it." All three adults found this quite amazing. Timmy went back to the sofa to resume his artwork.

Earl's secretary interrupted him with a call from his wife. He excused himself and told Shannon he was in the middle of a tour with the Harringtons from out of town. Shannon told him she'd be late again this evening, and Earl said, "Again! For heaven's sake, Shannon, this is the second time this week. Okay, we'll have dinner without you." He quickly got off the phone. Earl was agitated now. He wanted to get the tour underway and over with so he could get back to work. He still wanted to take off a little early today to go by and talk to his mother before their big day tomorrow. And Shannon would be working tonight until heaven knows when.

Erica and Perry could tell that Earl was eager to get finished with their visit, so they stopped their idle chatter. Earl told them he would walk them through the other four divisions and show them some features across the building, such as the recreation and exercise center, the dining room and the auditorium and theater.

Erica bid a silent farewell to her father's face in the painting. Then she, Timmy and Perry spent the next few minutes touring the modern Remington headquarters building.

They enjoyed their tour, and when it was over, Earl brought them back by his office so he could buzz for Arnold. While they waited, he showed them pictures of his family that sat in frames on his credenza, along with current photos of their father. Erica and Perry were glad to see these more recent pictures. Earl Remington, Sr. looked a little older, and his hair was white around the edges. Also, he no longer had a mustache, but he looked handsome. The two thanked Earl. Erica leaned over and gave him a slight, but unreturned hug and a peck on the cheek, and Perry shook hands with him again. They left the Remington Building and headed back downtown in the limousine.

Arnold could see that Erica and Perry were animated and excited. He figured Earl, Jr. must have given them the VIP tour, and from what he'd heard, that could dazzle the average Joe. But to be honest, Arnold was still trying to figure this whole thing out. Because here were these two illegitimate kids by Earl Remington and a black woman, and now everyone was acting all hunky dory. He'd have thought they'd all be going at each other like cats and dogs. But instead, they were acting like everything was just peachy keen. This was nothing short of weird.

Erica and Perry enjoyed their tour. It made them feel proud to have a relationship with the mastermind behind this modern operation. They liked the orientation video, and it looked like the people they encountered enjoyed working there. Then Erica talked on and on about seeing Thomas in the Remington video. She was still shocked at the coincidence and assumed Thomas didn't know about being in the video because he'd never mentioned it. Erica thought he'd be pretty proud of himself if he knew.

Back at their hotel, they thanked Arnold, who told them he would pick them up in the morning at ten o'clock. Then, Erica, Perry and Timmy walked around downtown until they decided on a place to have dinner before settling in for the evening.

CHAPTER
22

J.T. HAD TO act quickly. He thought of how hard it was this time compared to when Earl Remington was alive. When he was dealing directly with old man Remington, his airtight plan was as easy as taking candy from a baby. But then the old guy threw him a curve by not paying the money before he died. Now J.T. was embarking on what he intended to be his final job. While old Mr. Remington had not taken the bait, he hoped like everything Mrs. Remington would pay to keep her husband's past deeds from being smeared all over the tabloids. He had spent hours devising a new scheme. Now he had it, and he replayed it over and over in his head.

He had gathered and arranged a fascinating collection of photographs, pictorially displaying the lurid story of Earl Remington and Hattie Rose Williams. Heading this collection was a modern-day photo of Elizabeth Remington. J.T. had been lucky to find it in a local newspaper where she was photographed presenting a big monetary gift or something from the Remington Foundation to some arts organization. Her picture looked all right, but compared to the luscious young black woman whose picture was placed next to hers, Mrs. Remington looked haggard and old.

He also had photos of Earl Remington with his mistress, and he had photographs of their two illegitimate children from when they were younger. Additionally, his collection contained an article about Hattie's death, along with another picture of Mrs. Remington that intimated she might have had something to do with Hattie's death. Preposterous, maybe. But, more importantly, would it work? That was the real question.

J.T. wondered what Mrs. Remington would think of the following headlines splashed all over the cover of the national scandal magazines? EARL REMINGTON'S BLACK SECRET, or EARL REMINGTON'S BLACK FAMILY, or how about, THE TWO LOVES OF EARL Q. REMINGTON — ONE BLACK, ONE WHITE. Surely, he thought, Mrs. Remington and her family wouldn't want to face this kind of humiliation.

After testing the waters for takers of this juicy story among the national magazines, J.T. had struck gold with at least two major publications. Others were talking with him. He tried to think through how he would handle this thing if Mrs. Remington didn't pay. Certainly, he wouldn't want to be connected to this story in any way, or more definitely, to these photographs. Or, for that matter, anything that could point authorities his way for the blackmailing caper he'd pulled off the past two years. He sometimes worried that someone might be able to identify the source of the photographs, but that was a chance he was willing to take. If the Remingtons didn't pay, he'd just go with the sleaze magazine that made him the highest offer. He'd get his sweet revenge all right, though not all the cash he was banking on. J.T. really didn't want to think about that.

First things first, for J.T. now had someone to act as his intermediary. He laughed at the thought that this intermediary was a black private investigator. And judging by his previous communications with Lynn Davis, he'd already concluded she wasn't too bright. He wasn't the least bit impressed with her so far. The first time he called her office, he'd left a message. The second time, however, they actually had a conversation. When he got on the line with her, she was so stumped, she didn't know what to say — just stuttered and stammered and spit out a million stupid questions. He was confident she would not be a threat. He had to get a new message to her, and he needed her to cooperate. She had to get Mrs. Remington to pay the money. It was that simple.

He wrote the message out carefully and made some changes for effect. Then he gave it a few trial runs, practicing his accent and delivery. He wanted to get through the message without having to think about what to say. That way he'd only need to concentrate on his telephone voice. He thought his female impersonation was pretty convincing, and using that British accent was nothing short of genius. He had picked it up long ago as an understudy in a high school play. He was positive no one would ever connect that voice to him, especially with his usual Midwestern accent. He was proud of his wit, but at the same time he was feeling anxious about getting on with this maneuver quickly.

J.T. was also desperate; he needed to score big in the worst way. The old man hadn't fallen for his last demand. Maybe five million was unreasonable. Would four million be too much? Maybe. As much as he hated to do it, J.T. decided it would be best if he cut the amount drastically — all the way in half — to two and a half million dollars. And that may have to hold him, because, for reasons unknown, this whole thing felt shaky right from the start. But he was in so deep, it was going to take about a million dollars to bail himself out of all his bad debts. Then he'd just have to manage the rest of the money with discretion. Of course, if this didn't work, he could always come back for more, after the dust settled. If his plan was to be successful, he knew he had to proceed with extreme caution. Again, he looked over his written message to Lynn Davis.

* * * * *

On Wednesday morning, Rachel prepared a special breakfast in anticipation of Timmy's arrival. She had spoken to Erica on the phone last week and thought she sounded like a darling young woman. She even looked forward to spending the day with Erica's young son and wished it wasn't raining in case he wanted to run around outside. It had been a long time since she'd had a toddler around. She loved children, and at school they loved her back and she usually received from her students about a bushel of apples a year to prove it. The times she spent with her son's two kids were far too brief. Those two were growing up so fast. Jasmine was already eight and Nathan nine, and they lived in New York City. Yes, it should be fun to have Timmy around today.

At eight o'clock, Lynn picked up Erica and Timmy from their hotel and drove them to her mother's house. Erica looked stunning in a simple navy blue shirtdress with white buttons and trim. The dress fell just above her knees, and she was wearing navy and white pumps. With her trim figure, tasteful hairstyle and quiet makeup, Erica made a striking appearance. Lynn also thought her little son was a cutie, although he didn't say much.

It was a dark and rainy morning — a curl-up-in-bed-and-listen-to-the-raindrops kind of morning. It was also the kind of day that could make a somber occasion that much more so. Thankfully, the weatherman said the sun would come out in the afternoon. Actually, it was projected to be a scorcher with temperatures in the 90s.

Lynn asked Erica how she spent her day yesterday, and Erica told her about Arnold picking them up and taking them to Remington headquarters for an amazing tour of the facility, all arranged by Earl. "Earl Remington, Jr.," Lynn exclaimed in surprise.

"One and the same," Erica said with a puzzled smile. "And Perry and I both thought he was nice and friendly — not distant like he was the first time we met him. And that building, Miss Davis, is totally awesome. The grounds looked like a flowering campus. I mean I literally stood there with my mouth open, gaping at everything. It was just that impressive."

"I know what you mean. I've seen the headquarters," said Lynn. "It is very attractive."

Erica nodded in agreement. "But here's the thing we found the craziest of all. You won't believe this." Erica seemed very excited, whetting Lynn's curiosity. "Earl had this life-size painting of his father; well, I guess I should say *our father.* Anyway, this painting was hanging on a wall behind the desk in his office. Our father was a very good-looking man. Earl told us that up until he died, that picture had been in the lobby of the building. Then Earl showed us this film telling the story of the Remington Corporation, you know, a public relations kind of thing." Lynn listened and Erica continued.

"So there were all these people in the film, coming and going and milling about, and smack dab in the middle of the screen, who was standing in the lobby of Remington headquarters looking at our father's portrait, no less, but my ex-husband, Thomas." Lynn was taken aback, and Erica said, "That's right, Thomas Harrison — I just couldn't believe it. It was Timmy who first spotted him; I guess I had looked away from the screen for a moment."

Lynn found this all very interesting. She asked Erica how it had come about, and Erica told her, "Well, Earl said this video was made around two years ago. And then I remembered some time ago, back when we were still married, Thomas used to come to Cincinnati on business with the Remington Corporation. At the time, that name didn't mean anything to me, of course. But apparently on one of his trips here, they just happened to be shooting that film and Thomas just happened to be in it. He's only there for a few seconds, but I still couldn't get over it. It's such an amazing coincidence," Erica said, continuing to shake her head in disbelief.

"You're right about that," Lynn said, while thinking that it was indeed a pretty strange coincidence.

It took only a few minutes to reach her parents' home, and Rachel and Grady came outside to greet them, offering umbrellas as Lynn and Erica got out of the car. "Hi, Mom and Dad," Lynn said to her parents, and gave them both a quick hug and a peck which they warmly returned. Rachel was a tall, attractive brown-skin woman in her early 60s. She wore her black hair short and looked like she took good care of herself. Grady was much taller, around six feet, two. His complexion was light brown, he had curly black hair sprinkled with gray, and he was very handsome. Because of problems with his knees, he'd had to retire from his job at the post office a year earlier than he'd intended to.

"So this is Erica," Rachel said, reaching out her arms to greet her. Then she looked down to greet Timothy, but he turned his head away and held tightly to his mother's hand.

"Well, why don't we come inside," Rachel invited. Maybe Timmy was not accustomed to being around strangers, she thought. If so, it was probably going to be difficult for him when Erica left. It might help if they came inside and got acquainted.

Grady hung back to tell Lynn about her Uncle Ed's new boat. Lynn and her father put their arms around each other's waist as they walked up the sidewalk. Grady told her that he and Ed were planning to take the boat out this weekend and do a little fishing. Lynn was glad her father had some fun plans. She asked him about his knees. "I get around," he told her, then chuckled as he said, "but I don't think I'll be running a marathon anytime soon." Then he asked her if she had jogged today, and Lynn told him she had run five miles and it was exhilarating to run in the rain. "Be careful, baby, you don't come down with something," Grady scolded warmly.

Inside, Erica sat down to talk to her son. She told him she was going away for a little while and he would stay with this nice woman whose name was Miss Rachel. Timmy pouted, and she told him she would bring him back something special. Then she talked to Rachel about the kinds of things Timmy liked to do, what time he took his nap, that sort of thing.

Rachel tried to take little Timmy's hand to see if they could go off into the kitchen together, but he pulled back and held on to his mother. Lynn watched this and hoped Timmy wouldn't turn out to be more than she had bargained for, especially since it was she who had asked her mother to take care of him. He hadn't seemed irritable when they got into her car a few minutes ago. She didn't want to leave her mother with a little problem kid on her hands.

"Don't worry," Rachel said, noticing Lynn's concerned look. "Timmy and I will do just fine. Won't we, Timmy?" Timmy only glared at her through frowning eyes with his bottom lip poked out. Erica reminded him to be a good boy; then as she and Lynn left Rachel's house, she assured Lynn that Timmy was a good kid who shouldn't give her mother any trouble. He just had to warm up to her. Then Lynn drove Erica to the hotel where she and her brother would have breakfast together before getting picked up by Arnold at ten o'clock. It was only half past eight.

As Lynn drove, Erica said worriedly, "I hope Timmy doesn't give your mother a hard time. He really is a very good boy, and it's so nice of her to keep him for me."

"Look, Erica," Lynn told her. "You've got enough on your mind today. Don't worry about anything. Mother and Timmy will do fine." To herself, Lynn was thinking, I certainly hope so.

Meanwhile, inside the Davis home, Timmy sat on a chair near the front door with his arms crossed and his bottom lip still poked out. To everything Rachel proposed came an emphatic, NO! Did Timmy want anything to eat? NO! Did he want to play? NO! Did Timmy want to read a story? NO! Nor did he want to watch cartoons. And NO! He didn't want to go outside and sit on the porch and watch the rain and the squirrels. Well … maybe that.

So he got down from his seat and walked over to the front door where he stood and waited for Rachel to open it and take him outside. Their front porch was screened in so they could sit and watch the rain and hear the birds and see the dogs and squirrels running around in the rain. Timmy climbed up in a rocking chair and rocked himself as hard as he could. "Where's mommy? I want my mommy," he pleaded to Miss Rachel.

"Your mother had to go bye-bye," she told him. "She'll be back to pick you up later." Timmy looked very sad.

"I want my mommy," he cried, tears beginning to wet the corners of his eyes. "I 'ont want you! I 'ont wike you!" he shouted, his meaning perfectly clear.

"Why, Timmy? Why don't you like me, honey?" Rachel asked the little boy.

" 'Cause you're bwack," he said. Then he tried hard to spit to reinforce his point, but the bubbles just rolled down his chin.

"Yes, I am. But why don't you like me if I'm black?" she asked.

Angrily, Timmy answered, " 'Cus my daddy tole me."

Oh, dear, Rachel thought to herself as she instantly realized what was happening. This boy was merely acting out things he'd been taught. But she had handled tougher challenges, and she believed she could handle Timmy, too. She wondered if Erica knew her son's father was teaching him these things. And she wondered why he would teach this little boy not to like black people. After all, the child is bi-racial himself. Rachel asked, "And what color is Timmy?"

"Wite!" he said pointing to himself. Then he pointed to his arms and fingers and legs, and to each body part, he emphatically said, "wite, wite, wite, wite, wite, wite …"

Rachel knew this poor child didn't even understand what he was saying, but she felt his mother should be the one to re-educate him about race. And she would tell her about this later. So she said, "Listen, Timmy. Do you want to be sad today?" Timmy's tears had dried and he shook his head hard to indicate a decided *no*. "Do you want to have fun today?" And this time he nodded, his head moving in an exaggerated motion.

"I'll tell you what; do you want to go to the zoo and see some animals? Elephants, monkeys, birds?" To each animal she named, Timmy vigorously nodded yes. He started to smile while holding his head down so Miss Rachel could not see him turning happy. But then, Timmy said, "My daddy 'ont let me pway outside," and when Rachel asked why not, he said, "Becuz I'll get bwack." Um-um-um, Rachel said to herself of this boy's comments — his father teaching him to stay out of the sun. She told Timmy it would be perfectly all right because his mother had told her that he could play outside. Rachel wondered what else Timmy was being taught. She told him that first they would go back inside and eat breakfast. She asked if he wanted to eat breakfast and Timmy rubbed his tummy and said, "Yummy-yummy."

Rachel could see that Timmy was not going to be a hard sell. In spite of his teachings, he was already coming around. After all, he was so young. How committed could he be to these ideas; he didn't even understand them. She told him after they ate they would read some books, and when it stopped raining, they would go to the zoo. Right then and there Timmy decided to be happy.

Grady, Timmy and Rachel sat down to biscuits and jelly, eggs and bacon, and fried potatoes, and Timmy also ate a bowl of cereal. By now, he had settled down and seemed fine. Then Timmy just happened to notice an *Ebony Magazine* on the edge of the breakfast table. On the cover was Whitney Houston. Timmy pointed at the magazine and said, "Wook. Neegur, neegur." Grady looked up in disbelief at what Timmy said. Rachel looked at her husband. She shook her head and told him she'd explain later. Rachel told Timmy that words like that were not nice, so he should never use them. Timmy took a spoonful of cereal, and between smacks, he protested, "But my daddy tole me."

Rachel thought this was a very unfortunate situation. She knew this was sometimes how prejudice got started — parents passing their own beliefs on to their children. In this case, Timmy was a bi-racial child himself. He would surely grow up to be confused if he kept thinking blacks were bad people. Rachel remembered a colleague who had adopted a bi-racial boy who had been taught in foster care to be ashamed of his racial heritage. Out of shame, this child had actually tried several times to run away. He ended up needing serious counseling. She wondered why Timmy's father would teach him such damaging things. For certain, Rachel knew she would have to discuss this situation with Erica. But first she called Lynn to tell her what the little boy's father was teaching him.

Lynn was shocked. "Mom, I'm hearing all kinds of things about this guy." She told her mother. "Thomas and Erica divorced when Timmy was just a few months old. Erica says lately he's even been threatening to take Timmy away from her." Rachel thought to herself this man apparently has a serious problem with race, and she wondered why he married Erica if he did not like blacks. In her opinion, the worst part of this whole thing was that this little boy had to be exposed to such negative messages.

Rachel told Lynn that she and Timmy were already getting along all right, and that they were going to the zoo when the rain stopped. Later that morning, off to the zoo they went, and Timmy had a great time seeing all the animals. Other than for a few small snags, like the time Timmy saw the monkeys and almost called them *neegurs* and Rachel had to put her finger to her mouth and shush him, their day was fun and uneventful.

CHAPTER
23

AFTER LYNN HUNG up the phone from talking with her mother about Timmy, she thought of Thomas and wondered what he was all about. True, she didn't know the guy, but from everything she had heard, the picture shaping up of him wasn't pretty. Suddenly the phone rang and she answered it, realizing that Ella had already left the office and Janet was working at home. Lynn thought it might be Harvey calling her back as she had tried to reach him earlier. She answered the phone, and a voice began to speak. Right away, Lynn recognized that it was that person calling again. Her heart started racing, and she wondered, what now? She did not have to wonder too long, because the caller got right to the point:

"Miss Davis, since you have chosen to get involved in the Remington case, you are now going to have to do as I ask."

Lynn was instantly reminded of an earlier conversation with Ella who had said this character must be pretty dumb. After all, who in their right mind would involve a private investigator in a blackmail scam? She glanced at her caller identification, and it again registered *number unknown*. I guess he's not that dumb, she thought. She pushed a button on her phone to record the balance of the call. "Excuse me," she said in pronounced agitation. "Who are you anyway? Why do you keep calling *me*, and why on earth would *I* help *you*?"

J.T. did not want to stray from his written script, and fortunately, Lynn's question fit right in with what he was about to say next. So in his falsetto-accented voice, he continued. "Go to your car and you will find a large brown envelope just under the left front wheel of your Lexus." My Lexus! Lynn was aghast. This individual knows my car. This was very troubling.

"Open the envelope. Feel free to view its contents. Be a voyeur. Be my guest. I assure you, when you see the contents of this envelope, you'll understand more. This envelope is for Mrs. Elizabeth Remington, and as you will soon see, it will be in her best interest to receive it. But I caution you not to open the sealed private envelope addressed to Mrs. Remington. You got that? One more thing, you needn't waste your time noseying around for fingerprints, dearie. You'll find none."

Lynn said, "Wait a minute. Who are you anyway? What's this all about? Better yet, why don't you just leave me and these people alone?"

"Enough questions. Listen, you'd just better do as I've instructed you to do. Give Mrs. Remington the complete package, or your client will see her little family story on every major tabloid in this country, and, I might add, a few abroad. It's up to you. And who knows, we just might be able to cook up something to throw in on you, too. By the way, that's a nice beige suit you're wearing today with that cutesy little rose lapel pin you've got on."

Lynn froze in terror. This person actually knew who she was, her car, and what she had on, in detail. He had apparently seen her today, up close and personal at that! And now, he was even going so far as to threaten her with that tabloids comment. Lynn's uneasiness was laced with agitation. This person is getting beside himself, she thought, although she said nothing. The caller ended with the words, "So, you got that, girlie? Now just do as you're told, and if all goes well, we won't have to talk to each other again." Click.

Brother, Lynn thought, this stinks. This character knows me and I don't have the slightest idea who he, or she, is. He knows my telephone number, my car, and God knows what else. This has to be the same person who blackmailed Remington before. I guess he or she is determined to get more money out of the family or try to destroy their reputation. Who knows? And then Lynn played back the portion of the call she'd recorded and listened carefully, trying to identify something that might offer a clue as to the caller's identity. Nothing. Except that she was still convinced the caller was a man.

Lynn saved the recording and tried calling Harvey's office again. He still wasn't in, so again she left word. She was waiting for Erica to return from the reading of the will so they could pick up Timmy, but curiosity about this phone call got the best of Lynn. She had to see if there really was an envelope under the wheel of her car, so she locked her office and headed straight to the parking garage.

When she entered the underground garage, Lynn was sure she saw a darkly clothed figure lurking between some cars in her building's fairly well-lit garage, putting her ill at ease about proceeding toward her car. So she went back into the building and asked a security guard to escort her back to the garage. When she got to her car, she immediately noticed the promised brown envelope peeking out from under her left front tire. It was just as the caller had said. She picked up the envelope and thanked the guard for accompanying her to her car.

This is bizarre, she thought, as she remembered that first envelope saga — the mysterious one Mrs. Remington found under her windshield wiper a few days earlier that turned out to be the handiwork of her son, Earl, Jr. Lynn hurried back to her office. Shaken, she wondered had she actually seen that character back there in the parking garage. Worse, had he seen her?

When she was safely back in her office, she emptied the envelope onto her desk and examined its contents. Inside the large brown envelope was a smaller white one. It was sealed and addressed to Mrs. Elizabeth Remington. It was marked *PERSONAL AND CONFIDENTIAL*. Lynn placed that envelope back inside the larger one. There was also a large sheet of neatly folded newsprint. As Lynn began to open it, she saw it contained a layout of photographs. She quickly spread the newsprint across her desk to view it, then just shook her head.

The blackmailer had shrewdly concocted a shameful story of sex and half-truths with photographs. The first picture in the sequence was a recent newspaper photograph of Mrs. Remington, so unflattering Lynn wondered if it had been doctored. Next to Mrs. Remington's uncomplimentary picture was the portrait of Hattie Rose Williams looking extremely young, obviously black, and very pretty. In bold letters across the top of the page were the words, THE TWO LOVES OF EARL Q. REMINGTON — ONE BLACK, ONE WHITE.

There was an assortment of photos of Hattie Rose and Earl Remington together. Lynn instantly recognized some of the same photographs Mrs. Remington had found in her husband's blackmail file. And there were pictures of Erica and Perry that Lynn didn't remember seeing before. An article, along with the police report from Hattie's death, was included and another photo of Elizabeth Remington taken from a different newspaper article. The subtitle in bold, obviously prepared for effect by the blackmailer, read, THE MYSTERIOUS DEATH OF EARL REMINGTON'S MISTRESS: WAS IT AN ACCIDENT? It intimated that Elizabeth Remington had something to do with Hattie's death.

This whole collection painted a pretty dismal and convincing picture: Earl Remington had an affair with a young black woman, and together they'd had two children. The mistress died, and the cause of the automobile accident was questionable.

Lynn believed that neither Elizabeth Remington nor any of Earl Remington's six children would want to see these photos made public. She had to get this envelope to her right away. And of all times, she thought. She placed a call to Mrs. Remington, but she was unavailable, so she left word for her to return the call, saying it was urgent. Lynn thought, with the will being read today, this is the last thing Elizabeth Remington wants to see. She added, but unfortunately, it's the one thing she *needs* to see.

J.T. had waited stealthily in the garage to watch Lynn Davis pick up the envelope shortly after his call to her. He was pleased to observe that she seemed afraid to go to her car by herself and had to get an escort. He had wanted to shake her up, and it looked like he succeeded. A little fear in the equation might keep her from getting too smart. So far, so good, he thought. He wished he could have seen her reaction when she looked at the contents of that envelope. Oh yes, he thought. She will definitely deliver my little surprise to Mrs. Remington.

He thought of how easy it had been to learn who Lynn Davis was and where she parked her car. The first-floor directory listed her office number, and he had just waited by the elevator on her floor until he watched her arrive at her office that day. Even said good morning to her, and she had in turn, spoken back to him. He had carefully observed what she was wearing so he'd be able to mention her outfit in the phone call he was to make to her later.

J.T. had asked the young guy in the parking booth in the garage if he knew Lynn Davis, and the nitwit not only told him what kind of car she drove, but where she usually parked. He observed that she had seemed completely unaware of his watching her that day. Actually, getting information to Lynn Davis was the least of his problems. J.T. knew he could just as easily have left the package with the receptionist in her building. However, at least for this occasion, the parking garage scenario lent such sweet drama to the plan. He could almost smell his money.

CHAPTER
24

PARKER TOOK HER time getting to the family's Indian Hill estate. The impending reading of the will so symbolized to her the finality of it all, and she was feeling rather blue. The gray skies and gentle falling rain only added to her melancholy. As she drove along the tree-lined cobblestone drive of her family's Indian Hill home, Parker thought about her final good-byes to her father three months ago. Still missing him terribly, she whispered a prayer that he rest in peace.

Ferrel Whitmore had arrived at the house at ten o'clock and was sitting with Mrs. Remington and Earl, Jr. when Parker joined them in the living room. Jordan waited in the den and sipped iced tea, while a grim-faced Ross sat in the study wanting the meeting to begin. The sooner it started, the sooner it would be over. When Erica and Perry arrived a little later, the gathering was complete. Shortly before eleven a.m., everyone went into the study.

In preparation for the reading of the will, each family member had dealt with the matter at hand in his or her own way. Mrs. Remington had been unable to sleep the previous night. She'd tossed and turned as thoughts of her husband nagged and tugged at her. In a way, she wished the will had been read immediately after Earl's death. She thought that might have enabled her to more quickly come to a sense of closure.

Her thoughts were mixed. She remembered their many happy years of marriage. Of course, she was plagued with thoughts of his affair, and his unusual deathbed request weighed on her. She thought of how remarkable it was that she had been successful in bringing the entire group of his offspring together. Although she still searched for the meaning of this, she considered that some ultimate good would possibly come from it. In her heart, however, she still wished she had never known anything about her husband's affair with Hattie Rose Williams.

Jordan was in an unusually reflective mood, and she was very quiet. As she thought about her father, she thought with regret of the concern she had caused him over the years. She thought of how he once even came close to disinheriting her if she didn't get herself together. And amazingly, here she sat today, having done just that.

Young Earl was now the senior Earl Remington in this family and he was suddenly graced with an amazing insight. All his life he had walked in his father's shadow, looking up to him, emulating him, trying hard to please him. And he realized now that he had been so busy concerning himself with his father's view of him that he failed to focus on who he really was. As he reflected on his recent heedless actions intended to win him the seat of CEO, he knew now that he would have to make amends with many people. He was even prepared to change his personal priorities; while it was extraordinary, the role of CEO was not everything.

Ross had wanted to be alone for a while before the family came together. In spite of his father's character flaws, Ross loved him deeply. Although as a younger man, even though he never thought that much of the wealth and power that so epitomized his father, Ross still learned a great deal from him. He was continuing to learn about him and from him even after his death.

As for Erica and Perry, their day yesterday on the Remington tour had shown them who these people really were, especially their father, and they were truly in awe of them all. This morning as they approached the Remington estate in the limousine, they observed that the grounds at the Remington estate were even more spectacular than those at the headquarters had been. Beautiful floral gardens welcomed them with bursts of color, while sweetly scenting the air they breathed as they stepped out of the limousine and went into the house. Although they were taken directly into the study, they were completely awed by the grandeur of this magnificent home from the first moment they set foot inside it. They greeted their half-siblings, giving a special acknowledgment to Earl for the tour the day before. Then they approached Mrs. Remington to shake her hand. She returned a complaisant hello. They met the lawyer, and Mrs. Remington told Ferrel he could begin. The entire group sat around a conference-style table. Ferrel took a seat at the head of the table, and next to him was Mrs. Remington. The meeting got underway.

Ferrel Whitmore was a tall, well-built man with kind eyes and a pleasant demeanor who appeared to be in his late 60s. Dressed in a custom-fitted black pin-striped suit, he had a look of distinction, one befitting a counselor to the very rich. A Harvard man, Ferrel had been a counselor and friend of the Remington family for over 40 years. It was he who had encouraged Parker to choose Harvard for her law studies. It was also through him that Earl, Sr. had met Hattie Rose Williams, Ferrel's attractive young secretary, decades before. However, Ferrel did not learn of his friend's relationship with Hattie until after she died.

The lawyer spent the first few minutes explaining what the format of the meeting would be. He told the group this would partly be a video presentation delivered by Mr. Remington himself. He also told them Mr. Remington had given him two sets of video discs — one, a set of three, was for use should the people present consist only of his immediate family members. To this striking news, the Remington children looked at each other in bemusement. Ferrell explained that the second set of four videos was to be presented under the condition that the *additional* parties would be present. Everyone knew he was referring to Erica and Perry Harrington. He further explained that he had been directed to destroy the unused set of video discs after the reading. Thus, no one but himself would ever know what Earl Q.

Remington, Sr. would have said had the family not all come together. Secretly, however, Ferrel thought of how fortunate it was for all that he would be presenting the second set of videos.

Upon hearing these stipulations, there was a burst of gasps and throats clearing as the Remingtons shifted in their seats. The Remington children stole quick looks at one another, and Jordan and Ross whispered something to each other. They were thinking crazy thoughts. What if their father had decided to turn his entire estate over to his foundation had his last wishes not been complied with. They had heard of people writing their immediate families completely out of their wills. Of course, they realized the other set of discs could have been something altogether different, but they were suddenly glad their father's wishes had been carried out. At different times, they shot glances toward Erica and Perry as the object of their thoughts. Erica and Perry observed the group's reaction with interest, then looked at each other, nonplused. They could hardly believe the will being presented today was contingent upon their being present.

Ferrel waited a few seconds for the family to settle down and then resumed. "Are there any questions so far?" he asked. At first, there was silence until Parker spoke up. She asked him if he absolutely had to destroy the other set of discs. She thought they probably ought to be retained for the records. She couldn't bear the thought that anything her father had produced was being destroyed. Besides, she secretly wanted to know what was on the other discs. Ferrel assured Parker that Mr. Remington's specific request was that they be destroyed, and he was bound to follow his orders. Parker knew the answer, but it was worth a try. None of the others asked any questions, although secretly they felt the same as Parker.

"First," Ferrel said, "let me explain what I have here." He opened his briefcase and pulled out four video discs. "The first disc contains a joint message Mr. Remington brings to you all. In a few minutes, I will play that one. Then the others are confidential. Of course, one is for you, Elizabeth, and another for you four," he said, looking to Parker, Jordan, Earl and Ross. "And there is a disc for Erica and Perry Dodd. You will want to view these in private at your earliest convenience. The CD's have been transcribed and will be kept on record in my office." Then Ferrel noticed the strange look on Jordan's face and said, "Jordan, may I answer any questions for you?"

Jordan told Ferrel she was just trying to understand why her father would set up his will this way. Why all the secrets? This would only lead to suspicion among them. Ferrel told her that was certainly not her father's intent. He knew his private messages were not appropriate for everyone to hear, so he felt it best to keep their individual messages separate. In no way did this mean that anyone was being advantaged or disadvantaged by this. In fact, he told her that the terms of the distribution of his assets were to be shared with the group of them. The individual video discs were otherwise personal, and it was intended that they be viewed that way. Jordan accepted his explanation and said no more, although she still wanted to know what was on the other discs.

Ferrel said, "Then let's proceed, shall we." He placed the first disc into the player and asked all present to position themselves so they could view the large screen on the wall behind him. Some shifted slightly to get a better view of the screen. Using the remote control, Ferrel dimmed the lights, turned so he could see the monitor and pressed the play button.

Suddenly, larger than life, Earl Remington appeared on the big screen seated in the large brown leather chair in his study at the Butler County estate. He was wearing an elegant dark red silk smoking jacket, and despite his apparent frailty, he looked very stately. His favorite classical music, Chopin's Concertos by Artur Rubinstein, played ambiently in the background. Upon seeing their father, Jordan and Ross took each other's hands. Parker sat at rapt attention. In the meantime, Erica and Perry's eyes were riveted to the screen. Here was their father in his full splendor. They were intrigued. On screen Earl Remington clasped his hands and rested them on his lap, formed a brief smile and began to speak.

"Hello, my beloved family, Elizabeth, Parker, Jordan, Earl, Ross … and Erica and Perry." He spoke each name deliberately and thoughtfully, for this would be the final time he would call all their names together. "Now I know you will find this entire proceeding unusual — different from you might have expected.

However, I decided to address you this way so that, even though I'll be gone, you will know, unequivocally, my thoughts and feelings for you at this moment. I am grateful you are viewing this particular set.

"First, I must say, Elizabeth, you are indeed a wonderful woman." Tears began to form in Elizabeth's eyes. "That you are all together tells me something very important. It tells me you were able to find it in your heart to follow through on the request I intend to make of you. I know this will be a harsh burden to place on anyone, leastwise, one so undeserving of such a burden as yourself. But you have borne and abided it, and by doing so, you have honored me more than words could ever say. This means so much to me, and I thank you from the bottom of my heart."

At that, Elizabeth, who'd been sitting on the edge of her seat, dropped her head to conceal determined tears. Every eye turned her way. Sensing the mood, Ferrell momentarily paused the video. Parker, who sat on the other side of her mother, placed her hand on her shoulder. Earl tenderly rubbed her arm in comfort. Jordan and Ross left their seats and went to their mother, embracing her. Erica and Perry, uncertain what to do, sat and watched as they, too, fought back their emotions. Then when everyone was again seated, Ferrel resumed play.

Erica suddenly recognized the music of Chopin's *Romance: Larghetto*, and remembered a long forgotten ballet recital when she'd danced to the music of this very song and received a standing ovation from all the parents. Hearing the music now and seeing her father brought back the fleeting but powerful memory of the hugs and kisses she received from her mother, Hattie, for her performance, and later, from her father, Earl Remington. She was seven years old. And she remembered! It was magical.

Earl, Sr. formed a slight smile as he spoke his next words. "It makes me very happy to imagine all of you together. I only hope you will allow this to be the beginning of a long, enriching relationship for all of you. And so I say to you, Erica and Perry, welcome, my children. For so long I have wanted you to be a part of my life, just as I have wanted you to be accepted by my dear family." His voice cracked, and he paused a moment before he could continue. Erica and Perry were mesmerized by it all, for watching their father speak to them was surreal. However, hearing those words on the heels of her special memory jolt, Erica began to weep, and Perry put his arms around her to comfort her. Again, Ferrel paused the player and asked if Erica was okay and giving her a moment before resuming. Most of the others held their heads down.

Earl, Sr. continued, his voice sounding mostly feeble and strained. His weary eyes were moistening. "So now the answer to the big mystery — why was it so important to me to bring all of you together? I sincerely want you to understand, and in order to make that happen, I must share with you a part of my past none of you has ever known — not even you, Elizabeth, for I have long buried it deep within me. If it were not for the fact that this would clear things up for you which I am most determined to do, I would not dredge it up, even now. For you see, it's a sad story and difficult to tell." He paused to inhale deeply and sighed before continuing.

"Family means everything to me. I have always felt this way, even though my own early family situation was a complete wreck. My real parents were named Sara and Guy Jefferson. I was my mother's second child. I never really knew Guy until I was 16, but I'll come back to that later. Guy deserted my mother while she was pregnant with me, and my brother was just two years old. My mother struggled to take care of my brother, Marcus, and me, but she was very miserable. The struggle lasted for years, and when I was five and just ready to start school, my mother decided she could no longer live without my father. They got back together, but the only problem was Guy didn't want us kids around."

At this point, Earl, Sr. sighed deeply and continued in a somber tone, "So they solved that problem. They put my seven-year-old brother and me up for adoption. Oh, I believe my mother must have agonized over this painful decision, but in the end, the fact is she chose to be with Guy. Then if that wasn't bad enough, the worst of all possible misfortunes occurred. My brother and I were separated by adoption. I was adopted right away. Elizabeth, the in-laws you knew and loved, John and Mary Remington, were my adoptive parents. I'm sorry I never told you." He sadly added,

"All I was told was that Marcus went somewhere else to live. Where that was, I never knew. I missed my mother tremendously, and I ached with loneliness for Marcus." At hearing all this, Elizabeth lowered her head in sadness. Earl, Sr.'s children were astonished to hear about their father's difficult early life. They had known none of this and were eager to know more.

"From the beginning when I came to live with the Remingtons at the age of five, they told me I was adopted. They said that meant I was very special. By around age seven, I think, I was old enough to really understand what adoption meant, but instead of being contented or well adjusted, I went through a very difficult period that lasted many years. I felt sad, useless and bad, for why else would my father have walked out on my mother? And why else would my mother and father give me and my brother away to complete strangers?" Everyone was totally engulfed in Earl Remington's story.

The elder gentleman talked on. "I didn't handle this whole adoption matter very well. In fact, I'm ashamed to say I became a juvenile delinquent. I was in and out of trouble. Needless to say, my behavior caused my adoptive parents a great deal of grief. At the time I was glad, for I wanted to punish them for separating me from my brother. I did a lot of damage to our relationship, only to learn the horrible truth many years later that it was my birth mother and father who had permitted us to be separated. I thought they must have been truly evil. Miraculously, the Remingtons loved me unconditionally, and in spite of all the grief I caused them, they were always there for me.

"Then one day when I was 16, Guy contacted the Remingtons out of the blue and they let him to talk to me. You see, he told me my real mother had managed to keep track of my whereabouts over the years. Even so, I was totally shocked to hear from him," Earl's voice quickened. "Guy told me my mother was dying and she hoped to see me before she passed on. Of course, my adoptive parents were concerned about this new development. They knew how upsetting this was for me, a troubled and disturbed youth, and they wanted me spared any further distress. Still, they understood how important seeing my biological parents must have been for me, so with some chagrin, they allowed me to make my own decision. I chose to see them.

"Actually, the only reason I considered seeing either of my natural parents at that time was for the chance to see my brother, and I told Guy as much. But to my horror, he told me my brother, Marcus, had drowned seven years earlier at the age of 11." Hearing this, Jordan's hand flew to her mouth and she gasped. "Of course, I was devastated by this news, for I'd always believed my brother and I would be reunited one day. I wanted to curse my real parents for sending us away. I blamed them for his death. I despised my father, but consented to see him because now I really wanted to kill the man or at least do him great bodily harm." Then Earl, Sr. lowered his head for a few seconds, and when he raised it again, he said with grief etched in his face, "As you can see, this is very hard; bear with me. I'm obviously not proud of my story, but I will continue because it's important that you know all of it."

After a brief pause while the somber notes of *Allegro Vivace* filled the sound waves, he continued, "My adoptive parents drove me down to Lexington. When I arrived there, I wish now that I had gone directly to the hospital. Instead, I met my father at our appointed meeting place, and then wasted time engaging in a long, ugly battle with him. Yes, we actually fought. It was during this horrible encounter that I sustained this thing you know as a birthmark," he pointed to the half-moon-shaped mark over his right eye, then rubbed it gingerly. "My father did this to me with a broken bottle while defending himself, for you see, at that moment I wanted to kill him and tried my best to do so with my bare hands. Luckily I did not succeed.

"But this fight was a truly bad thing, not so much because I was hurt, but because it delayed our getting to the hospital. By the time we got there, my mother had been dead only minutes. Naturally, I was devastated. My father was heartsick, too. It was a terrible thing. They patched up my head at the hospital, and I stayed in Lexington for a couple of days so I could attend my mother's funeral. Fortunately, my adoptive parents stayed, too, for I was so despondent I don't know what I might have done had they not been there." As she listened, Parker looked on in disbelief and grief. She, like her siblings, had never been aware of any of this. It made her unbelievably sad to hear of her father's terrible early years and sadder that he had never confided in her about this.

"It was after my mother died that I had my first real conversation with Guy Jefferson. It was then I learned the real truth about why he left us, and why my brother and I were given up for adoption. It didn't make it right by any stretch, but it did enable me to understand it for the first time. This is an even more difficult story, but I'll keep it brief. Guy told me he had been injured while in the military — an injury that rendered him sterile. He could not biologically father children, and yet his wife, our mother, became pregnant. Twice." Hearing this, Elizabeth shook her head. Her dear husband had indeed had a troubled youth.

"Guy Jefferson had been the only image I'd ever had when I thought of my real father," the senior Earl continued. "I can't deny this bothered me to no end, for now I desperately wanted to know who my biological father was. Marcus' father? Since my mother had passed, I realized I would never know." Earl Remington's family sat mesmerized as he bared the amazing saga of his difficult childhood and teenage years, a saga none of his family had ever had even the slightest inkling of.

He went on to tell them how his father actually forgave his mother's infidelity the first time she got pregnant, for he loved her and knew how much she wanted a child. However, my mother did not know Guy was sterile. When she became pregnant a second time, he told her about his injury. They fought and he left her. Earl Remington said this man, Guy Jefferson, had a terrible mean streak, and it was a miracle his mother survived her adultery. But in spite of her betrayals, she still loved him deeply and was strongly dependent on him. As time passed, her yearnings for him only grew stronger.

"So when I was five, Guy agreed to take her back on one condition. No kids. He had been so hurt by her unfaithfulness he still wanted to punish her for it. My parents were obviously two very miserable people," Earl, Sr. said and paused at the thought and dropped his head momentarily. "From my mother's standpoint," he finally continued, "it was apparently him or us, and we lost out," Earl said, then explained that his mother and Guy agreed that the two boys could be adopted separately because the adoption agency tried but was unsuccessful in getting anyone to take two older siblings.

"This man I had believed was my father told me our mother was broken-hearted over giving us up, and she only went downhill after that. Actually, it made me somewhat happy to learn she'd kept track of our whereabouts over the years. When she found out my brother had drowned though, she tried to kill herself." Earl, Sr. told them Guy, his so-called father, was brutally honest with him. While he respected and appreciated that honesty, Guy could still only tell him what he knew and nothing more. It was his mother who had answers to the questions he so desperately wanted to know. "Even given her ultimatum, how could she have given us up? Who was our father? Had Marcus been adopted? I had many other questions. But I would never know the answers," he said, "for now she was gone."

The family was to learn how, in spite of his mother's death, Earl, Sr. felt as though a heavy weight had been lifted from his heart. He told them how, after the funeral, he returned to his adoptive parents' home with a new spirit. While he hadn't received the answers he sought, he did have a much greater appreciation for his parents for all their efforts in providing a loving home to him. He said he never saw or heard from Guy Jefferson again.

"The Remingtons did all they could to give me a normal life. At this point, I completely turned my life around and pledged myself to doing good. I wanted to repay them for everything they had done for me. I wanted to do this by becoming a decent, hardworking person." Then Earl told how after becoming serious about school, he finished high school and was awarded academic scholarships. He then finished college at the age of 21 with a determination to be successful. He attained wealth right away, took very good care of his adoptive parents and, "You know the rest.

"What I could never reconcile myself to was how I followed in the exact same footsteps as Guy Jefferson and my mother. Just as they turned their backs on Marcus and me, I walked away from two of my children, Erica and Perry. I know I also did untold harm to you, Elizabeth, and to our children. There is no way I could have made matters any worse than they were, except to have left them that way. But I must tell you this — the only way I know to leave here in peace is to bring all of you together. Of course, I will pass on not knowing how this will work out, but I dedicate my dying breath to the hope and prayer that it will — beyond your wildest imaginations.

"Elizabeth and my children, Parker, Jordan, Earl and Ross, please open you hearts to Erica and Perry. They are my children, too. They never asked for this. Their being in this world is purely a function of choices I alone made. Furthermore, I deserted them. I know personally what being deserted by my father did to me. So I just had to right this wrong. Please try to understand this." He paused as weariness was overtaking him, then he looked hauntingly into the camera. "None of you ever knew about the sad state of my early years, or how it shaped my belief about family togetherness. However, you who knew me have always known how important a stable family life has been to me. I am confident that deep down, you feel the same way. And now I pray that as I tell my story, you will finally understand," Earl, Sr. said.

"What I did, my extramarital affair, was wrong. Elizabeth, it was wrong to you and our children, and it was wrong to Hattie Rose, too. I won't try to make it right with excuses. Instead, I beg your forgiveness, all of you. It's not just for me that I ask you to forgive me, for when you hear this, I'll be gone. But I'm asking that you do this for yourselves. I cannot bear to think of any of you carrying hurt and anger in your hearts. It could ultimately destroy you and our family. The knowledge that my behavior could devastate my family in this way is unthinkable to me. Won't you please try and move past this."

Finally, after pausing momentarily, Earl, Sr. gave a look of resolve that he had finally finished his say. With his voice weakening to not much more than a whisper, he said, "Remember this, a family by any other name is still a family. You are my family, one and all, just as you are family to each other. I am proud of all of you. So till we meet in the life beyond, I love you all." He blew a soft kiss and said, "Farewell, my precious ones." At some point while he was speaking, the music had changed and now the wailing sounds of Albinoni's *Adagio in G Minor* played softly in the background and the screen slowly faded.

Everyone was wiping tears from their eyes. No one could move or speak. For the Remingtons, the notion of accepting Erica and Perry had been a thorny one. However, after hearing why this was so important to Earl, Sr., and how the circumstances of his life had affected him, they not only understood, but were moved to abide by his wishes. Erica and Perry, themselves, were extremely touched, knowing how much doing *the right thing* by them meant to their father.

As ambient music trailed, Ferrel had the good graces to wait for a moment as family members dealt with their emotions before he slowly brought the lights back up. He even casually dabbed at the corners of his own eyes, then suggested a short break. Jordan and Ross hugged each other, Parker and Earl sat in deep thought. Erica and Perry sat motionless. After a while, Earl got up from the table and walked over to them and shook their hands. This single gesture said volumes. Then Parker did the same, and Ross and Jordan gave them hugs. Elizabeth observed her children's gestures with gratitude.

During their break, Elizabeth thanked her children for opening their hearts to their half-brother and sister. To Erica and Perry she said, "My husband made his wishes quite clear. It will take time, but for now I want you to know you are welcome here."

When everyone was once again seated, Ferrel said, "I know Earl would have wanted me to express his gratitude to all of you for your attention and apparent responsiveness to his last request. So now, if you are all ready, I will read the distribution portion of the will." Elizabeth Remington glanced around and gave him the okay to proceed.

CHAPTER
25

O<small>NLY THE IMMEDIATE</small> family sat in on this reading of the entire distribution of assets. Other beneficiaries were scheduled for a separate reading at Ferrel's office downtown later that same afternoon. The specific bequeaths went quickly. Earl Remington had a net worth of well over a billion dollars. He awarded each of his children by Elizabeth five million dollars, and ample trust funds to be administered by an executor were created in each of their names. With good justification, they could access additional funds from the trusts. The generous trusts had a stipulation that college tuition for all grandchildren, in perpetuity, would be provided, as well as other allowances as deemed appropriate by the executors. The distribution of their inheritance was to be made in equal installments over three years, with supplemental amounts added to the trusts every five years. Erica and Perry and all their offspring, in perpetuity, received a similar inheritance as Earl's other four children.

Finally, to Earl's loving wife, Elizabeth, went a significant portion of the balance of her husband's estate, amounting to several hundred million dollars. This included 51 percent of his shares in the Remington Corporation. Additionally, she received several pieces of property, including the home in Indian Hill, their great family mansion in Butler County, the yacht, several luxury vehicles and vacation homes around the world, including a private island resort off the Gulf of Mexico and a villa in the South of France. Ownership of the other 49 percent of his shares in the corporation was to be split equally between his six children with important stipulations as to their continued ownership. Lastly, an enormous sum of money went to the Remington Foundation, the family's charitable organization. This amount would ensure the Foundation's existence indefinitely.

Later that afternoon Arnold Taylor, his loyal driver, would learn of the generous sum he was to receive: $750,000. Arnold was also deeded the Mercedes four-wheeler, which of all the Remington vehicles was Arnold's favorite. He would be forever grateful.

Several other relatives and long-time employees of the family, including Mrs. Remington's secretary, Fiona, were also to receive handsome awards. Some 45 people were in attendance at the afternoon reading. Each person left feeling very proud and pleased at Earl Remington's generosity.

Some time later, awed by the entire proceedings of Earl Remington, Sr.'s will, the family disbanded, each person needing his or her own private time to process the day's amazing events. Separately, and in their own time and space, they would all view their individual video messages.

That very afternoon, in a state of free-flowing emotions and reverie, Elizabeth viewed her husband's personalized message to her. Earlier that morning, Ferrel had arranged for her to view in private the disc that was addressed to the whole group prior to the gathering at eleven. It was in that early morning session that she had first learned the shocking secrets her deceased husband would disclose to the entire group later. Earl had wanted her to know before the others. However, she was reviewing her private message for the first time. Elizabeth listened and watched with her mind, body and soul as Earl talked of many things.

Earl, Sr. spoke of special moments long ago and more recent ones, too, and Elizabeth loved hearing his recitations of their life together. With a special glint in his eye, he briefly retraced their 40 years of marriage. He told her how she used to drive him and all the guys crazy in the early days when she would run her fingers through her long, luxurious blond hair. He reminded her that she would comb it away from her face with long graceful fingers and let it fall gently and tantalizingly back in place to drape her beautiful face. Her skin had been flawless, and he had always loved the rich golden hue of her skin. Earl described in detail her exquisite loveliness and told her that today, she was still one of the most beautiful women in all the world. She was touched.

With fondness and longing, Elizabeth realized she had never once doubted Earl's adoration which was manifested in so many special ways. Sometimes he would walk up behind her as she stood before the dressing mirror, one hand would tenderly cup her midriff; the other would stroke her hair while gently pulling it away from her face. Then he would lift her hair, tenderly kiss the nape of her neck, then stare adoringly at her mirrored reflection, smiling in a way that simply melted her. How she loved those memories. Yet even as she relived the precious moments of her relationship, she forced herself to think honestly of the ten-year-period of Earl's affair. In that span of time, was he less attentive, less affectionate? To be totally honest with herself, she had to answer *yes*. But Elizabeth had to acknowledge that she, herself, was not perfect either, so the subtle change he underwent seemed fitting at the time. But Earl had more than made up for this relapse in the second half of their marriage when his attitude toward her had been the very epitome of devotion, affection and love.

As Earl approached the present years, he spoke warmly of how happy he had been that night three years ago aboard their yacht. Elizabeth remembered that special night. It had been filled with music, dancing and champagne, and had ended with a beautiful romantic interlude. That extraordinary evening had ended all too soon and it would be their last time together in this precious and intimate way. She had spent many evenings reliving that final act of sexual fulfillment between them. On that evening, just as he had done for 40 years, he had satisfied her most completely.

After that night, he could only partially fulfill her needs, and it was just a matter of time before even those attempts would finally cease.

While their lack of intimate relations the past three years left Elizabeth feeling empty and full of yearning, she tried to understand and accept the fact that Earl's illness had left him sexually incapacitated. To compensate for this lack, he had buried himself deep in his work. To fill this void, Elizabeth was left with only her memories, her brandy and her cigarettes. Suddenly, on this day, she felt she no longer needed the latter accouterments and decided right then and there to end her dependence on them.

If there was one thing Earl said in this video that stood out for Elizabeth above everything else, it was that she must never think that anything she did drove him into another woman's arms. He told her she had been the perfect wife and no man could have ever asked for more. His indiscretions were the product, he said, of his own "macho, immature sense of entitlement that drove him to stray." He'd never intended for one moment for his feelings to have become so entangled in the web. Earl made no excuses for having had this prolonged affair, telling his wife that he alone was to blame for his indiscriminate behavior. He told her he would not dare ask for her understanding of his transgressions for he certainly did not deserve it, but he hoped to gain her forgiveness, though he said he hardly deserved that either. These words did more to allay Elizabeth's hurt and nagging guilt over her husband's affair than anything he could have said, and she was grateful he had said what he did about that.

Earl then thanked his wife for honoring his last wishes, telling her he knew just how tough it had to have been for her to do so. Then he thanked her for being his loving partner for over 40 years, told her to enjoy the balance of her life to the fullest and closed with a wish and prayer for her happiness. Finally, with a weak but glowing smile, he blew a faint kiss and ended with the words, "With a love that knows no bounds, so long, my precious Elizabeth."

Something strange happened to Elizabeth Remington that afternoon as she viewed her husband's private message to her.

His voice, his words, something about them had an amazingly cathartic effect on her. Ever since that fateful day in April when he told her of his affair, she had prayed a hundred prayers for something she believed unattainable — peace of mind and the ability to forgive him. Almost daily, she had been tormented by resentment, anger and hurt, and she didn't know how she could ever get past this ordeal. In her very soul, however, she knew she must one day release the anger and open her heart to forgiveness. After turning off the disc player, she felt herself finally letting go. She sat still for a long while. All at once, Elizabeth began to speak words of healing. In a voice she did not know she had, she talked freely to her husband for the first time since his death.

"Earl, today you have given me something very special. For so long, I have wondered how this thing could have happened and if I could have prevented you from going outside our marriage. Of course, I was angry with you and hurt beyond words, for I never understood how you could you have done this terrible thing to me? Indeed, that will probably always remain a mystery to me. At least, now I am assured I did not drive you to Hattie Williams.

"As you must have known, I was appalled and saddened to learn of your painful childhood. These things I never knew, Earl. However, by revealing how you were driven by your strong family values to bring your other two children into our family, I can now understand what compelled you to make such an unusual request of me. I do believe everything will work out. Erica and Perry are dear young people who are part of you, and I no longer think it will be impossible for me to bring them into my heart. It's more than I had hoped, but our children have already shown their acceptance, too."

Elizabeth felt as though this painful chapter of betrayal for her was over. She closed her conversation with her departed spouse saying, "Thank you, too, dear Earl, for being a part of my life for so many wonderful years. I love you. I will miss you. And, damn you, Earl, darling, I do forgive you." In her mind's eye, Elizabeth could see her husband's relieved smile, and she smiled back, for she now felt lighter, and suddenly very free.

* * * * *

The four Remington children viewed their father's video together that afternoon. His message to them was permeated with love, caring and well wishing. They were deeply touched as their father discussed his extramarital affair. "I am leaving this dreadful burden with your mother to pass on to you. I wish I could have faced telling you myself. But I would rather have faced a firing squad than to have looked into your faces and told you of my deception.

"It will take every ounce of gumption I have to tell your mother. This was a secret I would willingly have carried to my grave, and into eternity, whatever the consequences. But outside influences forced me to change my position. Of course, I am speaking of the blackmailer, that despicable worm. I am sure you know of this by now. But the truth is, this thing happened. And although I find the actions of the blackmailer reprehensible, a part of me realizes that he actually did me a huge favor by forcing me to bring this deep, dark secret out into the open. Otherwise I do not know if I would have the courage to bring all of you together this way.

"I am not proud of myself for what I've done. I know I was wrong, and I wronged you four just as I wronged your mother. I make no excuses, nor will I try and explain my actions away. I can only ask once again for your forgiveness." As he spoke, each of his children felt that their father was looking directly into his or her eyes. Then magically, his children looked into each other's eyes and silently communicated to each other their forgiveness of their father and their willingness, already demonstrated, to comply with his wishes that they accept Erica and Perry.

"No more secrets. No more lies," Earl Remington said with sad relief and conviction. "I only wish it had not taken so many years for this truth that has haunted me for so long to come out. But no matter what you think, I never stopped loving you. No man could have been more genuinely blessed than to have answered the call when each one of you said, Father."

Finally, Parker, Jordan, Earl and Ross received biddings from their father to be good and decent people, to live by principles, make wise choices, and to make their lives count for something.

He told Earl, Jr. that one day he would head the corporation. This was sweet music to his son's ears. When that day comes, the senior Earl told his son, "You will lead and guide the family business into the future." He told his eldest son to stay focused on the people, goals and values of the corporation and he would do fine. And he told Earl something that he had waited his entire life to hear. "I'm proud of you, son." This single message meant more to Earl, Jr. than anything his father could have said.

Earl, Sr. told Jordan how proud he was of her, too, for pursuing her passion for art and photography. He said he loved her free spirit, and told her to stay focused on her dreams. His message to Parker privately reaffirmed her special place in his heart. Among other things, he told her how he cherished and appreciated her daily visits and their many conversations. He said she had made him very happy, and he wanted her and Dale to have a happy life together. Ross learned that his father was delighted that he was his own man, refreshingly unaffected by societal conventions. It had only been during that recent bedside conversation that Ross had finally realized how much his father thought of him. And he was warmed by Earl, Sr.'s praise. Their father closed his message with love and appreciation to them, one and all.

* * * * *

Privately viewing their father's message, Erica and Perry instantly saw their video as an unbelievable dream come true. Their father had gathered photos, films and even letters from their mother and created a treasure on film. Heretofore, they had seen only a handful of photos of their mother. Their father's gift to them was a video collage of film clips and photographs of Hattie Rose. It was incredible. For the first time in 20 years, they saw their mother in motion, heard her voice, and saw her laugh and play. They saw their mother, resplendent in a white sequined evening gown and their father in an elegant black tuxedo aboard his fabulous yacht; and on a different occasion, in bathing suits, romping around the deck of *The Rose.*

Erica and Perry saw themselves as toddlers, being coddled and kissed by both parents. And there was even a special clip showing their grandmother, Sophie, dancing with little Erica. One photograph showed a very young Perry in the limousine with a young chauffeur named Arnold behind the wheel. Another showed Hattie singing a lullaby to her son. When Perry heard the song, he choked with emotion. "I knew I remembered her singing that song to me," he said affectionately of this cherished moment.

Their father told them he had found their mother to be totally irresistible, and once their relationship started, it was impossible to stop. "Oh, Hattie was a special woman, beautiful, fresh, fun and vitally alive, and I never felt more alive than when I was with her. And, oh, let me tell you," he said laughingly, "one look in Hattie's eyes, and one was charmed for a lifetime." She had a refreshing childlike sweetness and innocence about her. Yet this demeanor belied her true essence, for she had the wisdom of a person much older. Earl, Sr. looked as though he was almost in a trance. He appeared to be happy and contented at that moment and sounded as if Hattie's image was as real to him today as it had been during their relationship. "I dearly loved your mother," he told them. "She was my rose.

"I cannot condone what I did in establishing a relationship with her," he continued, his voice broken. "You would have to have known her as I did to realize there was something truly compelling about her. I'm so sorry you did not get that chance." He told them he had fallen in love with so many things about her — her charm and beauty, her sweetness, her intelligence, her sensitivity and her loving ways. "I can honestly tell you I still love your mother to this day," he said as he looked away from the camera momentarily and dabbed at the corners of his eyes. Looking back again, he said in a choked voice, "She touched my heart in a way I could never have imagined." Then, to recover his poise, their father paused again for a moment.

He looked up again, this time to read a portion of one of their mother's letters in which she described her undying love for him and their two beautiful children. Again, his voice cracked with emotion from reading Hattie's tender words. Erica dabbed her eyes. Perry did, too. Earl, Sr. then said to his two children by Hattie Rose that he only wished he had known them better and had had the chance to watch them grow up. Earl Remington looked troubled by what he was about to say next. "Erica, Perry," he paused. "I can no longer ignore the question that I am certain you most need answered. Why did I desert you all these years?" He looked away while determining how to proceed. "This is the most difficult thing for me to say to you. For I have no words to make you understand what I hardly understand myself. Oh, I could say that having the two of you in my life would have unduly complicated matters, and you were better off with your grandmother, and things were best left as they were. But words like this sound so weak in the grand scheme. The fact is, I've asked myself this question over the years, and I really never came up with a good answer. What I know was that losing Hattie was the hardest thing I ever had to deal with. In order to allow time to heal the wounds of such a tremendous loss, I felt the need to distance myself from any and everything that concerned her. In my thinking at the time, that included you."

Still looking pained he said, "Somehow I felt that after I got over Hattie Rose, I would make a point to see you from time to time. Of course, time slips away, and that never happened. I never even knew of your grandmother's death until years after it happened. I just prayed that you were somewhere in the world in a good place. I've never forgotten either of you. In fact, I thought of you two often. Each year on your birthdays, I wanted to do something special for you. Every Father's Day, I thought of how you were not with me. In a sad way, I felt that my not seeing you was my punishment. Perhaps it was, but I never thought of how it was punishing you, too. The only thing I can say to you is I never stopped loving you. And I am truly sorry."

Erica and Perry were deeply touched by this sincere, long overdue apology. They knew their father was correct — words could not make it understandable or right. But at least he had owned up to what he had done, and he chose to address it. That meant everything to them, and they would think about his words for a long time.

While still pondering his apology, they were surprised by what he was to talk about next. Their father touched on the topic of their racial makeup, telling his son and daughter, "Of course, you children are bi-racial. One part of you is black like your mother," he said, tenderly picking up and viewing a photograph of Hattie Rose, "and," he added, "another part of you is white like me. Even so, society will likely regard you as African Americans alone. Unfortunately, as you know, our society has not been kind to black people simply because of skin color. This is an abomination. For there is good and bad in every race, and none is superior to the other.

"I hope you will always be proud of your racial heritage. You have every reason to be. Your mother and I believed our love for one another blended to give you the cherished gift of life and the best of both our worlds." He paused momentarily. "So again I say, be proud of who you are, my children, as I am proud of you." Erica and Perry were extremely moved by their father's mention of their racial heritage and by his encouragement that they see this as a positive attribute versus a negative one. They were proud to know how he felt about the race issue.

Neither Erica nor Perry could have predicted what their father would say to them next, for it was very unusual. He told them their mother had what he called a keenly developed extra-sensory perception. She always seemed to know when something was in the air. And in the latter period of her life, she had begun to experience a recurring sense of impending doom. It was frightening her, but she knew not what to do about it. And neither did he, and it frightened him, too. He told them he felt she knew that something was going to happen to her. As their father talked, Erica thought of her mother's haunting memoirs that seemed to allude to her imminent death.

Their father said the night Hattie died was the worst night of his life. His whole world was shattered, and he virtually fell apart in anguish. He felt like dying right along with her. He said he wanted them to know the circumstances of her death. He told them that, "First of all, Hattie was not a big drinker; only occasionally would she sip a glass of fine wine. Alcohol did not cause her accident," he said emphatically. "I tell you this because there are some speculative accounts of her death that indicate otherwise. Nor was it an automobile malfunction. The authorities checked thoroughly and determined her car was not in any way the cause of her accident. The misfortune that claimed her life occurred when she lost control of her car in the rain and skidded down a steep embankment."

Their father said that he and their mother had been together the evening she died. She had brought up the subject of marriage, and his response to her as it had always been was that marriage was, unfortunately, out of the question given his situation. Their mother had been upset with him when she left, and may have been driving too fast. As he spoke about this event, his voice broke and trailed off. Although hearing these details was difficult, Erica had previously wondered before if her mother had possibly taken her own life. Her heart was lifted to learn now that she had not.

Then he said to his two children, "You have now met my wife, Elizabeth, and our four children — your half-brothers and sisters. Your being here alone should tell you just how special Elizabeth is, for she obviously had a choice of whether or not to honor my wish to bring you here. Elizabeth was a good wife and a marvelous woman. Please show her your respect and gratitude for bringing you into the family."

After a moment, he said, "Two wrongs don't make a right, and it was wrong of me to deny you. And while I can never right a wrong, I can finally do what I feel in my heart is the right thing. Although shamefully, it is 20 years late, I am intent on bringing you into the Remington family, and it does my heart proud to know that you are here." He welcomed them again into the family and told them he hoped this would be the beginning of a rich new life for them and a wonderful association with the Remingtons. Lastly, he said again that he loved them, and with that he said good-bye.

Erica and Perry were enraptured, warmed and touched by their personal video message from their father, Earl Q. Remington, Sr., and by seeing their mother in the flesh, moving, talking, singing — it was absolutely phenomenal. The two of them freely allowed their true emotions to surface while giving each other consoling hugs. They both were eager to play their disc a second time, but on top of everything else, it was entirely too much for now. They decided to put some time between viewings, but reflected a great deal on his presentation to them.

For some time afterward, something her father said still nagged at Erica, and it chilled her. Particularly, it was his comments about this sixth sense their mother had and her feelings of impending doom. Erica wondered if she had inherited this attribute from her mother, because sometimes she had a *way* of knowing things herself. For example, when she received the box of her mother's personal items, she just knew that somehow, even though she never discovered what it was, there was a clue to the identity of her birth father in that box.

And for quite some time now, she had also been experiencing a strange sense of foreboding. At times, she would get a frightful feeling which she had chosen to ignore. It felt like something very near her was the source of her apprehension. Hearing of her mother's gift made Erica more willing to acknowledge her own feelings. Before, she had kept this to herself, but now she decided to tell her brother about it for the first time. Perry found it all very interesting, but he told his sister he did not know whether or not he really believed in such a thing. For now, Erica left it alone.

Earl Q. Remington, Sr. had left his family quite a legacy. Further, all who received his personalized video messages knew and greatly appreciated the massive effort he made to put it together, particularly in his weakened state. It was an even more powerful signal that his love for them was strong and unrelenting — a love that transcended the boundaries of life and death. And in spite of the unusual circumstances of the reading of the will and his request that his family try and accept one other, everyone was left with a strange feeling of peace that was hard to put into words. They knew none of them would ever know what message had been contained in the other set of videos. However, this was fast losing its importance to all of them.

* * * * *

Later that day, Erica and Perry sought out Mrs. Remington to thank her again for what she had done for them. They asked if she was available to meet with them for a few minutes. She agreed to meet with them, and in a large study the three sat facing each other. "Mrs. Remington," Erica began, "this day has probably been the most wonderful day in our lives, even though the reason we are here is a sad one. We know how difficult our father's request was for you, and Perry and I both want you to know just how deeply appreciative we are at your decision to bring us here." Perry nodded. Mrs. Remington smiled slightly and waited for Erica to continue. "From what we can tell from the filmed messages, Earl Remington was a unique individual, and although our being here is the result of unfortunate circumstances, we just want to say that we're proud to be united in kinship to him ... and to this family."

Sharing his sister's sentiments, Perry added, "We want to thank you, Mrs. Remington, with all our hearts. We believe we can appreciate the difficult choice you were asked to make in our behalf. We will be forever grateful to you for welcoming us here."

Elizabeth Remington was very relaxed when she told Erica and Perry how right they were. This had been a difficult choice to make, but she now believed it had definitely been the right one. "I also realize how overwhelming this must be to both of you, too, but I believe that over time, things will level out and become much smoother between all of us. I am sure we will eventually come to know each other much better; in fact, I'm looking forward to it." Erica and Perry departed the study, leaving Mrs. Remington to contemplate the special sweetness of her husband's two children by Hattie Rose Williams.

* * * * *

Later that afternoon when Erica and Lynn drove over to Rachel's house to pick up Timmy, Erica told Lynn that their day had been simply amazing. She told her she'd seen videos of her father and of her mother, and how she and Perry felt an acceptance into the Remington family they would not have thought possible. Erica said she could not believe that she was now unbelievably wealthy. Lynn was intrigued by Earl Remington's filming his will. Moreover, she was very pleased for Erica and Perry. However, Lynn was still concentrating on the matter of that envelope. And she still had to tell Erica what her mother had said about Timmy's behavior.

Erica's exhilaration was replaced by dismay over what she learned about her son's actions. She was visibly shaken and upset, and even more so when Rachel, herself, described his behavior to her. Erica felt embarrassed and angry. But although she was upset that Rachel had experienced what she had with her son, in a strange way she was grateful that it happened, for she might otherwise never have known about this. Timmy had never, ever talked this way around her.

Erica would talk to Timmy this very evening. She definitely had to get these shocking prejudicial ideas out of his head. And just now, as she thought of Thomas teaching her son such horrible notions, that sense of imminent doom returned to overshadow her joy.

* * * * *

When Lynn talked to Donald that evening, she gave him a quick update of the latest saga. He expressed concern over Lynn's well-being and offered to drive her to and from work, at least for a few days. However, she told him that other than the eerie feeling she'd gotten when she went into the parking garage, she really had no fear for her own safety. Donald reluctantly did not push her.

CHAPTER

26

ON THE MORNING following the reading of the will, Lynn was feeling quite antsy about the blackmailer's envelope which she'd now been holding a day. Even after a second phone call the evening before, she had not yet talked to Mrs. Remington nor received a call back. Lynn finally reached her late that morning. Elizabeth Remington informed Lynn that she was aware she had tried to reach her the day before, but there had just been too much going on to speak with her. As it was, things were still hectic as she was having all the children over for brunch. She said everyone was already at the estate except Erica and Perry who were arriving a little later because they had a prior engagement with someone named Bertha Waters. However, hearing the reason for her call, Mrs. Remington promptly invited Lynn out to the Indian Hill home in the early afternoon.

Lynn's mood was contemplative as she drove out to the Remington estate. She was searching her mind for answers to the blackmailer mystery. Last evening, Harvey had finally called her. After she told him about the phone call and the envelope she'd received that day, he agreed with her thinking that the reason the blackmailer was using her as the delivery person was that she was his best way to get to Mrs. Remington. Harvey told her not to be surprised if that person continued to communicate through her, as that appeared to be the best and surest prospect. Lynn didn't like the idea of this contact with the blackmailer being an ongoing deal, but she had to concede it would probably be his most expedient way. As a safety precaution, earlier this morning she had asked building security to keep a regular check on her car.

"Oh, by the way, Lynn, Brownlee looks okay," Harvey said. A few days earlier, she had told him about Jeremiah Brownlee and the missing pictures. Harvey had taken the information Lynn had on Jeremiah and run a check on him. "He retired a few years ago, and word is, he made a good deal of money in the stock market. It's been verified. He looks clean." Lynn had already begun to believe this Jelly was not their man, especially with yesterday's developments which just did not seem like the antics of a lovesick 60-year-old spurred on by a decades-old crush.

She had asked Harvey, "If Jeremiah didn't have anything to do with blackmailing the Remingtons, what do you suppose his mother and aunt were afraid of?"

"Who knows? They could be thinking someone is trying to pin something on him. Hell, Jeremiah could be thinking somebody is trying to pin something on him. You never can tell. Every black man in America knows he stands as good a chance as the next one of being accused of something bogus. So ole' Jeremiah and his people might just be playing it safe."

"You could be right," Lynn had added, "especially since his mother and aunt just told him last week that a private investigator was looking for blackmail pictures. He'd almost have to be completely nuts to turn right around and call *me* to get me involved in the act. Besides, that telephone voice really didn't sound like an African American man. I know, you really can't tell by the voice."

After speaking to Harvey, Lynn had called her Uncle Ed to tell him what Harv said about Jelly. Her uncle told her he figured that was where she would come out. After they talked, Lynn once again considered some of the other possibilities, from that old guy named Huber, to Arnold, the chauffeur. She even ran through each of the Remington children in her mind, and Erica and Perry, and all their spouses and significant others, too. And what about business associates or Remington Corporation employees?

Now as she drove, melodious classical music engulfed her as she found her way through the winding roads of Indian Hill and past all the gorgeous estates, each with its multi-acre grounds. Lynn's mind was deeply immersed in the quest for answers. She began to get a strange, almost tingly feeling. She felt baffled but oddly excited, like she was just on the verge of discovering something important. She wondered if the answer was right in front of her face.

The sudden appearance of a police vehicle in her side view mirror shattered her thoughts. A ranger had pulled up alongside her and was signaling for her to stop her car. He stepped out of his vehicle and approached her window.

"Hello, ma'am. Mind telling me where you're headed?" Lynn was disturbed at having been stopped. Although she hadn't driven around much in ritzy Indian Hill, she was having no trouble finding her way, nor had she been speeding. Impatiently, she told him the address. The ranger studied her curiously as if he recognized the address and couldn't figure out why a person such as herself would be heading up to the Remington house. Those weren't his words, of course. He actually said, "Are you sure you've got the right address, ma'am? There are only a couple of homes up that way. Where exactly *are* you going again?"

Before the ranger asked her to stay seated in her car, Lynn had unfastened her seat belt and was out standing face to face with him. Noting his name and badge number, she told him she was going to the Remington estate, and gave him a look that made him think twice about questioning her further for no reason. His entire demeanor suddenly changed. He politely said, "I see. You know these roads can get pretty tricky at times. Tell you what, why don't you follow me. As a matter of fact, I just happened to be headed that way anyhow."

Lynn got back into her car and observed the ranger making a special note of her license plate. There was a several minute delay before they took off, and she knew he was checking her out. The very idea was unnerving. As he pulled away, she observed him talking into his mouthpiece and thought he was probably calling the Remington security office to see if they were expecting someone who fit her description.

When the ranger drove up the winding road for a short distance and stopped at her appointed destination, Lynn clearly saw that there had been no need for an escort. At the time she was stopped, she was not two minutes from the Remington home. The ranger stepped over to her car and told her this was the place. In a tone expressing her displeasure, she told him that she was a former sergeant with the Cincinnati Police Department and wondered why he felt the need to escort her to her destination. He looked at her rather sheepishly and told her she'd be surprised at how many people got lost in this area. Then he tipped his cap, got back in his vehicle in a hurry and drove off.

Being a woman, Lynn had not been stopped by police for no reason before. On the other hand, Donald had, on more than one occasion. Now she knew first-hand why it angered him so whenever this happened. While this incident annoyed her, she had more pressing matters at hand. Mrs. Remington had to see the contents of this envelope right away. Otherwise, she might still have been engaged in discussion with that ranger, for she was definitely looking for a better answer to why he had stopped her than the one he had given.

The security guard opened the gate onto the grounds and pointed Lynn up to the house. As she pulled her car into the wide cobblestone circular drive at the front of the place, she suddenly found herself in a whole different world. She took an absorbing look around and discovered this house was as grand as anything she had ever seen. The acres of grounds were immaculate and decorated with breathtaking floral gardens. The grass was like a rich green velvet carpet. There, up the white marble steps, a beautiful verandah lined with majestic marble pillars spanned the entire front of the house. Other than perhaps in the movies, Lynn had not seen a home as magnificent as this one.

Scanning the panorama, she slowly ascended the stairs. As she admired the beautifully sculpted, mahogany-carved door, she rang the doorbell. The butler, an older, tuxedo-clad Englishman, cordially invited her inside. Lynn stepped inside and found herself in a huge entry parlor with polished marble floors. Her eyes took in the gilded antique furniture, life-sized bronze statues, ornate lighting fixtures and colorful wall paintings. Huge tropical plants, delicately carved wood molding and Tiffany glass windows stained in blue-green, red and gold graced the area. The ceiling looked to be at least three stories high. The focal point of the entryway was a lovely winding staircase. Here, ornately carved molding offset a skylighted dome that illuminated the staircase, giving it an enchanting golden glow. Lynn was shown into a study where she remained standing and continued to take in the beauteous surroundings.

The butler went to inform Mrs. Remington of Lynn's presence as she continued to look around. Lynn realized she hadn't known quite what to expect, but found the Remington home to be extremely bright and airy. It looked to be a virtual gallery of art. Lynn thought she would love to tour the place, and didn't realize she'd been thinking out loud when Elizabeth Remington entered the room, interrupting Lynn's admiring gazes.

Lynn noticed right away that Mrs. Remington looked exceptionally striking today. She seemed radiant and glowing. "Good afternoon, Miss Davis," she said, extending her hand.

Lynn told Mrs. Remington she couldn't help from admiring her lovely home, then said, "I'm sorry to interrupt your lunch, but you'll agree this could not wait." Elizabeth assured her this was not a problem. She looked curious and Lynn got right to the point. "As I told you on the phone, the blackmailer called me again yesterday."

Upon hearing this, Mrs. Remington's expression changed noticeably. The color drained from her face. She had been on such a strange, peaceful ride since yesterday's presentation of her husband's will, even replaying her personal message again before retiring last evening. But now, hearing this from Lynn, her peace was shattered.

"Please, Miss Davis, sit down," Elizabeth said, realizing the unpleasant seriousness of this visit.

"Not only that," Lynn continued as she took a seat, "he came into the parking garage of my office building and left a package underneath my car for me to give you." Mrs. Remington looked stunned. Lynn opened her briefcase and pulled out the envelope as she talked. "I asked him why he expected me to help him, and he just told me to look inside the envelope and I'd know what to do. Well, I looked," Lynn said, shaking her head. "And there is some pretty ugly stuff in there. There's also a sealed letter addressed to you which he instructed me not to touch and which, of course, I did not."

Mrs. Remington listened wearily. This was indeed a dreadful development. "So my guess is he's probably after money," Lynn continued. "It's tough that this is happening, Mrs. Remington, especially now. But I knew you'd want to see this right away." Lynn handed her the envelope. "Better give a look."

Elizabeth sighed and took a deep breath and said, "My heavens. This is most awful." Taking the envelope from Lynn, she tentatively removed the poster-sized sheet. Then carefully opening it, she viewed in dismay the shocking collection of photographs and the horrible bylines accompanying them. She looked from one picture to the next, each one evoking in her a greater sense of despair than the prior one.

She made no effort to conceal her dismay. She had seen several of these pictures among the original set of blackmailer's photos, a fact that confirmed for her that these pictures came from the same person who had been blackmailing her husband previously. She studied each picture closely, reading the article about Hattie Williams, seeing the blackmailer's cruel attempt to implicate her in Hattie's death. Finally, after sighing and taking another deep breath, she glanced up at Lynn, shook her head and said resignedly, "Well, let's see how much he wants." Then she opened the sealed white envelope bearing her name. In a quiet voice, she read the computer-generated letter aloud:

TO: MRS. ELIZABETH REMINGTON:
ON JULY 22, THE PHOTOGRAPHS YOU SEE HERE WILL BE SENT TO THE TABLOID PRESS. SEVERAL PUBLICATIONS ARE READY AND EAGER TO PUBLISH

THIS ACCOUNT OF YOUR HUSBAND'S ILLICIT RELATIONSHIP WITH HIS BLACK MISTRESS, THEIR TWO ILLEGITIMATE CHILDREN, AND THE SUSPICIONS SURROUNDING THIS WOMAN'S MYSTERIOUS DEATH.

ONLY YOU CAN PREVENT THIS FROM HAPPENING. TO DO SO, YOU MUST DEPOSIT THE SUM OF TWO MILLION, FIVE HUNDRED THOUSAND DOLLARS ($2,500,000) IN A BANK ACCOUNT IN SWITZERLAND. THE ACCOUNT NUMBER IS LISTED BELOW. THAT IS ALL YOU HAVE TO DO. WHEN THIS HAS BEEN DONE, MY COMPLETE COLLECTION OF PHOTOGRAPHS AND NEGATIVES WILL BE RETURNED TO YOU AND YOU WILL NEVER HEAR FROM ME AGAIN, EVER.

YOU HAVE UNTIL SIX P.M. EASTERN STANDARD TIME, NEXT TUESDAY, JULY 21, TO COMPLETE THE TRANSFER. ONCE COMPLETED, I WILL BID YOU ADIEU AND VANISH FROM YOUR LIFE. HOWEVER, IF YOU CHOOSE NOT TO PAY, YOU CAN SAY HELLO TO THE WORLD OF THE TABLOID PRESS AND GOODBYE FOREVER TO YOUR PRIVACY AND PRECIOUS REPUTATION.

THE CHOICE IS YOURS. I WILL CHECK THIS ACCOUNT LATE TUESDAY TO SEE THAT THE DEPOSIT HAS BEEN MADE BEFORE SENDING THIS PACKAGE OUT TO EIGHT OF THE NATION'S LARGEST TABLOID NEWSPAPERS WHO ARE EAGERLY AWAITING IT.

"This is bad," Lynn said after hearing the note. Bewildered by the ugliness of it all, Elizabeth placed the package on the table. Massaging her forehead with the fingers of one hand, she stared into space and rubbed her hands together. "I think I need a drink," she said as she rose to pour herself one from the bar. Her earlier resolve to give the alcohol a break would have to wait. When she spoke moments later, she looked helplessly at Lynn and said, "Miss Davis, I frankly do not know what to do. What can you tell me?"

"Of course, I will do everything I can to find this guy and get him out of your lives."

"Yes, I know you will. However, in the meantime, I'd better

speak to my accountant about arranging this bank transfer. It could take a couple of days to pull this together."

"You're not thinking of actually paying the money, are you?" Lynn asked her.

"If it comes to that, of course I will pay it. While I'd love to see this person caught, believe me, I will do whatever I must to protect my family and the company. They come first. It would be too much for my children to bear if this information were to reach the general public, and there's no telling how this might negatively effect business."

At that moment, Ross and Earl knocked at the door of the study and stepped in. They wanted to know what Miss Davis was speaking to their mother about. Mrs. Remington wanted all her children to know what was going on. She asked Parker and Jordan to join them. When everyone was assembled, she recounted the new developments, including the telephone call Lynn received the day before and why Lynn had been unable to reach her until today. Then she handed Earl the letter and he read it aloud, while Ross looked over his shoulder. Parker and Jordan were mortified.

"Two and a half million dollars!" Earl exclaimed angrily. "Who the hell does this character think he is? Does he honestly think our family is just going to roll over and turn that kind of money over to some screwball? No way. Mother, we must come up with a way to outsmart this guy. We can't let him rip our family off like that. If we pay him now, you can believe we'll not have heard the last of him."

After Earl voiced his reaction, Mrs. Remington showed her children the photographs. They studied them incredulously, and as they did so, each became more upset, but they were also fearful of the possibility that this information could get out and destroy their family image. Ross, like his brother, first thought his family should take a tough stance. After viewing the pictures, however, he wondered if they shouldn't just pay the money, especially as he considered the possible effects of something like this on his mother, his siblings, the corporation, and his father's image. Even on Erica and Perry.

Earl, Jr. held firm. He said, "It looks like we have a couple of days to work this thing out. Miss Davis," he said to Lynn. "If you are going to help us get this person, I also want to help in any way I can. The idea that someone thinks he could come in and wreck everything our family has stood for and built is preposterous. This character must be insane."

Lynn told Earl she would be staying on the case, and if he had any ideas she would be happy to hear them. Then she explained that although the blackmailer still used a fake woman's voice and an accent, she was relatively sure it was a man's voice disguised. Lynn could sense the fire raging in Earl, and she was impressed to see this kind of fight in him. Earl said maybe they could set this guy up and catch him in the act. Hopefully they could figure out who he was and get to him before he got to the press.

Mrs. Remington's spirit of battle was wearing thin. She almost felt ready to give the blackmailer what he wanted and try to catch him the next time. After all the stress she'd been under for so long, starting with her husband's illness, then everything else, she wasn't sure how much more she wanted to handle. However, she did not express her skepticism because a part of her definitely wanted to get the blackmailer for what he put her husband through and was now trying to do to her. She asked Lynn to hold on to the blackmailer's package, and Lynn put the pictures and the demand letter back in the original envelope and returned the envelope to her briefcase.

Some time later, Erica, Timmy and Perry arrived. They were shown to the study. Erica and Perry greeted the Remingtons and Lynn. Lynn looked at little Timmy and noticed he seemed subdued. She figured Erica had addressed his behavioral issue. Subdued or not, Timmy still managed to cast Lynn a spiteful glance.

Lynn briefly brought Erica and Perry up to date, telling them that the blackmailer had contacted her again; this time he demanded two and a half million dollars. Erica and Perry were shocked. Lynn described the phone call and the blackmailer's involvement of her.

Then Earl, Jr. chimed in to say that while he definitely didn't want to see the family maligned in the tabloids, he felt confident that if they all stuck together on this, they would figure out a way to outwit and catch the culprit. As Earl spoke, he sounded more and more determined, and in the end, everyone, including Mrs. Remington, agreed to stand together to try and catch this person rather than succumb to his demands.

Lynn made certain everyone knew how to reach her and left the Remington home. This time she found her way back through Indian Hill without a chaperone. She was still troubled over being stopped by the ranger earlier and decided that rather than just be upset, she would heed her mother's lifelong advice and deal with these situations in a proactive fashion. In that spirit, she would write a letter to the ranger chief of that community and explain what had happened and advise him to be certain his officers did not arbitrarily stop *certain* people on a whim.

After deciding how she would handle this situation, Lynn was able to relax and drive. But as she drove, that feeling returned — the one she'd had earlier of being right on the verge of something. She felt as if the identity of the blackmailer rested right on the tip of her tongue. She had a feeling he was inadvertently handing her his identity. Who was he?

Back in her office, Lynn briefed Ella on her visit to the Remington estate. Ella said it certainly sounded like Earl, Jr. was wanting to take a lead in resolving this issue. She told Lynn that Miss Bertha had just called to find out if they knew anything yet, and Ella wanted to call her back and allay her and Miss Lela's concerns about Jelly. But she and Lynn didn't want to get the little old ladies' hopes up too high just yet in case anything else came up about Jeremiah Brownlee and they would have to dash their hopes again. However, they decided it would be appropriate to let Miss Bertha and her sister know they were looking in a different direction for now.

Ella called Miss Bertha who told her warmly, "Those children of Hattie Rose visited me today. They were all grown up and just as mannerable as they could be. That was kind of you to tell them about me and Lela."

"I'm glad they were able to come by for a visit, Miss Bertha. In fact, they were really excited when I told them about the two of you. You know, they were just so hungry to learn more about their past. Especially from someone who knew their mother and grand-mother. I'm sure they appreciated being able to spend time with you."

"Oh yes, indeedy. We had a very nice visit, child. We sat around here and had some lunch together and I talked up a storm, and they laughed and asked questions. I told them I never heard from Sophie after Hattie died. But, oh, they loved hearing how their mother could charm the socks off just about anybody. Yes, sir, all the boys, including our Jelly, was real crazy about her. I told them Jelly thought she was just about the prettiest thing he'd ever laid eyes on. But she never did pay him or any of them no mind.

"I showed them what pictures I had and told them I had other ones, too," Miss Bertha said, adding " 'course now, those other ones could still be around here somewhere." Then she said reflec-tively, "I guess you're wondering how I got so many pictures of those folks. Well, Sophie showed me the ones with Hattie and that man, you know, boasting and everything. Then she forgot and left them, and I forgot about them, too, until years later when I found them stuck down in my sewing box. Now Jelly came up with some pictures, too. Said Hattie gave them to him. But I don't think you need to be worrying about Jeremiah blackmailing any-one." Then Miss Bertha paused a minute and said, "We love that boy to pieces. He went off and made something of himself. It just wouldn't be like him to be blackmailing anybody."

Ella wished she could have told Miss Bertha squarely that Jeremiah was off the hook. Instead, she played it safe and said, "Well, to tell you the truth, Miss Bertha, we don't know who did the blackmailing yet, but we do have reason to believe someone else was involved. Of course, until we find out for sure who did it, we're checking out every possibility. That is why we were inquir-ing about Jeremiah. It's pretty much standard procedure, you un-derstand. We'll be sure to let you know when we finally catch this person. But in the meantime, I want to thank you for everything — your hospitality, good conversation, and that refreshing home-made lemonade. I can taste it now. Ummm, ummm," she said, smiling.

"That's all right," Miss Bertha said, clearly pleased at what

Ella just said. "Oh one more thing, dear, I almost forgot to tell you. The last time you were here you must have forgot and left some money right over there on that table." Ella was glad they found it and glad she'd thought to leave it, especially since Miss Bertha and her sister were making those long distance calls trying to locate Jeremiah on her behalf.

However, before she could say anything, Miss Bertha said, "Now don't you worry. We were going to hold it for you till the next time you came by. But, I went ahead and gave your ten dollars to that young lady, Erica. Told her you must have accidentally dropped it when you were here, and she promised she'd give it to you for me. Was that okay?"

"Oh, Miss Bertha, you shouldn't have done that," Ella said. "I really wanted to pay you and Miss Lela for making all those long distance calls."

"Now, honey, we heard you say that before," Miss Bertha said. "But I guess you probably didn't hear us say no, thank you. Me and Lela both said it; we sure did. 'Cause, child, we know people work too hard for their money to leave it laying around. Besides, Lela calls her son 'bout every day anyway, so we wouldn't think of asking you to pay for her long distance telephone calls. You can just look for that young girl to give you your ten dollars back.

"And listen, those young people promised me they would stay in touch, and I want you to stay in touch, too. Perhaps you can come by again sometime, and we'll just visit. Maybe you can go to church with me and Lela some Sunday. You married?"

Ella was smiling as she listened to Miss Bertha. She told Miss Bertha that she was married and she and her husband, Ben, would be happy to go to church with them some Sunday. When the conversation ended, Ella was glad to have spoken with Miss Bertha, for this sweet little old woman had a way of reminding her just how wonderful people can be.

Back in her office, Lynn took a call from Erica. She asked Erica how their visit with Miss Bertha and Miss Lela had been. Erica said she and Perry had had a great time and that the two old sisters told them about how Miss Lela's son, Jelly, had this wild crush on their mother. Erica also said that Miss Bertha had given her ten dollars and asked her to be sure she personally handed it to Ella, so she was holding on to it until she saw her. She said that she and Perry were definitely going to stay in touch with those two special little ladies.

Then Erica explained that the reason for her call was to tell Lynn that she, Timmy and Perry were going to Columbus to visit their folks for a couple of days, but they would return to Cincinnati on Sunday evening. She and Perry needed to be back in town next week to sign some papers the attorney was to draw up for them.

Erica then told Lynn she talked to Timmy about his behavior at her mother's house and his inappropriate teachings. "He seemed to understand. And this just blew me away," she said. "Timmy said his dad told him he could go and live with him and Cathy. I couldn't believe Thomas would say such a thing. You know, I told you Thomas has said he would take me to court to try to get custody of Timmy. I never really took him seriously. But now I'm wondering if maybe he was serious about his threat and wants to make trouble. I cannot imagine why he would do this. Frankly, this is scary."

Lynn did not know quite what to make of the strange actions of Erica's ex-husband. She was beginning to wonder if he was on drugs or something. Erica told Lynn she had even tried to call and talk to Thomas about this, but his girlfriend had thrown her another zinger. Cathy said she hadn't seen Thomas in several days and she had no idea where he went, but that he'd taken his things. They'd had an argument over something, and Thomas left. Erica said she was very surprised at this because she thought Thomas and Cathy were getting along just fine.

Then she told Lynn, "You know, I feel I should be flying high right now. Instead I've been having these weird feelings that something terrible is in the air. I guess it's all this blackmail business. Do you know what I mean?"

"I know exactly what you mean," Lynn said. "You see, I get that way sometimes, too. It's like I know something is about to happen. In fact, I've had that feeling about this case, too. I feel like I'm on the verge of discovering who this character is. These feelings come at strange times; sometimes I even get them in my dreams. As a matter of fact, it was something like a dream that helped me decide to leave the police force."

Erica said, "I'm glad you understand. I don't feel comfortable telling other people about these feelings. By the way, Miss Davis, I did not know you were a police woman."

"Oh yes, for eight years," Lynn answered thoughtfully. "I was a sergeant. But I gave it up some time after my partner was killed in the line of duty. After Jack died, I just couldn't deal with it any longer. Even still, I had loved being on the force, and it took me a while to decide what I wanted to do next. You know, they say some people, women especially, seem to get more in touch with their ESP or intuition. At times, they seem to just know things. It's a pretty special thing. But occasionally it's a little unsettling, though."

"In his video to us, our father told me and Perry that our mother was that way — that somehow, she seemed to know she was going to die."

"Is that so?" asked Lynn.

"But he also assured us her death was strictly an accident. He said the two of them had been having a heated discussion and she left in a huff. Then, the car wreck happened … and she was killed."

"I'm very sorry, Erica," Lynn said. "You're having to deal with so much right now. Are you okay?" Erica said she was fine. Lynn continued, "Listen, I'm going to stay on this while you're away. Why don't you leave me your parents' phone number in Columbus and call me when you get back to town on Sunday."

Erica gave Lynn her folks' telephone number and said she'd call her in a couple of days.

CHAPTER
27

J.T. SAT IN his hotel room that evening and let his thoughts take him on an emotional roller coaster ride. By now, he figured the old lady had seen his offer, and he could hardly wait until Tuesday so he could get his money. Already stoned, he drank one cold beer after another while this whole deal ran through his head. He knew that by now the Remington will had been read, and he figured old man Remington was probably real generous to his family, maybe to the tune of millions. After all, the paper said he was worth over a billion dollars. He figured that even the two kids by his black girlfriend were included in the will, and J.T. jealously wondered what they ever did to deserve the old man's money.

J.T. was very clear. If anyone deserves Remington's money, it's me, he thought. I'm the one whose life was shot to hell when I was misled into marrying a black woman. That woman betrayed me, passing for white, making me fall in love with her. She looked white, all right, but in her heart she was black as coal. Even though they were now divorced, he had never forgiven Erica Harrington for deceiving him.

Thomas Jefferson Harrison had been reared to believe in white supremacy. He had caustic memories of elementary school when he was teased shamelessly by his friends for being named after the former president who was rumored to have fathered slave children by his black mistress. To redeem himself, Thomas cleverly reversed his initials to come up with his nickname. He became known as J.T. to his friends and family, carrying that tag throughout his life. Only Erica called him Thomas.

He had been taught early that the races weren't supposed to mix, and he accepted those teachings unquestioningly. Never in a million years would he have knowingly taken anything but a pure white as his bride. What a shock it was to learn he'd been married to a black girl for four years. This fact had undeniably ruined his marriage and cost him a great deal of peace of mind. J.T. thought often of the promise he made to his father the last time he saw him alive — to uphold his race. By marrying black, he had failed to keep his promise, and at times this fact distressed him almost more than he could bear.

Now she was coming into an inheritance, and it upset him to know that if he and Erica were still married, he'd be entitled to half her money. Of course, Thomas had tried to keep that black investigator from finding her and her brother just to keep things simple. He figured eventually someone would locate them, but for now, he wanted her out of sight. If she ever saw those pictures, the crap would hit the fan! But Lynn Davis didn't heed his warning, damn her. Now, the only thing he could figure was if his blackmail didn't work, he might have to take custody of his son. That way, Erica would have to give him plenty of dough for Timmy's care. After all, she was ruining his son by letting that black fellow, Porter, come around all the time. Fortunately, as a concerned father, Thomas Harrison was teaching his son, Timothy, to stay away from certain people. He taught Timmy what to call them, too.

Thomas again recalled the streak of luck that had literally dropped those priceless pictures in his lap. Erica had found them in a box of mementos once belonging to her birth mother. That's when she first shocked the hell out of me, he thought, showing me that picture of her mother. And that's when she *claimed* to have first found out she was black! What a crock! Thomas aimlessly switched the television set on and off. He could only concentrate on Erica.

He remembered how her news had ripped him apart. So much so, he became obsessed with finding out everything he could about her past. He figured more secrets lay hidden in that little wooden box, and he intended to find them. Thomas thought that if Erica's momma's picture was in there, maybe her papa's was too. She had carefully hidden the box but, of course, he located it in their second bedroom. Then he studied its contents. That's when he had the pictures copied.

When Thomas first saw these photos, he couldn't believe his eyes. Was it possible he recognized the man in the photographs? He was sure he'd seen him before. But where, when? At first he struggled to remember, but upon examining the man's face closer, he saw that queer-shaped scar over his right eye. Suddenly, bam! It came to him. He had seen this man's picture hanging in the lobby of Remington Corporation's headquarters in Cincinnati a few years before when he met with some executives there on that shopping center deal. Yep, it was him all right. Small damned world, he thought in amazement. That grotesque mark above his eye was a dead giveaway. The plaque underneath the man's portrait had read, EARL Q. REMINGTON, FOUNDER AND CEO, THE REMINGTON CORPORATION. So this guy was a big shot. Probably had lots of money, too. Thomas even remembered meeting the man's sissy-acting son by the same name.

All at once it hit him. Earl Q. Remington was his wife's father. He knew at once these pictures were an undisputed gold mine, and he had every intention of cashing in on them. Man, what a find! He was quite proud of his exciting discovery. What an opportunity these pictures afforded him. He could use them to get back at the very person who caused his marriage to fail when he chose to play sugar daddy to that black woman and father those two kids, one of whom I happened to marry, he thought, regretfully. And to get rich at the same time; this is fantastic!

Thomas smiled as he remembered how Erica had been so worried about who her real father was. But I knew who he was almost from the start, he bragged, so proud of how easily he'd put two and two together. Even prouder of how he'd gotten the photographs blown up and then sent the package off to Mr. Remington. The sucker swallowed the bait, hook, line and sinker. It was almost too easy. Should have probably asked for more money, especially since Remington was so willing to cough up the cash, he laughed.

It was plenty obvious that guy didn't want his little wife to know about his shenanigans with that woman. And who could blame him? After all, here he was messing around on his wife with some black chick. Bet his wife would never have forgiven that. Thomas laughed aloud thinking of how, had she found out, Mrs. Remington would probably have taken old man Remington for all he was worth.

He remembered again the horror he'd felt when he first learned he had been married to a black woman. The fear that his family would learn about his wife was stifling. His anger returned as he replayed that dreadful episode in his mind. Initially, he was snookered, actually believing Erica hadn't known what her race was before. But after he thought about it a minute, it didn't make any sense. Erica was, after all, a pretty big kid by the time her momma died. "Come on, Erica. Cut the dumb act," he said aloud, vividly reenacting the ordeal in his mind. You knew exactly what you were, but you led me to believe you were lily white.

All at once, Thomas' anger dissolved as he remembered how absolutely crazy he had been about Erica. She was so beautiful, and real sweet, too. And she was fun and exciting to be with. They used to have such a time laughing about things that happened on their jobs, going to the movies, taking long walks and dreaming big dreams for their future. They were building a good life for themselves, and he thought they would be together forever. But on the other hand, he just couldn't stand being deceived like that. It was hard for him to accept that he'd actually been married to someone black. He remembered how those people used to talk against interracial marriage something awful when they came to his house for their meetings. Sometimes his father would let him sit with the grown folks and listen to their discussions. He learned so much from just listening. He uttered pathetically, "If my folks knew about this, my dad would've jumped straight up from his grave and kicked my ass. My mother, well, if words could kill, Erica would be dead. Hell, my mother would've killed me, too, for contaminating our family line."

Thomas knew all about why Erica was going back and forth to Cincinnati these days. She has a nerve, he thought, asking me to keep the boy while she comes here to collect her millions. Erica isn't too bright at times. Thomas had been promising Timmy he could come and live with him one day. It was probably time to act on this promise. Maybe I should just go on up to Columbus while Erica's in Cincinnati and pick up Timothy from my former in-laws, he schemed. That would fix her, he plotted vengefully. However, just as quickly, the very notion of hurting Erica in any way was almost more than he could bear, for in his heart of hearts, he never wanted to truly harm her. Thomas was troubled and confounded.

For certain, his heart was broken. He had loved this woman dearly. Still did as a matter of fact. But staying true to his early teachings, he accepted the ending of his marriage to the one woman in this whole world who could lift his heart and make it practically soar like the eagles. She had been the love of his life. Although he had all these mixed feelings, he knew that in the deepest recesses of his heart, an endearing love would always abide for Erica Harrington. She was the only woman he would ever love. Oh, Erica. Why did you do this to me, he cried out. He pined for her; he missed her so. And in a way, he hated her.

Thomas also thought of his girlfriend, Cathy, now sitting home in Minneapolis, hoping he would come back to her. But I've had enough of her, he thought, as he realized Cathy was no better than any of the other women who had come in and out of his life since Erica. She could never hold a candle to Erica, he uttered aloud as he finished the last beer from his six-pack and fell across his bed to sleep off his stupor.

* * * * *

"Hi, Lynn," a neighbor said while strolling down the street with her huge Golden Retriever. "You look fabulous! How was your run?" Still breathing heavily as she began to run in place,

Lynn answered, "Hey, Frances. It was great." Then she caught her breath and added with a smile, "But the best part is the stopping!" The two women parted, and Lynn trotted toward her house. It was Friday morning, and she had run her usual three miles before dressing for the office. She found jogging especially therapeutic and stress-relieving, which came in handy in her line of work. It provided her a good time to clear her head.

While running this particular morning, however, Lynn's mind had been plagued with thoughts of the blackmailer and the events of the last two days. Who on earth was this character? Her thoughts only generated more questions, but she felt the answers were close at hand. Lynn removed a stylish light gray suit from her closet. Even as she dressed for work, she could not get him out of her head. She still felt like she was on the brink of discovery. The answer to this mystery was near; she was sure of it. Oddly, she could not get Thomas Harrison off her mind either. His actions were nothing short of bizarre. Was this guy going to keep making trouble for Erica, she wondered, and thought it was highly probable, especially since Erica now had money.

Lynn sat in her office with the door closed, asking not to be interrupted unless it pertained to this case. Needing to focus, she stared straight ahead in deep reflection. The blackmailer! Apparently, this person had seen her on Tuesday because he had described what she wore that day. She recalled his cryptic compliment about her beige outfit. He'd even gotten close enough to describe her lapel pin. Not only that, he knew her car. She kept asking herself how he could possibly have known these things? He had to have actually seen her. Wait a minute, she wondered, have I possibly seen him? Lynn felt certain she must have, and this both excited and weighed heavily on her.

It was more than just seeing that figure lurking in the parking garage, which she was now convinced had to have been the blackmailer. The possibility of there being another encounter was what she wondered about. Could he have been in this building?

Lynn decided the blackmailer's fake female impersonation was no doubt intended to throw her off track, have her looking for a woman. She was convinced more than ever there was a man behind that voice and, most likely, the same man blackmailing Earl Remington before. After all, his stash of pictures included all the ones used before. Would he be in drag, she wondered, while quickly ruling that possibility out, unable to see the benefit of his dressing as a woman since he was operating behind a telephone.

Lynn retraced her normal routine. She always went from the parking garage directly to the building lobby, where she would take the regular elevators up to the fourth floor. Lynn could not remember a time that day when she noticed anyone peculiar, although she did remember that Mr. Thompson from the parking garage was not there since he had had a heart attack, and a temporary employee was filling in. People come and go in this building all day long, she thought, so it would not be out of the ordinary to see someone she did not know roaming about.

But something still gnawed at her. What is it, Lynn asked herself. She tapped the desk with bright red fingernails and began speaking aloud as she rehashed the sequence of events racing through her head. Suddenly, something started to come to her. She felt excited as she remembered a particular occurrence, so she began to talk it out — a practice she often resorted to in order to think things through clearly. "On Wednesday morning when I arrived at my floor," she said quietly, "I remember … there was a man in a plaid shirt waiting … waiting by the elevator on my floor. When I got off the elevator, this man spoke to me. In fact, we spoke to each other. That's not particularly unusual … but, as I recall … this man did not get *on* the elevator when I got *off*, even though it appeared that he was waiting for it to come."

Lynn remembered turning back to look at him because she could almost feel his eyes piercing her skull. He looked down, and that's when she noticed the elevator call light was not even on. "Yet the man was still standing there," she quietly exclaimed. "I remember he appeared to be preoccupied with his newspaper or something. For some reason, at the time that didn't strike me as strange. But if the elevator light had been on, that would explain why he did not get on mine. He would have been waiting for another elevator going in the opposite direction."

Lynn's voice was a whisper, "So what was that guy doing, just standing there?" She was suddenly curious, mostly because she remembered the way he peered into her eyes when he spoke. It was like there was a hidden message behind those eyes. "So okay, Lynn, what's so strange about this?" she asked herself, then answered, "I'm wondering why he did not get on the elevator? Could he have been waiting for someone?"

Lynn recalled that she had arrived earlier than usual that morning to open her office since she was going to have to leave to take Erica and Timmy to her mother's house. The other offices on her floor didn't usually open until around eight-thirty. This guy was definitely not a tenant on her floor because she knew the other fourth floor tenants. So if the other offices weren't open for at least another hour, what was this man doing just standing there, she wondered.

Lynn tried to remember what he looked like, but that part of her memory was fuzzy. However, she was becoming strangely aware that the more she thought of this man, the more something was telling her she was on the right track. Could that possibly have been the blackmailer? A quiver ran down her spine at the very idea, and Lynn's thoughts began to flow like a tidal wave.

She wondered how the blackmailer could have known that Mrs. Remington and her family already knew about Erica and Perry. His original ploy had been to threaten Mr. Remington to keep his wife from learning about his affair. If this was the same blackmailer as before, he might have put two and two together and figured that Earl Remington told his wife about it before he died.

Lynn still couldn't figure out why the message in his first call was about not searching for Erica and Perry. What is with this guy? Lynn's thoughts were interrupted by a phone call. "Lynn Davis speaking." She was surprised to learn that Earl, Jr. was on the other end.

"Miss Davis, this is Earl Remington. I wanted to call you to make sure you realize how much we want to get to the bottom of this before Mother gives this blackmailer any money." Lynn acknowledged his point, and he continued. "Well, I told you I wanted to help, and I've been thinking a lot about something lately. Can we talk now?"

"Yes, please go on, Mr. Remington," Lynn told him. She was clearly interested in any new ideas he or anyone had about this case.

"Well, you see, something has been troubling me. On Tuesday afternoon, Erica and her son, Timmy, and Perry came over to headquarters for a tour. It was during the viewing of our public relations video that my sister spotted her ex-husband in the film." My sister? My, how things have changed, Lynn thought, hearing Earl refer to Erica. Earl said, "She may have mentioned this to you already."

Lynn said that Erica had mentioned it, and that she had been pretty surprised to see Thomas in the film. "I got to thinking about that guy," he said. "We did some business about four years ago with his firm, Runyon. Then it was over. I'm aware of no more business dealings we've had with them after that. We did not have anything going on with him two years ago at the time our corporate film was being made. See what I'm getting at? This guy wasn't doing any business with Remington two years ago. So I can't understand why he would be in our building, and why he was studying that portrait of my father."

"That's a good point," Lynn said, and as she thought about it, Earl had made an excellent observation. But was he suggesting that Erica's ex-husband, Thomas, had something to do with this scam? Was Earl possibly implying that Thomas was the blackmailer? Excited by that possibility, Lynn replied, "Mr. Remington, this is very interesting. As a matter of fact, there are some real strange goings-on where this guy, Thomas, is concerned." She was thinking about how Thomas was giving Erica a hard time over custody of their son, and how he had been filling his son's head with negative racial messages.

Earl, too, was puzzled. Then a chilling thought suddenly occurred to Lynn. "Listen," she asked, "do you happen to remember what Thomas looked like? Or on second thought, I wonder if I could view your corporate video?" Lynn asked this as the stranger at the elevator suddenly came into view in her mind. She pictured him clearly now. He was tall, around six feet with a slightly stocky build. She seemed to remember he had thick dark brown hair worn with a part on the side. Mostly, she remembered his eyes. They were dark and penetrating, and he had thick, dark eyebrows and rather heavy sideburns.

Earl said, "Yes, vaguely. Fairly tall, stocky. No facial hair. Average looking guy. But better yet, you can see the film yourself. If you want, you can come over to my office and view it here, or I can have Arnold run a copy downtown to your office."

"Let me come there and see it, and I may want to borrow a copy for a while."

"No problem. What time will you get here, Miss Davis? Perhaps we can talk for a few minutes when you arrive."

"I'll leave right now and I can get there in a half hour."

Lynn arrived at Remington headquarters, which was as she remembered it, and as Erica and Perry had described, quite a distinguished-looking place. What seemed especially nice was the tranquil atmosphere that seemed to surround the place.

Earl had alerted his secretary that Lynn was coming, and Brynn Jamison invited Lynn to wait in his office. The wait was short, but long enough for Lynn to study the portrait of Earl Q. Remington, Sr. that hung behind Earl's desk. It was an imposing portrait. Earl, Sr. was a strikingly handsome man who had an air of power and importance. However, there was also a warm and sensitive look about him. Lynn thought it was probably his eyes.

When Earl Jr. came into his office, he greeted her warmly as if they were now a team working together collaboratively. After chatting briefly, Earl said, "Mr. Remington feels far too formal, don't you think. Mind calling me Earl?"

"Certainly, no problem," Lynn answered. And you can call me Lynn. Okay."

"Sure thing, Lynn, it's a deal," Earl said, smiling and extending his hand to shake on it. Then noting how she was studying his father's portrait, he showed her some more recent photos of his father. In his later years, Lynn noted that he was still very stately and handsome. The mark over his right eye was ever the focal point of his face. What was strange was that Lynn could not remember the number of times she had seen Earl Remington's picture in magazines or in the news, but she had never before noticed that mark over his eye which now seemed quite prominent.

Earl invited Lynn to have a seat and told her he would play the portion of the film where Thomas appeared, and then she could take a copy and keep it as long as she needed it. The video was already cued for the right segment, and when he pressed the play button, the lobby scene appeared on the screen. At the precise moment Thomas was spotted, Earl pressed the pause button.

Lynn felt like she'd been struck by a lightning bolt. "Oh, my goodness," she exclaimed. The man standing there viewing the portrait of Mr. Remington *was* definitely the man she had seen standing by her elevator Tuesday morning. Although in the video his face was at a slight angle, certain features were all too obvious — those sideburns, for one thing, his build, and those heavy eyebrows. Lynn was positive. "That's him," she uttered in disbelief, shaking her head. Earl had no clue what she was talking about, and Lynn told him about the man waiting by her elevator two days before. She reminded Earl of how the blackmailer had described the color of her outfit that day, and how she had an eerie sensation when she thought about how this guy was just standing there by the elevator early in the morning before any offices on her floor were open. They had even spoken to each other. And she was sure, no, positive, it was the same person. Earl zoomed in to get a closer shot of Thomas, and Lynn just sat back in disbelief.

Earl was excited now. Could they be pinpointing the blackmailer? He said he would make copies of that particular frame so they could ask around and see if others in the building had ever seen this guy. He pressed a couple of buttons and momentarily handed Lynn several color copies of the close-up of Thomas Harrison. Lynn was elated. She said she wondered if Thomas had been in town at the times of the previous blackmailing. Earl told her that they did not know the actual dates his father had turned money over to the blackmailer, although if bank records were checked, they might be able to pinpoint the dates of suspicious withdrawals. He told her he would have that checked on that right away.

Earl buzzed his secretary to come into his office. When he

asked Brynn if she recognized the person in the picture, she studied it. Then she thought for a minute and said, "Of course, that's, hmmm, I think his name is Thomas something." Earl and Lynn looked at each other. Brynn continued, "It's something like Thomas Miller."

Miller? That was unexpected. Brynn said, "He comes around here from time to time, and you know, I don't know who his contact is here. But," she said, perking up. "I'll tell you who might know." Earl listened up. He was curious about who could shed light on Thomas' business at Remington. "Arnold could probably tell you," Brynn said. "I think he knows the guy. I've seen them talking, more than once. Why don't you ask him?"

Arnold? Now that came as a surprise. After all, he was the family and corporate driver. Why would he be talking to this man? Earl summoned Arnold to his office. When Arnold received the page to come to Earl, Jr.'s office, he thought, well, here goes. He knew one day the time would come when Earl would finally jump him for ratting on him. He was extremely uneasy as he stepped cautiously into Brynn Jamison's office.

"Hello, Miss Jamison. I was just paged to come up here." Actually, he was hoping she would say it was all a big mistake. Instead, she said, "Yes, Arnold. Mr. Remington would like to ask you a question. You may go in."

Here goes nothing, Arnold thought to himself as he walked into Earl's office, and was surprised to see, of all people, Lynn Davis, the private investigator Mrs. Remington had been working with to find Remington's two kids. He said, "Uh, excuse me. I was paged to come up here. Shall I come back?"

Earl told Arnold to stay and asked him how things were going. Arnold didn't quite know how to answer, because he didn't know what this summons was about. He spoke with reservation, saying things were going pretty well at this time. Earl said, "Arnold, we are trying to figure out who this guy is right here," handing Arnold one of the color pictures from the video. Earl told him they believed this guy came to the building from time to time, and he was trying to determine what his business was here.

Whew! Was Arnold ever relieved. Is that all Earl wanted? He

was quite happy to tell him that, sure, he knew the guy. He was from out of town, in fact, Minnesota. But he comes to town two or three times a year. Arnold said he wasn't sure who the guy came to see. Other than that, he said he knew him pretty well, since they talked from time to time. "Really nice man. His name is Tom Mailer."

TOM MAILER! Lynn and Earl were stunned at that name. This guy's name was Thomas, all right. Thomas Harrison. Earl's secretary had said she thought his name was Miller. Why did others know Thomas Harrison by another name? What was this all about? Lynn suddenly had a strange notion: It was that name that had her going. She could only think of how *Mailer* could be shortened from *blackmailer.* Surely not, she told herself, but I've got to admit, this is very unusual.

And why would he be talking to Arnold? They sure seemed unlikely candidates for a business relationship — Arnold, a chauffeur, and Thomas Harrison, an executive with Runyon real estate developers of Minneapolis, Minnesota. Earl thanked Arnold for coming up, and said, "Arnold, this discussion is confidential. I want you to be perfectly clear about that."

"Sure, confidential, no problem," Arnold told him, relieved to get the heck out of Earl's office.

Earl and Lynn were astounded. It might be they had just stumbled onto something here. Lynn was glad Earl had come up with these questions about Thomas' business with Remington. Something suddenly occurred to her. She said, "Earl, it just dawned on me that, as much as we've passed the blackmailer's photographs back and forth, the people who have never seen them are Erica and Perry. You know, Erica found some photographs belonging to her birth mother three or four years ago. If she could look at those pictures, she might recognize them. Surely she would know if any of them are from the same group of photographs she had. And if they are, especially with all the other unusual developments, this would definitely suggest that Thomas Harrison is involved. Certainly he would have had access to those pictures."

"That's right. But didn't Erica and Perry go up to Columbus to visit her parents?" Earl asked. "Erica could hold the key to this whole mystery and doesn't even know it."

"I have her parents' number in Columbus back at the office. I'll phone her when I get back there and see what I can find out. I definitely want her to see these pictures. I hope she'll be able to come back to Cincinnati before Sunday night. If she can't come back early, I'll take the pictures up there myself."

"I wish you could call her right now," Earl said, pointing to his telephone. Lynn agreed this was nothing to sit on, so she called her office and told Janet where to find Erica's parents' number in her office. When she got the number, she placed the call.

Lynn lucked out. Erica answered the phone and excitedly told her, "My parents said that Thomas was in town earlier this week and he came by their home on Wednesday expecting to see Timmy. He didn't know I had Timmy with me in Cincinnati. This is really crazy. I'm very concerned about Thomas' peculiar behavior. Even my folks thought it was strange. I wonder what he's up to?"

With every word Erica spoke, Lynn became more and more convinced that Thomas, with his unusual behavior, was the key. "Erica, listen, as crazy as it sounds, what you're telling me may be related to some breaks we are just now getting in this case. I'm meeting with Earl, Jr. right now in his office. Now here's why I'm calling. It's very important. We would like you to come back to Cincinnati before Sunday if possible. Do you think you can do that?" Lynn paused momentarily as Erica quickly digested what she was hearing. First, there were some new breaks in the case, which was great news, and second, that it could have something to do with Thomas?

"Of course, I'll come back," Erica answered. "What do you want me to do?"

Lynn answered, "Erica, look. I need you to look at the black-mail pictures and tell us what you know about them. This is critical. If only I'd shown them to you and Perry yesterday while we were at the Remington estate, but I had put them in my briefcase before you all arrived and didn't think to pull them back out." Lynn wanted Erica to see these photographs as soon as possible and considered faxing them, but she quickly decided that would not be the best way. Besides, she wanted to see Erica's reaction to the photographs.

Erica was intrigued at the idea that she could be part of the solution. She told Lynn she and Perry had dinner plans that evening with their parents and wondered if tomorrow morning would be soon enough. She said she could leave early and that no doubt Perry would want to come, too. Lynn told Earl, Jr., who said he could send the company plane up to Columbus to pick her up. Earl, Jr. got on the telephone, and they arranged a time for them to be at the airport.

"Tomorrow morning then," Lynn said, wishing it could be sooner, but still glad that Erica could flex her schedule. Tomorrow morning was just a few hours away. They arranged to meet at ten o'clock in Lynn's office.

Lynn told Earl. "This could be the answer we're looking for, Earl. Wouldn't it be something if it is? Thanks so much for your help. I'll phone you tomorrow to let you know how the meeting turns out."

"Lynn, if it's all the same to you, could I join you?" he said. "I'm really interested in finding out more about this guy, especially if he turns out to be our blackmailer. Furthermore, if he isn't, we won't have much time left to figure out who is. I definitely don't want Mother to transfer that money into that Swiss account Tuesday."

Lynn said, "Definitely, Earl, that's fine with me. I can understand how you'd want to be here. I will see you at ten."

"Righto. I'm really glad you came to the office, Lynn. I'd appreciate if you'd let me know if you learn anything else about this guy."

"Will do," Lynn said as she left Earl's office, feeling excited about these new developments.

CHAPTER
28

BACK IN HER office, Lynn viewed the entire Remington film. It was well done, painting a picture of the Remington Corporation as a strong, healthy business run by happy, productive employees. When she got to the end of the film and again viewed the scene in the lobby with Thomas standing below Earl Remington's portrait, she had no doubt that the man she had seen at the elevator three days earlier was one and the same.

Lynn was getting a bad feeling about Thomas Harrison. She wondered if he was a mental case, dangerous, on drugs, or what. The thought that she had been within just a few feet of him was disconcerting to say the least. However, she noted with interest that her feeling of being on the verge of something had ceased. Was this finally it?

Lynn made a note to ask Erica for a picture of Thomas. She especially wanted to see those eyes. Then she thought again about how the blackmailer sounded like he knew that Mrs. Remington was aware of her husband's affair, and she wondered how he might have known. If Thomas is the blackmailer, could Erica possibly have unwittingly fed information to him, she wondered. Lynn remembered how her mother said Timmy acted and how Thomas was teaching him such despicable ideas. Why? And why had he been so hateful to Erica, threatening to fight her over custody of their son. At this point, Lynn's mind was made up. Thomas Harrison, otherwise known as Thomas Mailer, was the object of their search.

On Saturday morning, Arnold was to pick up Erica and Perry from Lunken airport and bring them downtown for their ten o'clock meeting. Earl, Jr. was punctual, arriving at Lynn's office at a quarter to ten. Lynn offered him something to drink, and the two sipped iced tea and reviewed what they knew as they waited for Erica and Perry's arrival. Ella also came in, and for a few minutes the three of them sat in Lynn's office and discussed the case. Earl was civil and cordial, and Ella saw that this was not the aloof, self-righteous young man she had first met just a few weeks earlier.

Erica and Perry arrived moments before ten o'clock along with little Timmy. Ella offered to take Timmy to the outer office to keep him busy, and Lynn observed with interest that he went with Ella willingly. Earl asked Erica and Perry about their visit with their parents in Columbus, and both answered that it had gone swell. Then Earl explained that he had asked Lynn if he could be included in the meeting. Lynn nodded her head, repeating that she and Earl had met the day before. They all took a seat around Lynn's desk.

Lynn said, "Erica, like I told you, it didn't occur to me until yesterday that I failed to show you and Perry these pictures on Thursday when I was out at the Remington home. See," she looked at Perry, "I had put them away just before the two of you arrived and didn't think about it after that. That was a big oversight. So that's why you're here. It's extremely important, and I thank you for coming back early." Then, as she looked them both directly in the eye, she cautioned, "Now let me warn you, this could be hard for you." Erica and Perry looked wary. Lynn paused for a moment before proceeding, then asked, "Ready to take a look at these photographs?" They nodded.

Lynn reached for the 8" x 10" pictures Mrs. Remington had found in her husband's private file and handed them to Erica, telling her and Perry that these were assumed to be the original blackmail photos that had been found at the home office of Earl Remington, Sr. The first picture was the one with Earl, Sr. and Hattie standing by the Rolls Royce and Arnold sitting in the driver's seat. Erica did a double take and said, "Where'd this one come from? Did you say this is one of the blackmail pictures?" Lynn looked at Erica with a serious expression on her face and nodded. Erica looked shocked. "But, I know this picture," she said, studying it for a long moment as Perry looked over her shoulder. Then she passed it to Perry, telling him this was an enlargement of one of the pictures she had found in her mother's box. Perry, seeing it for the first time, studied it curiously.

Erica looked at the next two pictures and shook her head in disbelief. "I've seen these pictures, too," she exclaimed with a half laugh, confounded. "In fact, I have them. Is this a crazy coincidence, or what?" Excitedly, Erica snatched up the fourth picture — the portrait of Hattie Williams, and instantly her hand flew to her mouth in shock. She stammered as she told Lynn that this was an enlargement of the very same picture she had shown Thomas when she first told him about her mother. The *very same picture*. In pencil, she had written *I love you, Mom*, on her original. Although there had been an attempt to erase these words, they still showed ever so faintly on the copy. Reality was dawning on Erica. "These are *my* pictures. How could the blackmailer have gotten his hands on these to blackmail our father?" she asked in exasperation, then became at once dismayed as the dreadful truth hit her like a lightning bolt. "Thomas?" Erica whispered her ex-husband's name as a question. But she knew the answer. She nearly cried.

Perry watched his sister's reaction, then reached for the other photographs and examined them, one by one. The only one he had previously seen was the one of their mother — the one Erica had sent him long ago. He had not seen these other pictures of his mother and Earl Remington. He studied them intently and thought about the time he had confronted his sister about not sharing these with him before. Still holding the pictures in his hand, he studied them once again, looking closely at Earl Remington. "Erica," he said, "Thomas had to have something to do with this." Erica looked at her brother hopelessly and shook her head.

Lynn said, "There are more." She told them that this week the blackmailer had sent additional pictures and had made up a sordid story to go with them. It was this package, she explained as she picked up the brown envelope from her desk, the blackmailer left for her on Tuesday for her to take to Mrs. Remington. Delivering this envelope, she told them, was the reason she had been at the Remington estate on Thursday.

Lynn opened the envelope and handed the folded newsprint to Erica, who reached for it with trepidation and trembling hands. Perry looked disbelieving. As Erica opened the layout and viewed the blackmailer's shocking headlines and the pictures, her worst fears were more than confirmed. A huge lump formed in her throat and when she could speak, she quietly said, "God, no!" She so wished this did not mean the obvious, but it was all too compelling. "Why, why?" she uttered. With tears forming in her eyes, she searched the pictures again, looking for some small shred, anything to negate this horrible reality. Unfortunately, Erica could find nothing but the truth, and no matter how she looked at it, it would not change. Perry had viewed the layout with Erica. He was quiet, and now he knew what Erica did. When she finally looked into Perry's eyes, hers were filled with tears. "It's true — Thomas," she whispered in desperation. Perry was speechless. "Thomas was blackmailing our father. Now he's after Mrs. Remington." Then she let down her guard and cried. When she was able to speak again, she said that, except for the newspaper photos of Mrs. Remington and their yearbook pictures, every picture was an enlargement of the ones in her private collection hidden away in her mother's little wooden box. The high school pictures must have come from her very own senior high school yearbook.

All eyes were turned to Erica, but no one spoke. Strangely, for both Lynn and Earl, Jr., the absolute identity of the blackmailer was now almost anti-climactic, for they had already figured out that it was Thomas. Finally, Perry said, "Sis, this is unbelievable. I know how you must feel and I'm so sorry. I feel badly for you, but I'm also mad as hell."

Erica looked at Perry as her brother added angrily, "I just can't believe it. That no good son of a ... I always thought there was something about that guy. In fact, sometimes I wondered why you ever married him. That scumbag stole your pictures and used them to blackmail the Remingtons." Perry's face held the look of disgust. "That means he figured out who our father was a long time ago and kept that information from you. He had to know how important that would have been for you. I mean, we might have even been able to meet our father while he was still alive if only we had known. I just can't believe it."

Erica was tormented. Not speaking to anyone in particular, she said, "I can't believe it either." Then she paused in very deep thought and said, "Yes, Thomas knew how much this information would have meant to me. But all he was interested in was using it to extort money from a wealthy man. He is a cruel, cruel person. But how could he do this?"

Perry put his arm around Erica's shoulders to console her, doing so even as he realized he needed to calm down himself. Then he asked, "How did he ever get his hands on these pictures?"

Erica signed helplessly. "I hid the little box I found in Mom's attic in my sewing room, actually my other bedroom. Its contents were too precious and personal to me, and they were much too intimate to share with anyone else. I surely never intended for Thomas to see them. I only showed him the one photo — the one of our mother. And, boy, that's when everything hit the fan. But I guess his curiosity got the best of him, and he sniffed around until he found my box." As she listened, Lynn wondered if Erica told Thomas about her racial background for the first time when she showed him her mother's picture. Guess he didn't take that information too well, especially if that's *when everything hit the fan.* Then she thought about the little boy in the outer office and knew that one day he might have to know these terrible things about his father.

All the while Erica talked, she kept shaking her head in astonishment. "Wait a minute," she said abruptly. "Now I'm suddenly remembering something else. Three years ago, when I took the pictures to the photo shop in my neighborhood to have some copies made for safekeeping, I remember the clerk acting like he recognized the pictures, especially the one with the Silver Cloud. In fact, he said he'd copied them before. Naturally, at the time, I thought that was absurd, so I told him he was mistaken. But now, I believe he did see those pictures. Thomas must have had every one of them copied and enlarged at the same shop," she said, pointing to the larger photographs. She sighed and said, "Oh, my goodness. This is just too horrible," and gave an apologetic look to Earl.

"Well, Thomas always was persistent. But how do you suppose he knew the man in the picture was Earl Remington?" Perry asked.

"I think I know," answered Earl, Jr., who had been listening to everything being said. "Four years ago, our company did some business with Runyon Developers out of Minneapolis." He looked at Erica, who acknowledged the company where her ex-husband worked. Earl continued, "The Runyon representative we dealt with happened to be Thomas Harrison. In fact, although he worked mostly with one of our other presidents, I now remember having at least one meeting with him, myself.

"What did it for me was when we were watching the corporate film Tuesday and little Timothy spotted his father. Well, that started me thinking," Earl, Jr. said earnestly. "We hadn't done any business with Runyon in at least four years. But after asking around, it turns out that several people had seen Thomas in the building much more recently. And you'll remember in our film, he was studying Father's portrait. It's possible he may have been checking to see if he had the right man. Of course, our father is easy to identify with that distinctive mark over his right eye. As you see, it shows up very clearly on these pictures," he said pointing to Earl, Sr.'s scar.

Lynn was impressed with Earl. No longer the pontifical, arrogant character she first met, he seemed sharp, clear thinking, even likable. She chimed in, "I watched the film, too, and I am absolutely certain that Thomas is the man I saw Tuesday morning when I got off the elevator on my floor. You see, when he called, the blackmailer commented on the color of the outfit I was wearing that day. He even described a lapel pin I had on. I figure he had to have seen me and pretty closely at that to be able to describe the rose pin I was wearing. Then I decided I just might have seen him, too. I started thinking about people I had encountered that day. And that's when I remembered this man standing by the elevator as I was going into my office that morning. I mean, he was pretty distinctive, too," Lynn said. "He was nice looking and had rather heavy, dark sideburns and thick eyebrows. Probably six feet tall, muscular build."

"That's Thomas," Erica replied. "I wish I could say it weren't so, but you've described him to a tee. If nothing else, you can always spot Thomas a mile away by those sideburns." Then, looking at Earl she said, "Somehow I feel like this is all my fault. I'm so sorry."

"You can't have known, Erica. You had nothing to do with it, and it certainly isn't your fault. What that guy does is on him," Earl reassured her. "You couldn't have even known he was capable of something like this." Erica was grateful that Earl did not blame her. She appreciated his solace and accepted it with relief.

Lynn said, "If I had any doubts, they vanished the minute I saw the Remington film." She pulled out one of the color photos of Thomas that Earl had printed. "You see, this is from that film, and I'm convinced this is the man I saw in my building. Erica, do you have a better picture of Thomas?" Erica retrieved a photo of Thomas and Timmy from her wallet to show Lynn, who pursed her lips, then quietly said, "That's definitely him."

Earl, Jr. added, "Here's one for you. Arnold, our chauffeur, knows this man. They even talk regularly. But Arnold knows him as Thomas Mailer."

"Mailer," Perry said in surprise. "Where'd that come from?"

"Couldn't have anything to do with the word *blackmailer*, does it?" Lynn asked in puzzlement.

"Oh, no," Erica said. "Mailer is actually his mother's maiden name. But it is an amazing coincidence. I guess he didn't want to use his real name with Arnold for some reason. I wonder what Thomas had to talk to him about?"

"Probably pumping him for information," Earl, Jr. said. "I mean, how else would he have known some of the things he did? Like how would he have known about Lynn Davis, for example?"

he asked, looking toward Lynn.

"That's right," Lynn said. "It makes sense he probably got my name from Arnold. I don't know how else he would have known it. In fact, at first I was even a little suspicious of Arnold. But I learned that your mother trusted him implicitly. He does seem to be on the up and up. If he is giving out information, I bet it isn't intentional."

Earl said, "You're probably right."

"Thomas probably bilks it out of him," Erica said. "He has a way of charming people to get what he wants. He probably calls Arnold up, pretending to be a concerned and casual friend, and gets him to talk about all sorts of things. I can see Thomas doing something like that. I really can." Shaking her head again, she said, "I'm wondering how I could have ever been married to such a disgusting person. At least I'm not married to him anymore."

"I couldn't agree with you more," Perry said. "But what do we do now?"

"That *is* the question," Lynn replied. "We need to stop Thomas Harrison from maligning the Remington family reputation. And we need to get him for extortion, past and present."

"But how can we get him?" Erica asked. "Thomas can be very slippery, and I'm sure he'll just deny everything."

"Maybe so," Lynn said. Then, she looked at Erica and the others and said, "I'm don't have all the answers just yet, but I'm convinced we *will* get him."

CHAPTER
29

LYNN AND EARL called for a gathering to be held at the Remington Indian Hill home to discuss how to deal with Thomas Harrison. It was midday Sunday, and there was great hubbub at the Remington estate. Lynn brought Ella and Harvey along with her. Erica, Timmy and Perry were present, as were the four Remington siblings and Earl's three youngsters. And because he, too, was to have a major role in their plan, Arnold Taylor sat in the meeting.

Timmy was taken to a children's room where he and Earl's six-year-old daughter, Farrah, played gleefully under the watchful eyes of a caretaker. The adults sat in the lavishly decorated living room under the glistening crystals of a huge chandelier that hung regally from the tall ceiling. First-timers to the Remington estate could hardly contain their awe as they looked around to behold the very finest in furnishings, art and style.

An antique white Queen Anne grand piano holding a crystal candelabra shared one corner of the room with houseplants and exotic flowers. The walls of the room were upholstered in a muted off-white print that matched the fabric in the draperies. Two lacquered Louis XV bombé chests inlaid with ivory and mother of pearl flanked the magnificent black marble fireplace and a beautiful Persian rug adorned the floor. The room was spacious, airy and bright.

Erica and Perry had not had an official tour of this place, and they, too, viewed with amazement this finely appointed room for the very first time. Arnold had previously only stood in the doorway of this great room. Today, he sat there proudly feeling like a valued family member or friend, and he derived a special feeling of importance from being included in this way.

Hors d'oeuvres were served, and everyone quickly turned their attention to Elizabeth Remington who said, "All of you now know there have been some important new developments in our situation. The point of bringing everyone together now is for Miss Davis and Earl to fill you in on the missing pieces of information. Earl has been working with Miss Davis, and Erica and Perry, and obviously, we are extremely relieved that they have discovered who the blackmailer is." As Elizabeth spoke, Erica felt exceptionally bad because of her connection to the blackmailer.

Yesterday afternoon after leaving Lynn's office, Earl had filled his mother in on everything. Needless to say, Mrs. Remington had been shocked but she was greatly relieved at the discovery they'd made. She did not hold this against Erica. Reluctantly, Earl had also divulged his misguided plot to trap Jake Huber to his siblings. They had been amazed that their brother would do such a thing, but were much more interested in hearing how they found Thomas out. As they talked today, Elizabeth's other children naturally questioned whether Lynn and Earl were positively certain they had the right man — that this was not just some bizarre coincidence. This question was satisfactorily answered in the animated discussion that ensued.

Earl spoke with authority and conviction. "As you know," he said proudly, "it was Erica's young son, Timothy, who made one of the key discoveries that helped us solve this mystery." The group listened with rapt interest as Earl retold the story of how Timothy had been the first to spot his father in the Remington video. That the youngest member of the clan was instrumental in this discovery was fascinating to all.

Earl and Lynn told how they had arrived at their early suspicions about Erica's ex-husband. They were planning to compare the dates of suspiciously large bank withdrawals made by Earl Remington, Sr. in the last two years to the times Thomas was in Cincinnati. "That was our only avenue, but as it turns out, it was not necessary," Earl said, adding, "When Erica and Perry came back to town early, Erica helped confirm our findings by identifying the photos in the blackmailer's package. And by the way," Earl told them, "other than some school pictures of Erica and Perry likely taken from Erica's own high school yearbook, all the other photographs in the blackmailer's package, other than those of Mother, were copies of pictures Erica had in her possession.

Then Lynn said, "Although Erica had not known at the time that the man in the pictures was her biological father, Thomas apparently figured it out. He had first viewed the senior Earl Remington's portrait in the lobby of the headquarters building when he did a project with Remington some years before. Probably when he saw pictures of this man with that distinctive mark over his eye, he pieced the puzzle together. He took a chance that Earl Remington was Erica's father, and quickly saw a way to capitalize on this knowledge through blackmail. Thomas probably felt he had nothing to lose, and if he was right, this thing might pay off big. Needless to say, he figured right, and he collected a substantial sum of money from Earl Remington before he passed."

Between Lynn and Earl, all the details were told. The whole group was fascinated by the way Thomas may have discovered Earl Remington's identity. Fascinated, too, that he had actually shown up in Cincinnati this week to scope out Lynn Davis. And they were appalled at how he first obtained some of his critical information, inadvertently through Arnold.

The prior evening, Earl and Arnold had had a long talk. As before, when Earl called Arnold into the study at the family home after returning from Lynn's office, Arnold thought his goose was cooked. However, instead of reaming him out, Earl suggested to Arnold that they put that unfortunate envelope incident behind them. Earl told Arnold it was wrong to have involved him and he needn't fear repercussions from him for telling his mother. Besides, they had much bigger issues to deal with. Poor Arnold was relieved and thankful. He was happy to prove his gratitude by working like crazy on this case with the family.

Earl told Arnold why he had asked him about the man named Thomas Mailer the other day at the office. When he told him what they suspected Thomas had done, at first Arnold could hardly believe it. When he learned his so-called friend was probably the very person who had been blackmailing Mr. Remington and was now coming at the Remington family again using information he may have obtained from him, Arnold was fit to be tied. This got his dander up quicker than anything else could possibly have, for if there was one thing that never needed to be questioned, it was his strong loyalty to the Remingtons.

At the mere thought that he may have involuntarily aided the blackmailer with key information, Arnold became enraged. He knew he'd been used. And the old vengeance mentality he'd developed in his early years suddenly overtook him. Arnold was ready to hurt this guy for tricking him into betraying his fine employers in this way. At that precise moment, all he really wanted to do, in his own words, was to "kick this guy's sorry ass and put out his lights."

Arnold never had any idea who the blackmailer was. He figured somebody had probably seen Mr. Remington and Hattie together and decided to take advantage of the situation. He even thought it might have been some of Hattie's relatives behind this. In a way, it was, he mused, as he realized Thomas, who would have been Hattie's son-in-law, was the culprit. Arnold was ready and eager to help in any way he could.

"Here's what we decided," Earl told the group. "Thomas is expecting the money to be deposited in his Swiss account by Tuesday afternoon. But we are not paying him a dime." This caused a mild stir. "We have a plan," he continued, "and we're confident it's a good one."

Mrs. Remington had already agreed to their course of action. Others needed to hear more before they could get comfortable taking such a bold position. After all, they asked, what if the blackmailer mails the pictures to the tabloids anyway? How can we actually catch the guy in the act before he tries something? Can't we just confront him? Shouldn't we let him know we're on to him? These questions and a barrage of others were hurled through the air in rapid succession.

"Listen, everybody," Earl said, "Basically, Tuesday will be business as usual. We believe that when Thomas learns the money has not been transferred to his account, he will make contact at least one last time before sending his package of photos off to the press."

Harvey spoke up, saying it will probably be Lynn who will be contacted. "Then again," Harvey conceded, "Thomas may try and find a way to finagle something out of Arnold. Either way, we have a plan. Arnold is prepped to be a key player should that happen." Lynn expressed her agreement, and Arnold glowed with self-pride.

Earl explained that, fortunately, Thomas had no idea they were on to him. "What we want is to get this guy," Earl said, "not just for what he's trying to do to our family now, but for what he did to our father in the past." As Earl explained the rest of the plan, his mother, sisters and brothers listened resolutely. Deep down, his family was impressed with the take-charge way Earl, Jr. was dealing with this. In the end, everyone supported the strategy.

The plan began to unfold. As agreed, no Remington money was transferred to the Swiss accounts. Tuesday evening, just after six o'clock, Lynn received the expected phone call from the blackmailer demanding to know what was going on. Again, she taped the phone call to study later. Lynn could tell the caller was very upset, which they'd hoped he would be. They wanted him to be shaken up so he probably wouldn't be thinking too clearly and possibly figure that something was up.

The voice made threats, "Don't these people know I'm not playing games? If I drop these packages in the mail, their reputations will never be the same, the bloody fools." Then he asked, "What are they going to do? You're their messenger; you tell me because I am prepared to act now. Do I make myself clear?"

Lynn said, "Wait just a minute. I wouldn't do anything rash if I were you. I delivered your information to Mrs. Remington, all right. And she was prepared to transfer the money. But she was also torn by a deathbed request from her husband. See, you're not the first person to come after Mr. Remington. Someone did it before, and he pleaded with her not to succumb to the demands of a blackmailer."

Lynn hadn't been certain how to prepare for this call since she did not know what Thomas was going to say. She knew she'd have to think on her feet, and in preparation had mentally walked through a variety of scenarios. She definitely didn't want to slip up and call him Thomas. The caller did not know what to make of what she told him. Thoughts raced through his head. So the guy actually told his old lady about me. So now what? What the hell is she going to do, he wondered angrily.

Lynn continued, "The first person blackmailing Mr. Remington was a man." Then she paused to sound hesitant, and slowly said, "But somehow I wonder if you aren't one, too, just disguising your voice. Am I right? Yes, that must be it. I bet *you're* the person who was blackmailing Mr. Remington before."

This agitated the blackmailer. He figured they would probably think he was the same person hitting the old man up before; he just did not want this black private eye analyzing him like this. He didn't respond to her question, but angrily snapped, "Shut your trap! No one asked for your opinion! I guess that old broad's husband doesn't give a damn about his family then. Didn't he care about their reputation, their honor? Because I can strip it all away, and it won't take me but a hot minute to do it. So what'll it be, you? The Remington honor or my money?"

Lynn was glad to have exasperated the caller so. She noticed that as his frustration rose, he'd slip up and momentarily forget the accent or the female impersonation. Her job was to make the option of having the money transferred into his Swiss accounts far less attractive than receiving ready cash. She and the others believed that if they dealt with cash, they stood a better chance of smoking him out in the open. She needed to get Thomas to demand his payment in cash.

Lynn began her campaign. She told him Mrs. Remington struggled with the decision, but eventually decided not to abide her husband's request. She decided instead to pay him his money, but she was going to have great difficulty transferring such a huge sum. A team of accountants, auditors and lawyers tightly managed her assets, especially now that her husband was deceased and the distribution of her husband's assets had not yet taken place. Therefore, this group tracked every expenditure to the penny. And Mrs. Remington did not want to get into that level of scrutiny over this matter with them. It would just hold things up longer, you see. Lynn did not have a clue if anything she was saying made any sense. But something was working, for she could hear Thomas' heavy, excited breathing and sighing.

"However," she kept talking, "there is another way. Mrs. Remington does have the ability to withdraw cash, no questions asked, which she could then transfer to your foreign accounts through a different bank. Now, she is going to have to set up a new account at another bank to keep the auditors out of her regular business. No problem, though, because she'd been advised that this type of transfer process would take only a few days to complete. Probably no more than five to seven days at the most." As Lynn talked, she only hoped Thomas did not realize that wire transactions, even of this size, could be completed in hours, versus days.

The caller was starting to panic. A few days? Five to seven days! He tried unsuccessfully to hide his concerns as he nonchalantly said, "Oh, that is just far too much time. No, that will never work."

Lynn smiled inwardly as she pictured the caller buying her story, and she continued painting a convincing picture of red tape including how tedious and time-consuming the bank transfer would be. She explained that this second process would be much better and less problematic than transferring the money directly from Mrs. Remington's account.

The caller abruptly stopped Lynn. He was thoroughly unhappy with the time it would take to get the money into his foreign account, but he was extremely pleased to hear that he'd get his money after all. He tried to sound harsh as he said, "Listen, if you're saying what I think you're saying — that your client is going to cough up the money, then I'm willing to give her a few extra days." He added gruffly, "These newspapers are pressuring me for the photographs, but I'll try hold them off to give her time to get it together."

Then Thomas decided, what the hell, it was far more trouble than it was worth to fiddle with the money transfer. Cash would be better. "I'll tell you what," he said. "You can also tell the old lady don't bother with my foreign accounts. Instead, I want her to be prepared to deal with me in cash. I'll call Thursday at three o'clock to see if she has the money. I'll tell her what to do with it then, too."

It worked, Lynn said to herself, glad for Thomas' naiveté and apparent inexperience in international transfers. To the caller, she said, "You're barely giving her any time here. I don't know if it's enough."

"Hey, you heard me. I'll give her until Thursday at three o'clock. Not a minute longer. You let her know what my terms are. Got it?"

"Yes, I have it," Lynn said, satisfied that the caller was reacting the way they'd hoped he would. When she hung up, she called Mrs. Remington and Earl, then Harvey Chapman to alert them about the call.

CHAPTER
30

W ANTING TO GET a sense of how the Remingtons were dealing with this situation, Thomas Harrison, a.k.a. Thomas Mailer,
thought it was time to check in with his old buddy, Arnold. He
placed the call. Lynn and the group had anticipated this call, and
Arnold was prepared for it.

When Thomas asked how things were going, Arnold jumped
in gear to do his part in the plot to catch a blackmailer, giving
Thomas an earful. He told Thomas that he was under so much
stress lately, he was about to burst. He said it didn't help that Mrs.
Remington had been acting real strange, even seemed scared these
days. He was certain something was in the air, but he didn't know
what it was. He said he'd been running his boss lady back and
forth from one bank to another, for what, he didn't know. Lord
knows, the woman had enough money. "Even has me running
around to news stands picking up those trashy scandal magazines.
I've bought them all. I can tell you about the 47-pound woman
from Mars who was carrying Elvis' baby, or anything else you
want to know," Arnold laughed.

Thomas chuckled, too. He was real pleased to learn that the
Remington woman was running scared. Arnold told him she was

getting jumpy. "In fact, jumps every time the phone rings — like she was expecting a call from the dead or something. But come to think of it," he told Thomas, "every one of those Remingtons seemed edgy these days. Don't know why, though." Arnold told Thomas all he knew for sure was the old broad was treating him like dirt, so frankly, he didn't care what was going on. Whatever it was, she had it coming. Thomas couldn't help but smile. He liked the sound of this update. To him it meant all was not well in Remington Land, and they were getting his money together.

Then Arnold baited the hook. He told his friend he was going to let him in on something personal. Thomas didn't want to waste time hearing about Arnold's pitiful little life, but he made an attempt to seem interested; now was not the time to burn bridges. He was glad he listened, for Arnold told him some really juicy things, like how, after working for this family for over 30 years, he'd pretty much had it with them. He said things were really tough for him right now because he had gotten screwed royally by the Remingtons. "The old man was decent to work for, you know," Arnold said pathetically, "but now he's dead. And as for the rest of the Remingtons, I can't stand any of 'em if you want to know the truth." Thomas' ears perked up.

Arnold told him that before old man Remington died, he promised to pay off these huge-ass medical bills Arnold had racked up on behalf of his invalid mother — over $50,000 worth! He said Remington was even supposed to put him in his will. "Ha!" he spewed, sarcastically, "Guy's worth a billion dollars, and what do I get out of the deal? Ten damn thousand dollars. He could have kept that and I could have sure told him what he could do with it. And now, Mrs. Remington and her stingy-ass kids don't want to make good on the old guy's promise. Said they had no proof of Remington's intentions. I know what's happening. They're just trying to screw me out of what's rightfully mine. I feel like an old piece of meat around here. So needless to say, man, I'm fed up with the whole business. I wish I could tell 'em to take this job and stuff it where the sun don't shine." Arnold continued his rampage as Thomas listened with growing interest. Then, abruptly, Arnold stopped and said, "Hey, man, I don't mean to bore you with my worries. This isn't what you called me about. I'm sorry, dude," he added in a low voice.

"Listen, pal, it's okay. Just go ahead and vent," Thomas said, not wanting Arnold to stop now. This was starting to sound very promising. Warmly, he continued, "Shoot, everybody's got a beef at some time or other. Go on and let it out; you'll feel better. I don't mind being a sympathetic ear and you need one. Like they say, that's what friends are for. Your employer sounds like the scrooge of the century. It must be going around 'cause, hell, you ought to hear what I go through at work sometimes."

"Thanks, man," Arnold said. "I hope you never have to deal with anything like this. 'Cause this is bad. Creditors trying to take everything I own. The way I see it, that family owes me a lot. And now, with the old man gone, they're trying to hold out on me. But I'm not taking it. I just haven't figured out what to do about it yet, but I will. Meantime, they can all go to hell for all I care." Arnold was feeling like an Oscar-winning actor as he fed this line to Thomas. Now he was ready to hook him and reel him in. He added artfully, "Tell you what, I'd sure like to break camp and get the hell away from these snooty-ass people, and this town, too, for that matter. Sad thing is I can't go anywhere 'cause I'm head over heels in debt. But believe you me, pal, if I could split, I'd find a way to stick it to 'em first for what they did to me." Then he added, "Like I said, sorry to dump on you, old buddy. You just happened to catch me at a bad time."

Arnold's words were sounding like music to Thomas' ears, and while Arnold talked, Thomas was having an inspiration. As the image of cold, hard cash danced in his head, his idea seemed so perfect. He would invite Arnold in on this deal. He could hardly believe that a possible partner could be emerging out of this conversation, and an insider at that. This was almost too good to be true. And for the time being, Thomas was too excited to be suspicious at his amazing luck. Instead, he jumped at the bait, knowing that a unique opportunity now awaited him. Arnold's ploy had worked.

Based on what Arnold told him about how Mrs. Remington had been acting, his running her back and forth to the bank, and buying all those tabloids and all, Thomas was now totally confident he would get his money. Lynn Davis had pretty much said so, too. Furthermore, he did prefer to go after the cash versus using his Swiss account. Trouble is, he could use some help, and the good thing was, now he knew who could help him. He was getting energized and excited, so he decided, what the hell. Go for it. Again, he told Arnold he understood. After all, he said, everybody needed to blow off steam once in a while, adding that those Remingtons definitely sounded like a tough pill to swallow. Thomas decided now was the time to enlist a partner, and this gullible little fellow was definitely the perfect one.

"I want to let you in on a little secret, pal," Thomas said, as he cunningly proceeded to tell to Arnold that quite coincidentally, he too had a bone to pick with the Remingtons. His voice began to take on a sinister edge. Matter of fact, he said, he didn't care about them one bit either. And wasn't it remarkable that the two of them would both had similar sentiments toward this family? Just one more thing they had in common, he told him.

Arnold acted totally shocked. He said, "You're bullshitting me, man. What could you have against the Remingtons?" Thomas told Arnold he was now undergoing some pretty bad financial times of his own, and it was all because of a Remington deal gone sour. This wasn't entirely untrue, as the picture of himself waiting fruitlessly in the park that cold April day flashed through his mind. In fact, he told Arnold, he was about to go under, and just like Arnold, he sure would like to get his hands on a bundle of Remington money, too. Arnold egged him on.

Daring to go for it, Thomas told Arnold he had an idea that could land him a huge sum of money. And it was virtually risk-free. He listened closely to see if Arnold sounded interested. To his delight, Arnold seemed eager. Thomas could see the beginnings of a lucrative partnership with his old buddy unfolding.

He excitedly invited Arnold to join forces with him, telling him it would get them what they both wanted — big money. And the good thing was, the Remingtons would get what they deserved out of the deal. Thomas could see dollar signs, and at that moment he was positive that collecting cash would be a better plan than using that foreign account he had set up. He was glad he told

Lynn Davis to have the old lady get the cash. Besides, he would need the cash to pay Arnold off. Thomas said, "Look here, buddy, I don't want to say too much more over the telephone. Can we meet and talk about this? I'm feeling real good about what we can do together." Arnold said he was available, and Thomas told him where to meet him. Shortly, they were face to face.

Thomas told Arnold his scheme was blackmail. Arnold acted shocked and impressed. Thomas said nobody would get hurt and his plan had zero risk, and Arnold grunted and laughed. Continuing, Thomas said he'd come across some extremely telling photographs of Mr. Remington and a woman he'd had an affair and two children with. Excitedly, he told Arnold that if that weren't already bad enough, it was a black woman at that! What a story!

Arnold said, "Wow, man. I knew the old dude was known for foolin' around. But I didn't think he was fool enough to ever let anyone find out about his little honeys, especially the black one," he said laughingly, intimating that he knew all about her, too. Thomas was pleased he seemed to be hooking Arnold. He went on to say that he could use these pictures to get Mrs. Remington to part with a couple of million dollars or face seeing them spread across the front pages of the country's largest scandal sheets.

"A couple million! Hey, man, you don't fool around, do you? But seriously though, all jokes aside, you'd really do that?" Arnold asked, sounding pleased.

When Thomas exclaimed, "Hell, yes," Arnold said, "Dude, you're the man!" Then Arnold listened while Thomas explained his scheme. Arnold was very proud that the blackmailer was falling right in line with his plan. He was tasting sweet revenge against this character who had tricked him, used him and extorted money from his employers.

In a devious tone, Thomas said, "Say, Arnold, I could sure use a little help with this." Then he paused before adding, "Do you suppose I could count you in, partner?"

"Are you kidding, man? You'd let me in on this? I don't even need to think about it. Of course, I'm in. In fact, I want to thank you, man, for asking *me*," Arnold sounded sincere. Oh, how he wanted to get this guy for faking friendship just to get information on the Remingtons. And all I wanted was a real buddy, he thought, somebody who thinks I'm a pretty good guy, especially the way my mother's constantly shooting me down. He'd somehow believed that in Thomas he'd found that buddy, and now he felt embarrassed for having been so naïve and trusting. But more than embarrassed, he was angry that Thomas had taken advantage of his vulnerability. Thomas shouldn't have done that.

Arnold told Thomas his plan sounded like a winner. To show he was willing to do whatever it took, he even told Thomas he'd let him in on a giant secret. Eager ears awaited this new secret. Arnold told him this blackmail he was planning wouldn't be the first time the family had someone stick to them. He said it actually happened once before and, in fact, it was he who had delivered the money to some character every few months for the past couple of years. "No way, dude," Thomas said, royally hooked as he now realized he had a partner with both guts and spunk. After milking what information he could from Arnold about the prior blackmailing, Thomas smiled inwardly, hearing from Arnold that old Earl Remington would have continued paying him the big bucks for the rest of his life. It had been just that successful, but now, thanks to Remington's death, it wasn't that easy any more.

Thomas told Arnold he would get it all set up. He would demand two and a half million dollars for the photographs. And all Arnold would have to do was deliver the money as he had done before, but for a cool $50,000 cut. He could then pay off all those medical bills. Thomas nearly choked when Arnold told him that $250,000 was not nearly enough. This was more like a 50-50 deal, what with the risks he was expecting Arnold to take. Thomas had no intention of splitting two and a half million dollars with this loser.

But Arnold was a determined negotiator, and eventually, Thomas reluctantly agreed to a half million dollars for him. He was none too thrilled about agreeing to such a large cut for Arnold, but he had to face the facts. It was either cut him in with a fair share and still have two million dollars, or possibly end up with nothing at all. Plus, now Arnold knew. Thomas told Arnold he would call him as soon as he worked out the details.

* * * * *

Thomas had not expected the Remingtons to renege on transferring the money that Tuesday. Seems they were throwing him curves every time he turned around. So he would have to devise the perfect plan. But now, he had a partner.

The mastermind went to work plotting through the night. He only had until three o'clock Thursday to come up with a failproof plan. Not even 48 hours. With a stroke of genius and much exacting forethought, he crafted his game plan. It seemed guaranteed for success. The net effect would be that Thomas would be rich and the authorities would never come looking for him. He would literally drop from the radar screen. He laughed with much assurance at his shrewd idea.

Thomas had been fortunate in his profession to gain firsthand knowledge of different methods of demolition. Also, living in Minneapolis, the land of 10,000 lakes, he, like many others, owned a boat and knew a boatload about navigation. For his plan, he would put his expertise to work. He would need a small boat and found he could rent one from a nearby marina. Then he'd find an out-of-the-way dock where he'd be able to set up. He didn't need any interference from other boats that might happen by. And then he would rig the boat to operate by remote control. He'd do this tomorrow along with building an explosive device and rigging it to the same remote control unit. He'd tell old lady Remington to deliver or send the money to the remote boat dock. Then, after Arnold headed off to the appointed destination to deliver the money in a black duffel bag, the two of them would meet first to make certain the money was real and accounted for. Thomas will have filled an identical bag with paper and a few single dollar bills. Then at Thomas and Arnold's appointed pre-meeting, they would exchange bags.

Since Thomas was sure Arnold would be followed, they needed to be able to make their detour to exchange duffel bags without being detected. After the switch, Thomas would be in possession of the real money and Arnold would leave with the worthless bag. Thomas knew that if he couldn't find a way to get around it, he would also have to cut Arnold his share at that time.

Then both he and Arnold would separately head over to the boat dock where he was sure Remington security would be waiting for Arnold to show up. Thomas would hide while he used the remote control device to operate the boat. He would have to find a high enough point where he'd be able to view the river traffic. Arnold would go directly to the dock and throw the duffel bag into the boat. Security would see the transaction taking place as planned.

Then the boat would start up and take off. In the dark of night, it would give every appearance that Thomas, himself, was manning it and heading away with the money. In his mind Thomas could see the boat swiftly moving away from the dock, and behind him would be the Remington security force and maybe even the Coast Guard. But at the speed he was planning to move that boat, they'd never even get close.

When the boat got a good distance away from the shore and he could see that the pursuers were a safe distance behind, he would press the magic button on the detonating unit, and KA-BOOM! An explosion would blow the boat to kingdom come. The moneybag will have been pre-treated with a flammable solution to ensure that it burned rapidly and completely so there would be nothing left for the authorities to examine. When the boat's motor was examined later, it would be found to have a potentially hazardous fire-causing defect. It will be concluded that this boat was not fit for rental.

Everyone would conclude that the blackmailer had met his fate, and there'd be no proving otherwise. They'd assume that the money was gone, too. By the time the fire department arrived, there would only be a few charred remains of the boat and nothing of Thomas except, of course, some pieces of ripped and burned fabric from some clothing that would have been strategically placed on the boat.

They wouldn't have any idea of the blackmailer's identity. Assuming he'd been blown to pieces by the blast, they would never come looking for him again. He'd be free. And he'd be rich! Thomas could then do whatever he pleased and no one would be any the wiser. Hot dawg, he thought, this was one damn good plan. He had to smile.

One other small detail needed to be attended to. Thomas realized the Remingtons would want to collect the photographs and negatives in return for the money. So he would place them in an envelope somewhere near the boat, like on a retaining wall or something if he could find one. Of course, Thomas was smart enough to keep plenty more copies of the pictures in case he ever needed to use them again.

He would rig a light on the wall that he could also operate remotely. Then, as soon as he saw the duffel bag being thrown into the boat, he would switch the light on and off. He would tell Remington that as soon as the light flashed twice, their person should go to the flashing light, pick up the envelope and leave. Everyone would assume the blackmailer was operating the light from his boat.

Thomas decided to schedule his pickup for Saturday evening. This would give him a day to get set up. He thought about the Swiss account transaction which would have been the safest and easiest route. But after learning from Lynn Davis how long it would take to transfer the money, he decided, to hell with that. Why bother with all that red tape when I can have my cash in hand? Besides, this foreign account thing had been the plan before his new partner happened into the picture. Now he had no reservations about collecting the cash, especially since it was being hand delivered by his old pal, Arnold.

* * * * *

In her office Thursday afternoon, Lynn had just taken a phone call from Tracy Billingsley, her former partner and office-mate, about the group's reunion dinner next month. The six investigators who used to share an office and once dreamed of becoming the biggest, most successful private investigation firm in the country still got together at least once a year to find out how each other was doing. All six were still doing investigative work and looked forward to catching up on the news at their annual get-together.

A few minutes later, at exactly three o'clock, Lynn's phone rang. She was waiting in her office to take the call, which Ella answered and said, "This is it." Lynn took a deep breath. She was set to execute her part of the plan and had to do it convincingly. The first thing she told the blackmailer was that Mrs. Remington had the cash and would pay up. Thomas breathed easy. He'd been pretty sure she'd see things his way, but until he heard the word, he could not relax. Lynn told him, of course, Mrs. Remington wanted to collect all his copies of the photographs and negatives. She also said Mrs. Remington wanted to know she had his commitment and promise never to come back to her again for any more money. In his phony female voice, Thomas excitedly said, "Yeah, yeah, she's got it, whatever she wants."

Getting right to the point, he told Lynn to have Mrs. Remington gather the money in unmarked, mixed denominations and stuff them in a large black duffel bag. He told her exactly what kind of bag to get and where to get it. He gave her the precise dimensions, style, color and brand name of the bag to use. Suddenly Thomas pictured the real dough sitting in the bag, and he beamed inwardly at the thought. Next he told Lynn to tell Mrs. Remington to bring the money or have it delivered, he didn't care. But get it to the dock at a small marina on the eastern edge of the city and be sure there were no cops and no funny business going on. Thomas said he would have someone at a lookout point who could see everything in case they tried anything. And if they did, the next time they saw those pictures it would be on the front pages.

Thomas was confident Mrs. Remington would not bring the money herself. His plan would only work if the delivery person was Arnold, and it would be Arnold's job to make sure he got the delivery job. Then Thomas gave Lynn the exact location. He preferred a late timing and told Lynn to tell Mrs. Remington to make sure she, or whoever, was alone and to arrive at eleven o'clock Saturday evening. But now that Thomas knew she had the money, he'd loved to have been able to tell Lynn to have it delivered today and forget all about Arnold and his cut. It was too late for that, of course, because now Arnold knew everything. Besides, his plan was good, and he would need a couple of days to get everything set up. So Saturday was fine.

When he hung up the phone, he called Arnold to discuss the arrangements and to agree on a place to exchange bags before going down to the river. Thomas suggested a nearby park, but Arnold, keeping with the plan, proposed Lunken Airport. Remington Corporation had a private jet, and Arnold said he had the key to their hangar. The airport was in a remote location and was pretty deserted at night, so they would be able to go inside the hangar, examine the money and Arnold could collect his share. Besides, Arnold said, in case he was being followed, there was a private road he could take to get to the airport that no one else knew about.

He told Thomas he needed to be certain nothing pointed to his involvement in this thing in any way because he had important business to take care of before he could leave Cincinnati, like moving his mother to a nursing home for one thing. Jerk, Thomas thought, but agreed to meet at Lunken Airport. It was not such a bad idea really. It's just that a big part of him was still reeling over the thought of Arnold's demanding a half million dollars of the money he had worked so hard for. He still hoped to think of a way to keep from parting with quite that much of his precious loot.

* * * * *

The Remingtons preferred not to bring the police into this case, at least on the front end. This way, they could avoid certain unwanted publicity. Lynn and Harvey, working with Earl and Arnold, developed a plan aimed at catching Thomas squarely in the act. They already had a couple of tape-recorded conversations between Thomas and Arnold discussing the heist, and Arnold would be wearing a wire that night. Somehow, Arnold would have to get Thomas to implicate himself on tape. Then, they would turn Thomas and all the evidence over to the authorities.

On Saturday evening at eight o'clock, the team of Remingtons, Harringtons, Lynn Davis, Harvey Chapman and Arnold sat inside the study at the Remington estate running through the details of the plan. Lynn and Harvey walked them through the drill of the catch — where each person would be, exactly what each one was to do. Included in the catch would be Remington Security Chief Johnson, and several of his men as backups, as well as Lynn and Harvey.

"I want to go along," Erica said suddenly, surprising everyone by her outburst. They hadn't seen her quietly enter the room. She explained, "I still can't believe Thomas would do the things to me that he did. First of all, to have known who my father was and not tell me is just unbelievable. He knew how much it would have meant to me to know this. And then, to blackmail him.

"And this matter with Timmy is just awful. I'm so angry with him, he'll be lucky if he ever gets to see his son again. I want to see his face when you catch him. I want to ask him why he did these things to me. I just have to know why he was so determined to hurt us. After all, Thomas and I did have a life together at one time." Then, reading the negative expressions on Lynn's and others' faces, Erica pleaded, "Please, I need to see him. I won't get in the way."

They listened as Erica rambled on about Thomas. She seemed so desperate and out of character. Everyone knew this would never work. As much as Lynn believed Erica needed to bring closure to this ugly saga, they absolutely could not jeopardize Thomas' capture by having her along; she'd only hurt their plans. The answer, Lynn told her, unfortunately, was *no*. Erica was extremely disappointed.

CHAPTER
31

THOMAS SET UP the rig and tested the entire system several times. Then he did a dry run to ensure that everything was working as needed. The system worked perfectly. The only thing he did not test was the explosive gadget. But Thomas had enough experience with these types of explosions to make them almost infallible. He drove the route to Lunken Airport to be certain he could find it without any problems, and he drove from Lunken to the marina.

Hooking up with Arnold had been a godsend. He was excited, and could still hardly get over his luck of finding the perfect partner. Also, coming up with such a slick plan had him feeling smug. He looked forward to executing it, but mostly he looked forward to tomorrow when this would all be behind him. He would have his fortune, and he'd be able to go back to Minneapolis and get his life and financial matters straightened out, quit his job. Then, no telling where he'd go.

By seven o'clock Saturday evening, everything was ready. He sat in his rental car in Eden park overlooking the city. With several hours to kill, Thomas mentally went over every single detail of the plan again and again. There were no weak spots. This plan would clearly work. He looked down on the river and tried to relax. Everything seemed so calm and peaceful. No one would ever dream what was in the works.

The sudden sight of a police car cruising through the park brought him instant panic. "Damn!" he uttered under his breath, worried that something about him might look suspicious and cause the police to stop. He knew he didn't have anything incriminating sitting unconcealed on the seat of his car. But he did have a semi-automatic nine-millimeter Baretta tucked under his seat out of view. Thomas knew that if for any reason he were searched, he'd be a goner.

His fears subsided for the moment as the cruiser slowly made its way through the park. Even so, he worried that there might possibly be some telltale evidence in view, like maybe some of the explosive wires dangling from his trunk. What a nerve-racking thought. He knew he'd been extremely careful, but he never expected to get spooked by a cop right now either. Damned close call, he thought as he felt an instant surge of relief when the police car drove out of sight. He took this as a sign to move on. Realizing he hadn't eaten in hours, Thomas drove down to a fast food restaurant and bought himself a hamburger, fries and a Coke. But he was actually too excited to eat. He sipped his drink for a while and nibbled on his French fries. Then he pitched the entire bag of food and drink into a trash container.

He tried to listen to the radio, but again, he could not concentrate. Since he hadn't been able to sleep the night before, he thought about closing his eyes and taking a quick nap. But he was too afraid he'd fall into a deep sleep and, God forbid, not awaken in time. So he sat anxiously in his car in the parking lot of the fast food restaurant and waited for time to pass.

As he often did, Thomas thought of Erica. And as was often the case, his thoughts ran from one extreme to the other. At times he hated her; other times, he loved her with all his heart. They'd had a special relationship and a damned good marriage. That is, until she told him she was the daughter of a black woman. That had spoiled everything. He still cursed the day he learned the truth.

Erica was so beautiful — probably one of the prettiest women he'd ever known. She had a fresh, girl-next-door innocence and sex appeal about her, and Thomas was aware that other men often drooled when they saw his wife, especially if they thought he wasn't around. She had supported him completely by moving with him to Minneapolis because of his job when she could have taken a much better job herself in Washington, D.C. Erica was everything any man could possibly have wanted in a wife. But the wicked race card had brought an end to his marriage. Once he knew she was half-black, he just couldn't stay married to her any longer; he just couldn't.

His folks had always taught him the importance of racial purity. He knew he would never be able to forget or forgive Erica. At times, he wanted to crush her for ruining his marriage. But Thomas actually loved her so deeply, he would have gladly died for her. But he couldn't be married to a black woman. It just wasn't right. Somehow, none of this made any sense to him right now.

Sitting here reminiscing about Erica and the trauma that ended their marriage, Thomas remembered being taught very early in his childhood the importance of staying away from certain people. His memory served up a painful time when at a very young age he was reprimanded for running up to a water fountain in the park to take a drink just after a little black kid had finished drinking there. His father yanked him away from the fountain so hard, he almost tore his arm out of its socket. Then his mother dragged him by his ear until they were away from other people.

His mother and his father scolded him but good, reminding him that he was never, ever to touch anything that one of those people had touched. They told Thomas that those were very bad people, and he had to stay away from them. This had been hard for him to comprehend because those people hadn't seemed so bad. But his parents stayed on him day and night until they were satisfied he finally understood the rules.

Thomas thought about the time that sometimes brought a smile to his face. It was the age of innocence. One day in the first grade he learned about Abraham Lincoln. Later, when he and his mother talked about his school day, she had asked him what Abraham Lincoln was famous for, and the six-year-old proudly answered,

"He freed the *slays*." His mother was amused at his pronunciation and asked him to tell her what a *slay* was. Thomas simply replied, "It's something you ride on in the snow." Years later, his mother would relay this story to him laughingly, too, for she now knew her son was very clear about what a *slay* was and everything else.

Frankly, Thomas never fully understood what the big deal was really, but at some point, he resigned himself to obeying his parents' teachings. He worked hard to role model the lessons he learned about people of other races, and this meant black people were off limits. Oh, he occasionally associated with some of them when he was in the military and also during his college football days. But being married to one was strictly a horse of another color.

"Why, Erica?" Thomas lamented. As he reflected on his years with her, he realized how much he still loved her, but he also hated her for her deception. In spite of this hatred, his feelings of love for her still surfaced often. He'd had a string of girlfriends on the rebound, hoping they would help keep his mind off Erica, and he had splurged big time on his women with his Remington money. He thought about Cathy. Nice girl, wrong place, wrong time. He felt kind of bad for walking off from her like that since she hadn't done anything wrong, but their relationship was over. Thomas could not imagine any woman in his life except Erica. Certainly none could ever take her place in his heart.

And now he would have plenty of money. Thomas was very confused as he daydreamed that he and Erica could now have lived like kings and queens. But hell, he thought, Erica probably has plenty of money now, herself, what with her old man sticking her and that brother of hers in his will. His rage returned as he thought about the money. And here I am, he sneered, having to sneak around, risking prison just to get my hands on what should be rightfully mine. And Erica lands it without lifting a finger.

She doesn't deserve that man's money. What did she do to earn it? And what will she do with it? Spend it on that Porter dude? Expose my son to all kinds of people? "Not if I can help it," he uttered under his breath. He was still curious about where Erica had taken Timmy the week before because he had been all set to take off with his boy when he stopped by his former in-laws' house in Columbus. But Timmy wasn't there. Where was he? With Larry Porter? Oh boy, Erica, you're pushing me too far with this black business.

Thomas' thoughts turned to the mess he had made of his life and his marriage. He had promised his father on his deathbed that he would uphold the proud Harrison family tradition of racial purity. Now he deeply regretted having made that promise. At times he hated his parents for teaching him to hate other people. They're crazy, all of them, he thought. I don't need anybody. I've got everything I need.

For the next several minutes, his thoughts continued to race to crazy places in his head, his emotions ran wild — hot one minute, cold the next. Thomas looked at his watch. It was nine-thirty. Suddenly, his eyes turned steely cold. It was time to go. Damn 'em all, he thought.

CHAPTER
32

THOMAS AND ARNOLD were to meet up at Lunken Airport at ten-fifteen. Thomas had given Arnold specific instructions on the rendezvous, but he wanted to arrive early to be sure there'd be no slip-ups. He drove into the parking lot of the administration building at the airport, but much to his dismay, a tall steel locked gate blocked the road to the hangar. What now, he wondered?

Inside the building he could see one or two people moving around. Otherwise, the place seemed almost forsaken. At one point, a security officer stepped outside the building, stretched and looked around. Then he lit a cigarette. Thomas did not know what to do, so he slid down out of view and waited until the guy went back into the building. Only a few other cars were parked at the airport, and those were near another hangar. Thomas could see that there were no lights on in or around the Remington hangar. Good spot, Arnold, old boy, he thought. Now let's just get in there.

The night was still, and the grounds around the small airport were pitch black. The woods surrounding it were even blacker. Only a few stars lit the night sky. Thomas counted the seconds as he waited for Arnold. He couldn't wait to exchange duffel bags so he could examine that money closely. As he waited, he mentally walked through his plan one last time. Arnold should be arriving momentarily.

At precisely ten-fifteen, the Mercedes Benz rolled into the lot. Arnold looked over at Thomas and passed him a knowing glance, then drove up to the gate and used a card key to open it. The gate closed behind them. Arnold and Thomas drove slowly over to the Remington Hangar. Arnold beckoned Thomas to get out of his car and come in.

The first thing Thomas looked for was the duffel bag. Arnold had it! Two and a half million dollars! Thomas was so excited, he could think of nothing else at that moment. He removed his pistol from underneath his seat and slipped it under his belt and covered it with his jacket. He didn't intend to use it, but wanted to be prepared for anything that could happen. Then he got out of his vehicle. Picking up the other duffel bag filled with highly combustible paper, he walked stealthily over to the hangar door.

He told Arnold, "That locked gate back there had me worried there for a minute!" Arnold only shrugged, and Thomas added, "Well, buddy, I guess this is it. Are you ready for the big time?"

Arnold gave a wry smile and a wink and opened the door. It creaked in the quiet night, and Arnold made his way to a nearby light switch that lit up a small office on the right side of the building where the pilot and co-pilot reviewed their flight plans. He told Thomas, "Let's go in here and spread out."

Thomas followed him into the small office, but with every step he took, he had to ward off the temptation to take his gun or something hard and heavy and knock Arnold out cold, take the money and run. He figured Arnold would never find him. After all, he didn't even know his correct name. But Thomas didn't know how he'd get back through that locked gate. He decided not to succumb to his baser instincts.

He looked around, and in that darkened hangar he could see one of the Remington Leer jets perched proudly in the center of the floor. Its dark shadowy figure stood erect as light from the open door cast haunting shadows in his direction. Money, Thomas thought. These people sure had plenty of it. He followed Arnold into the office. It was hot and stuffy and cramped for space.

"Is the money in there?" Thomas asked Arnold, his attempt at whispering sounding more like the gleeful exclamations of an excited kid. Arnold sat the bag on the desk and unzipped it. There it was. Two and a half million dollars in crisp, beautiful new greenbacks. Thomas wanted to kiss it, and at that moment, he could have kissed Arnold, too. He picked up a stack of thousand-dollar bills and quickly leafed through it. In the bag, he could also see hundred dollar bills, fifties, and other denominations. Then they both riffled through the money checking for markings and authenticity. Then they started to count.

Thomas asked Arnold how it felt carrying all this money around. He wanted to know how the Remingtons presented it to him, who gave it to him, what they said. He wanted all the details. Thomas was completely immersed in the beauty of his plan, but Arnold ignored his questions and pretended to concentrate on counting. He was actually concentrating on what he had to do. Arnold's mission was to make sure Thomas said something that would clearly identify him as the mastermind behind this whole plot, as well as the previous blackmailing of Mr. Remington. Thomas said as if thinking aloud, "Man! I was just going for small potatoes before. But this is the big time!" Arnold saw an opening and nonchalantly asked him what he was talking about, but all Thomas said was, "We've struck gold, man. This is the big time." Arnold could see this wasn't going to be automatic.

"You got the pictures?" Arnold asked. "The old lady wants to be sure I bring back the pictures, the negatives, everything."

"Don't worry. That's taken care of. I mean, Guy, this shit's beautiful. Remember, all you have to do is watch the blinking light and pick up the package on the adjacent wall. I already showed you where they'll be anyway. Same place." And then Thomas winked at Arnold and said, "Yeah, man, you're going to see fireworks tonight."

"You're all set up?" Arnold asked.

"Is the blue sky blue, dude?" Thomas answered. "I've gone over this thing a hundred times. Believe me, I'm ready."

Arnold said, "Well, I'd say it's all here. Let's get my cut out of here. Five hundred thousand dollars. Damned sweetest deal I've ever made, and the easiest. Now I'm set for life." Each stack of bills Arnold picked up was like a stab in Thomas' heart, but Thomas forced himself to go along with the program, at least for now. He'd love to have just split with his cash, but there was too much at stake, because if he executed his plan right no one would ever come looking for him again. He had to stay the course. For now, he just wanted to get everything over with here and get down to the river for part two.

Arnold still needed Thomas to implicate himself in the prior blackmailing scheme. Thomas had almost said something a few minutes ago, but stopped, so Arnold tried a different angle. He said, "Well, I'll tell you one thing — the guy who was blackmailing the old man before — now that was one slick character. I've never seen anyone pull off anything as smooth as him. Geez!"

With animated gestures and exaggerated facial expressions, he continued to describe the genius behind the first blackmailing. "I mean, this guy put a plan together that was just plain brilliant. And I'll tell you what; it worked like a charm. No slight intended to you, man, 'cause this all seems pretty cool, too. A little complicated, but it's working. But my hat's off to that other guy. He was just plain smart. Now there's someone to team up with if you ever want to pull off a job without a hitch. Problem is, I don't know where or who in the hell he is."

Arnold was getting into his spiel, and he knew it was coming off convincingly. He continued, "It was pretty obvious to me this guy was a genius. I mean, Old Man Remington told me he'd probably keep paying him forever. By the way, I heard he had some pretty juicy pictures, too."

Hearing this praise, Thomas could feel his chest swell. He began grinning from ear to ear. He felt very smug. Since Arnold was speaking so highly of his past deeds, Thomas even decided to try and forgive him for taking his cut of the money. He was feeling pretty invincible right now and wanted his due adulation. He had to do speak up, he just had to. He had to boldly declare himself the original blackmailer, the one, the only.

Thomas bragged, "Yes, it was pretty slick, if I must say so myself." Then he smiled and gave Arnold a knowing glance and a wink. "I mean, I really had the old man going. That guy sure didn't want his old lady to see those pictures."

"What are you saying? You saying it was you, man?" Arnold exclaimed in feigned surprise. "Naw, I don't believe it. Are you telling me you're the one who was blackmailing Mr. Remington before?" He exaggerated his amazement and seeming admiration.

"What can I say? You bet your sweet boots, it was me, all right," Thomas said, as he finished counting Arnold's cut. "When you're good, you're just good, son."

"So that's what you meant when you said you were just going for small potatoes before. I can't believe it was you, man. Are you putting me on?" Arnold shook his head and laughed. Then he continued, "It was really you blackmailing the old man before? Well, if it was, I gotta tell you something — my hat's off to *you*, buddy." Arnold extended both arms upward as if to bow to the king of blackmail. " 'Cause you were damned good. I always wished I coulda figured out how to get something out of it, myself. I mean, like I said, the old man was pretty good to me, true. But like I told you before, the rest of that family isn't worth two cents, if you get my meaning."

"Hey, I hear you," Thomas said, smiling. "Well, look here, old buddy, it was good working with you. Who knows, just maybe we'll team up again, what do you say? Because you don't think I was stupid enough to turn over all my pictures and negatives and everything, do you? These pictures will have earned me nearly three million dollars, and the way I figure, there's more where that came from. You think I'm going to just hand over my treasure chest? Think again, dude.

"Man, I'll tell you what. You aren't ever going to see me again. Like I said, I'm set now. I'm getting out of here just as soon as I can. Who knows, I may head down to Mexico."

Thomas handed Arnold his money, and Arnold stashed it away in a money belt he was wearing. It was stuffed so full, it emphasized his short stature and made him look practically as wide as he was tall. Then Thomas looked at his watch. It was exactly half past ten. He said, "Well, let's go do it."

Suddenly the door to the small office flung open, and Harvey

Chapman stepped inside with a handgun pointed at Thomas. Harvey said, "I don't think you'll be going anywhere, my friend."

Thomas jumped like he was seeing a ghost. His tanned face turned ashen as he glanced up at Harvey and three other men standing just outside the office door. "Hey, man, who in the hell are you?" he questioned. Then he turned his puzzlement to Arnold and yelled, "Were you followed, man? What the hell is going on?" as Harvey came forward, patted Thomas and collected the Baretta from his belt.

This surprised even Arnold, since he hadn't known Thomas was armed. Thomas gripped his duffel bag tightly as if there might be a chance he could still get away. But he quickly assessed that he was in a tight little room and the only door was blocked. There were no windows. There was nowhere to run. He was trapped.

He held the bag with one hand and raised his other hand in the air. "Shit, Arnold, man, do something. Where'd these people come from? And how the hell did they get in here?" Arnold didn't answer. "What are we going to do, man? Do something, damn it!" Thomas yelled.

Harvey said, "Face it, Thomas, you're through. This is it." Then Harvey started to empty Thomas' weapon, but when he pulled out the magazine clip, he told security, "It's not loaded." He looked at Thomas and just shook his head.

Thomas exclaimed excitedly, "Who the hell are you, man? How do you know my name, anyway? Are you trying to rob us or something? Well, aren't you nothing!"

At that moment, Lynn Davis stepped into the office. Thomas hadn't noticed a woman in the group before. She said, "Well, well, well. So this is the caller with the British accent, the one who's been calling me. Thomas, is it? Or is it Miss Thomas? I'm Lynn Davis. But then, you know that already, don't you, since we've spoken several times. And I see you've already met my associate," she said pointing toward Harvey. Then Lynn added, "You should know that I don't like being threatened. And oh, by the way, you probably shouldn't get a private investigator to be your go-between in your little scams. Not smart."

Thomas looked at her. He felt hopeless. Glaring hatefully at her, he said, "You're crazy, you know that." Then with outstretched arms, he said, "Here's the goddamn money. Is this what you want?" At that moment, he could only see red. He wondered how Lynn Davis had figured all this out? Just then, however, the possibility of a double-cross dawned on him, so he asked, "Arnold, man, what's going on here? How'd these people know we'd be here?"

This was Arnold's chance to tell Thomas a thing or two. He gave Thomas a hard, cold gaze, and said, "I guess I must have told them, buddy." Thomas jolted in shock. At that moment, he could have torn up this little runt with his bare hands. He lunged toward him, but two security guys jumped in and grabbed Thomas' arms, causing him to drop the duffel bag.

Arnold was unruffled. He said snidely, "In the first place, I'm not your buddy. In the second place, when I learned how you had been using me all this time to get your little information to black-mail the Remingtons, I decided this needed to be your last stupid mistake. I'll tell you something. I've been wanting to kick your ass every since I found out how you were using me. Man, don't you know I could just break your face? Playing me was your first mistake, and thinking I would be part of your stupid little plan was your last!" With that, Arnold threw the duffel bag filled with paper at Thomas' feet, and said in disgust, "Here, man. Take this. You deserve it."

Thomas looked at Arnold in disbelief, and for the first time he was speechless. So that's how Lynn Davis knew. This little clown had told. He couldn't believe that Arnold had actually double-crossed him and quickly realized he had underestimated this guy, taking him for some pitiful little chump. He never fig-ured Arnold had the smarts to outwit him.

Suddenly Thomas thought of an angle. Blame Arnold. He said, "Can't you people see what's happening. This no-account is try-ing to point the finger at me. He's the mastermind behind this whole thing. He told me so. He's the one who used to take money to some blackmailer before — or so he claims. He's the no-good blackmailer. Can't you see what he's doing? I'm glad you got here in time. This guy was all set to take this money and run. Look in his money belt if you don't believe me. It's loaded. He conned me into getting involved. That's the only reason I'm here."

At that moment Thomas heard another voice. It took only a second before he realized it was his own. Harvey was holding the tape recorder up and playing back Thomas' own words: "Well look here, buddy, it was good working with you. Who knows, just maybe we'll team up again ... These pictures will have earned me nearly three million dollars, and the way I figure it, there's more where that came from." Thomas looked aghast as he listened. He could think of nothing else to say. Several of the officers began to move in on him. He felt hopelessly defeated.

But he froze, then melted when he heard the next voice saying, "Why, Thomas? How could you do this?"

"Erica?" he uttered in disbelief, as Erica walked through the group before anyone could stop her. She walked directly toward Thomas, who cried, "What are you doing here? Are you part of this?" He paused for a reply, but she didn't speak. "How did you know I was here? It was those damn pictures. I should have known it would be you. Once again, Erica, you've betrayed me."

Erica was amazed. Thomas had done these terrible things, yet he was behaving like she was the one who had done wrong. She tried to shake that off by giving him a look of utter disbelief. Again, she asked, "Why, Thomas? Why did you do this? Why didn't you tell me who my father was? You knew how desperately I wanted to know. Did you hate me that much?"

"No, Erica, sweetheart, I never hated you," cried the helpless man. "I only loved you. Don't you know that? I didn't want to hurt you."

"But you blackmailed my father," Erica exclaimed, surprised at, but ignoring the endearing name he had called her. "I can't understand how you could do these things, Thomas. You're even teaching our son all kinds of terrible prejudice. You've blackmailed the Remingtons; you've used and hurt people. What did I ever do to you to deserve this?"

"No, no, Erica, you've got it all wrong, baby. You never did anything. Well, I mean, not intentionally. But you've got to believe me. I never wanted you to be hurt."

"I am sorry for you, Thomas, for what you have turned into.

It didn't have to be this way. I loved you."

"I was angry because you deceived me. Don't you see?" Thomas said as his voice trembled and his eyes got weepy. The tough blackmailer was gone. In his place was a pathetic, besotted, defeated man. "I'm so sorry I hurt you, sweetheart. I didn't mean to. You gotta believe me, Erica." Then he dropped his head and sobbed like a baby.

Harvey watched Thomas for a moment, then said, "I think we'd better get this guy out of here. Good job, people."

Thomas raised his head as they walked him outside. He achingly looked back at Erica, who had turned and was slowly walking away crying. He yelled, "Erica, when this is over, we'll talk, okay?" Then he stopped to watch her as she kept walking, and cried, "Erica, listen to me! Erica! Come back; please, don't walk away! It's going to be okay. We'll talk soon. Okay?"

As Erica walked into the hangar, ignoring his pleas, Thomas suddenly realized that the world as he knew it had come to an end. Everything was crashing down on him. He faced jail and some real mean loan sharks, and worse, he had blown any chance of ever getting Erica back. It's all over, he thought, I'll never get through this. And in that instant he decided he had no choice. He didn't want to hang around to face the consequences. Thomas yanked his right arm away from the guard's grasp, and in the same fluid movement, he reached down and grabbed another small handgun from inside his boot. "Stay away!" he shouted as he instantly pointed the gun to his head.

Harvey and the other men froze in their tracks. It hadn't occurred to Harvey that Thomas would have another gun. The first one had been empty. This time they might not be so lucky. Slowly reaching his hand out, Harvey said, "Hold it, fella. Don't shoot. Why don't you give me that?"

Thomas cried out in anguish, "It's over. Don't you see? Erica, please forgive me."

Erica turned and saw Thomas with a gun to his head. She quickly ran out of the hangar and headed straight over to him. Harvey grabbed her. At that moment, she wanted to help Thomas. Yes, there was no doubt she had been completely devastated by all the hurtful things he had done to her and her father, and what he was now doing to their son. Even so, she felt a pang of sadness toward him. He had been her very first love, her husband, her child's father. She wanted him caught, stopped cold all right. But she didn't want him dead. She pleaded, "Thomas, please. Put the gun down. Please don't do this." Thomas stopped momentarily to hear Erica's words. She didn't know what to say, but had to think of something quickly to keep him from shooting himself. She remembered the words of endearment he had used when he spoke to her tonight and decided to return them.

She shouted, "Thomas, sweetheart, put the gun down. Look, I know you never wanted to hurt me. You could never hurt me. Don't do this, please! Put the gun down. Think of Timmy; he needs his father ..." On she pleaded until Thomas looked like he was finally listening to her. He began to lower his arm. Erica was so relieved at that point, she completely lost it. Thinking things were now going to be okay, she exclaimed, "Thank God," and dropped to her knees, her head in her hands.

A shot rang out, and Erica screamed, "Oh, God, no!" She jumped up and tried to run toward Thomas, but someone held her back. There was now a tussle going on. Harvey and another guard had successfully wrestled the handgun out of Thomas' hand. Amazingly, they got to him just as he started to fire, but not soon enough to keep him from putting a bullet through his right thigh as they tried to wrestle the gun away from him.

Fortunately, Thomas was not too badly hurt. In the skirmish he sustained a nasty gunshot wound. He fell to the ground holding his leg, groaning and writhing in pain. Blood spewed everywhere. Erica pulled away from the arms that were holding her and ran to him, touching him. Then, with great relief, she exclaimed, "Oh, Thomas, you're going to be all right."

Thomas only looked at her with glazed eyes as he moaned, "I'm sorry, Erica!"

"Call for help," someone yelled. "Call 911!"

In the aftermath of events that followed, Thomas was taken by ambulance to the hospital. Fortunately, he would survive to have his day in court. The explosive rig and remote control unit were located in the trunk of his rental car, as were the pictures and other incriminating evidence. Lynn took the envelope containing the photographs. The other contents of his car, the taped conversation and other evidence of Thomas' criminal activities were turned over to the local police. The rented boat sat docked at the drop site. The authorities checked it out. The boat had been rented to one Thomas Mailer. An investigation showed it was rigged to blow.

Erica could have blown the whole thing. After pleading to come with them and Lynn telling her she could not, Erica had looked for a way to go along. Somehow she managed to hide in the empty back seat of one of the vehicles going out, and it was only when everyone was exiting their cars to go into the hangar that Harvey and Lynn realized she had come with them anyway.

Lynn had been upset with Erica, but it was too late to send her back to the Remington home. She told Erica that she understood how much she wanted to be a part of this, but her being there could put herself and others in danger and their plans in jeopardy. Erica acknowledged she should not have come and willingly agreed to stay in the background. But while she was listening to Thomas, something snapped and she just had to step forward to confront him. She realized now this might have been the worst mistake of all.

She was stunned by this whole ordeal and relived it over and over in her mind. It seemed she would forever smell Thomas' blood on her hands. For hours afterward, the memory of him holding the pistol to his head and his haunting words rang in her ears, especially his proclamations of love to her. Poor Thomas, she thought to herself, you don't love me. I wonder if you ever really knew how to love anyone — me, Timmy, and most of all, yourself. Although she had been disappointed to see her marriage end, she was very relieved to have gotten out of a bad situation.

Erica suddenly thought about that special gift she apparently shared in common with her mother — her extra sensory perception. She realized that her looming sense of foreboding, of impending doom was gone. And although she was sickened by this whole series of events, she sensed a strange and welcomed peace.

She offered a sincere apology to Lynn, Harvey and the others for interfering in their plan to catch Thomas.

Earl, Jr. had stayed back at the family home with the others. He was especially proud of the way his family had stuck together in solving this huge problem of capturing the blackmailer. Furthermore, they had openly accepted their new family relations admirably. At that moment, he was extremely grateful about his mother's decision to bring Erica and Perry into the picture. After all, had they not been around, no one would have ever been able to identify the source of the blackmail pictures, and Thomas could probably have gone on forever, taking his family for millions. It's amazing how things work out, he thought.

As the eldest son and now the senior Earl Remington, he had decided that his mission was to preserve their precious family bond. He knew this was what his father would have wanted, and he discovered it was what he wanted as well. Earl now saw for the first time that family ties meant more to him than any corporate title could ever mean, and he felt happier and more at peace than he had ever felt.

CHAPTER

33

IN THE DAYS following the capture of Thomas Harrison, Lynn spent time tidying up loose ends on the Remington case. She had a full agenda planned for each day of her short week. On Wednesday evening, she and Donald would celebrate the third anniversary of their relationship. Then she would take Thursday and Friday off to participate in her family reunion this weekend. Lynn was looking forward to seeing everyone, and one of her happiest times had already come when she saw her brother, Jeremy. He and his family had arrived from New York on Saturday, but it just so happened she had been busy catching a blackmailer that day. With the case solved, she enjoyed horseback riding with them on Sunday and playing chess with her niece and nephew. Life was great!

Monday was catch-up day in the office. Lynn had been happy to learn when she came in that day that Mr. Thompson from the parking garage was out of the hospital and recovering nicely at home from his heart attack. She knew that had he been at his booth in the parking garage that day, Thomas would have never been successful learning where she parked her car or what car she drove. She sent him a "get well and hurry back" card.

That afternoon, Lynn met with Erica and Perry, two new

multi-millionaires, connected by blood to one of the nation's most powerful families. These young people had gone through quite a lot in the last few weeks and had handled it well. And they seemed to have made a special connection with the Remington family. "What are you going to do now?" Lynn asked them as they sat in her office.

"Well the first order of business for us, Erica said smiling, is to introduce our folks to the Remingtons. We spoke with Mrs. Remington about meeting them, and she said she would be happy to meet our folks. They have been wonderful parents, and they certainly have a right to know the people we are now calling our biological relatives."

"That's right," Perry interjected. "We have already picked a date next month, and our folks have agreed to come down from Columbus and, of course, Erica and I will be in town for this, too. Mrs. Remington has invited all of us to her home for dinner. The brothers and sisters will also be there. We're excited about this."

Then Erica spoke up, looking radiant and happy. She said she would leave her job in Minneapolis and she did not plan to work for a while, for it was obvious that Timmy needed a great deal of direction and love from her. "I've got to help him unlearn some of the negative stuff Thomas taught him." She also explained that she would have to help Timmy understand and adjust to not seeing his father again for a long time, because if Thomas was convicted it could be years before Timmy might see his father outside of prison walls. She thought of how Thomas, in the spirit of cooperation, had his lawyer tell Lynn Davis where the rest of the pictures and negatives could be found, and Lynn had collected them. He was finished blackmailing anyone. Erica said she would consider relocating to Columbus to be nearer her parents. "Everything's up in the air now. I'll just be glad to take some time and decide what's right for us."

Perry told Lynn that Earl asked him if he wanted to come to work for the Remington Corporation. "And I might give that some thought. I could do engineering which I'm good at, but the real reason I'd think about it is that this is the business our father built, and the idea of being part of it does appeal to me somewhat. I've got a lot of ties in Chicago, so it's certainly not a sure thing, but I'm definitely going to think about it."

Erica and Perry said they hoped to build stronger relationships with their newfound half-brothers and sisters. Of course, they had a tremendous regard for Mrs. Remington and definitely would stay in touch with her. Also, they couldn't wait to do some special things for their adoptive parents, such as buy them a big new house and let them both retire if they wanted to. Paul and Kitty Harrington loved to travel. Erica and Perry wanted to send them anywhere they wanted to go — anytime. "Actually, we're setting up a big retirement fund for them so they can do whatever they want," Perry offered.

Before returning to their homes, they would go to Ft. Davis for a short visit with their Uncle Wilbur and Aunt Bessie and were eager to meet these family members. Wilbur and Bessie had welcomed the news and told them when they arrived, they would have a big family gathering so they could meet all their cousins and their families.

* * * * *

Ella also had things to wrap up. She paid a visit to Miss Bertha and Miss Lela to tell them the good news about catching the blackmailer. Miss Bertha was simply astounded by the news that it was Erica's ex-husband. "Child, that just about beats all. But don't you know we were kind of worried about our Jelly for a while there. He was so fond of dear little Hattie, we couldn't have sworn to anything where she was concerned. Poor Jelly never could get her out of his system. 'Course now, that's all changed since he met his new lady friend, Angel," she added with a chuckle, then said, "let me show you a picture of Jelly and his Angel."

Finally, Miss Bertha told Ella how Erica and Perry promised to stay in touch with her and Lela, which just pleased them to pieces. Their conversation ended with Miss Bertha inviting Ella over for a nice visit one day. Miss Bertha reminded Ella that she and her husband were still invited to attend church with her and her sister. Preferably the Sunday after next, 'cause she and Lela were in the senior choir, and they were scheduled to sing a duet that day. Ella knew she'd have to be there.

* * * * *

On Tuesday, Lynn was surprised to be invited to a meeting of the Remington CEO search committee. Interestingly, Earl, Jr., had given her name as a character reference. She was described to the committee as an investigator, a Yale graduate, and an intelligent business woman who'd had some dealings with the Remingtons. The setting was the executive boardroom. Lynn observed the posh, yet tastefully elegant surroundings, and figured many major business deals had been consummated in that very room.

James Reiner, head of the search committee, asked for her input on Earl, Jr. By her brief association with Earl in solving the blackmail case, Lynn had gained a good insight into his character. Naturally, the committee was not to know the details of the Remington family matter, but Lynn was able to speak highly of Earl, Jr. She told the committee that he exhibited maturity and strong leadership in a clear-thinking manner. He also showed a refreshingly intense family and company loyalty. Lynn explained to Mr. Reiner and other members of the committee that because of Earl, Jr., they were able to satisfactorily conclude a very serious matter. His proactive approach had been both welcomed and helpful. She gave Earl, Jr. high praises and meant every word she said.

The committee was very impressed with the evaluation of this attractive Yale graduate. They found her extremely credible and professional. Some of the members silently wondered if she might be interested in coming to work for the Remington Corporation, as they were aware the company needed more diversity at the top. As a woman and a minority, Lynn Davis would be an excellent addition. They appreciated Lynn's input and thanked her for coming, and she left feeling glad to put in a good word for this bright young leader. From what she had seen of Earl, Jr., he could no doubt run his father's company very capably.

At the elevator, Lynn ran into Earl who had known, of course, that she was meeting with the search committee. Lynn told him the meeting went well. Then she told him how impressed she had been with the way he got involved in this case and helped work through it. He smiled and thanked her, and was about to shake her hand, when instead he opened his arms wide and hugged her warmly. She returned the gesture just as warmly. "Good luck, Earl!" she told him.

* * * * *

Earl was headed down to the lobby to pick up a visitor. En route, he recalled the events leading up to this meeting. He had gone into his office on Sunday following the capture of Thomas Harrison to pick up a file that his secretary was to have pulled for him. However, she left a message on his desk that the particular file he wanted was locked up in his father's desk. So Earl went over to his father's office to retrieve it.

Entering the office, Earl had felt very strange; he could almost feel his father's presence in the room. Taking a seat behind the desk, he slowly unlocked it. Earl didn't know why, but somehow, going through his father's things made him feel like he was trespassing. He just wanted to find the folder and go.

Earl had opened his father's desk before, but he didn't remember seeing the file in question. When he opened the center drawer, the folder was indeed there. He pulled it out and happened to notice a white sealed envelope. It was slightly creased and appeared to have been stuck at the side of the drawer. The envelope was addressed to him. Right away, Earl recognized his father's handwriting. Hesitating for a moment, he picked it up and wondered what it was. He decided against tearing into it, and chose instead to open it when he got to his mother's house. Once there, Earl told her how he had come across the envelope, but he thought it best to have a witness to its contents, whatever they were.

A handwritten note from his father simply said that he had made a gentleman's agreement with a man named Jake Huber to make him whole. Huber had incurred huge losses on some valuable property he owned as a result of a business deal with the Remington Corporation, and Earl, Sr. asked his son to follow up with Mr. Huber for him. His father said he had told Huber that the corporation would help him acquire another piece of property, up to a value of a million dollars.

As Earl read aloud the note, he was taken completely aback

by what it said. He was shocked, not to mention instantly remorseful over the way he had talked to Mr. Huber several times. And he felt terrible for trying to set him up with that fake bomb scam. Now Earl's heart told him that no matter how hard he had worked to justify his actions, what he did was clearly wrong. "So Huber was right all along," he said, thoughtfully feeling a strong need to make amends.

"It looks that way, son." Elizabeth saw her son's angst as he realized what he had done to Mr. Huber. Then she studied the date scribbled on the note. It was written back in March. Today was July 26. Mrs. Remington added, "I think you'd better take care of this right away. It looks like your father intended this to be handled before now." Earl assured his mother he would take care of the matter promptly. Subsequently, he met with the board chairman to review his plan of action, and then called Jake Huber in to meet with him in person. Earl was prepared to explain what had happened and, importantly, to apologize and make the offer. As Lynn was leaving Remington Headquarters that Tuesday, Earl was on his way down to the lobby to pick up Mr. Jake Huber.

* * * * *

Later that afternoon, Lynn was to have a final meeting with Elizabeth Remington. She had been invited out to the Remington home in Butler County to meet with her and officially close the case. Although this was her first time going to the Remington mansion located up Interstate 71 some 40 miles from downtown Cincinnati, the address was easy to find. As she approached the home, Lynn was awed seeing this massive structure. It was situated on more than a hundred lush green acres. Lynn had heard that the Remingtons owned race horses, and driving up the lane she noticed about a dozen beautiful horses grazing in an area framed by an endless white fence. She saw a trainer leading one of the prized animals away. She had heard this house had more than 50 rooms, and as she entered the colossal entryway it felt at least that large. Stepping into this grand home was like stepping into a magnificent art gallery, and she eagerly took in the view.

She was shown by the maid into the living room. While she stood waiting for Mrs. Remington, Jordan came into the room and said, "Hello, Miss Davis, welcome to our second home. Well, actually it's our primary residence. It's just that we're at our other little place so often — whenever we have business in town." Lynn was amused by Jordan's reference to their Indian Hill home as *our other little place*. Jordan continued, "I'm glad to see you because I really wanted to thank you." Lynn looked slightly surprised. "You know, since Dad died, our family has been in a downhill slump. Our father was such a powerful influence in all our lives that without him we've practically been at a standstill." She explained, "You definitely helped us get back on track." While Lynn was happy with the job she had done for the Remingtons, she wasn't quite sure where Jordan was coming from and asked her what she meant.

"Well, going through this crisis helped all of us a great deal because it forced our family to come together. Now my sister, Parker, and I talk more than we have in years. It's nice. My brothers are also building a stronger relationship than they've had since they were kids. And I'll tell you, we're all so proud of Earl for what he did to help the family stick together.

"Furthermore, I don't think my mother ever thought much about her racial viewpoints," Jordan said, contemplating how her mother had reacted years before when she brought her black college friend, Gerald, home for a visit. Then she added, "However, going through this situation obviously made her deal with it. Had it not been for you, I know she wouldn't have been able to get past the fact that our father's mistress was African American. Nor would she have been able to accept Erica and Perry. So now we have two new siblings, and I would never have dreamed it possible to reconcile this. My mother has definitely come a long way. In fact, we've all come a long way in a very short time. Believe me, Miss Davis, you made a difference. And I want you to know my sister and brothers feel the same way." To Lynn's look of surprise, Jordan added, "Yes, even Parker. So long, Miss Davis." The two shook hands good-bye.

* * * * *

Elizabeth was enormously relived that this matter was now over. Earl's other two children were now in the mix, and the blackmailer had been stopped. Although she would have gladly paid to protect her family from harm, Lynn Davis had given her the confidence to fight. Elizabeth was proud that she'd had the foresight to put Lynn on the case — and to keep her on it.

She looked forward to meeting with her today. In fact, she intended to continue her association with this young woman to whom she had taken a real liking. Lynn exhibited characteristics not unlike her own when it came to making things happen. She admired and respected that in her. Plus, Lynn was attractive, poised, well educated and easy to be around. Elizabeth wanted to do something special to show her appreciation. She recalled their very first meeting when she had told Lynn Davis to expect a bonus for a satisfactory job and Lynn had clearly stated that would not be necessary. Elizabeth had intended to abide her decision, but she changed her mind. She wrote some personal sentiments on a card, and then she wrote a check and inserted it inside the envelope along with the card. There!

When Elizabeth came into the room, the first thing Lynn noticed was how incredibly radiant she looked. Although she usually looked stunning, today she was absolutely gorgeous. She had a plain, smart hair-do and was wearing a fabulous two-piece chartreuse suit and similarly colored fashionable Manolo Blahniks. Mrs. Remington looked 20 years younger than her age. Wow, Lynn thought to herself of this classy woman who stood before her. Elizabeth seemed quite relaxed as she invited Lynn to sit down. Lynn took a seat in a tall wing-back chair, and Elizabeth sat across from her on the divan.

Refreshments were offered and they both took a cup of tea. Out of force of habit, Lynn looked for an ashtray and wondered where were the usual trappings — a cigarette and Courvoisier. Mrs. Remington caught that look and said, "Cigarettes? You know, I haven't had one of those things in several days. I discovered I really don't need them — or the brandy."

Sitting upright with her fingers laced around her knees, Elizabeth explained to Lynn how this whole situation had been so unreal she still found it hard to believe at times. She said she never had any idea that matters would unfold as they did when she hired her several weeks ago to locate Erica and Perry Williams. She said, "Miss Davis, you were just what we needed. I cannot thank you enough for finding my husband's children and helping bring us together and, of course, for working as you did through the blackmail situation. You did a wonderful job for us." Lynn thanked Mrs. Remington and reminded her that without Earl, Jr.'s help, they might not have been so successful, and Elizabeth appreciated Lynn's acknowledgment of her son's involvement.

Then she told Lynn, "Erica and Perry turned out to be a pleasant surprise. I plan to get to know them better, and I'm no longer prompted to do this because of my husband's wishes alone. I'm not sure what I expected, but I found them to be very fine young people. I intend for our relationship to grow beyond where it is today."

"They are interested in having a relationship with you, too," Lynn said. "I know from speaking with them many times that they have tremendous respect and regard for you for everything you've done for them."

"I'm glad to hear that," Elizabeth said as she shifted her position to lean back and cross her legs. "I want to tell you one other thing. By engaging you in this case, I must say that I learned something very important about myself. It's rather interesting actually, and it's definitely been quite a revelation for me. At first, it was hard to confront some of my own beliefs, and as a matter of fact, I've had to come to grips with some I'm not particularly proud of."

Lynn figured Mrs. Remington was talking about the racial issues related to this case. Elizabeth continued, "I've thought so often about this, and through it all, I have grown. I've certainly become more aware of others. You have been a tremendous help to me, more than you'll ever know."

"Mrs. Remington, I assume you're referring to the fact that Hattie Williams was African American, and her children with your husband are bi-racial," Lynn said. Elizabeth gave an upside down smile and nodded, and Lynn continued, "I appreciate your openness in addressing this sensitive topic. I don't think most people ever realize just how big the race problem really is, that things occur daily to keep the races from coming together. It's a huge social issue and, you know, I've concluded the more things change, the more they stay the same."

Elizabeth asked her what she meant. Lynn thought about it a minute, then told her that racial unrest was no stranger to Cincinnati. She cited some local incidents, some of which had generated tremendous national publicity. Elizabeth Remington appeared unconvinced and said the same could probably be said of all big cities. Lynn agreed, but stated that even though Cincinnati may have been status quo, it still left much to be desired. She then decided to tell Mrs. Remington about her first drive out to her Indian Hill home a few weeks before when she had been stopped for no apparent reason by a ranger and *escorted* up to the Remington estate. She described the episode.

A shocked Mrs. Remington listened intently, abhorred by this account. It upset her that Lynn Davis had been subjected to such an indignity, and she wanted to do something to remedy the problem. "Something must be done about that," she said in a concerned voice. However, Lynn assured her she had already taken care of it and explained what had transpired so far. "The fact is, though, what I did addresses my specific incident, not the general problem of racial profiling. I can guarantee that since that day, there have been many more incidents like mine, and there will be more tomorrow. Like I said, the more things change ..."

The two talked generally for a bit longer, and after a short while the conversation ended with Lynn being highly impressed at Elizabeth Remington's openness. Lynn thanked her for her concern. She was definitely proud to have been instrumental in helping Mrs. Remington work through this tough aspect of her case and happy to have had an open discussion with her on one of society's toughest issues.

Elizabeth was not content just to know that such a huge problem existed. She was not proud of her lack of prior awareness, but now that she had been enlightened to some extent, she wanted to know more and to do something. As Lynn had been talking, an idea began to stir in her head. The Remington Foundation could get involved. Perhaps it could underwrite a study to develop remedies to some of these terrible social problems. After all, that was what the foundation was for — to fund projects that would improve society. I'll propose this topic to our Foundation board, she decided.

* * * * *

With a resolute shake of her head, Elizabeth looked at Lynn and said, "Now I believe I once heard you say you wished to tour our Indian Hill home. Would you care to have that tour here instead? You may have heard of our extensive art collection. Much of it is here, and I am always happy to show it off." A surprised Lynn remembered thinking out loud of her interest in touring their lovely home on her first trip out to the Indian Hill residence. She hadn't realized Mrs. Remington had heard her comment, and this offer was more than she had hoped. She readily accepted, and for the next hour she accompanied the lady of the house on a breathtaking walk through the incredible Remington manor.

Years before, Lynn had seen this house featured in *Architectural Digest*, and she was excited to have the chance to see more. As they began their walk down the long corridor and into the various rooms, Lynn's attention was drawn at once to the extensive collection of paintings decorating every wall. Seeing Lynn's admiring glances, Elizabeth Remington stated, "As I said, I have a real passion for art. And obviously for antiques as well." She informed Lynn that their family owned over 300 paintings ranging in style from late-Renaissance and Baroque, to Chinese and Japanese art.

In the large dining hall, a single 17th-century Brussels tapestry dominated an entire wall. Magnificent gilded antique mirrors, marble statues of humans in various stages of undress, exotic floral arrangements and elaborate oil paintings were further appointments of this stately room, which Lynn figured with its enormous walnut table and chairs could accommodate a dinner gathering for dozens.

The drawing room off the dining room was one of three grand reception areas. Here, rich, bright peach velvet and brocade seating was arranged in attractive groupings around a black marble fireplace which featured a bright-colored poplar fireboard painted in oil. The other two reception areas were equally grand, both boldly furnished with eighteenth and nineteenth century antiques, colorful silk rugs, and stylish treatment on windows that looked out onto the picturesque Remington grounds.

On they walked up and down corridors and into different rooms. Lynn found each room she entered as interesting and beautiful as the previous one. Every room had its art and its unique history, which Mrs. Remington graciously shared with Lynn. Clearly, the artistry throughout the entire place was almost indescribable. Lynn was shown several of the 20 bedrooms in the house. Each looked fit for royalty. She learned which rooms three U.S. Presidents had slept in.

As the tour neared its end, they made a quick pass through the late Earl Remington's quietly elegant study. Lynn was fascinated at how even she seemed to sense his quiet presence in this room. His study featured a huge ivory-inlaid carved mahogany desk, occasional consoles, plush leather chairs, and rich, aged leather-bound books on walls of shelves, impressive family oil paintings, and finely woven, colorful silk pile rugs which partially covered the dark walnut floors.

After the grand walk through the interior of the great house and viewing the theatre room, the indoor tennis courts, heated pool, sauna and exercise facility, Mrs. Remington showed Lynn the grounds with their impeccably manicured floral gardens, flanked by peaceful rolling green pastures in every direction. Lynn was enthralled by the exquisite landscape and exotic array of floral aromas, just as she was by the interior of the place. The interior design was an obvious reflection of Mrs. Remington's love and exquisite taste in art and finery. Lynn concluded the tour, happy to have had a supremely intimate look into the personal lives of this interesting and special family.

Because she had been so wrapped up in solving this bizarre case, Lynn hadn't realized how much she was beginning to feel a special connection with Elizabeth Remington and her family. Mrs. Remington was a beautiful woman, gracious and fascinating. Her children were cool, especially Earl, whom Lynn had come to know a bit better than the others. Lynn thoughtfully mused, how does one even think about billionaires? To some degree, with awe and fascination — you have to be impressed with someone who has attained this much wealth. But, she told herself, you also have to realize that they, too, are only human, and but for fate and happenstance, the tables could easily be turned.

It was now time for Lynn to leave, and she felt both glad and a little sad. As she gathered her purse and prepared to depart, Mrs. Remington handed her an envelope and told her it was a token of her appreciation. Lynn thanked her and they parted warmly. She smiled as she placed the envelope in her purse and started her drive back downtown, knowing that closure of this case signaled a huge success for the Lynn Davis Agency.

As she drove, she became suddenly aware of that little nagging sensation — that feeling she had come to rely on so well. It told her greater surprises were in store.

EPILOGUE

WHEN LYNN ARRIVED at her office, she still had that sense of expectancy that something was up. Sitting at her desk preparing to review the contents of her in-box, and still thinking of the satisfying close of the Remington case, she suddenly remembered the envelope Mrs. Remington had handed her as she was leaving and immediately pulled it out of her purse and opened it. As she began reading, the handwritten note on the card brought tears to her eyes. Mrs. Remington wrote:

Miss Davis,

I cannot begin to tell you how much you have done for this family. Thank you for your unrelenting search for Earl's two children, and for the blackmailer who seemed determined to interfere in our lives. Because of your efforts, we have grown in many ways, one being in our acceptance of others. Our lives are surely richer for it.

You have also done a great deal for me personally. For out of this experience, I can now go forward with a light heart, free from debilitating anger and pain that had so filled my soul.

Our family has increased in size by three. And even though we may not all be Remingtons in name, as Earl used to say, "A family by any other name is still family." How true.

I consider you a friend of this family, and I am sure we'll meet again. In the meantime, please accept this gift as a token of my appreciation for a job that far exceeded my expectations.

Elizabeth

My goodness, how sweet, Lynn thought. Through moist eyes, she stared at the lovely card for a long time and was warmed by its message and her thoughts about this case. The successful ending of a case always brought Lynn a deep sense of satisfaction. This one certainly had that effect on her.

She never dreamed that when Mrs. Remington phoned her that fateful Sunday afternoon, the case she offered would bring such fascination. Pondering Elizabeth Remington's note, Lynn reflected on how great it was that the Remington family had worked together to bring this case to its successful close, and importantly, how the Remingtons seem to have genuinely accepted Erica and Perry. In doing this, they created a significant bond between two families and in a small way, two races. Lynn found herself choking back her emotion for she was truly proud of the way things had turned out.

Lynn thought about the Earl Remington quote in Elizabeth's note, "a family by any other name …" Mr. Remington apparently had very strong family values. It reminded Lynn of how her mother, too, had always exalted the importance of family. Rachel felt it didn't matter if you were related by blood or not; she always said, "family is as family does."

Inside a slot in her card, Lynn noticed what appeared to be a check. What's this, she wondered, for she'd already been paid in full. Then she remembered her first meeting with Elizabeth Remington when she quickly told her a bonus would not be necessary. Lynn thought of how well paid she had been for her services on the Remington case. For a solid month, nearly her every working hour had been dedicated to this case at a substantial hourly rate. In addition, there were Ella's hours and Harvey's services. Even though she had spoken in haste of her disinterest in a bonus, she had no regrets, for with money earned from this case she would be able to pour some right back into the business and set a little aside for renovations to her own office building. She looked forward to the day when she could move her investigative practice there.

Still, Lynn was actually surprised to see it was a check. She pulled it out and gazed upon it. She saw the number five, but what she couldn't quite follow were the zeroes after it. For some reason, her mind started playing tricks on her and she couldn't see for looking. She felt like she was in a trance. She blinked, and looked again. Finally, it registered, and in something of a delayed reaction, Lynn squinted her eyes, then gasped, then she shook her head and even pinched herself to make sure she wasn't dreaming. Then she counted out loud the zeroes on her bonus check. All … of them.

"What the…!" was all she could say, as her little nagging sensation instantly vanished. This is it. This is the bonus Mrs. Remington talked about, and she gave it to me even though I told her it would not be necessary, Lynn thought. My God, is she generous or what! Lynn wondered for just a moment if she would keep the check. It didn't seem like hers, even though her name was plainly written on it. What to do? Her telephone rang, and Lynn jumped before answering. An unknown female voice on the other end said, "Ms. Davis, I must see you immediately. There is a matter of grave urgency I must talk with you about." An abrupt tap on her door made Lynn realize that she had been daydreaming — thinking back to the day over a month ago when she had spoken with Elizabeth Remington for the first time.

Janet ducked her head in and said, "Donald's on the phone."

Donald was in a chatty mood, but Lynn was obviously preoccupied. "Honey," she said excitedly, "let me call you back in half an hour. I've got an important errand to run." Donald said, no problem, and Lynn hung up the phone. She'd made an important decision. Although Ella was not an equal partner, Lynn was certain she'd be thrilled with her portion of this generous bonus. She quickly wrote out a thank you note to drop in the mail to Mrs. Remington. Then she placed the check in her purse, headed out the door and began smiling. She smiled for many reasons: happiness, pride, amazement, satisfaction. And she kept right on smiling — all the way to the bank.